STRIPPED BARE

Lowri Turner

Stripped Bare

headline

First published in Great Britain in 2003
by HEADLINE BOOK PUBLISHING

10 9 8 7 6 5 4 3 2 1

Cataloguing in Publication Data is available from the British Library.

ISBN 0 7553 0257 5

Typeset in RotisSerif by Avon DataSet Ltd, Bidford-on-Avon, Warks

Printed and bound in Great Britain by
Clays Ltd, St Ives plc

HEADLINE BOOK PUBLISHING
A division of Hodder Headline
338 Euston Road
London NW1 3BH

www.headline.co.uk
www.hodderheadline.com

For my mother Shirley, sister Catrin and son Griffin.

Thanks also Elaine, Lizzy, Tracey and Jay.

Chapter One

'Running up . . . speed.'

'Action!'

Valerie Chancellor swept a stray tendril of long red hair behind one ear, to expose more of her better, left side, and began to glide up a flight of stairs. Valerie was tall, five foot nine in slippers; not that she wore slippers. According to Valerie, slippers were for people who couldn't afford under-floor heating. However, as the presenter of *On The House*, Futura Productions' prime-time homes and gardens makeover show, most of whose viewers were lucky if they had a fully functioning fan heater, she reserved this view for private, off-screen moments.

As Valerie moved towards the camera, the fluffy turquoise collar on her jacket fluttered slightly around a neck whose tendons stood out as if corrugated. Valerie wasn't just thin. She was TV thin. To achieve this, it is necessary to starve yourself until your body no longer appears to be able to support your head. Most TV presenters have large (as well as big) heads. It works better if their face fills the screen. Still, without her clothes, Valerie looked like ET.

At forty-four, Valerie was virtually pensionable for a TV presenter. Of this she was acutely aware. She had only to open one of the glossy men's mags to see her younger, firmer rivals in all their kitless glory. The only magazine to request a photo shoot with Valerie recently was *Saga*. Nevertheless, a bit of soft fill light under the chin and a reflector to soften harsh shadows, not to mention a key light so strong enemy spies could have used it to send signals across the Channel during World War II, and she could pass for thirty-five, or so she thought.

The job of shaving years off Valerie today belonged to Beth Davies, *On The House*'s newest director. At thirty-seven, with a pale complexion, grey-green eyes and short dark hair, Beth had been poached from *Guess That Hymn!*. This brave attempt to break the mould of religious broadcasting had bombed, but Beth's achievement in getting the Archbishop of Canterbury into a pair of cargo pants had not gone unnoticed.

Until recently, *On The House* had been TV's number one makeover show, but rival programme *DIYSOS* had now overtaken it. Ratings for the last series had slipped and research afterwards was less than positive. The focus groups had practically gone into a coma. The new series was just about to go to air. Anastassia Frink, Director of Factual Entertainment, Commissioning Leisure and Lifestyle Programming and Production, National and Regional – woe betide you if you left one of those off – at Channel 6, expected it to do much, much better. If it didn't, she would axe the show and they'd all be out of a job, Valerie and Beth included.

'This week we've come to the north-east...' The edge of Valerie's lip curled almost imperceptibly. She had tried to have it written into her contract that all filming take place within a two-mile radius of Knightsbridge, but this demand had been refused. Valerie had won the battle of the wardrobe, however. Beth had suggested she don a boiler suit, as a nod towards the content of the show. Valerie had given her a withering look and called her agent. This was what she did whenever she was displeased; consequently her last mobile bill had been £1,456.28.

At that moment, Beth was also slightly regretting her decision to head up the A1 to a two-bedroom back-to-back in Newcastle upon Tyne. While Valerie swept regally up the stairs, Beth was squashed into one corner of the house's whiffy upstairs loo, studying a video monitor. She'd seen rabbit hutches that were more roomy. A section of wall decorated with broken tiles was digging into her shoulder and she had cramp in one foot, which was jammed up against a peeling skirting board.

Still, Beth wasn't really the type to throw a strop. Her physiology was against her. To give really good flounce, you have to have long limbs, hips the width of a six-year-old child and cheekbones you can cut someone else's throat with. At barely five foot, with a round face, and legs that, while useful on a member of the former East German shotputting team, were somewhat wasted when the heaviest lifting you did was lug the shopping in from the car, Beth was the wrong shape for megastropdom.

This was not to say that she was unattractive. On a good day she could look like a young Liz Taylor. On a bad day, well, she didn't wear her glasses to put on her make-up. Men might not have traversed oceans to reach Beth, but she'd never had a problem encouraging them to roll up their trouser legs and have a bit of a paddle. For the last five years she'd been married to Richard, also in TV. They had a one-year-old son, Stanley, and a house in north London with a mortgage on it the size of Wales.

'We're here to meet Michael and Julie . . .' Valerie's voice was as soft and voluptuous as she was brittle and uptight. It was like listening to melted butter drip off a piece of toast. Beth would have quite liked a piece of toast right now. Instead she shifted her weight to get the feeling back in her foot and tried to concentrate on the monitor.

Valerie was an ATP, an Actor Turned Presenter. Ten years ago she had been Bev, the sexually voracious barmaid with a drink problem and an addiction to lip gloss – she wore so much grease on her mouth, her lips could have swum the Channel – in daily soap *Jubilee Road*. During emotional scenes, Valerie's lips quivered dramatically. As with the Formula One winner who has shaken up a bottle of champagne, the camera had to stay at least ten feet away to prevent the lens being spattered. Valerie's thespian past and her endless harping on about it was usually a pain in the neck, but at times like these, when she had to walk across hard surfaces, it came in useful. Thanks to years of treading the boards – panto rather than Pinter – her expensively shod feet were soundless, even on peeling lino.

Valerie's smile was just as practised. One moment she could be wearing a scowl that could strip gloss paint off banisters at twenty paces. The word 'action', however, and it was like switching on a light bulb. All trace of ill-temper disappeared, replaced by a smile of such intensity that onlookers were routinely advised not to stare directly into it for fear of temporary blindness. From the safety of her video monitor, Beth found herself marvelling at Valerie's grin. It was the perfect mix of mumsy approachability and mistressy seduction. It was the quintessential presenter's smile and, for

Valerie, an essential tool. Indeed, it was the only tool she used on the show.

Valerie claimed to be allergic to power drills, wallpaper steamers, strimmers and secateurs; indeed, anything that might chip her French manicure. The production team had been forced to create a DIY and gardening exclusion zone of at least two metres around her. Woe betide you if you accidentally brushed past with a sheet of sandpaper or a bag of compost. Even momentary contact and Valerie would insist she had to lie down in a darkened room. This could delay filming for several hours.

Even so, Beth, along with everyone else, knew not to argue with Valerie. She was 'The Talent'. Anyone who appears in front of camera is 'The Talent', and the thing is, none of them, including Valerie, seem to realise the term is ironic. Two months of working with Valerie had led Beth to the conclusion that an averagely intelligent donkey could have done her job. And Muffin wouldn't have spent so much time in make-up or demanded sushi for lunch.

'Michael is in computers,' continued Valerie. 'And when Julie saw his attempt to fix a leak, it was *she* who wanted to press the delete button.'

On The House was a makeover show that specialised in helping those who had made a mess of things in the house or garden. Bathrooms with pipework like lawn sprinklers, patios so uneven you needed crampons to reach the barbecue. That sort of thing.

Today, the team had arrived to rescue Michael, who had responded to a leaky sink by shoving a length of grey plastic guttering into the ceiling above the stairs. Every time anyone washed their hands, a fair proportion of the water now poured through the hole in the hall ceiling and ran down the guttering into a bucket wedged into the crook of the stairs. It was a scene unlikely to feature on the pages of *World of Interiors*.

Valerie had now reached the bucket. She paused, still smiling. The only hint of her distaste was the angle of her body. It veered away from the grubby water like a human Leaning Tower of Pisa.

'So, can we turn this horrible hallway into a stairway to heaven?' she was saying. 'And in just three days? Stay with us to find out. But first it's over to our very own antipodean heavenly body, Jack...'

Jack Taylor was *On The House*'s resident Australian handyman. All makeover shows need a handyman. Their role is to look good in a pair of shorts. Since most presenters, even those who do deign to pick up a screwdriver, know as much about DIY as they do about hang-gliding, it's also useful if the handyman is actually handy. Jack knew his way round a socket set. He knew his way round other things as well.

Like a young Brad Pitt, only with a more self-conscious wave to his highlighted blond hair, Jack was the housewives' choice. He liked to return the favour. When he went missing on shoots, which he did frequently, the crew mounted a house-to-house search and usually found him ensconced with a star-struck female neighbour. He invariably claimed to be changing the plug on the toaster, putting up some shelves or fixing her tumble drier. Well, some sort of a tumble was going on, anyway.

A slight hitch for the production team was the fact that Jack and Valerie didn't get on. That was putting it politely. They hated every molecule of one another. She thought he was a jumped-up Aussie wide boy. He thought she was a toffee-nosed Pom. They had a half-hearted stab at covering this up on screen. Indeed, many viewers thought they were a married couple, which said more about the state of the average British marriage than about Jack and Valerie's acting abilities.

Suddenly Beth heard whispering. She peered out of the open door of her pongy cupboard. Saffron, the runner, was saying something to Tim, the cameraman. Saffron was nineteen, and painfully shy. Her brownish hair was cropped short; she was wearing no make-up and her usual shapeless clothes in an attempt to hide the puppy fat that was hanging on a bit. In fact, Beth often felt Saffron was not unlike a depressed beanbag. Still, she was efficient in a quiet way. Beth couldn't hear what Saffron was saying now but she was gesturing towards Valerie. Beth stared at her monitor. She couldn't see anything wrong with Valerie. What was going on?

Beth peered round the monitor and looked again at Tim. When a boy dreams of being a cameraman, he visualises himself dodging bullets in Beirut, a lone desperado bringing back the story come what may. Most end up pointing a camera at two people in bad jumpers sat on a sofa. Still, Tim was the real thing, an ex-SAS sniper who now specialised in filming documentaries on survival in extreme environments. A lithe five foot seven with cropped blond hair and piercing blue eyes, when he wasn't ice-climbing in Finland, he was setting camp in a jungle in Costa Rica. And when he wasn't doing either, he had an even tougher assignment – working with Valerie.

Tim mouthed something Beth couldn't make out. She cupped one hand to her ear to mime deafness. Tim pointed past Valerie at the wall behind her. Valerie was oblivious, which just went to prove that self-obsession had its uses.

'. . . He's out in the garden with Hamish . . .' Valerie ploughed on.

Beth squinted at her monitor, using the cuff of her *On The House* fleece to dislodge a layer of brick dust from the screen. She looked again at Valerie and then she saw it. On the wall behind her there was a faint scribble. It wasn't ink or paint, though, which was why she hadn't spotted it before. Someone had used a wet finger, presumably dipped in the bucket of water, to write in the dust. But what did it say?

Valerie was still speaking. 'They're going to be constructing an exquisite Japanese water garden out of old council paving stones and industrial ducting . . .'

Beth began to be able to make out the letters. The first was a V, then an A. Val, it said Val, but Val what? The former queen of soapland had her lollipop head in the way and Beth couldn't see the next bit.

Valerie was getting to the throw, the end of the link where she passed the presenting baton to Jack. It was all pre-recorded, of course. Jack was actually gulping a mug of tea and chewing a bacon sandwich in the kitchen at this moment. Still, it was filmed to look as if the two were having a cheery live chat.

'How's it going, cobber?' asked Valerie, shifting her position to reveal the whole message behind her.

It read: 'Val is a tight-arsed Pommy bitch.'

There was a deathly silence, then a titter from Saffron, followed by a stifled laugh from Tim. Even Beth found herself smiling. The only person not smiling was Valerie. She knew something was up. Without a word, she turned slowly to face the wall behind her. She was motionless for a good five seconds. When she turned round, her face had gone a cherry colour which clashed horribly with the turquoise of her collar. Then there was a rumble that seemed to

8

come up from her stomach and into her throat before finally exploding out of her mouth. Beth half expected her head to spin round and green gunge to come out.

'Saffron!' Valerie bellowed.

Saffron craned her head round to meet Valerie's furious gaze. 'Yes, Valerie.'

Valerie's brown eyes had turned almost black. They glittered with anger. The muscles in her face were twitching ominously.

'Get my phone. I'm calling my agent!'

Beth looked round the *On The House* office. It was on the top floor of a once grand, now exceedingly shabby house in central London. When new people saw it, you could see them thinking, Hang on a sec. Doesn't this company do a makeover show? The carpet was brownish, the walls were greyish and the lighting was fluorescent, so even the most fresh-faced recruit looked like a serial killer.

The overwhelming impression was of stuff. Stuff everywhere. Desks were jammed into corners next to piles of papers that teetered on the brink of collapse, which was how you felt when you finally reached the office. It was on the fifth floor in the one-time servants' quarters of the house, and there was no lift.

At the far end of the room, Beth spotted Siobhan O'Hanlan, assistant producer, Beth's number two and best friend. Siobhan was twenty-nine, with shoulder-length blonde hair and eyes the colour of cornflowers. She was gorgeous, but she wore her beauty casually, without a trace of arrogance. Looking the way she did, Beth should have hated her. As it was, she adored her.

The world is divided into two sorts of women: those who can put on a cropped top and baggy combats and look really sexy in them, and those who can't. Beth belonged to the latter group. She had tried combats – for about ten seconds. That was long enough to convince her that she looked as if someone had taken a foot pump to her thighs. Siobhan, however, was today sporting navy combats and a navy and khaki sleeveless tank, revealing her toned, twenty-something upper arms. She was on the phone with her back to the room. Beth began to walk towards her.

'No, no, it's not you. It's me.'

She was obviously talking to a boyfriend, and by the sound of it, she was chucking him. This wasn't unusual. Siobhan had a complicated love life. When it came to men, she had a kamikaze instinct. For the last four years, she had been in love with Simon, an airline pilot. Unfortunately, Simon was married to Elaine and had three lovely children, a Range Rover and a mock-Tudor semi in Surrey. Every so often Siobhan would come to her senses and break it off. This was when she went out with other people. Lots of other people.

Like the ex-smoker who takes up knitting, Siobhan's romantic freneticness was a sort of desperate displacement activity. Still, in the same way that for a serious smoker, knit one, purl one is never going to supply the same hit as a drag on a Capstan Full Strength, no matter how many other men Siobhan tried, none of them erased Simon from her thoughts. The longest one of Siobhan's Simon-free phases had lasted up to now was a month. This time, she was going for a record. Her self-control had remained unbroken for three. But it was hard.

Beth took a couple of steps forward and tried to catch Siobhan's attention.

'I didn't say that . . . You're very mature,' Siobhan said gently.

Ah, so it was Kevin she was talking to, thought Beth. The name of Siobhan's current squeeze was actually Darren, but Beth had taken to calling him Kevin the Teenager on account of his extreme youth. Siobhan wasn't exactly sure how old he was. Twenty? Twenty-one, maybe? She'd met him at the Reading Rock Festival. It was somewhere she knew she wouldn't run into Simon.

'No, I don't think we need to talk about our relationship.' Siobhan's voice had taken on an incredulous tone. 'We don't have a relationship! We have just slept together a few times, that's all . . . I am *not* commitment-phobic! . . . Look, this has nothing to do with *my issues*. I just don't think I can go out with someone who doesn't know who Lesley Judd is.' There was a pause. 'She was on *Blue Peter* . . . No, before Katy Hill . . . No, before that . . . No, Shep belonged to John Noakes . . . Look, it doesn't matter. You're too young for me. For Christ's sake, Darren, I've got shoes older than you!'

Siobhan put down the phone and turned round.

'Men,' said Beth. 'Shag them once and they think you're in a *relationship*.'

Siobhan smiled.

'Come on, let's go and get a coffee at that new place and you can give me all the gory details,' Beth said.

Beth and Siobhan looked around. This was their first visit to Fresh and Earthy and they were beginning to regret it already. All they wanted was a shot of caffeine. Instead, they were about to have a Zen experience – whether they liked it or not.

Fresh and Earthy was a juice bar of the sort that required you to take out a high-interest personal loan to afford a gluten-free muffin. Fortunately, the owner had realised the need to offer customers plenty of places to sit down and recover from the shock of the bill.

Bamboo and hemp stools were arranged in pairs along one tree-bark-covered wall. These were punctuated by low cubes masquerading as coffee tables. You couldn't actually get your knees under the tables, so sitting down was massively uncomfortable. It was a wonder they didn't provide hair shirts and bunches of beech twigs so you could really punish yourself for committing the mortal sin of consuming anything other than fresh air.

'Shall we make a run for it?' Siobhan whispered.

Beth shook her head. 'We're here now anyway, let's just get a drink and sit down.'

Opposite the stools ran a long counter. Beth and Siobhan moved towards it. Behind it, assorted staff in aprons made of eco-friendly green cotton – they knew that because it said 'made from eco-friendly green cotton' on the front – juiced. One slight hitch to the whole Zen, 'my body is a temple' juicing thing is that juicers are very loud. Attempting to order anything over the din was like trying to have a quiet chat on the deck of an aircraft carrier.

Beth tried to catch the attention of a thin girl facing her. She had her eyes closed, which wasn't very helpful, but she was the only one not actually pushing things into a machine. As Beth gesticulated wildly, the thin girl wrapped her arms around her body in a painful-looking yoga pose. She breathed out loudly. At that moment Beth wanted to kill her. Instead, she decided to try shouting.

'Do you have a—' *Whizzzzzzzz* went a juicer. Beth waited for a mango, three carrots and a lime to be pulped.

12

'I said, do you have a—' *Whizzzzzzzz* went the juicer again. This time, half a greengrocer's stall appeared to be going in. Beth had no choice. She lifted her voice even further to a bellow and tried again.

'I said, have you –' the juicer stopped – 'got a coffee?'

Beth's voice bounced off the walls, ceiling and floor and ricocheted off a stool. A pasty-looking teenager operating a juicer was momentarily stunned, standing frozen, holding an avocado and a bunch of organic vine tomatoes in mid-air.

The thin girl opened her eyes disdainfully, taking a brief pause in her yoga routine.

'Chicory coffee only. Or Aloe vera juice.' This was said with the sort of weary contempt teenagers reserve for a parent who doesn't know how to set the video.

'Aloe vera? I thought you put that on your hair,' giggled Siobhan.

The thin girl was not amused. 'And there's a special offer on wheat grass,' she announced, rocking her head back and forth. Now Beth really wanted to kill her.

'I think we'll give that a miss,' said Beth. 'I don't think it's quite, er, us.' She turned to Siobhan and, in a whisper, added, 'Mouldy hedge clippings.'

Beth and Siobhan scanned the menu.

'Oh look, that one's got guarana. That's about as much of a hit as we're likely to get in here,' said Beth. 'Two Citrus Bursts, please.'

Siobhan and Beth sat down on the bamboo stools. Siobhan immediately caught her knee on a splinter.

'Ow,' she exclaimed.

She rubbed her leg and gradually recovered her good humour.

'Actually, all we need is fishing rods and we could be garden gnomes,' she observed.

Beth smiled. 'You know they're back in fashion? I saw Liam Smith on TV the other day and he had covered an entire lawn with them.'

'Really?' asked Siobhan, frowning.

'Yeah, he'd grouped them together to spell out the words "horticultural" and "kitsch". Apparently the punters have already ripped it out and stuck in gravel, railway sleepers and a shedload of slate chippings instead.'

Beth had tried to get Liam for *On The House*, but had failed. He was a makeover superstar. An interior designer, he had now transcended that world to become a celebrity interior designer. Actually, his position had recently elevated even further. His job title was now redundant. He was now known as TV's Liam Smith, which is the celeb version of being knighted. The only two rungs further up the showbiz ladder are for your surname to be dropped by the tabloids and, at the very pinnacle, for the TV bit to go too. The day a headline referred to him simply as Liam, he would have become a celebrity saint. Liam Smith, patron saint of MDF.

'Anyway,' Beth continued, putting him out of her mind, 'what was all that before? Have you dumped Kevin?'

Siobhan took a sip of her Citrus Burst. It was like drinking Cif Lemon, only more tart. 'Darren. His name's Darren. But yeah, did you hear . . . ?'

'Some of it. Still, he was a bit of a non-starter, wasn't he? Did you ever find out how young he was?'

'No, but . . .'

'What?'

'When I woke up this morning, his uniform was hanging up on the back of the door.'

'Please tell me it was a fireman's uniform.'

'Nope.'

'Policeman's?'

'Nope.'

'Army? Navy? Not clamper man?'

'It was a school uniform.'

'Siobhan! How could you?' Beth's mouth was wide open in shock. She started laughing.

Siobhan blushed. 'Reading's not the Riviera. At the festival it rained a lot. It was sort of murky. You couldn't see very well. Anyway, we were in the tent most of the time and it was dark in there,' she replied.

Beth raised an eyebrow. 'Well, at least you got out fast.'

'Not fast enough.'

'What do you mean?'

'His mum came in to bring him a cup of tea this morning, and she—'

'His mum! Don't tell me he lives with his parents!'

'Yup.'

'And you didn't know that either?'

'Well, they've got a weekend cottage in Snowdonia, so they weren't around. They only came back last night.'

Beth shifted in her seat. 'Let me get this straight. He took you back to his place. You had your wicked way with him and then, this morning, his mum comes to say hello? What happened?'

'I shook her hand.'

'You what?'

'I shook her hand. I couldn't think what else to do.'

'Quite ladylike, I suppose.'

'Not really. The duvet slipped down and she ended up saying hello to one of my nipples.'

Beth and Siobhan were now laughing so hard, Citrus Burst was spraying out of their noses. Siobhan covered her mouth with a napkin and passed one to Beth. Even without the napkins, they were incapable of speech for a good two minutes.

When they'd calmed down, Beth started again. 'So that's why you dumped him, because of his mum?'

'Not really. The sex was . . .'

'What?'

'Have you ever tried to walk a Dalmatian puppy across a busy road?'

'No.'

'Well, they're completely uncontrollable. Very affectionate and sweet, but all over the place.'

'And is that how Kevin –' Siobhan gave her a look – 'Darren was in bed, then?'

'Yeah. Lots of energy, no focus. Actually, I wanted to dump him after Reading, but I thought I'd get him to reprogram my laptop first. You know these teenagers and new technology.'

'And did you?'

'No, he was too busy being a Dalmatian puppy. Anyway, I've met someone new.'

'Jesus, that was quick. Who is he?'

'His name's Kyle. He's South African and we're going out tonight.'

16

'Well, you know the rule.'

'Yes, yes, no sex on a first date.'

Beth shook her head. 'I don't think I could hack it being single now. At least Richard's seen all my dodgy bits. I'm sure that's why so many women stay in bad marriages, you know. It's not because of the house or anything. It's so they don't have to go through the trauma of someone new seeing their cellulite.'

'Well, I'm not going to be naked, so don't worry.'

Beth stirred her drink with the straw, hoping it might improve its taste. 'Thank God for boring middle-aged monogamy. It may be dull, but at least you don't have to hold your tummy in.'

Olivia Timney rolled her eyes to the ceiling, ran an elegant hand through her long dark brown hair and suppressed a scream.

'Yes, Valerie ... yes, Valerie ... If I could just ... Yes, Valerie ...'

Olivia was wardrobe designer for *On The House* and the third musketeer to Beth and Siobhan. They formed a tight and loyal triumvirate. In theory, it was Olivia's job to ensure all the on-screen talent looked good, allowing for a sprinkling of cement dust and the odd dab of creosote. In practice, she was forced to spend 99.9 per cent of her time pandering to Valerie's rampant egomania.

'The thing is, Valerie, the budget won't quite stretch to Chanel couture ...'

Olivia was at JFK airport, returning from a friend's wedding in New York. All had been going smoothly until Valerie's call. Well, as smoothly as it can go when you're attempting transatlantic travel with four kids. Olivia had so much luggage she needed a sherpa to negotiate the departure hall. Instead she had Colin, her husband.

Colin was widely regarded as The Perfect Husband, on account of having given up his job as a graphic designer to look after the kids. This sometimes annoyed Olivia, usually when she had to leave home for a meeting with Cruella De Vil, aka Valerie, and Colin was sat on the sofa with the kids watching *Teletubbies*. But she would have died of boredom if she'd been stuck at home. Colin's domestic existence meant he was no Arnold Schwarzenegger. Slight and bookish-looking, he was the sort of man who had to have a cup of coffee to recover from getting a book down from a high shelf. He was now having trouble steering two heavily laden trollies towards Olivia.

Olivia herself was a glorious, glamorous image of old-fashioned femininity. Her features were as regular as a china doll's, but she wasn't just beautiful. Olivia was sexy. It was something to do with the way she carried her body. On this occasion, however, she wasn't at her best. She was crouched on her haunches next to check-in, a mobile clamped under her chin, trying to reason with Valerie while also desperately searching an overflowing handbag for the tickets and passports.

Chaos was something that clung to Olivia like expensive scent. Before Colin took over responsibility for all the domestic arrangements, the family had frequently been plunged into darkness on account of an unpaid bill. This had nothing to do with lack of money. Olivia was of independent means. She'd had an upper-middle-class upbringing with bells on – boarding school so expensive no one bothered to pass any O levels, but everyone knew how to plait a pony's tail and make salmon en croute.

When Olivia reached twenty-one, her trust fund had kicked in. She was just too posh to get it together. She exhibited that brand of aristocratic vagueness that saw her going shopping and buying designer clothes by the armful, but then forgetting where she'd parked the car. But then her mother was also on the batty side. Were she not distantly related to the Duchess of Kent, she'd have been carted off by men in white coats. As it was, she did her gardening in a nightie and everyone pretended not to notice.

'No, Valerie, Gucci is not really an option either.'

Apart from Siobhan, Olivia was Beth's closest friend. They felt an affinity for one another. If you looked past Olivia's designer label wardrobe, she and Beth were actually quite similar. Both were staggering under the weight of trying to have it all. Obviously, Olivia had the luxury of Colin at home, but then she had four children to Beth's one.

Beth had been slightly stunned when Olivia had confessed to her quartet of offspring. She found one knackering enough. Olivia had explained that it wasn't deliberate; she wasn't a Mormon or anything. She'd just been too shagged out to remember to take the pill on a regular basis. She had a point. The week after Stanley was born, Beth had gone to the greengrocer, left him outside, forgotten she had him and headed for home alone. Someone had had to run after her down the street.

'Look, I'm going to have to go, Valerie. No, I can't call you back. I can't use the phone on the plane ... Because it might crash, Valerie ... No, I don't think they'd waive the rule on the grounds that you're having a fashion emergency. Bye.'

Olivia shook her head in exasperation and put the phone in her pocket. Then she leant forward to grab three-year-old Seth's ankles and haul him off the luggage conveyor. Anouska, eighteen months, was standing a foot away, spinning slowly round.

'Don't do that, sweetie,' Olivia cautioned her. 'You'll make yourself dizzy and—'

Anouska careered into Seth and the two of them fell in a heap.

'Fall over,' finished Olivia.

'Waaah!' screamed Anouska, closely followed by more shrieks from Seth.

Olivia hugged Anouska, simultaneously rubbing Seth's elbow. The commotion woke the twins, Mia and Daisy. Just seven months old, they had been asleep in a double buggy. Now they too began to cry. The combined effect of four sets of lungs was deafening.

Colin arrived next to Olivia puffing with exertion. 'Sshhh,' he cooed, rocking the buggy and picking up Anouska, sitting her on his waist. 'There there.'

Seth wrapped his arms round Olivia's leg. She stroked his head. 'I tell you what,' she said to Colin. 'I'll be glad to get back to work. It'll be a bloody rest. Whose idea was it to bring the kids, anyway?'

Colin took the tickets and passports out of his pocket, where they'd been safely stowed all the time, and put them on the check-in counter.

'As always, Olivia, yours,' he replied.

Anastassia Frink pressed the button marked 'Play'. The familiar jaunty melody of the *On The House* theme tune filled her Channel 6 office. The box from which she had pulled the video that was now playing lay in front of her. 'Rough Cut, Programme One' was written on the side in black marker pen.

Anastassia sat back. While more modest members of staff were lucky to get a folding picnic chair, Anastassia's bottom was nestled on £2,000 of fully ergonomic executive-model swivel chair, with tilting back and fully sprung seat. The amount of shouting she'd done at the facilities man, plus the fact that if she'd sued the company for so much as a twinge of back trouble she'd have got damages equivalent to the gross national product of an average-sized South American country, ensured her bottom touched only top-of-the-range furniture.

Anastassia frowned. She saw herself as a vamp in her sexy little suits. And with her expensively shorn, dyed black hair and long, polished nails, from a distance she didn't look too bad. Close up, however, the image crumbled. Anastassia always wore too much make-up. It settled into her forty-something lines. Her collagen-plumped lips were too red, her mascara cloggy. *On The House*'s cheery theme music was noticeably not rubbing off on her mood. She picked up a pen lying on the desk and scribbled in a notebook. Then she returned her attention to the TV. A couple of minutes later she was writing again. This continued until the tape finished thirty-five minutes later.

When the screen had turned black, Anastassia leant back, clasped her hands in a steeple in front of her and breathed in. Things were going to have to change at *On The House*, and fast.

Chapter Two

The wallpaper really was appalling. Huge flowers of a hue so bright they didn't appear to belong to any variety of bloom Siobhan had ever seen. Was there such a thing as irradiated chrysanthemum? The background was yellow and it was scattered with improbable bile-coloured leaves. Siobhan peered at the wall out of her peripheral vision. If she'd looked straight at it, she would have had to be sectioned immediately.

Siobhan's eyes scanned the rest of the room. A junk-shop wardrobe in mahogany-stained pine stood in one corner. One of the doors had dropped on its hinges and wouldn't close properly. Through the gap, she could see a jumble of clothes. She was tempted to go and have a rifle through.

Siobhan had learned the hard way that when dealing with a man and his clothes, it was best to assess what you were up against at the outset. Then you could work out how big a restyle was needed and whether he was worth the effort. White trainers and a mullet? Allowable if the rest of the package was halfway passable. Surf shorts, V-neck acrylic jumpers and grey slip-on moccasins? He'd have to have the face of George Clooney and the brain of Stephen

Hawking to justify the marathon effort *that* would require.

The reason Siobhan knew this was that she'd once dated a chap called Rupert who wore shoes shaped like Cornish pasties. At first she'd thought he had just the one pair. However, on peering inside his cupboards, she had discovered that he had racks of them. All the same. All revolting. Unfortunately, Siobhan didn't find this out until a month or two into the relationship, by which time she had become emotionally involved. The result was, she spent the next three months walking Rupert past shoe shops, attempting to interest him in 'a nice new pair of lace-ups'. It was useless. Rupert could quite legitimately point to the fact that he already had plenty of pairs of shoes – albeit neither nice, nor new – in his cupboard at home.

Things came to a head in what became known, between Siobhan, Beth and Olivia anyway, as the Petrol Station Incident. Siobhan and Rupert were waiting to pay for two litres of unleaded in a service station in Nuneaton when a coachload of senior citizens on their way to a 'Sounds of the 60s' concert crowded into the shop. Rupert had taken off one of his shoes to pull up his sock. An OAP in a mirrored mini dress and support hose mistook the shoe for a stray item of fast food and put it in the microwave. Only after an extended altercation was the shoe retrieved, steaming slightly. Siobhan ended the relationship there and then.

Fortunately, Cornish-pasty shoes didn't appear to be big in South Africa. Kyle Hoogstraten – or Hoog-something; Siobhan was having difficulty understanding his accent (or maybe it was just the number of glasses of wine she'd drunk last night) – was from Cape Town. He was over here working in a bar to fund a trip round Europe.

Despite her promise to herself and Beth, Siobhan had succumbed to Kyle's taut twenty-five-year-old body. And, having completed an hour of under-the-duvet aerobics, Kyle had gone to the kitchen to get food for them both. This was why Siobhan was staring at his awful wallpaper and deciding that she really ought to be going.

It wasn't only the chrysanthemums. Siobhan was honest enough with herself to know that her night of hot sex was not about to turn into the love of her life. She was still on the rebound from Simon, not to mention Darren. She really had to pull herself together. She was turning into a slapper. She'd be getting a tattoo of a butterfly on one hip and wearing a toe ring next.

Siobhan decided it was best to make a dignified exit. 'It's been fun but . . .' She glanced at her watch: 2.30 a.m.! She had to be up for work in a few hours. She pushed herself up on her elbows. Then she heard footsteps on the stairs. The door swung open to reveal Kyle, naked, carrying a tray.

'Hope you're hungry,' he said, smiling.

Siobhan was momentarily stunned by the vision before her. Six foot two inches of tanned flesh, totally starkers. Then the smell of hot toast and coffee drifted over to her, and that was even more appealing. Maybe she should stay for breakfast after all. She was feeling rather weak and it was only polite.

'Mmm, I'm starving, thanks,' she replied.

Kyle didn't move. He looked nervously towards her. Oh God, they weren't going to have the relationship discussion now, were they? She really had to stop sleeping with younger men. All this emotional intimacy stuff was just too exhausting. Siobhan hadn't had any sleep. She wasn't in any state to stroke Kyle's ego – her eyes dipped below the tray – or anything else for that matter. She looked up again. Still, if she could have just a bit of toast, she might feel up to it.

'Before we eat,' said Kyle.

Siobhan groaned silently. Damn those seventies mothers. Bring back gender stereotyping, she thought, lying back against the pillows and closing her eyes. If I ever have a kid and he's a boy, I'm going to dress him in blue, buy him an Action Man and arm the little tyke to the teeth.

'I suppose I should explain, um . . .'

Siobhan braced herself.

'I suppose I should explain what happened to my other testicle.'

At first, Kyle's words didn't penetrate Siobhan's tired brain. There was silence as he waited for her to speak and she struggled to make sense of the sentence he had just uttered. Finally she managed to murmur: 'Sorry? Did you say . . . ?'

'Yes, my other testicle. I was talking about my other testicle.'

'That's what I thought you . . .' Siobhan's voice trailed off. She pulled herself up to a sitting position and opened her eyes. She stared at Kyle's groin, her head tipping first one way and then the other, as if examining an especially perplexing work by Tracey Emin.

'Now you come to mention it . . .' she said.

'It is there,' offered Kyle, peering over his tray enthusiastically. 'It's just not completely . . .'

Kyle's detailed explanation of the fate of his one shy gonad was lost on Siobhan. She was transfixed by his lopsided nether regions. How had she not noticed it before? She really had to start paying more attention.

'You know what?' she said. 'I really think I should make a move. It's been fun and everything, but could you call me a cab?'

'OK, I've apologised to the mother of the boy that Stanley shoved, but I had to give her twenty quid for the jumper. That paint's not coming out.'

Richard slumped into his chair and picked up his brush again.

Creative Kidz was an establishment that offered guilty working parents the chance to spend quality time with their offspring while wearing hideous aprons. The idea was that you and your little darlings decorated ceramics together.

Inevitably, Stanley had taken one look at the plate put before him and decided he'd rather watch the video playing in the corner of the room. This left Beth and Richard to do the creative play bit, while Stanley's young brain atrophied in front of American TV pap. Then they, like all the other parents crouched intently over bits of pottery, would pass the results off as the work of their hugely talented child.

Beth daubed some lurid purple on to her already headache-inducing plate and smiled ruefully to herself. Before they'd had Stanley, she and Richard had made a pact that they wouldn't compromise their lifestyle just because they had a baby. They might be parents, but that didn't mean they had to turn into different people, did it? Not for them an end to all conversation unless it was about the price of nappies. Their weekends wouldn't be spent taking glum little trips to children's zoos to stroke manky-looking sheep. Their house wouldn't permanently pong of nappy sacks. They would be nonparent parents – Parents Lite.

Of all the resolutions Beth and Richard had made in that golden period before Stanley actually arrived to upset all their neatly made plans, the most fervent was that they would never, repeat, never, come to a place like Creative Kidz. And here they were.

There was a crash.

'Stanley, no!' shouted Richard, sprinting across to the TV. Stanley was bashing another, admittedly unpleasant-looking, tot over the head with a toy car.

'Now play nicely,' Richard cooed, dropping to his hands and knees.

Oh, for the days when Beth and Richard had gone out, not to paint plates, but to eat off them. Beth thought wistfully of the leisurely dinners-à-deux with a bottle of wine and three whole courses and coffee. Now they had to eat in relays, and whoever was on Stanley duty was lucky if they got a mouthful of food before he was demanding to get down and run about. Tugging at his baby reins impatiently, Stanley turned any trip out into an experience not unlike trekking across the Antarctic by dog sled, only without the sled or the chance to plant a flag on a mound of snow.

Still, Beth wouldn't have swapped days like this for her childless ones. In the year since Stanley's birth, her life had been transformed. She had watched herself waving goodbye to all her pretensions – aesthetic, culinary and otherwise – as if unhooking the carriages on a train. And she'd done it gladly. OK, so every item in her wardrobe had some unidentifiable splodge on it and she'd had to learn how to put her make-up on in the car, but she had got so much in return. They were a family now, a proper family.

Over by the TV, Richard and Stanley were sitting side by side, the wailing child having been removed by his disapproving mother. The height of the bench meant Richard's knees were crunched up under his chin. He had his arm round Stanley's tiny shoulder. Stanley was resting his head against Richard's chest. He had his thumb in his mouth and was mesmerised by some revolting woodland creature who spoke as if raised in deepest Brooklyn.

Richard too smiled ruefully to himself. He was thinking that before they'd had Stanley, they had vowed that they would never use the TV as a babysitter. They'd stimulate and entertain their child with a range of traditional wooden toys and old-fashioned things called books. Well, actually, it was Beth who'd said that. Richard had been rather looking forward to going out and buying a remote-control car, a Scalextric track and a Playstation. Still, he had kept his mouth shut and nodded enthusiastically.

The first beeping, squeaking piece of neon plastic had arrived even before Stanley was born. Now their home was awash with electronic gadgetry. Their no-video rule had also crumbled in the face of a tearful, teething Stanley. By ten months he'd worked out how to use the video by himself anyway. He now had a VHS library only slightly smaller than that boasted by the local Blockbuster.

Stanley's plumply cherubic face had a look of wonder on it. Richard loved it when he looked like this. He was overwhelmed by his feelings for his son. His son. He said it to himself again. It sounded good. Solid. Richard bent his head towards Stanley and, glancing around to make sure no one was looking, gave him a furtive kiss on the head. He still felt a bit uncomfortable kissing another person of the male gender, even his son, in public. People might think he was some sort of Italian, for goodness' sake.

'Woo-woo!' Stanley exclaimed, pointing at the screen.

'It's actually not a woo-woo, it's a squirrel, but good try,' Richard corrected him gently.

Richard had spent Beth's pregnancy being alternately terrified and excited. At the moment she'd told him they were going to be parents, he'd felt a surge of pride. It was like playing in a crucial football match at school and being the one to score the decider a minute before time. Richard had got a ball in the back of the net! If he hadn't thought Beth would have decided he was mad and therefore totally unfit to be a father, he'd have pulled his shirt up over his head and run round and round the living room shouting: 'One nil, one nil . . .'

Once Stanley was born, Richard had been determined not to be one of those dads who never saw their kids. He'd carried him in the sling when they went to the supermarket, so as to give Beth a break, and he couldn't have been prouder if it had been an Olympic gold medal he was wearing round his neck. Plus, from the very beginning, he had done his share of the feeding and the bathing.

Richard had to admit that he wasn't that keen on changing nappies. The first time he'd had to do it, he'd found the smell so overpowering he'd sprayed Stanley's bottom with some of Beth's perfume to try and mask the foul odour. This having been successful, he began to make a habit of it, until Beth asked him why Stanley reeked of Calvin Klein Obsession. He'd thought his idea was brilliant, but she'd gone mad and made him buy her a whole new bottle. Must have been her hormones or something.

Richard had heard all about hormones at Beth's antenatal classes. He'd got chatting to some of the other fathers and, in the break between discussing loft conversions and the correct fitting of car seats, those blokes who already had kids had filled the ones who didn't in. They'd muttered darkly about post-natal mood swings. They'd also all had a grey look about them, and, depending on how many sprogs they had, drove either a Renault Espace or a ten-year-old Volvo estate with the tax disc about to expire. Their cars seemed a sort of tragic metaphor for their lives.

Richard had been totally freaked-out by this vision of his future and had pushed it immediately to the back of his mind. Still, over the last twelve months, he had looked in on his own life and occasionally seen glimpses of those grey men and their wired wives, and it frightened the hell out of him.

Not that Richard didn't adore Stanley. He did. It was Stanley's effect on their lives that he didn't always like. Why couldn't he just have his old life back, but with Stanley in it? Beth seemed to have adjusted to all the new routines and responsibilities of motherhood, but something in Richard rebelled. Yes, he wanted to be a dad, a good dad, but he didn't want to be forced to grow up to do it.

In the last year, Beth had transformed into a mother, and she seemed to have done it effortlessly. The fatherhood bit, now that was a different thing entirely. It was going to take Richard a whole lot longer to work that out, by which time Stanley would probably be a seventeen-year-old heroin addict who mugged old grannies and then told the judge it was all Richard's fault for being such a crap dad.

Richard looked over his shoulder at Beth. She was engrossed in her painting. She *had* changed, and he was ashamed to say it, but he didn't like it. He knew she'd had to, but, secretly, he wanted the old Beth back. The one who wasn't tired all the time, who wore make-up, nice bras and gave him neck massages. Yes, he knew it was selfish, but he couldn't help himself.

But maybe this was what being married with kids was supposed to be like. Perhaps all those grey men with their horrible cars felt the same distant rumbling of discontent that Richard did. God! Maybe even his own dad had felt this way. The feeling wasn't unbearable. You could probably push it to the back of your mind if you wanted to. It was like the sound of a party a few streets away, not that they ever went to parties any more. Or if they did, they ended up in the kitchen discussing the price of babysitters with another shattered-looking couple.

Richard realised that Beth had looked up from her plate and was watching him. He felt guilty. He smiled and waved, his wave having a manic edge. She waved back.

While Richard had been in his silent reverie, Beth had been having thoughts of her own. She had been noticing how Richard's wavy dark brown hair was sticking out at all angles, just as it always did.

When they were first dating, Richard had been the owner of a motorbike helmet. Not the bike. Just the helmet. He used to sit in the living room wearing his helmet for at least an hour before they went out at night, in an effort to flatten his hair down. Now, at thirty-eight, he was thinning slightly at the front. Beth sometimes caught him examining ads for hair transplants, at which point she would say the words 'Elton' and 'John' and he'd snap out of it.

Richard's features weren't conventionally handsome. His nose was a little too long, his lips were unexpectedly feminine and his dark brown eyes now sprouted a fan of wrinkles at the corners. His complexion had the pallor that comes from too many hours in a TV studio. But Beth wouldn't have changed anything.

When she and Richard had met, they'd been runners for the same small independent TV production company. That was nine years ago. Richard was still passionate about his work and the cleverest man Beth had ever met. Plus, he could make her laugh so hard she had to cross her legs to prevent herself wetting her knickers, although, admittedly, since childbirth, reruns of Basil Brush could achieve the same effect.

When they'd first been together, Richard had wanted to be John Pilger. These days, he was executive producer of *Smart Talk*, a topical talk show fronted by a plump former hotel manager called Gordon Taylor. Gordon was a Real Person Turned Presenter, a category that was fast replacing the Actor Turned Presenter as a fashionable way to fill the screen. Largely this was because they were cheap. Bung a Real Person a hundred and fifty quid, plus a cheese roll, and they were happy.

Gordon had been discovered in a docusoap. His knowledge of current affairs was roughly equal to Prince Charles's acquaintance with Yardie patois. Still, Richard liked to feel he hadn't compromised too much. His programme on the Euro was up for an award from the Television Association, an accolade fortunately not contingent upon ratings. The show had been trounced by snooker on one channel and a documentary about a women's collective of quilt-makers in Namibia on the other.

Stanley was the image of his father, the same brown eyes and long nose and even the same male-pattern baldness. Beth did hope that there was a period in his life, however brief, when he might enjoy a normal hairline. When Stanley was born, Beth had been a bit miffed that he looked so much like Richard. Nine months of not drinking or smoking and he didn't have the decency to look even a little bit like her. When she first saw him, she felt like knocking back eight glasses of wine and smoking forty fags just to get even.

Beth suddenly realised that Richard had turned round. Their eyes locked. He smiled and waved. The wave was a bit odd. Maybe he was embarrassed by their surroundings. She waved back.

Richard turned back round and Stanley climbed off the seat and danced in front of the TV, hopping from foot to foot with his hands raised triumphantly in the air. He looked like someone at a rave, not that Beth had ever been to a rave. She had thought about a last-ditch spot of 'largin' it' in Ibiza before her Zimmer frame cluttered up the dance floor. However, since she tended to nod off during *Jubilee Road* these days, going to a club that didn't even open till three a.m. was a bit of a non-starter.

Beth sighed, suddenly aware of her own tiredness. Richard didn't understand how drained she often felt. His life hadn't really changed since Stanley. Yes, he did a bit of bathing and there had been that period, early on, when he'd insisted on taking Stanley to the supermarket in the sling. Beth would have preferred to take the pram. As it was, he'd swanned about being cooed over by fifteen-year-old check-out girls and she'd had to pack all the shopping into the car on her own.

Richard was fantastic at doing the showy bits of fatherhood. He was less expert at the hard grind. It would never have occurred to him to change the sheets in Stanley's cot, for example. But then, in all the years they'd been together, he had never once changed a loo roll. He could manage to call up the football results on Ceefax using buttons on the TV remote she'd never even seen, but an empty loo roll holder was beyond him. Beth wondered if there was something in the male chromosome that bestowed selective blindness. Richard was more than able to spot if she'd thrown out any of his mountain of old records. Yet he seemed incapable of noticing they were low on nappies, locating a chemist, going in and buying some. She had to do that.

When it came to the organisation life with Stanley required, that was all down to Beth too. If he was due for a jab, or was invited round to a friend's house, or had grown out of all his socks, Beth had to sort it out. She made the calls, did the shopping, juggled her diary. If Stanley was ill, it was Beth who took a day off. If someone had to get back in time to pick him up from nursery, it was Beth who left the office early. And if she couldn't, she organised a stand-in. Beth's life was now ruled by the wall planner. She was Wall Planner Woman.

Beth looked at the back of Richard's head. She felt love even for that. It wasn't a lack of feeling that was the problem. She loved Richard without question. She couldn't even say she was consciously unhappy with him. Most of the time she was fine. It was just that she felt ground down by the hard slog of daily life with him. She needed more help. She didn't like to nag. She hated being a nag, but that was what she was turning into. Sometimes she heard herself and cringed.

Beth realised that Richard was looking at her again. She felt guilty and smiled to cover it.

'Mama!' Stanley exclaimed.

Richard got up and headed back towards Beth, carrying Stanley. 'Time for a little rest,' he said. 'Then it's home to bed.'

Richard put Stanley in the high chair next to Beth, then sat down himself, opposite. 'I'm knackered,' he told her. 'I could murder a beer.'

You could probably go on feeling the way Beth and Richard did for years without doing anything about it. Then again, it would only take one of them to pick up a small stick of dynamite to blow the lot to smithereens.

Chapter Three

'Waah!'

Beth tried to open her eyes. Her lashes felt like they'd been Velcro'd together.

'Waah!'

When she finally managed to prise one eyelid open, she saw that the alarm clock, partially illuminated by a chink in the cream linen curtains, said 02:30. She groaned. When Beth was pregnant, she'd lost count of the number of mothers who'd announced smugly: 'Once the baby's born, you won't be able to remember what you did with your time before!' Well, she had no trouble recalling what she used to do at two thirty in the morning – sleep.

'Waah, waah!'

Beth dragged her legs out from under the white cotton duvet and lowered her feet on to the pale wood floor.

'Waah, waah!'

She wondered how one small baby could make such a lot of noise. She began to move, slowly, towards the door and into the hall.

'Waaah, waah, waah!' Stanley was getting more insistent. His cry was no longer monotone. It moved up at the end. Another couple of months and he'd be able to do 'Nessun Dorma', or more likely, something by Iron Maiden.

Beth felt cold in Richard's blue Paul Weller T-shirt. What was it with heterosexual men and Paul Weller? Gay guys had any number of icons to worship – Kylie, Jane McDonald, Keith from Boyzone. Straight men only seemed to have Paul Weller.

If only Beth had known about the Paul Weller thing when she was single. Back then, she'd had to use the fresh basil test to establish whether a prospective boyfriend was straight or gay. This involved following him round a supermarket. If he put fresh basil in his basket, he was definitely gay. This was on the grounds that straight single men found it arduous putting so much as a slice of pizza in the microwave. Sadly, the accuracy of this once fail-safe test had now been eroded by Jamie Oliver, so it was back to flicking through a CD collection for signs of Judy Garland or the Pet Shop Boys.

Beth's bare feet made a slapping sound on the hall floor. She opened the door to Stanley's room and staggered in.

'Waah, waah, waah, waah!'

She bent forward to pick Stanley up. His eyes were wide open. This, plus his semi-baldness seen through the hazy half-light given off by his globe nightlight, gave him an eerie Martian appearance. But then his eyes softened, he stared deep into hers and his lips quivered.

'Mama.'

Beth smiled sleepily. She gave Stanley a gentle kiss on his cheek. It was as soft and dusty as a marshmallow. She hugged him close.

'Mama,' he said again, squirming.

Beth settled herself into a chair with Stanley facing her on her lap. She began to hum quietly. 'Twinkle, twinkle, little star . . .'

Maternal instinct is a wonderful thing. No matter how ill, hungover or just plain exhausted a mother is, she will still get out of a nice warm bed, walk across a chilly hall and minister to a screaming child. This is behaviour that is beyond selflessness.

Beth looked at Stanley. He was sucking his thumb, his little cheeks going in and out like a pair of miniature bellows. While levering herself upright at this time of night was difficult, secretly she cherished these moments. They were her special times with Stanley.

People asked how she coped with getting up in the night and going to work the next morning. In fact, a night like this was perfect for mulling over work problems. As she rocked Stanley, Beth thought about *On The House*. There were rumours that Anastassia Frink was unhappy with the rushes of the new series. It was only a rumour, of course, but if true, some sort of executive shuffle had to be on the cards. What would that mean to Beth, Olivia and Siobhan?

Stanley was asleep now. His thumb had fallen out of his mouth and his arm was jutting out at an awkward angle. Beth tucked it in across his chest. He stirred slightly. She stroked his forehead, rearranging strands of his sparse hair across his bald bits. He looked like a miniature Jack Charlton.

Beth felt so tender towards Stanley. Yet she'd never yearned for children. In her twenties she'd barely thought about them. Babies had been like gallstones. She'd heard some people had them, but didn't really know what they involved.

It was when she reached her early thirties that Beth's feelings changed. She felt a tiny ripple of doubt cross the calm pool of her settled, childless existence. At first she'd vacillated. Did she really want to live life under a curfew? If they did go out, they'd have to be home from parties by eleven thirty because of the babysitter. It would be like being fifteen again, only the person sitting on the sofa waiting for you to come in would have emptied the fridge *and* expect you to pay for a taxi.

In the end, Beth adopted a bungee approach to having a baby. She did it even though she was terrified, because if she didn't, she might always regret it. But she hadn't regretted it for even one moment. Well, perhaps the moment she tried to wee for the first time after the birth she might have had just the merest smidgeon of doubt about her decision to procreate. But it had faded, erased by the sort of miraculous maternal amnesia that makes you want to have another baby even though the birth of the first was bloody hideous.

When Stanley arrived, Beth was shocked by the strength of her feelings for him. She found herself leaning over the crib when he was asleep, taking great lungfuls of his air, as if she could breathe him back inside her. She tried to be even-handed in her love, sharing it out between Richard and Stanley like a bag of liquorice allsorts. One kiss for you and one for you. But there was a teenage intensity to her feelings for Stanley. The closest thing she could imagine to it was if, at age nine, she'd been allowed to borrow Woody from the Bay City Rollers for the weekend. She'd probably have sat Woody on her bed and gazed at his tartan turn-ups with the same awe with which she now regarded Stanley's perfect fingers and toes.

Stanley was snoring, but Beth wouldn't put him down just yet. She pulled back one of the lilac nursery curtains and looked out through the glass. A street lamp threw a strange Tolkienish light over the street. It was empty of people. Beth stroked Stanley's shoulder and thought wistfully of the first night they'd spent together like this. He'd been only a few hours old and Beth had looked through the window just as she was doing now and had felt as if only she and Stanley existed in the whole world.

Next door, Richard turned over in his sleep. His arm went out automatically to touch Beth, but she wasn't there. He opened his eyes and looked round sleepily. The door was open and he could see the glow of Stanley's lamp coming from underneath his door. He grunted and wrapped the duvet tighter round himself. Then he hugged his knees up to his chest in a foetal position. The bed felt empty.

Valerie was staring at a copy of *Bravo!* magazine. A barely audible hissing was emanating from her tightly pursed lips, making her sound like she was having a slow puncture. She flicked over a page and the hissing was replaced by a sharp intake of breath, then a groan.

The reason for Valerie's ill-temper was spread across twelve pages of glossy paper. 'TV's Liam Smith welcomes you into his lovely Ibizan hideaway,' ran the headline, above snaps of sun-kissed gorgeousness. Here was Liam reclining on a sunlounger next to his Olympic-sized swimming pool. There he was inspecting the trees in his own private olive grove. In between, he could be seen stirring something in a pot in his peasant-style kitchen and flicking through last week's issue of *Bravo!* lounging on one of his many terraces.

On and on the pictures went, each one more fabulously luxurious than the last. Valerie felt sick. Here was Liam, nothing more than a jumped-up painter and decorator, living the life she should have had. Valerie would have screwed up her face in rage, but since her last batch of Botox, the most she was able to do was smirk weakly.

The last time Valerie had seen Liam, she'd been a panellist on *The Other Side Of The Letter Box* and his home had been featured. The panel had actually guessed him, an event so rare they'd mounted a brass plaque to him in the lobby of Channel 6, another source of Valerie's envy.

Well, if Liam could have a designer wardrobe, so could she. Valerie strode into her walk-in closet, the inky-blue silk of her lace-trimmed nightie and matching peignoir billowing behind her like an expensive parachute. She switched on the lights. They glittered off the polished wood. Her builder had warned against teak but Valerie had been adamant. What was the loss of an acre or two of rainforest against her wardrobe? They'd never even miss a few trees. It wasn't as if anyone except a few Indians ever actually went to the Amazon, was it? And they were probably too busy piercing themselves with bits of stick, according to Valerie, to notice the view anyway.

Valerie surveyed the racks of TV suits. TV suits are the same as other suits, only they come in brighter colours and have 'interesting' fashion details above the waist. She picked up the sleeve of a fuchsia number and then dropped it dismissively. She *had* to have some new clothes. Damn Olivia for being away. It would never have happened on *Jubilee Road*.

On *Jubilee Road*, Valerie had had a retinue of staff hanging upon her every word. She had a minion to carry her handbag and another to fan her when required. They hadn't even gone to the loo without asking permission first. Had Valerie got her way, her *Jubilee Road* drones wouldn't have had to do that either. She'd suggested they both have catheters fitted, so nothing, not even nature, would interrupt their twenty-four-hour devotion. That idea was vetoed, so Valerie had hired a couple of anorexics instead. They didn't have to stop work for meals and they were happy to run up and down stairs.

The copy of *Bravo!* was now sitting in the middle of the burgundy damask bedspread. Valerie glanced at it again. 'Age doesn't worry me,' Liam was quoted as saying. 'I think if you have a happy home life it shows on your face, doesn't it?' This jaunty sentence was accompanied by a photo of Liam with his 'lovely wife Soraya', a former Miss Singapore, and their many photogenic children.

This vision of domestic bliss was too much for Valerie. She was rumoured to be married to a man called Neville, except that no one had ever seen him. Neville did exist. He wrote the poems inside greetings cards for a living. Valerie was loath to take him out in public. At home, they had ceased to share a bed some eight years previously. Valerie had dispatched Neville to the spare room, along with Fluffy the cat, and a Baby Belling.

Liam's boasting about his happy home life underlined the deficiencies in Valerie's own domestic arrangements. She fell upon *Bravo!* like a hyena upon an antelope carcass, ripping pages from it and scattering them on the floor. Then she walked up and down on them, her walk becoming a demonic dance as she speared the pages with the stiletto heels of her fluffy mules. Finally she collapsed back on to the bed, beating the cushions with her fists.

'Why? Why? Why?' she shouted.

There was a timid knock on the door, followed by a disembodied voice.

'Can I come in?'

'No,' shrieked Valerie.

The door swung open anyway, and Neville's shiny bald head popped round it, offering a perfect reflection of the chaos in the room. He'd brought Valerie a cup of morning tea. He glanced at the pages of magazine strewn on the floor and attached to her heels. He sighed.

'Oh, dear. Prozac not working then, snookums?'

Beep, beep . . . Beep, beep.

Beth reached over in a panic to turn off the alarm, then leaned back and waited for her heart rate to return to normal. She glanced over at Richard. He hadn't moved, but then he could have slept through a Viking invasion. His mouth was hanging open and a tiny rivulet of dribble traced a line down his chin. He looked rumpled but adorable.

Richard turned over and flung an arm over Beth's stomach.

'What time it is?' he whispered without opening an eye.

'Seven. Better get Stanley up for breakfast.'

He pulled her towards him. 'No point waking him. Why don't we make the most of him being out for the count?'

Beth was torn. Part of her would have sold a kidney for some more sleep. She had eye bags you could balance a cup and saucer on and she hadn't shaved her legs for a month. She wasn't feeling exactly sexy. Still, they hadn't had sex for, how long was it, exactly? Five, six days? A week? It couldn't be two, could it?

Beth removed Richard's arm from her tummy. 'I'll just nip down and get a bottle in case he stirs,' she said.

As Beth climbed out of bed and headed off to the kitchen, Richard lay back against her warm pillow. He could smell her on it, sweet and musky. He wished she was here, rather than just her scent.

Richard saw Beth's all-consuming love for Stanley, and although he never said anything, he was jealous. He was ashamed of feeling that way, but he couldn't help it. He felt supplanted by Stanley, shunted into second place by his arrival. At times, he felt three again, the day his mother had brought his little sister home and he'd asked her to take the baby back to the shop.

Even when Beth wasn't fussing around Stanley, her baby antennae were up, just in case he should wake/need a bottle/ require changing/want a toy/fancy something to eat/whatever. Every moment Richard spent with Beth, he was aware that she was looking over his shoulder. He only ever had ninety-five per cent of her attention now. It was like listening to a radio station on a bad transistor. There was static all the time, a bleed-in from another station. Station Stanley.

Richard needed Beth to make him feel that he was still the most important person in the world to her. He used to feel like that when they made love, but these days they didn't have time for that. They had sex instead, or, more precisely, they had parental sex, which is a lot faster. Parental sex has to be accomplished in that tiny portion of free time when a) your child is asleep and b) you aren't. This makes it reminiscent of one of those 'How Many Cream Crackers Can You Eat In One Minute?' contests. You go like the clappers for fear of being interrupted by the buzzer, aka the baby's cry.

Richard sighed and glumly reached over to the bedside table. He found the remote and switched on the TV to watch the news. Might as well use the time before Beth got back ... When she arrived, she stuck the bottle on the bedside table and climbed under the duvet. Richard looked at her. Even without her make-up, he still fancied her. He kissed her and slid his right hand downwards to rest on top of her right breast.

Beth disengaged her lips. 'Do we have to have the TV on?'

'Well, you're always complaining that men can't do more than one thing at once,' replied Richard, smiling mischievously.

'I meant looking after Stanley, emptying the washing machine and answering the phone!'

Richard ignored Beth's comment. His hand travelled further down her body and up under her T-shirt. 'Well, this isn't very romantic either. Can you take it off? Don't know why you wear it.'

Beth could have launched into an explanation of how, since Stanley, you could read her bottom in Braille and it was saying 'Help!' But maybe Richard genuinely hadn't noticed, in which case she didn't want to draw his attention to it. If he had and he was just being too polite to say, well, she'd rather not know.

Beth luxuriated in the feeling of her naked skin next to her husband's. Getting married was something she had had her doubts about. It seemed terribly old-fashioned and fuddy-duddy. It was only when Stanley was born that they decided to do it. Now she rather liked the whole wife/husband thing. It felt uncomplicated. Sorted out.

Richard's head moved down Beth's tummy and disappeared under the duvet. Beth tried to lose herself in the moment, but over Richard's shoulder she could see the TV. They were doing a report about a new lap-dancing club opening on a quiet residential street. There were the usual interviews with appalled residents and a Tory MP with flushed cheeks and double cuffs. Then a blonde woman came on the screen.

The blonde was a lap dancer. Her name was Chastity. Just Chastity. Nothing else. Why did strippers do that, choose names that promised the very opposite of what they were being paid to deliver? Had they never heard of the Trade Description Act?

Beth ruffled Richard's hair to show appreciation. 'Yes, yes,' she offered half-heartedly.

'We're just providing a service,' Chastity was saying. She hadn't got a bad speaking voice. It was a bit put-on, though. It was a voice that hadn't so much been polished as scoured. There was just a vestige of an Essex twang left, clinging on like burned egg to the bottom of a frying pan.

'It's called free enterprise,' she said firmly.

Richard's head popped out from underneath the duvet. 'I don't expect a multiple orgasm every time, but it would be nice if you made a bit of an effort.'

'Sorry. Not a bad story, though,' Beth said. 'Might be good for *Smart Talk.*'

Richard watched for a minute. 'Yeah, "Would you want a lap-dancing club on your street?" sort of thing. Who is she?'

'Chastity something. You know these strippers, as careless with their surnames as they are with their bikini tops.'

They both laughed, and Richard found the remote and clicked off the TV.

'Now where were we?' he said.

He paused like a cross-Channel swimmer taking a lungful of air before plunging into the deep, and dived back under the duvet.

'Waah!'

Beth froze.

'Waah!'

Richard carried on doggedly kneading her thighs.

'Waah!'

'Look, I'll just—'

Richard interrupted her. 'He'll stop in a minute.' His voice was muffled from the duvet.

'Waah!'

'No he won't,' said Beth, peeling back the covers and starting to disentangle herself from his arms.

Richard didn't move. 'Just leave him.' Now he sounded exasperated.

Beth got out of bed, picked up the bottle and walked towards the door.

'You always do this,' said Richard. 'If you just left him . . .'

Beth was anguished. 'Look, we can have another go tonight.'

'You said that last night.'

'I know, but I was tired and . . . I don't think you have any idea of all the stuff I do that you don't even think of. When was the last time you cleaned his toys, or folded his vests, or boiled some organic bloody parsnips?'

Richard winced. He had made a fatal tactical error. He had started an argument with a woman suffering from sleep deprivation and working mother's angst.

Forget all those pamphlets on nappy rash and mastitis they give couples when they bring their baby home from the hospital; Richard wished he'd been given just one piece of advice: after a woman has given birth, Never Argue With Her About Anything Ever Again. The slightest disagreement is liable to escalate into an uncontrollable, one-sided torrent of dissatisfaction.

'... I mean, yesterday I spent half an hour cooking Stanley macaroni cheese and he wouldn't eat any of it. He just screamed,' Beth was saying tearfully. 'And when you come home he's all smiles. And, well, I am trying my best to hold things together. You know how things are at work. They're really piling on the pressure and there is talk that Anastassia isn't happy and someone new might be arriving on the show ...'

Richard was in real trouble now. Anger and tears, the female emotional double whammy.

Beth knew that expecting Richard to make a useful contribution to this conversation was like asking him to climb Everest. He simply didn't possess the right equipment to make the trip. He'd need a map and years of study before he could so much as tramp about in the empathetic foothills, let alone reach the emotional summit. But she couldn't stop herself. She was working up for the third wave of chest-clearing when Stanley came to Richard's rescue.

'Waah!'

Beth swung open the bedroom door and stomped out. Over her shoulder she saw Richard pick up the remote and turn up the volume on the TV. He leaned towards it, engrossed by the blonde lap dancer.

'She's interesting,' he said aloud, then looked round to see if Beth had heard. She hadn't.

'I have Anastassia Frink for you,' announced a brisk voice, followed by a click.

Patric Mortimer, boss of Futura Productions, was sitting at his desk. In his early fifties, his handsome face now lined and his tall frame gone a bit soft around the edges, he was still an impressive man. But he was nervous. It was seven a.m., and he'd been in the office since six, waiting for this call. It was the verdict on the new series. Patric wasn't expecting an easy ride. Even had Programme One been brilliant, Anastassia would still have given him a drubbing. She was notorious. She made Catherine the Great look like Pam Ayres.

Channel 6 was a commercial station and Anastassia's life was devoted to one thing: ratings. Given the choice, she would have preferred to fill her schedules with fly-on-the-wall documentaries about the sex industry, interviews with people who claimed to have been kidnapped by aliens, and anything on Nazis. However, there was the little matter of the station's franchise agreement. This stipulated that Channel 6 must provide a certain degree of 'quality programming'. In factual terms, this was meant to imply earnest documentaries of the it's-grim-up-north variety. But only one man and his ferret watched those. So the factual quota was filled with shows like *On The House*.

Patric raked a hand through his elegantly greying hair. It was long and swept back so that it touched his collar. Patric's hairstyle had nothing to do with fashion and everything to do with pissing other, balder men off. He braced himself as Anastassia's unmistakable Geordie tones exploded on to the line. 'What the fuck do you think you're doing?' she shrieked. 'It's crap, total crap.'

Listening to Anastassia was like going to an Ian Paisley rally, only Ian Paisley would probably have encouraged more audience participation. Anastassia just ranted. Patric, not normally a shrinking violet – he had, after all, built up a multi-million-pound business – tried to interrupt Anastassia, without success.

'Anastassia, if I could just–'

Anastassia ignored him.

'I could get better stuff if I handed a camcorder to my eighty-two-year-old grandmother. At least it would be in fucking focus. What is this, Ecstasy fucking TV? I didn't ask for arty crap. I just want a fucking makeover show, OK, Patric? If that's not too difficult for you.'

Patric had the receiver held about a foot from his ear. He was used to Anastassia's mouth-frothings. He wouldn't have taken this sort of abuse from anyone else, but he needed her and she knew it. He held his temper.

'I've had enough,' Anastassia bellowed. 'If you don't know how to make a fucking DIY show, then I know someone who does. Her name's Karen Newsome and she'll be arriving at the end of the week.' And with that she slammed down the phone, leaving Patric to wonder who Karen Newsome was, and what she was going to do to his TV show.

Chapter Four

'Twenty-four, twenty-five, twenty-six . . . Come on. Get your flabby ass into gear. Twenty-seven, twenty-eight . . .'

A black man the size of an oak tree, wearing a camouflage-print boiler suit, was standing over a small blonde-haired woman. He was shouting instructions and abuse in a loud American accent. She was face down, her expression one of grim determination. Her body was moving back and forth rhythmically as she did press-ups.

'Twenty-nine, thirty . . . You gotta gimme fifty o' these,' the man boomed, putting a boot in the small of the woman's back and pushing down.

Her spine began to collapse, but she fought it. Her face descended briefly into a quagmire of muddy grass.

'I said fifty! You lily-livered piece o' chicken shit! Get yo' white ass up here!'

The woman's frame stiffened and she pulled her back into a horizontal position again, brown smudges now decorating her nose and one cheek. She spat a bit of grass out of her mouth, gritted her teeth and continued her press-ups.

'Thirty-one, thirty-two,' he counted as she worked her way up to the required number.

When she had finished, she rolled over and lay on her back on the grass. The sun was just coming up over Regent's Park. The first geese were waddling into the water like plump Victorian bathers taking to the sea at Brighton. A heron flew low over the lake, its wings spread out as if it was wearing a Notting Hill Carnival costume. The sun glittered off the water and the squirrels bolted excitedly from tree to tree, disturbing the fresh dew. She saw none of this. She lifted her shoulders off the wet turf, totally focused on a series of sit-ups.

'One, two, three . . .' Now it was she who was counting.

'OK, that's enough f' today,' the tall man announced. His voice had softened and he was bending down to her level.

'But Brad,' she whined.

'No, really, I think that's enough.' He was being kind, but firm.

'I can do some more,' she insisted, her tiny frame – she couldn't have been more than five foot two and a size six – moving even faster. The effect was of a clockwork doll that had been wound way too tightly.

Brad was adamant. 'No,' he declared, exasperation creeping into his voice. 'You've already done a half-marathon and that twenty-two-K bike ride this mornin'. Time to take a break.'

Suddenly Barbie transmogrified into Lara Croft. 'Take a break! Take a break!' She was the one shouting now. 'I didn't hire you as my personal trainer so I could *take a break*. I am a winner and winners don't *take a break*!'

Her sit-ups went into overdrive as she bellowed: 'When I was at the boot camp in Venezuela, we did a full marathon every day, plus two hours of tree climbing, a ten-K white-water canoe ride *and* we had to carry the canoe home. We were given half a carrot and the water off a gura gura leaf to live on and I never felt better. I certainly didn't *take a break*.'

Brad shook his head in disbelief. 'You never heard o' just lyin' on a beach for a holiday? Why you gotta pay ten thousand dollars to be marched up an' down a jungle for a fortnight? What kind of dumb-ass idea is that?'

'I like to be challenged,' the woman answered, turning back on to her front, putting her hands behind her ears and arching her back up and down.

The man lay down next to her. He stared upwards. 'Y'know, you career bitches are the worst. Y'never know when t'quit. Always pushin' y'self too hard. Y'wanna try getting a life, honey. A man, kids, a home, y'know?'

'If I want to hear drivel like that I'll phone my life coach,' the woman spat, sarcastically.

'All I'm sayin' is you wanna try kicking back occasionally. Even in the Marine Corps we take it easy sometimes. Now, how about a cuppa coffee and a nice ol' chocolate brownie?'

At this, the woman exploded again. 'You're a soldier, man. Pull yourself together!' she screamed. Then she turned on to her side and, supporting herself on one elbow, began to move her leg up and down.

'Chocolate brownie? I haven't eaten a gram of fat since 1986 and that was only because I was putting my make-up on while I was on the phone and I accidentally bit the end off a lipstick. Come on, there's an hour before I have to start e-mailing.'

The man sighed and raised his eyes to the sky.

'OK, OK, we can do a five-mile jog, but no bricks in your back-pack this time.'

The woman jumped to her feet. 'You see, the mistake you make is to forget that you're not dealing with just anyone here. I am Karen Newsome, and Karen Newsome does not *take a break*. And neither do the people who work for her.'

'Damn!'

Wearing a slightly crazed expression, Olivia burst in to the *On The House* office. She was carrying an overflowing shoulder bag and pulling a suitcase on wheels.

Beth looked over at Siobhan and smiled. They both got up from their seats and walked towards their friend. Olivia abandoned her luggage and hugged Beth and Siobhan warmly. 'They only had *OK!* and *Good Housekeeping* on the plane! I practically had to inhale *Vogue* in the taxi on the way back from Heathrow just to feel normal.'

Beth smiled even more broadly. It was good to have Olivia back.

Siobhan broke up the happy reunion. She looked at her watch. 'Oh God, I'd better go. I'm off to do a recce in Swindon.'

'Not quite Milan, is it, darling?' said Olivia.

'No, I'm going to see a leaky kitchen roof.'

'Sounds attractive,' said Beth.

'That's nothing,' said Olivia, looking at Siobhan. 'Remember that house where that woman had taken up the living-room floor and her husband had his armchair balanced on rubble for seven years?'

'Oh, yeah. God, that was bad. I still think that poor couple who had to use a bucket to flush the loo for five years was worse, though. Imagine that, having to use a bucket!' laughed Siobhan.

'I had a boyfriend like that once,' said Olivia.

'Like what?' said Beth.

'Had a place in the Highlands. Sixteenth century. No running water. Owned half of London but liked to go native at weekends. Had to fill a bucket from a tap in the yard.'

'How did you cope?' said Siobhan incredulously.

'He had a very large penis.'

'And both balls, presumably,' said Beth, looking pointedly at Siobhan, who then looked guilty.

Olivia wrinkled her brow and looked at Siobhan questioningly.

'Tell you later,' Siobhan offered.

'Anyway,' continued Olivia, 'the large penis man's house did have electricity, and that was what really put me off him. You see, I caught him drying his pubic hair with a hairdryer.'

'Why would anyone do that?' exclaimed Beth.

'God knows. A bit of a turn-off, I can tell you.'

Siobhan turned away. 'Look, I'd love to discuss the sexual deviances of the aristocracy, but I've got to go. I'll see you later.' As she picked up her jacket and jogged towards the door, she narrowly missed Jack, who had rounded the corner.

'Hi, blondie,' he said as they did a dance to avoid a collision. Then he began sauntering towards Beth and Olivia. Siobhan turned to watch. He had rather a good saunter, she had to admit.

Siobhan walked out of the room and Olivia nudged Beth, stifling a giggle. 'Does Jason Donovan know what he looks like?'

Jack settled himself on the corner of Beth's desk, leaning forward enough for his denim shirt to fall open and reveal three inches of tanned, muscled chest. One of his legs was propped up on the desk, setting his strong thigh off to advantage. He nodded to Olivia before turning to Beth and fixing her with his blue eyes.

'G'day, Beth. You're looking prettier than a day-old dingo.'

Jack could go on like this for ages. It didn't really matter who he was chatting up. Almost any female would do.

'Hi, Jack. How are you?' asked Beth.

'No worries.'

'Good.'

'Wondered if you fancied a few tinnies later?'

Things must be a bit thin on the housewife front, thought Beth. But she didn't say that. Instead, she gave him a gentle brush-off. 'Oh, you know, Jack. Husband and baby to get back to.'

'You married Sheilas are no fun.'

'We have our moments,' said Olivia, raising an eyebrow and vampily flicking her hair over her shoulder.

Olivia was one of the few women Jack didn't flirt with. He didn't 'get' her. To him, she might as well have been a creature from the black lagoon, and the way he looked at her, that was probably where he thought she belonged. Olivia favoured the designer dishevelled look. It was a style that only other girls really understood. Men were never quite sure if what she'd got on was really, really expensive or had come out of a skip.

Jack swivelled his bottom towards Olivia and gave her a slow appraisal. 'You know, if you made a bit of an effort, you'd be a bonzer Sheila.'

'Thank you, Jack, though I'm not sure I should take wardrobe advice from someone who comes from a country where they hang corks from their hats,' Olivia commented drily.

Jack shrugged, swung his leg off the desk and walked away. When he was out of range, Olivia bent in towards Beth, whispering conspiratorially: 'I know he's an idiot, but he might be interesting in bed. Probably tie you to the headboard with his bush whip or something. Maybe he's got a snake, or a crocodile.'

'Don't be ridiculous,' Beth said. 'Anyway, I'm married and I've got a child!'

'Yeah, and I've got four and . . .' Olivia got closer to Beth. 'Well, I don't think there'll be a fifth, that's for sure. Chance would be a fine thing.'

'Things no better?' asked Beth.

'Well, I am getting a bit worried. It's supposed to be the woman who goes off sex after kids, but Colin's just not interested. Maybe he doesn't fancy me any more. What do you think?'

'Look at you, Olivia. You're fantastic-looking.'

Olivia pulled her shoulders back. Her expression suddenly reminded Beth of Mrs Thatcher on that tank, only without the head scarf. Olivia was resolute and determined.

'I've decided things have got to change. I've talked to Colin and we're both going to make an effort. Actually, we had a go on Friday night, but Seth threw up Alphabetti Spaghetti all over his Manchester United duvet.'

'Manchester United . . .?'

'I know, I know. Colin's mother bought it for him. Hideous, of course, but he loves it. A wardrobe full of Armani Bambino and he wants to sleep next to polyester! Anyway, I spent twenty minutes cleaning up vomit and by the time I'd got back to bed Colin was asleep. And I'd been to Agent Provocateur and got a basque and everything.'

'Did you keep the receipt?'

'Oh, Beth, always Mrs Practical.'

* * *

'So, just tell me again why you drilled all those holes in the ceiling?' asked Siobhan. She was standing in a kitchen in Swindon, clutching a notebook and pen and staring up at what looked like a colander overhead.

'Well, my mate – he's called Geoff – well, Geoff put his foot through the flat roof, right?' said Steve, homeowner and potential contributor to *On The House*. 'I reckoned the whole lot'd come down if I didn't, like, spread the load.'

'So you now have lots of little leaks rather than one big one?'

'That's about it, yeah.'

Siobhan scribbled in her notebook and pulled her cagoule tighter around her. Her feet felt clammy in her borrowed wellies. It was raining steadily in Swindon, and thanks to Steve's handiwork, it was as damp inside as out. Siobhan cast a pitying look at Michelle, Steve's other half. She was holding a pair of saucepans, attempting to catch at least some of the myriad drips coming from the ceiling. The fact that she wasn't succeeding was amply demonstrated by the growing puddle on the floor.

Brrng brrng. Siobhan's phone was ringing.

'Sorry, can you just excuse me a minute?'

It was a relief to be able to step into the dry living room. Siobhan retrieved her phone from her pocket and pulled back her hood.

'Hello?'

'Hi, it's Simon.'

Siobhan's energy drained from her. She felt dizzy, breathless, winded. It had been three months since she'd heard Simon's voice. Well, in real time anyway. She'd saved his answerphone messages, and when she'd had one too many glasses of Sauvignon Blanc she'd listened to them and cried great fat sobs of grief for the future she'd lost.

'Siobhan, are you there?'

She managed to stutter, 'Yes.'

At work, she'd been able to function, sort of. Beth and Olivia had covered for her when she couldn't cope. Once home, though, on her own, she'd climb on the sofa, hug a cushion and replay every moment of her relationship with Simon, where they'd been, what they'd done, what he'd said. She needed to anchor it in her mind.

Siobhan had tried to explain to Beth and Olivia why she loved Simon, but she hardly knew herself. On paper, it was crazy. He was a married man with three children. Even were he to leave Elaine, they'd never be able to walk off into the sunset together. There'd be maintenance to pay, and weekend access, and . . . But she couldn't help herself. Simon had a wounded animal quality about him. She wanted to look after him, nurse him back to health.

Siobhan knew Beth and Olivia didn't approve, but the fact that Simon hadn't left Elaine, far from putting her off, had actually strengthened her love for him. Had he been able just to up and leave his children, he wouldn't have been the kind, sensitive, caring man she loved. Indeed, he was the very opposite of the hard-hearted, selfish stereotype of the married man who plays away. Simon was racked with guilt, not just about Elaine, but about Siobhan as well.

Still, Siobhan had managed a rare moment of strength and had ended the affair. She hadn't wanted to, but the pain had over-whelmed what brief moments of happiness they shared. She was like a drinker who can no longer bear the hangovers. Now sober, she tried to remember the giddy feeling of being with Simon, but it had become distant until none of it seemed real at all. But it had been real, hadn't it? Four years they'd been seeing each other, allowing for a few gaps. That had to mean something. He had loved her, hadn't he?

'I love you.'

Siobhan felt the panic rise in her throat. If only Beth and Olivia were here, they'd tell her what to do. Without them, she could feel herself sinking into the quicksand of hope. It was the sort of hope that didn't just overcome experience, it pole-vaulted clean over it and landed the other side with a gymnast's flourish. She did have lots of experience with Simon. In four years, how many times had he let her down? How many times had he ripped out her heart and trampled all over it?

'I miss you.'

His voice wrapped around her like a warm towel after a hot bath. It felt deliciously comforting, cosily familiar. Her resolution began to ebb away. So what if she'd told him she never wanted to see him again? She'd tried going out with other people, and it hadn't worked. It was too hard. The ache in her stomach hadn't gone away. It had formed a stony knot of pain that sat heavily within her.

'Do you miss me?'

'Yes.' She said it quickly. The relief was enormous.

Siobhan began to walk up the hall. She opened the front door and stepped out. In the rain, no one would see her crying. First one hot tear then another and another ran down her cheeks. They stung, but they felt good too. They felt honest.

The words tumbled out. 'Oh, Simon, I love you and I miss you and I've been so miserable and–'

Simon interrupted her. 'Look, can I see you? Let's have a drink tonight. I'll meet you at that bar round the corner from your place at six thirty, the Illustrious . . .'

'Elusive Mermaid. It's called the Elusive Mermaid.'

'See you later.'

Long after Simon had put his phone down, Siobhan still had hers clasped to her ear, imagining she could still hear the echo of Simon's breathing. She was soaked, but she didn't care.

'Valerie doesn't do stairs.'

'What?'

'She doesn't do stairs. Well, she does, but only up, not down.'

Beth was in a minicab, being driven by an Albanian with bad English and a worse sense of direction. She was on the phone to a new researcher, explaining the delicate matter of the Valerie Stairs Rule. This stipulated that she could be filmed walking upstairs but never down. The researcher was calling from a tower block shoot in Telford. Unsurprisingly, perhaps, she was having a problem grasping the concept.

'I don't understand. Is she disabled?'

Beth had made the same mistake when she'd first arrived at *On The House*. Having been informed of the Valerie Stairs Rule, she had been about to order a Stanna stair lift when Tim, the camera-man, had taken her aside and filled her in. There was nothing wrong with Valerie's legs. It was her chin she was worried about.

Valerie had jowls. They were barely visible, but such was her paranoia about her age that she refused to be filmed from below.

So as to ensure that the camera remained always slightly above her, she had also attempted to make the height of the camera operator a contractual issue. Valerie wanted any cameramen under six feet two sacked or issued with compulsory heel lifts.

Valerie was not alone in disliking up-your-nose camerawork, otherwise known as Big Breakfast Syndrome. One rival female TV presenter of uncertain vintage was known to have stipulated that her camera be lifted an inch for every year she had her show. She'd been in TV a very long time. Her programmes were now shot from a scaffolding tower and rumour had it that the crick in her neck had become so severe she had to be fed from above like a baby starling.

Fortunately, Futura Productions had refused to accede fully to Valerie's wishes. A compromise had been reached whereby Valerie would not have to walk downstairs into camera. Gardening items would also, wherever possible, be conducted with Valerie occupying a specially dug trench.

Having ended the call, Beth looked blankly ahead of her and thought about her row with Richard. She hated arguing with him.

Maybe it was her fault. She had been up in the middle of the night with Stanley, which had probably made her tetchy. Richard hadn't ever actually asked her to do all the night feeds, but even after she'd gone back to work when Stanley was six months old, she'd continued to breast-feed him at night. Now she got up out of habit.

Still, it suited Richard, didn't it? There was that phrase he liked to use whenever a wash needed doing, a nappy needed changing or Stanley was lobbing toys out of his cot at three in the morning. 'But you're so much better at it than I am,' he would coo. It was the ultimate male get-out clause. When Cave Man couldn't be bothered rubbing two sticks together, did he turn to Cave Woman and say: 'You make fire, darling. You're so much better at it than me'?

Beth thought back to how she and Richard had been when they were first together. They'd leave restaurants and snog on street corners, totally unembarrassed by the people walking past. She wanted it to be that way again.

Brrng brrng. Beth was startled by the sound of her phone. She stuck the earpiece back in.

'What does Valerie need now?' she said grumpily.

'A warm personality?'

Beth laughed. It was Richard. She was so pleased she almost hugged the phone.

'Hi. I'm so sorry about our row. I hate us arguing.'

'Yeah, so do I,' he replied.

'Look, I'll make it up to you. What about tonight?'

'If you can stay awake.'

Beth bridled at this. 'Oh, come on.'

'I was joking. Jesus, you're so touchy.'

'I think it's called not having had a full night's sleep for twelve months. Anyway, I don't want to have another argument. I thought we might have lunch today.'

'Sorry, already booked.'

Beth was intrigued. 'Really, who with?'

'Well, it was your idea really. That girl we saw on the telly.'

Beth racked her brain. She couldn't for the life of her think what woman Richard might be referring to.

'You know, the dancer,' Richard prompted.

Beth was still clueless. Ballet? Tap? Bulgarian polka?

'The woman on the news. The one who worked at that club,' Richard finally admitted. 'You said I should get her on *Smart Talk.*'

'Oh, you mean the stripper!' Beth exclaimed.

'She's a lap dancer, actually,' Richard said, adding somewhat defensively, 'Anyway, you said I should get her on. So I'm having lunch with her.'

'Fine. Have a good time. I'm sure you'll find her fascinating.'

Beth was slightly miffed, but she had too much on her mind to be really annoyed. Never mind lunch: if the rumours about *On The House* were true, she might be out of a job by teatime.

Chapter Five

Richard had heard there were women like Chastity, but he had never actually met one. Until now. She sat across the table from him, her long, mini-skirted legs crossing and uncrossing. When not doing that, she was tossing her mane of straw-coloured hair or chewing the edge of her long, pink fingernails and pouting. Her behaviour had all the subtlety of a water cannon.

Richard didn't know how to react. In television, all the women had short hair and wore trouser suits. They didn't go in for hair-tossing or coquettish leg-crossing. Any female who tried that would have been clubbed to death by the sisterhood armed with their mobile phones. Richard bit into his jumbo chicken and ham sandwich and tried not to look at her.

A trickle of mayonnaise escaped from the corner of Richard's mouth. He dabbed it with a paper napkin, careful not to look up. The tables at Greed – 'The biggest lunch in town!' – were so small that, had his gaze shifted from the stainless-steel tabletop, he would have been confronted by two huge breasts, hovering just a few inches away.

'So, Chastity, the show's pretty simple, really,' Richard

explained, swallowing the last of his sandwich and shifting as far back as possible in his seat. 'You sit in the audience, like a normal member of the public. Only we mike you up. Then, after we've been to the MP, the vicar and the former prostitute – she'll be wearing a wig and glasses and will only be seen in silhouette, by the way – Gordon will come to you. Does that sound OK?'

Chastity leaned across the table. 'Well, I am new to all this,' she purred, flicking her hair over her shoulder and licking her already glossy lips. 'I just hope I won't be too nervous.'

Richard coughed self-consciously.

Chastity ran her finger round the rim of her cappuccino. She dipped it into the froth, then transferred this into her mouth. Richard's eyes almost popped out of his head. He swallowed and shifted again in his seat.

'No need to be nervous, Chastity. I'm sure you'll be fine.'

'Well, I'm in your hands, Richard,' she replied, raising an eyebrow.

Richard normally had trouble reading female body language. He and Beth would have a row, and to him it would have come totally out of the blue. Beth would insist he must have known she was upset for days, weeks even. He hadn't spotted any of the clues. It was as if they spent their lives both looking at the same optician's alphabet board, but while he could only make out the giant letters, she could manage the tiny print at the bottom.

Today, however, he was having no trouble reading the message flashing up in neon lights from across the table. Chastity was definitely coming on to him. Not that he would do anything about it, of course. Still, he warmed his ego in front of the blowtorch that was Chastity's attention. Here was a twenty-three year old, and a pretty damn gorgeous one at that, and she was flirting with him. Not bad for a thirty-eight year old with thinning hair and an empty bank account.

Richard pushed his shoulder blades back. OK, so he could probably do with a few sessions down the gym, but he was holding up pretty well. A week or so of sit-ups and he could get rid of his beer belly. It wasn't even a beer belly, really, more of a relaxation of his stomach muscles. They were resting. He just had to wake them up. Maybe he didn't even need to do that. He could still pull a blonde with huge breasts – he wasn't being sexist; she had put them on display, hadn't she? – even though the last bit of exercise he'd done was walk up the stairs at the office when the lift broke down.

Suddenly Richard felt a pang of guilt. He tried to pull himself together. But then his eyes fell upon Chastity's cleavage. He let them rest there, wallowing in the pillowy softness, telling himself it was all completely innocent, harmless. It was *only* lunch.

Chastity dipped her head and peered at Richard from under her sooty eyelashes. 'Actually, I could really do with your advice. I've been hoping to make the move into telly for a while and, well, you have so much *experience.*'

She paused, then reached over and touched his arm. He felt the hairs stand up on it.

'I know it's a lot to ask, but do you think we could meet up again so I could pick your brains? We could have a drink, or dinner. I would be *so grateful.*'

Now this wasn't *only* lunch. She was talking about a drink or dinner! Alarm bells started going off in Richard's brain. He was on the edge of a precipice and he knew it. He could step back, and he'd be safe. But who wants to be safe? He might be pushing forty, but wasn't there a bit of the spirit of adventure still in him? And what was wrong with that? Then again, if he took that step forward and accepted Chastity's invitation to a drink or dinner, he would plunge who knows where.

Richard couldn't decide what to do. This was a key moment in his life, and he vacillated. Still, male logic quickly kicked in. If in doubt, delude yourself. Richard pretended he hadn't seen the hair-flicking and the finger in the cappuccino. He pretended Chastity's hand wasn't on his arm. He pretended he wasn't about to betray his wife and son, and risk his marriage.

'Well, if it's *only* dinner . . .' he said.

Beth was hovering. She could have sat down. There were two chairs available. However, they were designer chairs. Once you sat down on one, it would take a couple of Def Leppard roadies and a block and tackle to get you out again. Beth decided not to risk it.

It was a quarter to nine at night, and Beth had been waiting for twenty minutes to see Patric. Marcia, Patric's PA, had called and asked if she could 'pop over' when she had a moment, which was secretarial code for: 'Get yourself round here now!' Now she had gone to get Beth a coffee, so Beth was left to scan Marcia's desk to pass the time. Her gaze was caught by a little pink teddy bear. There was a tag round its neck reading: 'Because you're luvable.' Yuck! If Richard ever gave her anything like that, she would divorce him immediately.

Marcia James fascinated Beth. Here was a woman almost totally defined by what she was not. She wasn't young, but she wasn't old either. She could have been anywhere between thirty-five and forty-five. She wasn't pretty, but neither was she ugly. About five feet four, Marcia had medium-length mid-brown hair, which she wore pulled back into a ponytail with a scrunchy. She was make-up-less and her clothes were of the Alexon school of fashion, circa 1982. They were sensible, but bland, and so was she. If Marcia James had been a paint, she'd have been honeysuckle white – the colour for the terminally noncommittal.

What intrigued Beth was what Marcia did when she wasn't at work, if that situation ever arose. Marcia appeared to always be in the office. Beth suspected she didn't go home at all and that she was actually half-woman, half-bat. At the end of a hard day at the PC, Marcia would simply hang upside down in the corner of the office, so as to be on hand for an early start the next morning.

If Marcia was bland, her boss was not. If you were a female Futura employee, then Patric's management style was openly flirtatious. Here was a man who liked women, and had obviously enjoyed the company of a great many. About the only female he didn't cast a roving eye over was Marcia. She was somehow off limits.

'Here you are, Beth,' said Marcia, returning to her desk. 'Milk, no sugar, right?'

Beth nodded.

'I also brought some biscuits.' She lifted a plate up to Beth's face. 'There's Hobnobs, Bourbons, gypsy creams and some oaty ones.'

That was another thing about Marcia. She was fearsomely organised. Jesus, she was probably one of those people who actually read their bank statements, thought Beth. She waved away the biscuits. Her eye was caught once more by the luvable teddy bear on the desk.

'Do you like my teddy?' asked Marcia eagerly. 'I collect them. I've got a hundred and thirty-seven others at home. I'll bring some of them in if you like.'

'No, no. That's all right, Marcia,' said Beth.

'It's no trouble.'

Beth cast about desperately for some way to change the subject and so avoid death by stuffed-toy boredom. She had a brainwave. It was a brave strategy, but she had no choice. 'How's the toe?'

Marcia had recently had an ingrown-toenail operation and was only too happy to talk about it.

'Fortunately they managed to save part of the nail. Did an amazing job really . . .'

Beth nodded, but she wasn't listening. Waiting out here for her meeting with Patric reminded her of the time, aged thirteen, she'd been caught wearing earrings at school and was sent to see the headmistress. She felt the same sense of dread. Back then, her punishment had been a week's detention, a pretty stiff sentence since it meant missing *Grange Hill*.

'. . . After that, they had to kill off the nerve.' Marcia was still going, totally unaware of Beth's lack of interest. 'That way it doesn't grow back. Would you like to see?'

Before Beth could say anything, Marcia had her left beige court shoe off and had unpeeled a stone-coloured pop sock. It was at that moment that Patric's head appeared round the office door.

'Would you like to . . . ?' Patric had spotted Marcia's naked foot up on the desk and it had thrown him '. . . um, er, come in, Beth?'

There was a pause as Marcia froze in embarrassment and Beth blushed in sympathy. Patric took in the vision of Marcia's pasty thigh where her pleated skirt had ridden up. His gaze then fell upon the discarded pop sock. He stepped forward, took a biro out of his top pocket and speared the sock. He lifted the offending item into the air and held it aloft as if it were a rare but poisonous mushroom.

'What is this?'

There was silence.

'Marcia, what is this exactly?'

If Marcia could have secreted herself in the one-inch gap between her desk and the filing cabinet she would have done so.

'It's a pop sock, Patric.'

'A what?'

'A pop sock.'

'*A pop sock.*' Patric dragged out the words like a small child stretching bubblegum. It wasn't that he was revolted. He wasn't even being deliberately mean. His expression was one of horrified fascination. He had been given an unexpected peek inside Marcia's lingerie drawer. It was a place he clearly had never expected to go. Now he'd got there, he was wishing he hadn't made the trip.

Marcia reached forward and took the sock from Patric, scrunching it up in her fist to make it disappear. Her shoulders were hunched. Her back was curved. She was literally shrinking into a corner. Beth suddenly felt sorry for her. OK, the toe thing was gross, but hosiery humiliation was too much for any woman to bear alone.

Perhaps Beth should demonstrate a bit of pop-sock solidarity – confess that she too had been known to wear them? Hell, she could also admit to having the odd comfy bra that had gone grey in the wash, and a pair of favourite opaque black tights that had a hole in one toe. Beth looked at Patric. Maybe not. She made a mental note to get herself a La Perla G-string when she had a free moment. That would be in about 2010.

Once inside Patric's office, he motioned Beth away from the desk and towards one of two sofas set at right angles.

Beth took a deep breath and started. 'The writing on the wall thing, I'm really sorry. I've had a word with Jack and he's promised good behaviour from now on.'

'Ah yes, good behaviour. Personally, I prefer the other sort,' said Patric, his eyes twinkling. 'What about you, Beth?'

'Oh, um, well, you know . . .' Beth had no idea what to say.

Patric was amused by her flailing about. 'It's all right. We can explore the subject of bad behaviour another time. There's something else I want to talk to you about.'

Siobhan took another sip of her wine. The glass was virtually empty now, but she didn't want to go up to the bar and order another one, because it would make everyone think either that she was an alcoholic or that she'd been stood up. And she hadn't been stood up. Yet.

Siobhan studied her watch from an oblique angle. She could have just looked right at it, but that would have made her seem even sadder. Simon was twenty minutes late. She sighed and stared at the bottles above the bar for the hundred and twelfth time.

Five minutes later she was still staring at the bottles above the bar, but she had a new drink. It was already half gone. The effect of the alcohol was kicking in fast. As the minutes ticked on – Simon was thirty-five minutes late now – and the wine took effect, Siobhan began to sink into a mixture of self-pity and self-loathing.

What am I doing? she asked herself. I'm wasting my life with a man who always lets me down. I am pathetic. Maybe it's my own fault. They say you get the relationships you deserve, so I must deserve to be humiliated. Perhaps I vandalised the *Blue Peter* garden in a former life and now, in this one, I'm paying the price. And I'm going to keep on paying. Ten years from now, I'll be like Marcia James, collecting teddy bears and going on and on about my minor surgery.

'Siobhan, I'm so sorry,' said Simon, breaking into her torrent of misery.

Siobhan was so relieved to be released from playing Sad Girl Getting Drunk that had it been Peter Stringfellow standing before her, she'd have kissed him – with tongues.

As it was, she smiled broadly and said: 'Oh, that's all right.'

'Look, I'll explain why I'm late in a minute, but I'll go to the bar first. Do you want a second wine?'

Siobhan couldn't bear to confess that this was already her second, so she just nodded. As Simon walked across the room, she studied him. He was wearing a leather jacket and jeans. She smiled. One of the things she loved about Simon was his optimism. He probably thought he looked like Tom Cruise in *Top Gun* in that outfit. But Simon had the kind of body that causes people to tell you, when you're in your teens and twenties: 'Don't worry, you'll fill out.' He was now forty-four, with no sign of any increase in bulk. He was a human pipe cleaner in a leather jacket. Siobhan smiled again. It made her want to feed him up.

Simon turned round and returned Siobhan's smile. His face was intelligent. Short mousy hair topped pale grey eyes. There was a delicacy about his features. His lips were thin, with a defined cupid's bow, and he had small hands with long, elegant fingers. Simon was the sort of bloke who other blokes think is gay, except he's sleeping with their wives/girlfriends. Siobhan was not his first affair, although she wasn't exactly sure how many there had been before her. She didn't really want to know. It might shatter the illusion.

'Josh walked into a door and we've been at A & E for most of the afternoon,' Simon explained as he sat down opposite Siobhan. He put a glass of wine and a pint of lager on the table and shrugged off his jacket. 'That's why I'm late. Sorry.'

When the affair first started, Simon hadn't talked about his children at all. But as time had gone on, he'd begun to drop little references to them into the conversation. Siobhan encouraged him because that way she felt less peripheral to his life, but it still made her jump.

Now she pulled herself together and managed to ask: 'Is he OK?'

'Yeah. They had to do a couple of stitches. But they gave him a Superman plaster, so he's chuffed to bits.'

Siobhan smiled and felt her top lip drag across her teeth. Her mouth was dry, despite the wine. She was nervous. Tonight was important. She hadn't seen Simon for three whole months. She'd said a few hard things when they broke up, given him an ultimatum really. In her rush of relief at seeing him, she didn't want to make a fool of herself by taking any of them back. She wanted to be tough. And yet she was so delighted to see him, her resolution was about as firm as one of those baths of custard people sit in for charity.

Most important of all, Siobhan didn't want to end up in bed with Simon. To this end, she had deliberately worn her oldest bra and knickers. They didn't even match. She hoped if good sense didn't save her virtue, vanity would.

'It's good to see you,' said Simon.

Siobhan smiled again.

'I really have missed you,' he added.

Siobhan was determined to be strong. She swallowed. 'Yeah, well, you know why we broke up. I don't want to spend my life being your bit on the side.'

Simon looked hurt. He put a hand on her knee. 'You're not my bit on the side. I love you. You know that.'

'But you're *married*, Simon. I shouldn't even be here now, really,' Siobhan replied, removing his hand from her knee.

Simon sat back and shrugged. 'You know my situation, Siobhan. I can't just walk out. What kind of man would that make me?'

Siobhan melted. It had taken her all of four minutes, but she couldn't hold on any longer. She leaned forward and touched Simon's arm. 'I know. It's just, I get so lonely.'

Simon bent closer. 'Come here, silly.' He wrapped his arms around her and went to kiss her.

'I'm not sleeping with you!' announced Siobhan as Simon's lips aimed for hers.

'I didn't ask,' he said.

Olivia picked a baked bean out of her hair. 'That wasn't funny, Anouska.'

Supper time in the Timney household was a cross between a paintball contest and a scene from *Annie*. Children and food were everywhere. Anouska and Seth were sat at a large scrubbed oak table. To one side, Mia and Daisy occupied matching beech high-chairs. Olivia was facing them.

'No, Seth. We don't put chips up Mia's nose.'

Olivia kept up a running commentary from the table, while Colin bustled round the pale green Shaker kitchen, taking things out of the Aga and wiping the slate worktop. There was only one word to describe Colin: nice. He had a nice face; round, with an apologetic wisp of a goatee. He had nice hair, short and brown. He wore nice glasses – silver-rimmed – and drove a nice car, a Mercedes people carrier. This was the flashiest thing about him. Olivia had chosen it.

'The health visitor popped round today,' Colin shouted from the kitchen.

Olivia was simultaneously wiping tomato ketchup off Seth and picking a pea out of the back wheel of a small toy car he had driven across his plate.

'What's she like?'

'It's not a she. His name is Nigel.'

'Bloody hell! Teach us to live in Hackney, I suppose. He wasn't black and in a wheelchair as well, was he?'

'No.'

Colin walked up to the table and began clearing plates from it. 'Now, I know what you think of health visitors.'

'You mean the breast-feeding police. You did hide the formula, didn't you?'

'Yes.'

'And the steriliser?'

'Yes, yes. Nige is actually OK.'

'Oh, it's fucking Nige now, is it?'

'Fucking, fucking, fucking,' repeated Seth, delightedly.

'Olivia! I'll get called in again by his teacher because of his swearing. Last time it was so embarrassing. I had to agree to man the tombola at the spring fayre, if you remember.'

'Sorry, I forgot.'

'We just had a coffee, that's all. I do need adult conversation occasionally, you know.'

'Yeah, well, you've got me now. And for the rest of the evening. What about getting the kids in bed early and you and me . . . you know?'

'Well, I was going to have a flick through my new Raymond Blanc. There's an interesting sea bream recipe I was thinking of having a go at. You cure the fish in salt and sugar and marinade the vegetables in rice vinegar and . . .'

Olivia sighed. It was great having a husband who could cook, but you could take things too far. Given the choice between massaging a breast belonging to a corn-fed chicken and doing the same to one of hers, she knew which bird Colin would rather fondle, and it had feathers on things other than a handbag.

Looking back, Olivia should have spotted the warning signs. On one of their first nights together, she had suggested Colin spread whipped cream over her naked body and lick it off. He had nipped to the all-night shop, come back with a tub of mascarpone and spent the rest of the evening making tiramisu. The irony of Colin and Olivia's situation was that, having produced four children, everyone assumed they must be at it like rabbits. Behind closed doors, however, they were fast turning into Donny and Marie Osmond.

Still, being with Colin was better than the alternative. Colin was Olivia's second husband. Her first, James, had been an investment banker. Sadly, he had invested rather too much time in his secretary, Allyson With a Y. That was how she always introduced herself, and God, how it had grated on Olivia, even before she found out they were having an affair. Allyson With a Y and James now shared a house in Hertfordshire, where they gave posh dinner parties. This despite the fact that when Allyson had met him, she thought an artichoke was a first aid procedure.

Olivia looked at Colin. He had begun to load the dishwasher. His glasses were sliding down his nose. Thank God she'd met him when she did. He was her best friend. So what if the sex wasn't exactly sizzling. They had so much other good stuff between them.

'Even Gordon Ramsay has sex occasionally, Colin.'

As soon as the words were out of Olivia's mouth, she regretted them. They sounded brittle, even a bit desperate. There is nothing more unattractive than a desperate woman. Forget Marie Osmond; she was turning into Blanche Dubois.

Clunk. One of the twins had dropped her bottle on the floor. Colin retrieved it. Olivia could feel his relief at the chance this offered to change the subject.

'So, how was work today?'

Olivia let it go. 'Rumours are flying about. Could be a new series producer coming.'

'But you're so close to transmission. Isn't it a bit late to . . .?'

'Yeah, well. Ours not to reason why and all that. Something's definitely up, though. That's for sure.'

Patric leaned forward conspiratorially. 'Between you and me, Beth, Anastassia Frink is not happy. She wants us to hit nine million this series.'

'She can't be serious,' gasped Beth.

'She is, and if we don't do at least six, she won't recommission.' Patric moved closer. 'Now, I don't like to put you under any more pressure, Beth ...' which meant that that was exactly what he was about to do '... but, at Futura, we'd be very sad to see the show go.'

Beth gulped. 'I can't see how we can do it,' she said. 'Short of getting Valerie to present all the gardening items in the pouring rain, wearing a T-shirt and no bra, that is.'

'I think you'll find someone else got there first with that idea,' said Patric wryly.

'Oh, yeah. So, what do we do?'

'Well, Anastassia feels that we need a little more experience on the show. Now, I'm not saying I agree with her. I think the work you did on *Guess That Hymn!* was excellent. But, anyway, Anastassia – and she's quite within her rights to do it – has appointed a new series producer.'

So the rumours had been true. There was to be an office shake-up.

'I'd like you to make her welcome. Show her the ropes, you know,' Patric said gently, placing a hand on Beth's shoulder.

'Who is she?'

'I don't know her personally, but Anastassia speaks very highly of her.' Patric paused. 'Karen Newsome. Don't know if that name rings any bells?'

Beth felt as if she'd been kicked in the stomach. Oh yes, she'd come across Karen Newsome. She hadn't so much come across her as been mugged by her.

When Beth had been a student, she'd been a runner on daytime show *Every Morning*, and Karen had been one of the day producers.

She had made Beth's life a living hell. On one memorable occasion, Beth had been put in charge of a canine fashion item. When the dogs arrived, they'd sent the wrong breeds. A little Burberry coat made to fit a poodle now had to go on a Great Dane. A wedding dress made for a red setter had to be pinned on to a King Charles spaniel.

The dogs did make it on screen. However, the spaniel cocked its leg over a corner of the sofa before enthusiastically humping the leg of the resident agony aunt. Karen was apoplectic. If Beth hadn't been working for free, she'd have been sacked.

'Er, yes, we did sort of work together once,' Beth said. 'Not that I was ever on her level, you know. I was just a minion. I'm sure she won't remember me.'

'You're too modest, Beth. If you worked together, I'm sure she'll remember you. How could she not? I'll sound her out.'

'No, that's all right . . .'

'Nonsense.'

Beth left the office in a daze.

'Bloody hell,' she whispered to herself. 'Karen Newsome!'

'So how was your day?'

Richard was already in the kitchen when Beth got home. He was opening a bottle of wine.

'Oh, fine, you know. Busy,' said Beth, as she walked down the last couple of steps into the basement. She skirted the black leather sofa. It made the room look like the reception of a hotel in Dubai, but at least it was more or less Stanley-proof. She dumped her bag on the glass-topped dining table and walked over to Richard, planting a peck on his cheek.

'I thought we could get a takeaway,' Richard said.

'Yeah, whatever,' Beth responded. 'You'll never guess who's coming in as series producer on *On The House*.'

'Who?' he asked.

'Karen Newsome. Remember, that horrendous woman I told you about from *Every Morning*.'

Richard shook his head.

'The dog woman. You must remember. She went mad when that pooch weed all over the set and then had sex with the old biddy's leg.'

'Oh, God, yes.' Richard laughed. Then he saw Beth's face. 'Sorry, but in retrospect, you have to admit it was funny.'

'Well, it won't be funny when she sees me at my desk. It'll be like *The Blair Witch Project*, only I won't be wearing a woolly hat.'

Richard got the cork out of the bottle and began pouring the wine.

'I'm sure it won't be that bad.'

Beth didn't look convinced.

'Well, no use worrying about it. Sit down and drink your wine.'

Beth made her way over to the table and began flicking through her mail. Richard opened a drawer and pulled out a pile of takeaway leaflets.

'Anyway, what did you get up to today?' Beth asked.

Richard had been expecting this question. He was prepared for it. He'd decided that, while he would tell Beth how his lunch with Chastity went, he probably wasn't going to mention the being asked out to dinner bit. No point getting Beth in a strop. It was *only* dinner, after all. He took a deep breath and tried to sound casual.

'I, um, had that lunch. What do you fancy, pizza?'

'What lunch?' asked Beth.

'With that, um, dancer. We could have Thai.'

Beth frowned.

'You remember. I told you. We saw her on telly. Or there's that good Chinese.'

A lightbulb finally fired up in Beth's brain. She looked up from her letters excitedly. 'Oh yes. How did it go? Were her breasts really enormous?'

'Well, they were quite big.' Richard put down his leaflets, then saw Beth's expression and began to backtrack. 'But I wasn't looking. I mean, I wasn't having lunch with her breasts!' he declared. 'I was having lunch with a contributor!'

'So, what, it was a meeting of minds, was it?' Beth asked sarcastically.

'It was fine. She was fine.'

'Well, you've got to tell me more than that,' ordered Beth.

'Look, it was *only* lunch.'

'OK, OK. Don't get your knickers in a twist. So what was she like?'

Richard now began opening his own mail. He concentrated on being engrossed by a letter offering discounted patio doors. He'd got over the difficult bit now. He'd told Beth about his lunch. He hadn't kept it a secret. Hadn't concealed anything. Well, not much anyway. He was like a racing car on the home straight. Now all he had to do was cruise past the finishing line without mishap.

'She was fine. Sweet, really,' Richard said. 'Not used to telly, of course. But she could be rather good. Quite bright actually.' Oops, he'd hit a pothole.

'And, no doubt, really mature for her age as well,' said Beth waspishly.

Richard tried to swerve round Beth's comment. 'Jesus, you women, just mention someone's a model or something—'

'She's a stripper, not a model,' corrected Beth.

'A lap dancer. Chastity is a lap dancer.'

Richard had now gone into a tailspin. The name Chastity stuck out of the conversation like a chequered flag being waved in both their faces. He rushed on.

'She has actually had a really difficult time. She didn't want to be a lap dancer. And it's only temporary. She's hoping to go into TV presenting.'

Beth almost choked on her wine. 'Not another one! The next time they interview the farmer on *One Man and His Dog*, the dog's going to pipe up that it is only herding sheep on a temporary basis and it fancies a spot on *Newsnight*.'

'Oh, for goodness' sake,' said Richard vehemently. 'If you're going to be like this, I'm going to the study.' Then he gathered up his post and strode upstairs. Beth was left looking at his empty seat. Still, she had more urgent things to worry about. Tomorrow would be Karen Newsome's first day at *On The House*.

Chapter Six

'Hello, sweetie. Patric said you were on board. Let's hope there are no pooches on *this* show, shall we?'

Karen Newsome's mouth was stretched into the sort of smile employed by the wolf who dressed up as Little Red Riding Hood's grandmother. Her teeth flashed threateningly and her eyes were cold. Beth shivered.

Karen was everything Beth was not. Inside she was a hundred per cent Rottweiler, but on the outside she was as fluffy and frothy as the top on a cappuccino. Today, Beth noted, she was wearing a T-shirt that bore the legend: 'I Like Boys'. Karen was thirty-nine.

Karen's modus operandi was just as disingenuous. She wrapped every comment or criticism in a pretty parcel of dishonesty. To deal with Karen, you had to wade through layers of 'darlings' and 'honeys', which you knew she didn't mean. It reminded Beth of when, as a little girl, she would find a stray chocolate button in her coat pocket and would have to pick the fluff off it before she could eat it.

Men invariably failed to spot Karen's true viciousness. 'But she's so sweet,' they'd say.

Yeah, and so's the sugar lump they used to give you your polio vaccine on, thought Beth.

No sooner had Karen arrived at *On The House* than she had convened a meeting, or 'chatette', as she insisted on calling it. Everyone assembled in Karen's new office. She perched herself on the edge of her desk, her legs dangling, and addressed the staff. 'OK, guys,' she began, sounding like a trendy vicar visiting a school for maladjusted teenagers and trying to pass himself off as one of the 'kidz'. 'We're all new to each other. Well, apart from Beth. We've crossed paths before, haven't we, sweetie?'

Beth nodded, trying not to catch Karen's eye lest it encourage her. Her tactic didn't work.

'Why don't you tell everyone that hilarious story about the dogs, Beth?'

Had Beth been in possession of a sharp object, she would have plunged it repeatedly into Karen's heart. But all she had was a cold cup of coffee and a half-eaten biscuit. Neither were exactly murder material.

'Oh, no. I'm sure you're far too busy for me to witter on,' said Beth.

Olivia turned to Beth enquiringly. Beth shut her eyes and shook her head from side to side as if to say, 'Don't ask.'

'All right then, darling. We can save that delight for another day,' said Karen ominously.

Nothing like prolonging the threat of public humiliation, thought Beth.

Karen shifted her attention from Beth to the whole group. 'First things first. Just so you know, I'm not here to sack everybody, ha, ha, ha.' She thought this was hilarious. 'Well, not right away, anyway.' She thought that was even more hilarious.

There was no laughter from anyone else.

Karen moved straight on. 'I'll be having a get-to-know-you session with each of you at some point, but I want to tell you what a marvellous job you're doing, and I'm sure if we all pull together we can make On The House even better.'

They began to file out. 'P45s by the end of the week, then,' Olivia whispered to Beth.

Siobhan lay back in bed. After last night, she'd decided to take the morning off. She stared contentedly at the ceiling. It was sky blue, as were the walls and the silk sari fabric of the curtains. Siobhan loved her bedroom. It made her feel calm and as serene as the pure white orchid in a pot that was sitting on top of her wicker chest of drawers.

The room was actually in a state of some disarray. The corn-flower blue silk throw that was normally thrown *just so* over the top of the white duvet had slid into a pile on the floor. An ornate gold and navy bolster lay discarded a few feet away, and scatter cushions in white and cream were, well, scattered.

Siobhan was toying with the idea of getting up and making a cup of coffee when the phone next to the bed rang. It must be Simon ringing to see how she was. How sweet, she thought.

'Hiya, sexy,' she purred into the receiver.

'I didn't know you felt that way about me,' said Olivia.

'Oh, sorry, I thought it was ...' Siobhan didn't finish her sentence. Having promised Olivia that she would remain chaste, she didn't want to admit she'd succumbed.

'It doesn't matter. Get yourself out of bed and into the office. We've got a new series producer.'

'You're kidding. What's she like?'

'Well, I haven't seen Beth look so pale since I told her the ra-ra skirt was making a comeback.'

Beth, Siobhan and Olivia were sitting in neighbouring cubicles in the Ladies'.

'If I'd known I was going to be out of a job, I wouldn't have gone to Cheap yesterday,' said Olivia.

'Yes you would,' said Beth.

'Oh, all right. Yes, I would, but I wouldn't have got the rhinestone jeans.'

A door to a cubicle swung open and Beth walked to the sink. Siobhan and Olivia followed. Beth spoke as she ran the tap. 'How much?' she asked.

'They were in the sale,' Olivia answered sheepishly.

'How much?'

'One thousand two hundred.'

'Olivia!' Siobhan exclaimed.

'I know, but it's not as if I do drugs or anything,' declared Olivia defensively.

'A coke habit would be cheaper,' said Beth, rifling in her make-up bag for her blusher.

'Probably. But I'd be so thin, I'd want to go shopping all the time as well.' Olivia was dabbing her nose with a powder compact. 'Anyway, this new Karen person, what's she like? She said you two knew each other.'

'Yes, we did *Every Morning* together. She was one of the day producers and I was on work experience.'

'Yes, and?' said Siobhan.

'Maybe she's changed, mellowed?' offered Beth.

'Bad as that?' asked Olivia.

'Look, I've got to go. Doing that garden in Halifax,' said Beth, moving towards the door. 'All I'll say about Karen is she had researchers in tears all the time on *Every Morning*. One was found hanging from a scaffolding tower. She'd tried to strangle herself with upholstery braid. She was OK, but it was a hell of a scare. Stuck her in the Priory. All hushed up, of course.'

Beth pushed open the door. 'See you tomorrow.'

'Jesus!' Siobhan exclaimed, looking at Olivia. She was really worried now.

When it comes to ways not to impress your new boss, digging up someone's dead pet while attempting to install a water feature is pretty near the top of the I Must Remember Not To Do That list. Digging up the contributor might be marginally worse, but only if they hadn't signed the release form first.

Beth and the team had arrived in Halifax to transform a garden that was little more than a patch of gravel with some plastic pots sprouting half-dead geraniums into a Moroccan oasis. That was the idea, but it hadn't worked out like that.

Beth peered under the corner of the lid of a muddy shoe box at what had once been Timmy the tortoise – his name was written on the box – and knew she was staring career suicide in the face. If Karen got to hear about this, she'd be working for the Travel Channel before you could say Costa Dorada.

Could Beth perhaps bung Timmy back? No one would ever know, would they? The light was fading. It would soon be dark. She was sure she could conceal Timmy's reburial. She was just eyeing up the hole whence he had come when she saw Hamish coming towards her.

Hamish McTavish was *On The House*'s resident gardener. Of Scottish extraction (the kilt was a bit of a clue), he had very short, bright red hair and an accent so strong that the production team were never quite sure if he was actually speaking English. Beth had become so desperate that she had got Jack to knock up a quasi–Ouija board out of some spare laminate flooring to communicate with Hamish. When she now addressed questions to him, he answered by knocking once for yes, twice for no.

At least Hamish's little band of landscape gardeners understood him. They were all imported from the Isle of Skye. As for the viewers, it didn't seem to matter. Hamish was a whizz at making huge things out of metal and craning them in and out of people's back gardens, which made good telly even if his explanations might as well have been in Walloon.

It was Hamish who had dug up Timmy in the first place. Typical of him to leave Beth to cope with the fall-out. As he lolloped towards Beth, she saw he wasn't alone. At his side was a small figure clutching a large rag doll. It was Phoebe, five-year-old daughter of the house. She had been a major reason why they were all here.

Karen had issued a memo stipulating that all *On The House* shoots must now include children aged nine or below. Small, cute kids were a sure-fire ratings winner, according to Karen. Older kids who were overweight and/or had acne were, however, to be concealed at all costs.

Beth looked at Phoebe and a terrible thought occurred to her. No, it couldn't be, could it? Timmy hadn't once belonged to

Phoebe, had he? Hamish was bringing her right this way. Beth hurriedly shifted the shoe box behind her back.

'Hello, Phoebe. How are you?' said Beth when the pair had reached her.

'Hamish is going to make a new cage for my guinea pigs,' announced Phoebe proudly.

Jesus! thought Beth. Bearing in mind the scale of most of Hamish's work – a recent Dorset tree house had been so large, planes had had to be diverted via Teesside Airport, rather than risk a collision – did Pheobe's parents realise they would need to build a new extension to house the rodent home? 'That's nice,' she said.

Hamish mumbled something unintelligible.

'What's that?' Phoebe had spotted the box. She was peering round Beth, staring at it.

'It's nothing important,' said Beth, dropping down on to her haunches, so as to be on Phoebe's level. She needed to find out if there was a connection between Timmy and Phoebe.

'Now, I know that rag doll's your friend, but have you ever had any other friends, special ones?' asked Beth. 'You know, like a pet or something?'

Phoebe applied all the concentration a five year old is capable of, which is considerable given that they don't have things like mortgages, relationships or whether they might be about to become unemployed to clutter up their brains.

'Well, there was someone. He was my best friend. I had him for ages.'

Beth was engulfed in doom.

Phoebe hadn't finished. 'But Mummy said I was too old for an *imaginary* friend, so George went away.'

Lowri Turner

Hallelujah! thought Beth, doing a virtual jig. The tortoise must
belong to a previous owner of the house. Her glee was short-lived.

'After George, Mummy said I could have a tortoise. His name
was Timmy. But he died. He's in heaven, you know.'

Hamish crossed himself and mumbled.

Beth prayed for salvation. She needed to get rid of Phoebe so
she could decide what to do with Timmy.

'Are you thirsty, Phoebe? If you go and find Saffron, she'll get
you a Coke.'

'Mummy says I mustn't have Coke,' said Phoebe primly.

Beth was exasperated. 'Well, a carrot juice then. Off you go,
Phoebe, there's a good girl.'

With her one free hand, Beth tried to guide Phoebe towards the
house. But she wasn't going anywhere.

'I want to stay here.'

Hamish was Beth's only hope, which didn't bode well for her
chances. She began waving the shoe box from side to side behind
her. The idea was that Hamish would see what she was doing, take
the box from her and discreetly slip it back in the hole. Phoebe
wasn't looking at him. He might just be able to get away with it.
At first, Beth swung the box just a little. Nothing. Then more
ambitiously. Still nothing. No reaction from Hamish at all. Beth
increased the arc of her wave. She was now almost swaying from
foot to foot. Hamish was oblivious.

Unfortunately, Phoebe was not. 'What's that?' she demanded.

'Nothing.' Beth was really panicking now. In a last-ditch attempt
to alert Hamish, she launched an even more frantic wave with the
box, but she'd forgotten something. The shoe box had been
underground. The cardboard was wet. That was how she'd been

94

able to lift a corner and see Timmy in the first place.

As Beth made a last desperate wave, the cardboard gave way. The bottom of the box fell to pieces in her hand, and Timmy flew into the air, somersaulting as he went. Beth, Hamish and Phoebe were all transfixed as Timmy, now reborn as a sort of reptilian Olga Korbut, performed acrobatics twenty feet in the air. Not for long, though. There was a dull thud, as Timmy plummeted to earth, followed swiftly by the wail of a small child.

Valerie picked up the remote and began channel-surfing. The first four channels featured Carol Vorderman, so she kept going. Sport was on the next. Channel 6 were showing a documentary about transsexuals, with an earnest psychologist discussing the emotional implications of the operation, interspersed with camcorder footage of someone Doing It Themselves in their bedroom.

Neville had retired to bed for a cheese toastie. He had recently augmented his Baby Belling with a sandwich maker, and now there was almost no need for him to come out of his room at all. Valerie had consumed two rice cakes and a low-fat yoghurt. She started flicking channels again and was just about to turn the TV off and go to bed when her attention was caught by something.

'Please welcome the man who put designer into des res, TV's Liam Smith!'

It was the Lucas Lieberman show and Liam Smith was a guest. Liam swaggered in, his mohican a luminous orange to match his suede jacket and trousers. Lucas and Liam did a lot of hugging and kissing and 'how are yous?' then sat down.

'So, Liam,' Lucas said. 'Was it a surprise to be named Britain's richest TV celebrity?'

Valerie unzipped one chocolate leather boot and aimed it at the TV. There was a huge bang as it went straight through the screen and lodged inside.

There were footsteps the other side of the living-room door. Neville had heard the commotion and come downstairs to investigate. He opened the door and peeped round. He registered the boot and the broken TV.

'Shall I get the Lithium then, dear?'

Richard and Chastity hovered on the doorstep.

'Would you like to come up?' she asked.

'Well, um, I don't know . . .' he answered.

It was a pointless conversation. They both knew what was going to happen. Still, they went through the charade, because to do otherwise would have been to expose the fact that the dinner they had just eaten was nothing more than an excuse, a way of marking time, allowing a decent interval before the inevitable happened.

Richard in particular was still clinging to the delusion that if sex occurred between himself and Chastity it wouldn't be premeditated, but spontaneous and therefore guilt-free. Planning was the difference between the murder of a marriage and its manslaughter. The result, of course, was the same. But he wasn't thinking in those terms. This wasn't an affair, it was *only* a fling.

How quickly Richard had moved from it being *only* lunch, to *only* dinner and now *only* a fling. The speed was essential. It blurred his vision of what he was doing. If he had actually stopped to think about it too much, he might have realised what he was putting in jeopardy. Instead, he let the excitement carry him along.

Richard should have felt guilty, but he didn't. He told himself he deserved this. Beth had Stanley and her job and him and she was happy with that. He needed more. He needed a bit of territory all his own. It wasn't that he was betraying her. He was having a marital awayday, or awaynight. They say a change is as good as a rest and Richard was recharging himself. Who knows, he might be a better husband afterwards. So Beth would get the benefit in the end.

Chastity had turned her key in the lock and pushed open the door. Richard could see the lace edge of her black bra peeking from inside her white shirt. Her lips were moist and shiny.

'Well, maybe just a quick coffee then,' she said, hesitantly.

Well, it was *only* a coffee, wasn't it?

Olivia was at the foot of the bed. Wearing black PVC thigh boots and a choker, but nothing else, she was on all fours.

'Yes!' she shouted. 'Yes!'

Colin was lying on the bed, spread-eagled on top of the duvet cover. He was naked. His wrists and ankles were attached by handcuffs to the cherry-wood posts that rose to support a muslin canopy above.

'Oh . . . oh . . . oh,' he moaned, his voice rising with each 'oh'. His body was arched. He was writhing, his wrists pulling the handcuffs taut. 'Oh . . . oh . . . oh. The cramp's getting worse.'

Well, that's some stiffness for once, thought Olivia, although what she actually said was: 'Sorry, darling. Just hold on.'

'I haven't got much choice, have I?'

'I know, sorry.'

The evening had begun reasonably well. Olivia had managed to tear Colin away from Rick Stein long enough to handcuff him to their bed. She'd walked up and down his chest a bit in her heels. She'd even detected some sign that the PVC might be working.

A shuddering had occurred, a crotch-level rumbling almost. It was as if Colin's Calvin Kleins contained the engine of an old car that had been kept in the garage too long. Olivia had switched on the ignition and he was slowly cranking into life.

However, she had mistaken the source of the rumbling. It wasn't Colin's nether regions, but his leg. He had got cramp, and as he writhed in agony, the key to his handcuffs, which Olivia had thoughtfully kept in the lock so they wouldn't lose it, had taken flight and clattered on to the floor. Olivia watched in horror as the key rolled across the floor and into the gap between two of the stripped floorboards.

She was now on her hands and knees, peering between the boards. She could see a glinting, but it was maddeningly out of reach.

'Oh . . . oh . . . oh,' moaned Colin.

'There's nothing for it,' Olivia announced in exasperation. 'I'm going to have to lift a floorboard.'

Colin said nothing.

'How exactly do I do that?' asked Olivia, frills being more her area than floorboards.

'Crowbar,' stuttered Colin. 'Cupboard under the stairs.'

Olivia scrambled to her feet and began to totter unsteadily to the door.

'You couldn't,' Colin called after her, 'flick on *Food and Drink*, could you? Might take my mind off the pain.'

* * *

Siobhan slid the plastic tray out of the microwave and on to the worktop. Then she attempted to peel back the corner of the plastic lid. A rush of steam burned her hand.

'Ow!' she exclaimed, licking her finger and hopping from foot to foot.

Perhaps she'd do better if she used a tea towel. She found one on the counter and wrapped it around her sore hand, then took another from a drawer and used it to hold the corner of the plastic tray. It reminded her of that kids' party game where you have to eat a bar of chocolate with a knife and fork, wearing a hat, scarf and gloves. Twenty years on she was a bit rusty.

After what seemed an age of struggling, Siobhan finally managed to get the lid off. Next she carried the tray of food across the kitchen to her plate.

'Now, if I can just—'

She was interrupted by the phone.

As if in slow motion, the tray slipped out of Siobhan's hands and her dinner landed face down on the floor. She watched as a puddle of white wine sauce, with flecks of tarragon in it, spread across the vinyl.

Brrng, brrng.

She stepped over the puddle to pick up the receiver. She didn't quite clear it completely, however. The heel of her shoe skidded in the liquid, twisting her ankle and sending her crashing on to one knee.

'Shit!' she exclaimed.

'I'm sorry,' said an unfamiliar female voice. 'Is that Siobhan?'

Siobhan scrambled to her feet. 'Er . . . yes, who's speaking?'

'This is Pauleen Merchant.'

The name meant nothing to Siobhan.

'Darren's mother.'

Siobhan's mind was still blank. Darren? Darren who?

'Oh my God, Kevin the Teenager!'

'I beg your pardon?'

'Sorry, I mean, what can I do for you, Mrs, um . . .'

'Do call me Pauleen. I think we passed the first-name stage the other morning, don't you?'

The memory of flashing her bare breast flooded into Siobhan's brain.

'I got your number off Darren's computer. I do hope you don't mind.'

'Not at all.'

'Anyway, the thing is, Darren's had an accident, been knocked off his bike. He's in the Royal Free and he's been asking for you.'

'Has he?'

'Yes. Do you think you could go and see him? I know you two have been having a few problems, but it would mean so much to him.'

'Problems? We broke up.'

'He didn't say. Never mind, he wants to see you.'

'Yeah, but . . .'

'It's not much to ask, surely? He is injured, you know.'

Siobhan was no match for a maternal guilt trip, even once removed.

'OK, I'll see what I can do.'

Three bowls of Frosties later, she had calmed down enough to make a decision. She definitely couldn't go and see Darren. Now that things were back on with Simon, she'd feel dishonest. What if he asked if she'd met someone else? She wouldn't be able to lie to him. Still, she couldn't just not turn up. That would be cruel. She'd have to find someone to go in her place.

Karen finished her three hundredth sit-up and slumped forward, her hands brushing the cream shagpile rug in front of her fashionably minimalist fireplace – a hole gashed in a slab of concrete with a Bunsen burner stuck in it, along with two pebbles and a rusty nail. She frowned and flipped on to her front, beginning the first of two hundred and fifty press-ups.

On The House was in trouble, and she, Karen, was not going to be the captain who went down with the ship. She was more like one of those emergency helicopters that arrive in the nick of time to save the day. But how? How was she going to boost the ratings and, more importantly, take all the credit for it?

Karen grimaced as she went into her second sit-up century. At work, she had to be Miss Fluffy. It was a useful Trojan horse. Here, in her own space, with her hair scraped back and a film of sweat on her shoulders, she could give herself over to what she really liked to do. Push herself to the limit, physically.

Exercise wasn't just a hobby for Karen. It was her friend, her lover, her salvation and her sanctuary. It gave her the instant satisfaction of a goal set and achieved. Other people were a constant disappointment to Karen. In her mind, they lacked drive, ambition and application. Women, especially, got all hung up on relationships, distracting them from effectively performing their duties. But Karen never got distracted.

When Karen was pounding the Stairmaster or slogging up a steep hill, she didn't have to think about anything else, about the boyfriend/husband she didn't have, the babies she hadn't conceived or the friends she didn't confide in. She was in the perfect relationship. It was just her competing against herself.

Having completed her last stomach crunch, Karen lay back against the carpet. She'd had an idea. It was pretty audacious and it would take some doing. Valerie for one wouldn't like it. But hey, you can't make an omelette without breaking eggs. Not that she ate eggs, except for the whites. Karen smiled to herself. Now all she needed was someone to do her dirty work.

Beth was sitting on the edge of her bed in the Val-U Lodge in Halifax, picking at the velveteen coverlet. Her mobile phone rang, interrupting her soft-furnishing contemplation.

'Hello, Beth?' It was Richard.

'Hello darling. Tell me you've had a better day than I've had,' Beth said.

'Well, I don't know about that,' he replied, clearing his throat nervously.

'Why are you talking so quietly?' she asked. 'Do you have a cold?'

Richard coughed. 'Well, I think I may have a bit of a bug, yes. You know, it's going round the office at the moment. Look, have you been trying to get me?'

'No, why?'

'Oh, my phone said "missed call" and I thought it must be you, and, well, if it wasn't, then it doesn't matter.' He coughed again. 'Anyway, how are you?'

'Fine. Well, actually, not great, we managed to dig up—'

Richard interrupted her. 'Glad you're OK. Look, I've got to go.

Boiled the kettle for some Lemsip. You know. I'll see you tomorrow. Love you.'

Beth didn't have time to wonder at Richard's brusque goodbye. There was a knock at her door. Her room service had arrived. When she'd tipped the waiter and he'd left, she removed the silver cover and stared down at her meal. What she'd wanted was beans on toast. But that wasn't on the menu. Instead, she'd got 'grilled fillet of sole on a red pepper coulis, with a coriander and chilli salsa and drizzled with extra virgin olive oil'. She surveyed the dish. It was a culinary car crash.

'Ainsley Harriot has a lot to answer for,' she muttered under her breath.

Richard slipped his mobile back into the pocket of his jacket, which was hanging off one of the bed posts. He was naked. He suddenly felt cold, so he folded his legs back under the duvet and laid his head on the pillow.

'Who was that on the phone?' asked Chastity, emerging from the bathroom.

'Oh, nobody. Just checking my messages,' Richard lied.

'You don't have to rush off, do you?'

Richard shook his head. 'I'm all yours.'

Chapter Seven

Beth couldn't believe she was doing this. After everything she'd said to Siobhan about Simon, here she was doing her a favour so Siobhan wouldn't feel guilty about having slept with someone else. As if he wasn't sleeping with someone else all the time – his wife! Really, she could strangle Siobhan sometimes. Still, she was Beth's friend, and when all was said – and a great deal had been said – and done, Beth would support her whatever she did.

Beth was making the detour to the hospital on her way back from Halifax. It gave her an excuse to put off returning to the office for the inevitable showdown over the tortoise débâcle. Karen was going to have a field day.

Beth pushed open one half of a swing door. The stainless-steel finger plate was covered in greasy fingerprints. The view the other side wasn't that much better. Marigold Ward was comprised of a large, long room with a row of iron beds painted institutional grey running down both sides. Each bed was decorated with a blanket, also grey. Some patients lay or sat up underneath these. Others perched on the edge of their beds, talking to friends and relatives in whispers.

Beth had been in multi-storey car parks with warmer atmospheres. She began to walk down, looking left and right as she did so. Punctuating the beds were little cabinets sporting bottles of orange squash and sad little flower arrangements in glass vases that had gone milky from being dish washered too many times. Plastic chairs were dotted about. Someone had stuck a poster up, a view of a Caribbean beach with sand, sea and palm tree. It said, 'Come to the paradise island of St Lucia'.

Beth wondered why it was that people gave the nastiest places the most inappropriately nice names. It reminded her of a shoot she'd done once in a place called Eden Road. Cars without wheels were parked in rubbish-strewn front gardens. More like Hellhole Street. As with Marigold Ward, the pretty name had merely underlined the foulness of the place.

'Can I help you?' A nurse had spotted her wandering aimlessly. 'Are you looking for someone?'

'Er, yes. Darren Merchant. Knocked off his bike.'

'He's over there.' The nurse pointed to the second from last bed on the right. A pair of orange and brown curtains of a hideousness that even the most slavish revival of seventies style could not have rescued were pulled around it. 'Are you his mother?'

Beth's jaw twitched in annoyance. 'I'm a sort of friend,' she said through gritted teeth. 'Well, a friend of a friend really.'

'Oh, right. Well, one thing you should be aware of. He's OK, but his short-term memory's been affected. Nothing to worry about. It should sort itself out.'

Beth walked over to the bed. On the way she passed a large Asian family. The father had his leg up in plaster. His wife was feeding him something out of a plastic container. Three children, ranging between about five and ten, were sitting in a neat little line on the bed. She smiled at the mother and gingerly peeled back one of the curtains. Darren was lying in bed, his blond hair ruffled up by the pillow. The thing that struck Beth immediately was his skin. It had the kind of ruddy glow only normally seen on the faces of choristers on Christmas cards. Wow! He really was a teenager.

'Hello, Darren, you don't know me, but I'm Beth. I'm a friend of Siobhan's.'

Darren's face lit up like a little boy opening a brand-new set of Hot Wheels on his birthday.

'Siobhan sent you. Great. I was getting worried. You know, she hasn't been to see me. She hasn't even texted me.'

'She asked me to come in her place. She's very busy. Work, you know.'

Darren looked upset. 'But she should have at least texted me. She is my girlfriend.'

'She's your what?'

'My girlfriend.' He said it with such certainty, as if he was pointing out that the sky was blue, the earth was round or supermodels were on the whole not the sharpest knives in the drawer. But surely Siobhan had chucked him? Beth had heard her do it. Then the penny dropped. Darren's short-term memory loss. The bump on the head had erased the fact that Siobhan had dumped him. He thought they were still together. Oh, God! Beth would have to explain things.

Beth took a deep breath and said, as gently as she could: 'The thing is, Darren, you and Siobhan agreed, er, to break up last week. Your concussion means you don't remember.'

He looked crestfallen. 'No, that can't be true. We were going to go away for the weekend. I got the tent out and everything.'

A vision of Siobhan in her kitten heels in a tent flitted briefly across Beth's imagination. But it was too ridiculous to contemplate. 'It's for the best, you know,' she continued. 'You'll get another girlfriend. Someone a bit, er, closer to your own age.'

The chatter from the family at the next-door bed had stopped. Beth could almost feel their ears pressed to the curtain. Chucking someone was bad. Chucking someone who was injured was worse. Beth felt awful. She wanted to pull the curtain back and bellow: 'Look, this wasn't my idea, OK?'

Darren had also fallen silent. There was a puzzled look on his face. 'One thing I don't understand. Why hasn't Siobhan been to see me?'

Now it was Beth's turn to look confused. Hadn't they just had this conversation?

'I mean, I am her boyfriend.'

Short-term memory loss, the nurse had said. Beth just hadn't realised how short term that was. Darren now had the memory of an amoeba. She had no choice, she'd have to dump him again. She took another deep breath.

'I'm afraid you're not her boyfriend, Darren. The two of you finished last week. You've had a bump on the head . . .'

Five minutes later and Beth had to repeat the process. Five minutes after, she did it again. And again. And again. It was like an emotional Groundhog Day. Each time, her patience grew more strained, her temper more frayed. By the eighth chucking, she had abandoned all attempts to soften the blow.

'She dumped you, OK? Have you got that, you pre-pubescent moron?' Beth was shouting now. 'She said you were totally crap in bed. Penis the size of a bloody cocktail chipolata.' She'd made that last bit up. Siobhan hadn't said it at all, but she was getting desperate. She hoped to shock him out of his concussion. Darren looked disconsolate. As she got to her feet and pushed her way through the curtain, Beth felt as if she'd just backed her car over a puppy.

Once she was the other side of the fabric, she tried to recover herself. She began to search in her bag for her scarf. When she looked up, her gaze was met by a line of horrified faces. It was the family at the next bed, plus the nurse, bedpan in hand. They were frozen with shock. They had heard the whole thing. Beth blushed. She wouldn't be getting the Kofi Annan award for diplomacy this year then.

Once outside, Beth breathed in the fresh air and looked for a cab. The sun was shining and she began to feel cheerful. She was just enjoying the view when her phone rang. She delved into her handbag to find it, and pulled something out. It was half a slice of stale bread. Also rattling about at the bottom was a teething ring, the wheel off a toy car and forty-two cashpoint receipts.

Aah, for the days when all her dainty baguette bag had contained was a wallet and some lip gloss. Now she heaved a bag the size of a fridge freezer on to her shoulder, containing everything but the kitchen sink.

Maybe birth control campaigners should consider commandeering a mother's handbag as a contraceptive. Not literally, of course, though Beth had once tried the female condom and could probably have brought the shopping home in it. No, they could use it as a warning to any broody teenager. GET YOURSELF

PREGNANT AND YOU WILL HAVE TO CARRY ONE OF THESE! TRY DANCING ROUND THAT IN A NIGHTCLUB!

Beth finally found her phone.

'Hello?'

'Hello, Beth, sweetie. It's Karen.'

Beth closed her eyes and braced herself.

'Just wondered whether you might be popping into the office today, *at some point*. I think we need to have a chatette.'

Beth was sitting at her desk. Well, not sitting as such. More crouching. Her body was crumpled into a semi-foetal position. Olivia was perched next to her, reading aloud from a newspaper.

' "TV Makeover Bosses in a Hole Over Timmy the Tortoise." That's the headline, and underneath there's a picture of a little girl. She's sort of crying and pointing. Do you want to hear the rest?'

Beth sighed. It was worse than she could possibly have imagined. Phoebe's family sold their story to a national newspaper, and they'd managed to do so at the speed of light. This was not the sort of PR *On The House* was looking for. Fortunately, when Beth had arrived back in the office, Karen had been out to lunch. But she'd be back any minute.

'OK, go on,' said Beth.

'There's a quote from the little girl. "Mummy told me Timmy was in heaven with the angels. Now I know it was a lie." That's bad.'

Beth groaned and began to rock back and forth.

'It goes on, but I don't know whether you want . . .' Olivia said.

'No, it's all right,' replied Beth.

'Well, after the bit about Timmy not being in heaven . . .'

Beth tensed.

'. . . it says, um, are you sure?'

'Yes.'

' "Now I don't believe in Father Christmas or the Tooth Fairy any more either." '

'Oh God. I've killed Father Christmas.'

'And the Tooth Fairy.'

'Thanks.'

'Well, it could have been worse.'

'How, exactly?'

'They could have spelt your name wrong.'

Beth and Olivia heard giggling. Valerie and Karen rounded the corner of the office. They were walking arm in arm.

'Well, Lucas Lieberman has definitely had liposuction,' said Valerie. 'And a face lift. Serena Tiverton told me when we were on *Jubilee Road* together. Did I tell you I was on *Jubilee Road*?'

'You might have mentioned it, yes,' answered Karen.

'I won Soap Actress of the Year three years running.'

'Yes, you said.'

Beth and Olivia exchanged horrified glances. Individually, Karen and Valerie were bad enough, but now they had bonded. It was like watching Hitler and Goebbels in designer skirts.

'Didn't take her long to suck up to Karen,' hissed Olivia.

'You know Valerie.'

'More intimately than most. I see her in a G-string, remember.'

'Don't.'

Karen and Valerie had stopped outside Karen's office. They were exchanging showy kisses. 'Mwaagh, mwaagh. We must do this again,' purred Valerie.

'Yes, let's,' chirruped Karen.

Olivia mimed sticking her fingers down her throat, a pose she had to rearrange rapidly when Valerie set eyes upon her.

'Ah, Olivia,' she shouted. 'Have you got those new things for me to look at?'

Olivia picked up a pile of carrier bags and walked towards Valerie. 'Good luck,' she whispered to Beth.

Valerie turned back to Karen. 'On *Jubilee Road* I wore Valentino. That was in the good old days. I understand Serena Tiverton now has to wear clothes off a market stall. I don't mean clothes that *look* as if they've come off a market stall. They really have!'

She swept out of the office, trailed by Olivia, whose progress was slower due to all the bags she was carrying. Valerie, of course, didn't deign to offer to carry a single one.

'Beth, got a minute, sweetie?' asked Karen.

Here goes, thought Beth. Tortoise bollocking coming up.

Richard stared out of the window of his office. It was a corner office, but that made it sound grander than it actually was. The windows hadn't been cleaned since about 1972 and had all the sparkle of a twelve-year-old boy forced to visit a stately home.

Richard was in the grip of Post-Infidelity Depression. Last night, he'd felt free and daring and young. Well, youngish, until Chastity suggested doing it standing up in the shower and his back had gone and he'd had to put her down. Now, he felt just one thing: guilty.

There was nothing for it. He could never see Chastity again. He'd had his fling. If Beth hadn't gone away it would never have happened. Still, no one had got hurt and Beth need never find out.

When she came home tonight, he was going to be really nice to her. And this thing with Chastity would never happen again. He almost had himself believing it.

'I said I wanted Cheap. This is . . . well, cheap!' Valerie was trying to read the label on a jacket, a job that wasn't made any easier by the fact that she was holding the garment it was sewn on to as far away from her body as possible. It was as if it was radioactive and she feared closer contact might contaminate her.

'Look,' begged Olivia, 'I know it's not from Cheap, but you know the budget.'

'Fresh Style.' Valerie read the rest of the label. 'Isn't that a *discount* place?'

'They do carry a certain amount of bankrupt stock, yes.'

Valerie's knees buckled and she sank to the floor. She was struggling for breath and frantically rifling in her handbag.

'Valerie, are you OK?' asked Olivia, wondering if she was looking for her medication. She'd heard rumours that Valerie might be taking something to run alongside her anger management counselling.

'No, I'm not all right,' Valerie answered, pulling her phone from her bag. 'I'm calling my agent!'

What was all this about? Beth had thought that Karen would pin her to the wall with the office nail gun at the very least. Instead she was being nice. Maybe she hadn't seen the newspaper. Then Beth looked over to Karen's desk. A copy of the *Morning News*, open at the tortoise story, was spread out ever so neatly. She'd seen it all right. Karen was like a moggy who'd dragged a vole back through the cat flap. She didn't intend to kill her prey immediately. She would torture it first.

'Patric and I were having a little pow-wow about you this morning.'

Oh, God, thought Beth. Patric knows.

'Patric's a teeny-weeny bit worried about you, honey,' continued Karen, the 'honey' feeling like a little jab to Beth's solar plexus. 'He wondered whether you might need some time off.'

Oh no, she was going to be sacked!

'I told him that I thought you'd prefer to carry on working. Is that right, Beth?'

'Oh, yes,' replied Beth, somewhat too enthusiastically.

Karen smiled in triumph. 'So glad I could help.'

Beth realised that she'd stepped straight into Karen's trap. She now owed her a favour. But it was worse than that. The Chinese believe that if someone saves your life you belong to them. Karen now owned Beth. Frankly, sacking would have been the better option.

'A couple of things,' Karen announced, with a smug look of victory. 'I need you to do another trip.'

Beth's face fell even further. The rule was that *On The House* directors took it in turns to go away. 'But I've only just come back from Halifax. I haven't seen Stanley for a couple of days . . .'

She realised her mistake immediately. Mentioning a child in front of Karen was like waving a bunch of garlic before a vampire. Karen's face was stony. Beth weighed up the options and knew she didn't have any.

'When do you want me to go?' she said.

'Tomorrow should be fine, darling.'

Beth sighed inwardly. The last thing she wanted to do was go away again. But what could she do? Karen had her in an emotional half-nelson. Beth was not in a position to say no.

'Which brings me to the other thing,' continued Karen. 'Liam Smith.'

'Yes?'

'I think we should give him a tinkle.'

Beth furrowed her brow. 'I don't understand.'

'I'd like you to call him and get him on the show, sweetie.'

'Well, yes, he's fab and everything. But we've tried to get him for a guest spot before and he's always unavailable.'

'No, I don't think you understand, Beth. When you work for me, there is no such thing as unavailable. You do work for me, don't you?'

'Yes,' answered Beth miserably.

'Good. Now I want you to call him and I expect results. Oh, and by the way, I'm not talking about a guest spot. I want Liam to present the show.'

Beth gasped. 'Jesus, does Valerie know about this?'

'No, and I don't think she needs to just yet, do you?'

Chapter Eight

Beth put her suitcase down in the hall. 'Hello? Hello?'

'I'm down here,' replied Richard. He was in the kitchen.

Beth walked downstairs. When she turned the bend in the stairs, she smiled. Richard was standing in the middle of the kitchen holding a bunch of flowers.

'Welcome home,' he said.

Beth walked over to him and took Richard's surprise gift. She looked at it. It was the quintessential boy's bouquet. A mix of carnations and roses, it had clearly sat outside a petrol station for some considerable time. The stem of one of the carnations had snapped and the head was now dangling sadly outside the cellophane. According to Olivia, only gay men and PRs knew how to buy a bouquet. Beth wasn't married to either so crap flowers were her lot in life.

Still, it didn't matter. Beth was so pleased to see Richard, and he her. He bent down and kissed her. His arms were wrapped around her shoulders and he held her close for a long time. When he finally let her go, he looked into her eyes.

'I've really missed you, you know.'

'And I've missed you.' Beth smelled the flowers. They were, of course, odourless. 'I should go away more often if this is the reception I get when I come back,' she said.

Richard looked serious. 'I hate it when you go away.'

Beth slipped an arm through his and stroked his shoulder. 'I know, but it's my job. You know that.'

'I just wish you didn't have to. I get lonely without you. At least you won't be away now for a while.'

'Um, well, funny you should say that,' Beth said, disengaging herself. 'Karen wants me to do another trip.'

Richard tipped his head back and groaned. 'No, when?'

'Tomorrow. Look, it'll only take a couple of days. I'll be back by the weekend.'

'Isn't there any way you can get out of it?'

'Not really. You know how things are.'

'I really don't want you to go.' Richard sounded desperate. Beth just didn't know how desperate he really was.

'No worries,' said Jack Taylor, leaning forward and aiming a felt tip at one bare buttock. 'That's a hell of an all-over tan, Hayley. Ever been to Oz?'

Hayley giggled and blushed, though it was difficult to tell because she was already the colour of Caramac. 'Is that an invite, er, Jack?' As she said 'Jack' she nudged her friend, who was a similarly distressing hue, only her hair was marginally more bleached.

'The lucky country always welcomes the ladies,' said Jack, handing the felt tip back to Hayley.

She pulled her jeans back up over her white acrylic lace

knickers, turned round to face Jack and flicked her hair.

'This is Charlene, by the way,' she said, indicating her friend.

'My mum was a big fan of *Neighbours*,' said Charlene. 'If I'd been a boy she was going to call me Scott.'

'Well, I for one am happier than a sheep shearer on payday that you were a girl. Can I get you ladies a drink?'

'Lager,' they chorused.

At this point Beth joined them. She was slightly breathless, not from physical exertion so much as anxiety. 'There you are. I've been looking all over the hotel for you.'

Jack gave Beth a wicked grin, put an arm round her shoulders and squeezed her to him. His body felt strange, wholly different from Richard's familiar physical topography. Richard's was a body of extremes. The sharp edges of his slim frame contrasted with areas of wobbliness. Jack's skeleton had a continuous padding of muscle. It felt like being hugged by a well-stuffed leather Chesterfield.

Beth struggled free. 'Jack, we need to have a meeting about tomorrow's filming. We have to go.'

The team were in Scarborough to install a koi carp pond in the garden of Fred and Edna, a retired couple. Fred had had a go himself, but having started digging had hit an underground stream. The back garden had swiftly turned into a swamp and he had resorted to keeping a few goldfish in a mixing bowl on the patio.

'I'll be with you faster than a 'roo with the runs,' Jack said. 'But first I'm off to the bar. You keep Hayley and Charlene company. You thirsty?'

'No . . .' Beth had no desire to keep the tanning twins company, but she had little choice. Jack was gone.

* * *

119

'Well, I'm keeping my anorak on.'

Olivia and Colin were crouched behind a sand dune. Colin wasn't happy. To be honest, Olivia wasn't that happy either, mainly because Colin had been whingeing for the last twenty minutes, but she was trying to stay positive.

In an effort to shake their sex life out of catatonia, Olivia and Colin had come to Camber Sands for some late-afternoon open-air sex. Colin hadn't been keen to start with, but Olivia had packed the kids off to Alton Towers with her sister, packed Colin into the car and headed for the coast.

Granted, it wasn't quite as warm as Olivia would have liked. What little heat there had been in the sun had now faded. As she pulled off her boots and put her bare feet on the damp sand, she wished she'd brought the car rug. She couldn't hide a shiver as she unpeeled her layers. She managed a smile, even though, once she was naked, you could have grated cheese on her goose bumps.

However, Colin wasn't holding up his end of things. His end was resolutely pointing down, as much as she could see of it underneath his anorak, that is. He had removed everything except this decidedly unsexy outer garment, and even had the hood up. His knees were bent and his arms were crossed over his chest, his hands searching for heat in his armpits.

Olivia shuffled Toulouse-Lautrec-style towards Colin and attempted to prise his arms away from his chest and on to her own. She snuggled up to him, as much to leach out some warmth as to kick-start things down below. The whole of his body, bar the important bit, was rigid.

'Have you never heard of the spirit of adventure, Colin?'

'Have you never heard of hypothermia, Olivia?'

120

'Look, we've come all the way here, we might as well give it a go. Close your eyes and imagine it's Jamaica.'

Colin lay down and even unzipped his anorak so he could wrap the ends round Olivia. They both had their eyes closed. Olivia began to hum 'Je T'aime'. They kissed. Suddenly, Olivia felt something warm and wet on her thigh. She'd obviously done a better job of revving up Colin than she'd thought. Too good a job.

'Oh, Colin, you could have waited!'

She sat up in a huff and opened her eyes. Another pair of eyes were staring directly into hers. They weren't Colin's. These were big and black. Above them sat a pair of furry ears; below, a set of sharp teeth and a large pink tongue.

'Rex! Rex!' yelled a female voice just the other side of the sand dune. 'Come here, bad boy!'

Rex was indeed being a bad boy. He had his leg cocked and was weeing all over Olivia's thigh.

Richard poured chilli sauce on his kebab and bit into it. It tasted greasy and depressing. He walked out of the shop into the cold, chewing. With Beth away again, he was indulging in high-cholesterol consolation. She'd arranged for Stanley to stay at her mother's, so all that waited for Richard when he got home was a dark hallway and a bottle of Gaviscon.

Brrng, brrng.

Still walking, Richard reached into his pocket for his phone, trying not to get grease all over his suit in the process. The phone felt slippery. He almost dropped it.

'Hello?' he said.

'Richard, are you all right? It's Chastity.'

Richard stopped dead in the street. People were pushing past him as if he was a Japanese tourist wandering about Trafalgar Square with a camcorder. He hadn't spoken to Chastity since their night together. He hadn't known what to say. He was confused by his feelings. Part of him was guilt-ridden, but as the days had gone on, another part craved the excitement. He hadn't trusted himself not to suggest a repeat performance so hadn't made any contact. Now here she was on the phone and he was flummoxed.

'Richard, are you there?' Chastity asked.

'Yeah, yeah. Sorry I haven't, you know, um, called or anything.'

'It doesn't matter.'

People swarmed past Richard as he stood in the middle of the street, holding a rapidly congealing kebab. Some were heading home, others were off to a night out. The air was expectant.

'I just wondered if you'd like to come over,' said Chastity.

Richard gazed at his kebab. It looked decidedly unappetising.

'Well . . .' he said hesitantly.

'I just thought it might be fun,' she coaxed.

Richard dumped the kebab in a bin and hailed a cab.

'Hello, Liam, it's Beth from *On The House.*'

Liam sounded vague. 'Cath?'

'No, Beth.'

Bang, bang, bang. Someone was hammering in the background. *Eee-aaaw, eee-aaaw, eee-aaaw.* A hand saw had joined in.

'Liam, can you hear me?'

'Sorry, Cath. They're building my bedroom.'

'It's Beth, actually. I didn't mean to disturb you at home.'

'Oh, don't be silly, darling. It's not *my* bedroom, it's my bedroom, if you see what I mean.'

Beth didn't.

'It's my new range of bedroom furniture. We're doing an Egyptian theme. They're putting it together, hence the noise. We're shooting an ad.'

The volume at the other end suddenly went dramatically up. 'No, no, not there! The sphinx goes OVER THERE!'

Beth was forced to hold the receiver away from her ear.

'I said OVER THERE! And it's the wrong way up! Have you never seen an Ionic column before?'

There was a low muffled answer. Beth couldn't make it out. Liam turned his attention back to her.

'So sorry, Cath. Comprehensive education has a lot to answer for. How could one mix up Ionic and Doric, I ask you? Anyhow—'

Brrng, brrng.

'Sorry, Cath, hold on. It's my other phone.'

There was a clunk as Liam put down phone number one and picked up phone number two.

Beth had decided to give Liam a call from her hotel room. Well, it wasn't as if she had much else to do. It was funny how when she was at home dealing with Stanley and all the normal domestic chaos she yearned for peace and quiet. Clean towels, an uninter-rupted hot bath and room service in bed with the remote were her idea of heaven. When she got her hotel room for one, however, she immediately felt bereft.

Liam's footsteps could be heard tip-tapping across floorboards. Calling him was like dialling the customer services department of a privatised utility. Beth was destined to spend ninety-five per cent of her time on hold. At least she wasn't listening to 'Greensleeves'.

Liam was talking. 'Hello? . . . A commercial for dog worming tablets? How much? . . . Not bad. The thing is, you know as well as I do, I don't have a dog. I am poochless . . . Oh, they'll provide one. Marvellous. What colour? . . . Oh, they come in breeds, do they? Well, I don't know. Something chocolate brown, bitter chocolate I think . . . Sort of medium size . . . Oh, I've heard of them. No, too frowsy country hotel . . . Basically, anything that looks like it's got a Kevin Keegan seventies perm is out. OK? Talk later, darling. Bye.'

Liam's footsteps advanced back towards the receiver. 'Sorry, Cath,' he said. 'Now what can I do for you?'

'Well . . .'

The volume shot up again. 'Is that my sunken bath? It looks more like a washing-up bowl. This really is too much. We're supposed to be remaking *Antony and Cleopatra*, not *Carry On Cleo*.'

Beth reckoned she had one and a half seconds to get her pitch in.

'I know we've asked you before, but I wondered about your availability to do a spot of presenting for *On The House*,' she gabbled. 'I'd ask you to lunch, but your agent says you're not free till April 2004.'

Brrng, brrng. It was Liam's other phone again.

'Hello, can you hang on a minute?' Liam said into phone two, before lifting his voice to a bellow. 'Is that blue really working, darling? Does it say Tutankhamun, or just Tooting?'

Beth's heart began to sink. Liam was busier than Harrods on the first day of the sale.

'Sorry, Cath, got to go, bit of a nightmare,' Liam said.

Nightmare was right. Only it would be Beth's nightmare when

she had to tell Karen that she'd failed to secure Liam's services for *On The House*.

Richard nuzzled his cheek into the pillow. It felt soft, comforting and warm. He considered his options. He could go home to an empty house, or he could stay here in this nice warm bed. He looked across at Chastity, who was sleeping beside him. Her shoulders rose and fell in time with her steady breathing. A few strands of blonde hair were hanging across her young, unlined face.

He hadn't meant to do it. He had meant it to be strictly a one-night thing. A fling. Now it was two nights. Did that make it an affair? And if it was already an affair, did it make any difference if it was a two-night affair or a three-, four- or five-night one? That Richard was even thinking in those terms was proof that his resolve was ebbing away. He had built a wall of good intentions around himself, but now it was collapsing like a sand castle washed away by incoming tide.

The trick was not to think too much. When he was with Chastity, he didn't think about Beth and Stanley. He pushed them from his mind. Then there was the lying. That was getting easier too. Well, they say practice makes perfect. If Beth asked him what he'd done tonight, he would simply tell her he got a kebab and came home. She'd probably even feel sorry for him.

The fact was, Richard liked the way he looked, reflected back from Chastity's adoring gaze. She made him feel clever and handsome and sexy. He felt like the man he used to be. Carefree, not careworn. When Richard was with Chastity, he wasn't a husband or a father, with duties and responsibilities. He was just him, Richard, only all fresh and new.

Being with Chastity was like being on holiday. She didn't make any demands of him. He didn't have to take the rubbish out, or wipe round the bath. He didn't have to make allowances for the fact that she might be tired or Stanley might wake up. He felt liberated.

The bottom line was that when Richard was with Beth, he felt like the man who couldn't do things, or got them wrong, or forgot to do them entirely. He was the man who was always apologising for himself. With Chastity, he felt like he could do anything. He wasn't yet in love with Chastity, but he was already in love with this vision of himself.

Beth sighed with relief. She pushed the window down so she could feel the London pollution wafting through the taxi window. She'd be home soon now. She'd missed Richard, of course, but the person she was really dying to see was Stanley. She wanted to feel his plump cheek against hers, breathe in the sweet smell at the nape of his neck and kiss the softly padded soles of his feet.

Damn Karen, Beth thought darkly. What Karen didn't understand was that in going away, Beth didn't just miss Stanley, she missed an actual chunk of his life. That was time she could never make up. It was lost. Or maybe Karen did understand and she didn't care. Beth had a strong suspicion that the fact that she had a child was not entirely unconnected with the fact that Karen was being such a cow to her. Was Karen, single and sprogless, visiting all her body-clock issues on Beth?

The traffic slowed to a crawl and Beth found herself looking out the window. Up ahead she could see the awning for the Sionara Gdansk. A Japanese/Polish fusion restaurant, it was *the* place to be seen eating at the moment. Olivia had been, of course. According to her, they gave you lots of little dishes with hardly anything on. It was for the woman who had everything except an appetite, had been her verdict. Obviously, there was no sign outside saying *Sionara Gdansk*. That would have been far too obvious. Indeed, this *eaterie du jour* prided itself on its elusiveness. Even if you did, by some miracle, stumble across it, the staff refused to confirm you were in the right place. The business cards were blank and the phone number unlisted.

Beth was just fantasising about what it must be like to have the sort of life where you went for expensive lunches at smart restaurants like Sionara Gdansk when the taxi lurched forward. Her handbag jumped off the seat and landed on its side on the floor. Biros and lipsticks rolled everywhere. It was like a re-enaction of the *Exxon Valdez* disaster in the back of a cab.

'Damn!' Beth said, getting off the seat and on to all fours to retrieve the rubble from the floor and restore it to her bag.

'Thanks for lunch,' said a female voice, just outside the window of the cab.

'It was my pleasure,' a male voice responded. It sounded familiar. Spookily familiar. Beth frowned. It wasn't, was it? No, it couldn't be. What would Richard be doing having lunch at Sionara Gdansk?

Beth didn't want to make a fool of herself if it wasn't Richard, so, rather than leaping up and confronting him, she inched herself towards the window to look out. She'd just have a peep.

'Well, I'd better be going then,' the woman was saying.

'Yeah, me too,' echoed the man.

There was no sound of footsteps, so neither seemed to have moved.

It definitely sounded an awful lot like Richard, but who was the woman? Beth felt a bit odd crouching in a taxi, spying on someone who might or might not be her husband. It was pathetic behaviour really. Still, she inched her eyes up towards the glass. The top of her head cleared the window frame. Another couple of inches and she'd be able to see them.

'Right then,' the woman said.

'Yeah,' the man responded.

Beth's eyes hit glass. She was no more than three feet away from them. Yes, it was Richard all right. But who was the woman? The traffic suddenly cleared and the taxi jumped forward. Beth was flung towards the partition, hitting her head on it.

'Ow!'

She scrambled back on to the seat and turned round to catch another glimpse of Richard. He was walking away from her, but the woman was in clear vision. She was young and blonde and vaguely familiar. Who was she and what was she doing having lunch with Richard?

When Richard got home, Beth was upstairs with Stanley, putting him to bed.

'Hello?' he called as he closed the front door.

'I'm up here,' answered Beth.

She had a compulsion to run down the stairs shouting: 'Who was that woman you were having lunch with today?' But she was determined to play it cool. She didn't want to be one of those pathetic women who interrogated their husbands about their every movement.

Richard climbed the stairs to Stanley's bedroom.

'Dada, dada,' shrieked Stanley as his father appeared in the doorway. He got to his feet and began rattling the bars of the cot.

'No, no, darling. Time to go to sleep now,' Beth admonished him. Richard walked towards them and gave Beth, then Stanley a kiss. Then he picked up one of Stanley's toy cars. 'Car's tired. Car's going to sleep,' he said. 'Kiss car goodnight.'

Stanley kissed and hugged his mini Ferrari and obediently lay down.

Richard picked up a book and began to read. 'It was Danny the Digger's first day on the building site . . .'

Beth got up and went to the door. She looked at Richard and Stanley. He was the image of New Man. If they ever made a sequel to that postcard of Muscly Man Holding a Baby, then this image would be it: Father Reads Story to Son.

Beth walked downstairs. As soon as she reached the hall, however, a terrible compulsion gripped her. She gingerly slipped a hand into Richard's jacket pocket. When she pulled it out again she was holding a taxi receipt and half a packet of chewing gum. She put them back, ashamed at this invasion of his privacy. But she couldn't stop herself.

She could hear Richard's voice coming from upstairs. ' "Hello Tommy," said Danny, as Tommy the Truck trundled past . . .' She dipped into the other jacket pocket, then went through the inside ones. What was she looking for? A scrap of paper with a number on it, a name, a note? She didn't find anything.

She was overcome with shame. What had she become? She heard Richard's step on the stairs and hurriedly put the debris she was holding in her hand back where it belonged. She composed herself.

'Is he down?' she asked overly brightly.

Richard nodded. 'What's for dinner?'

'Don't know what we've got in. Let's go and have a look.'

On the way down to the basement, Beth tried to be calm. She'd shocked herself with the level of her insecurity. She knew Richard, she told herself. He'd never do anything to betray her. Still, he had been slightly odd lately – short-tempered and a bit distant. The feeling of dread wouldn't go away.

And there was something about the way he had looked with the blonde woman, something about their tone of voice. They had seemed at ease. No, that wasn't quite it. The scene had looked intimate.

Beth opened the fridge and poked around among the packets and boxes inside. 'We've got chicken casserole and some of that fried rice from the other night,' she said.

Richard didn't say anything. He was reading the local free sheet.

'Or there's some cheese. What about Welsh rarebit?' offered Beth.

Richard still didn't answer.

Beth felt a tingle of annoyance. She was having an emotional crisis and he was reading about cuts to the mobile library service!

She couldn't stand it 'I think I saw you today,' she said.

'Hmmm,' Richard replied, not looking up.

Beth's anger was building. 'You were coming out of Sionara Gdansk. With a woman.'

Richard's heart practically exploded out of his chest. Beth had seen him and Chastity. He knew it had been a bad idea, but Chastity had persuaded him. She'd heard Lucas Lieberman went to Sionara Gdansk and he hadn't been able to say no. Whatever he felt about Chastity – and he wasn't exactly sure what he did feel – he didn't want her to think she was some sort of secret sex toy. To be honest, this was more about the vision he had of himself than her. He may have been shagging a woman who wasn't his wife, but he liked to think he was still a nice guy. Anyway he had made sure they had a table in the corner and he'd sat with his back to the room and thought he'd got away with it. Apparently, he was wrong. He said nothing, playing for time.

Beth couldn't tell if Richard really was concerned about the availability of large-type books for the over sixties or if he was stalling. It took a good five seconds for him to answer.

'Yeah, um, I did pop out for a while,' he said evenly.

Pop out! Pop out! This from the man who always insisted he didn't have time to pick up so much as a tube of toothpaste at lunchtime because he was chained to his desk. Beth had always suspected that the real reason he wouldn't nip to the shops was that he didn't want to be seen by his colleagues lugging carrier bags back to his office. It wasn't manly or something.

Beth struggled to stay dignified. She hid behind the fridge door.

'Who did you *pop out* with?' Oops, that sounded bitchy.

'Oh, just a contributor, you know.'

'No, I don't know,' Beth replied coldly.

'I don't fancy cheese on toast. Shall I pop out and pick up a curry?' said Richard, changing the subject as if he was a passenger in a car who had just grabbed the wheel and forced a left turn.

Here Richard was offering to pop out again! Beth grappled the wheel from him and steered the conversation back in the direction she wanted to go. 'I don't want a curry. What contributor?'

Richard realised that he wasn't going to win. Sweat was

breaking out on the back of his neck. He turned away from Beth, bent down and began to unload the dishwasher. Anything to avoid having to look her in the eye.

Bastard! thought Beth. Now he decides to help with the housework!

'It was your idea, remember, that girl we saw on TV. The, um, lap dancer. You said I should get her on the show.'

Beth frowned, closed the fridge door and walked towards Richard. 'But didn't you already have lunch with her?'

'Yeah, but she's nervous.'

She hadn't looked especially nervous when Beth had seen her on the street today.

'Is it usual to spend Channel 6's money on *two* lunches with one guest?'

Richard carried on unpacking plates. He found the banal nature of the task comforting.

Beth didn't like the way she was sounding, which was shrill. Still, she couldn't stop herself. 'Well, is it?'

Richard stood up. He had no choice. He would have to employ the Make Her Think She's Mad defence against potential accusations of infidelity.

'What is this? Why are you getting so hysterical? It was your idea, remember. And now you're having a go at me. A lunch. That's all it was. Jesus, if you're going to make this kind of fuss every time I have a business meeting, well, I had no idea you were so insecure.'

That last bit really hit Beth between the shoulder blades.

'I just thought . . .'

'I'm going to check my e-mails.'

Richard strode out of the kitchen, leaving Beth to wonder. Was it really all her own insecurity, or was something going on?

The Tweenies were warbling incessantly and Beth had a huge urge to throw a brick at the speaker which lurked just above her head. But that wouldn't have solved anything. At the Funky Food Factory, they had a seemingly inexhaustible supply of speakers pumping out naff kiddie muzak.

The idea behind the Funky Food Factory was brilliant. Get a few plastic tables and chairs, fixed at the most uncomfortable distance from one another, add a logo of a roller-skating parrot and a play area and hey presto! you'll have parents queuing up. Money for old rope, which was what the hamburger buns tasted of.

Olivia ate a chip. 'Right,' she announced. 'What's the problem?'

'I didn't say there was a problem, did I?' Beth answered.

'No, but you've got something on your mind.'

Colin had taken the twins to baby massage class – what next, baby caviar-eating class, or possibly baby lounging on a chaise-longue being fed grapes class? With the babies otherwise engaged, Olivia and Beth had brought Anouska and Seth to the Funky Food Factory. The children were now playing happily on the slides, leaving Beth and Olivia to talk.

Beth sighed. 'Well, it's more a feeling, really. I saw Richard coming out of Sionara Gdansk–'

Olivia interrupted her. 'I had no idea Channel 6 had that kind of money.'

'Yeah, well, they did make a bit of dosh on all those *Big Sister* phone votes, didn't they? Anyway, he was with someone. A woman. When I asked him about it, he was sort of defensive. I mean, it's probably nothing. Let's face it, Richard's not the type to have an affair.'

Olivia raised an eyebrow. 'Who is she?'

'Her name's Chastity.'

This time Olivia's eyes widened in disbelief.

'I know. Awful name, isn't it? Anyway, she's, get this, a lap dancer, and he's getting her on one of his shows, and maybe I'm overreacting, but, well, he's not that kind of man, is he?'

Olivia bit into a chip. 'And what kind of man is that?' she asked. 'One with horns and a tail? They're all that kind of man, Beth.'

For Olivia, the memory of her break-up with James always hovered just below the surface. She'd been like an apple that had been cored. Her centre had disappeared, cut out by a vicious vortex of anger, grief, doubt and betrayal. It wasn't until she met Colin that she'd started to rebuild herself. And it wasn't until she'd had Seth that the void inside started to shrink. Olivia now wrapped herself in the love of her children as if it was an old-fashioned eiderdown. The pain of James's betrayal was still there, but it was muffled by the touch of soft little arms and legs.

Olivia looked at her plate and wrinkled her nose. 'She's a lap dancer, you say?'

'Yeah, nothing like going upmarket, is there?' laughed Beth, but it was a thin and joyless chuckle. 'The thing is, what do I do, or do I do nothing?'

'Oh, no. You definitely don't do that. I think you need to neutralise the opposition.'

'How?'

'Invite her over.'

Beth looked appalled. 'You are joking?'

'Remember that stuff about keeping your friends close and your enemies closer?'

'But I don't know if she is an enemy yet.'

'Fine. What's the worst that can happen? You make a new friend.'

'I haven't got time to see all the friends I've already got,' said Beth.

'Look,' said Olivia firmly, pushing her plate away from her, 'all I'm saying is it would be wise to get to know her and make sure she gets to know you. It's much harder to sleep with someone's husband if you know the wife. Not impossible, but more difficult. Just do it before it's too late.'

Feminine subterfuge was as unfamiliar to Beth as a fifties girdle. It pinched and poked her conscience. How women of her mother's generation had managed when manipulation was their only weapon, she had no idea. No wonder half of them were on the sherry by four o'clock.

Beth peered over the top of her newspaper. She and Richard were having breakfast. Stanley was sitting on the floor, contentedly rolling cans of baked beans.

'You know, I've been thinking,' said Beth. 'Maybe we should have a dinner party. Just a small one.'

'Why?' said Richard, lowering his paper and taking a bite out of his toast and marmalade. 'You hate dinner parties. You say they're for people who want to show off their new three-piece suite.'

'Yeah, well, never mind that,' Beth spluttered defensively. 'We're becoming really boring. I think it would be fun to have some people over.'

'Fine, if that's what you want,' he said, lifting his paper again.

Beth paused. She could hear crunching sounds coming from the other side of Richard's wall of newsprint. Neutralise the opposition, Olivia had said. 'I thought you could invite your lap-dancing friend.'

'Chastity!' Richard exclaimed from behind the paper. If she'd suggested he remove all his clothes and tap-dance to *The Best of the Crankies* in the street, he couldn't have sounded more surprised. 'Why?'

'It would be nice.'

There was no reply from Richard.

'And I'd like to meet her.'

Richard didn't drop the paper, but there was a very long pause. His brain was working at triple speed. He was trying to work out two things. First, did Beth wanting Chastity to dinner mean that his efforts to persuade her she was just being paranoid had failed? Did she now think something was going on? And second, how the hell was he going to get out of this one?

'I don't think inviting Chastity is a good idea,' he said finally. Was that panic in his voice? 'I mean, well, I'm sure she's busy.'

'Nonsense,' said Beth firmly. 'If she has the time for *two* lunches with you, I'm sure she can fit in one dinner with both of us, don't you?'

'Well, um . . .' Richard was floundering.

'I'm not taking no for an answer.'

Chapter Nine

'How does Madonna do it?' Beth had one foot in front of the other and her knees were bent. She was wobbling madly. Siobhan and Olivia were doing only slightly better. When Siobhan had suggested the three of them go to a yoga class, Olivia and Beth had thought it might be restful. Now they were hurting in places they hadn't even known existed half an hour ago.

None of the other twenty or so lithe women were complaining. There was also a smattering of men, some of whom appeared not to be wearing pants under their shorts. According to Siobhan this wasn't sexual harassment, it was 'sort of ayurvedic', whatever that meant. Everyone else wore expressions of inner calm to match their insouciant little T-shirts and pyjama trousers.

That had been Beth's first yoga faux pas. She'd climbed into the leotard and cycle shorts she'd bought when she last joined a gym. Halfway through a spinning class, she'd been convinced she was having a heart attack. Her clobber had sat in a drawer ever since. When she looked around her now and saw the pitying looks of her yoga classmates, she wished she'd left it there. 'You tragic person. You think this is an exercise class,' those looks said. 'We are here to develop our spirits, not our bodies.' This was rubbish, of course. Had Mahatma Gandhi had cellulite, they wouldn't be contorting themselves like Crazy Straws now.

Around the class, the only sounds were breathing and the soft whine of an Indian sitar coming from the ghetto blaster in the corner. This was partly to drown out the roar of cars thundering overhead. The sports centre where this yoga class was being held was built under a dual carriageway. Occasionally there was the discreet jangle of an ankle bracelet.

A man's voice broke the silence. 'Breathe.' It was the teacher, Asif, who was rumoured to have 'practised' with Sting and Trudie Styler.

'I wonder whether Sting wears pants under his shorts?' whispered Olivia.

'Yuck!' said Beth.

Siobhan said Asif's real name was Neil and he lived in a one-bedroom flat in Ealing, which rather destroyed his mystique. Still, he'd taken the trouble to grow a ponytail, so he was obviously committed to the yogic lifestyle.

'Now raise your arms above your head and put your palms together as if you're praying,' said Asif.

'More like begging for mercy,' said Olivia.

A girl in a lace-trimmed thermal vest and expensive-looking jersey trousers, roughly hacked off below the knee, gave her a filthy look.

'This is called the warrior posture,' said Asif.

'If this is a war, then I'm surrendering,' hissed Olivia, collapsing into a heap.

Beth sat down beside her. 'Do you fancy a drink?'

'I wish I'd had a stiff G and T before I got here.'

* * *

Beth, Olivia and Siobhan settled themselves into a sofa at the Frog and Lettuce. Formerly the Windsor Castle, it had been given a radical revamp. Out had gone the flock wallpaper and ketchup. In had come moody black-and-white photos and sundried tomato pesto.

'Thanks to you, Olivia, I've now got to cook the bloody woman dinner,' said Beth.

'At least you don't need to bother with cheese and biscuits. She'll get up on the table after pudding and dance around in her G-string.'

'Perhaps you should invite her round for Christmas at your place, Olivia? She could give the whole family a demonstration of pole technique with a mop after the Queen's Speech. It would make a change from charades, wouldn't it?'

They all laughed.

'When's she coming?'

'Next week sometime, I hope. Richard's being vague. Keeps saying he's leaving messages on her answerphone but she doesn't call him back.'

Beth saw Olivia's expression. 'Don't worry. I'm not bottling out. I told him I'd call his secretary, get her number and call her myself if he didn't organise it.'

'Actually, Beth,' Siobhan said, sounding suddenly serious, 'I meant to say earlier. I've got a message from Karen for you.'

Beth winced.

'She caught me just as I was coming out of the office. She said to say she'd booked Sian Jones for next week's job.'

Olivia and Beth made horrified faces.

'Look, I know she's got a reputation, but she's not a bad designer,' said Siobhan.

'Ever the optimist,' Beth replied.

'You know those old pictures of Welsh women wearing those black pointy hats?' said Olivia.

Siobhan nodded.

'Well, in Sian's case, she's got the broomstick to match. Rather you than me, Beth.'

'I don't think I have a choice after the tortoise incident, do you?' Beth replied.

At that moment, Siobhan's phone beeped. 'It must be Simon. He said he'd text me.' She began pressing buttons. 'Shit.'

'What?' said Beth.

'It's Darren.'

'The schoolboy lover?' asked Olivia.

'Which one?' asked Beth. 'You seem to be having a run of boyfriends who haven't started shaving.'

'Kyle wasn't a boyfriend. He was a one-night stand!' protested Siobhan loudly. A couple of men at the bar turned round and smiled a tad too warmly for Siobhan's liking.

Siobhan dropped her voice. 'Anyway, he was a mistake, and so was Darren. I love Simon. You know that. And we're back together. It's just Darren keeps texting me. Look, it's another one of those sad faces.'

Beth and Olivia leaned forward to study the screen on Siobhan's phone. 'God, I hate those,' said Beth. 'They're the modern version of those seventies "Love is . . ." notelets. And how naff were those?'

'He wants to know when I'm coming to visit him.'

Beth threw her a look. 'No.'

'What?'

'Before you ask, I am not going back up there. The nurse already thinks I am a complete cow.'

'And I'm not going either,' said Olivia firmly. 'I've had enough embarrassment for one week.'

'Oh, yes,' said Beth, giggling. 'How is the last of the red-hot lovers?'

'It's not funny. We were followed by other dogs all the way back to the car and now Colin is even less keen. I don't know what I'm going to do.'

'He'll come round. He's a man, remember, and no man can go without sex for more than a few weeks.'

'What about Cliff Richard?' asked Siobhan.

'Maybe you've got a point. I'm married to Cliff Richard.'

Siobhan put her phone back in her handbag and took a sip from her wine glass. 'I do hope Simon's all right.'

'What do you mean? Hasn't he called?' asked Beth, incredulously.

'No, and I've been reading a lot about deep-vein thrombosis. Flight crews are especially prone to them, you know—'

Olivia interrupted Siobhan. 'Or maybe he's been kidnapped by a crazed air stewardess and is being held captive on a desert island.'

'Don't make fun of me.'

'It's just that, well, haven't we been here before?' asked Beth.

'Oh, Siobhan, face facts,' said Olivia. 'He's married.'

'I know, but he said—'

'Never mind what he said. He's got what he wants now. You won't hear from him for weeks.'

Siobhan had been forced to confess that she'd slept with Simon, and now the others were giving her their 'I told you sos'. Still, Olivia's vociferousness was more about her history than Siobhan's future. Beth understood this, but still thought she was being too harsh. 'Hold on, Olivia,' she said. 'Give her a break.'

'No, she needs to hear it.'

Siobhan put down her wine glass and reached in her handbag for a packet of cigarettes.

'I thought you'd given up!' exclaimed Beth.

Siobhan looked down guiltily. 'I know you think I'm an idiot, but at least I feel passion, which is more than both of you. When was the last time either of you had a decent shag?'

Siobhan's comment hung in the air like the smoke from her newly lit Marlboro Light. Olivia and Beth were too shocked to answer back. Finally, Beth decided things needed to calm down. 'Look, this isn't a contest. We just think you could do so much better.'

Siobhan exploded. 'It's all right for you. You're both married. You've got someone.'

'Even if he is called Cliff,' Olivia added drily.

Siobhan started to cry and Beth put an arm round her shoulders.

'Simon is my one chance,' sobbed Siobhan. 'I know he's married. But he doesn't love Elaine. He loves me.' She saw Beth and Olivia's faces. 'No, he does. He's just in a really difficult position. He only married her because she got pregnant with Hannah.'

'So what about the other two kids?' said Olivia. 'Is he especially potent, especially unlucky, or do they perhaps sleep together rather more regularly than he would have you believe?'

'But if he's not happy?' asked Siobhan.

'Well, then he should sort it out, not have a sordid little affair.'

'That sordid little affair . . .' Siobhan was crying so hard now, she couldn't get her sentences out whole. She'd abandoned her now sodden cigarette in an ashtray. '. . . has taken up the last four years of my life.'

'Exactly,' said Beth as gently as possible. 'It's been four years and he still hasn't left Elaine. Don't you think it's time to move on?'

'I know you're right, but I've tried and I can't do it. I'm not as strong as you.'

Siobhan was looking at Olivia, who reached forward and put her arms round her too. The three of them clung together.

'You're not on your own,' said Beth.

'I can't.'

Olivia sat back. 'Look, the world is full of single men.'

'I think the title of the book was *The World is Full of Married Men*, actually,' said Beth.

'What I mean is, there is life beyond Simon. You just need to give it a bit more of a go. Look at the guys in here. There are loads of good-looking ones. That one up at the bar, for instance. He's been staring at you since we came in.'

Beth and Siobhan swivelled in their seats and surveyed a dark-haired man in jeans sat on his own with a bottle of beer in front of him.

'Not bad,' said Beth. 'Sort of Ralph Fiennes-ish.'

The man turned his head and just caught Siobhan's eye before she looked down.

Olivia rummaged in her handbag for a tissue and a mirror, both of which she gave to Siobhan. 'Here, clean yourself up, girl. By the way, when you go to the bar, mine's a white wine.'

* * *

Sian Jones strode into the fifteenth-century cottage and exclaimed: 'Concrete!'

'Concrete?' Beth wasn't sure she'd heard right, her attention having been distracted by the large sling Sian had her arm in. 'What happened to your . . .' She didn't get a chance to finish her sentence.

'And gravel, and maybe a bit of galvanised aluminium.'

Beth decided to leave the arm-in-a-sling issue for the moment. She had more pressing things to deal with. 'This place is fifteenth century. It needs a bit of work, granted. But you don't really want to skim the beams in concrete, do you?'

'There is a reason some of us are *directors*,' Sian said, spitting out the word as if it was a cherry stone, 'and others are designers. Designers, such as myself, have vision.'

Beth had known Sian would be trouble. She was well known in telly for being the woman who uprooted a copse of two-hundred-year-old oak trees and installed a star-shaped swimming pool in their place. The swimming pool hadn't contained any water. It had been 'a conceptual space', according to Sian, which meant it was filled entirely with pink ping-pong balls.

With her brunette crew-cut, sharp, unsmiling face and stern Gil Sander suits, Sian could have been an especially dour governor of Prisoner Cell Block H. Her attitude to design was certainly rigorous and she brooked no challenge to her authority. That she and Karen got along was perhaps not surprising. They might have been polar opposites, looks-wise, but their personalities made them like a pair of evil twins.

'I'm sure your vision is gorgeous, Sian. It's just that I don't feel our contributor had, er, concrete in mind. He wanted more of a—'

'And since when did we let *members of the public* design rooms?'

'Well, of course, you are the expert, but don't you think—'

'I don't think. I feel. And what I'm feeling now is concrete. I've already told Jack to organise it. Twenty-five tons of ready-mixed is arriving at four o'clock. Anyway, I've got to go. I'm due back at the Real Homes Show at Olympia in an hour.'

Sian began walking towards the door.

'Sorry, Sian, just one more thing before you go. Did you have an accident? Your arm and the sling, I mean?'

'Too many autographs,' announced Sian, turning on her heel and marching off.

Somehow, Beth didn't think the owner of this house would be queuing up to add to Sian's problem.

Valerie had a manicured hand placed on a middle-aged man's shoulder.

'OK, George, open your eyes.'

George Marshall, once the proud owner of a fifteenth-century house, contemplated his new concrete dining room, with its gravel floor and galvanised aluminium table and chairs. He didn't speak.

'Well, George, what do you think?'

Not a word came out of George's mouth. His complexion did the talking all on its own. He was progressing through a series of shades of pink. First baby, then rose. He had now reached fuchsia and was heading for cherry.

'Sian's very pleased with it,' said Valerie, panicking slightly. Twenty seconds of silence is a long time on TV. She knew she had to get something out of him, even if it was just a yelp. Still nothing. She'd have to fill. 'I think it's one of those looks that needs bedding in,' she said. 'Once you get used to it, I'm sure you'll love it.'

Without a word, George turned to Valerie and planted a perfect left hook on her cheek. She crashed to the ground like a felled larch, one elegant arm grazing a galvanised aluminium chair as she went.

Siobhan studied herself in the mirrored door of the bathroom cabinet. She looked like the 'before' picture in an ad for vitamin supplements. No wonder Simon hadn't called. Who'd want to sit across a dinner table from someone who looked like Pauline Fowler after a rough day at the launderette?

Another wave of sickness welled up inside her. Siobhan hurriedly emptied the tooth mug and filled it with water from the tap. She took a long drink, enjoying the cool feeling as the water ran down her throat. Maybe it wasn't a bug after all. Maybe she was just tired.

She went into the kitchen. Eating some breakfast would make her feel better. Perhaps she'd just have a bowl of cereal. She opened the fridge. No milk. She got some muesli out of a cupboard and walked round the kitchen shaking the packet so the interesting bits rose to the top. This was one of the moments when she relished being single. She had no one to answer to for picking out all the nuts and raisins.

The nausea was beginning to recede. Probably just need an early night, Siobhan thought as she took herself and her packet of cereal back into the bedroom. She sat down on the bed and tried to decide what to wear, dipping her hand in and out of the packet, and then up to her mouth. As she did so, she scattered bits of oat and dried banana on the sheets. This was another time she was glad she was single. No one to moan about crumbs in the bed either, she thought as she swept the debris on to the floor.

Eight a.m., and Beth was in the office. The call came almost immediately.

'Hi, it's Marcia, could you drop by? Patric would like a wee word.'

Arriving outside Patric's office, she was greeted by Marcia looking even frumpier than usual. Olive-green below-the-knee skirt and matching cowl-neck sweater.

'Coffee?' said Marcia.

'I won't, thanks. Trying to cut down, you know.'

'I like camomile tea myself.'

Beth had once had a boyfriend who drank herbal teas. He kept a travel kettle under his desk and a little box of tea bags next to his phone. (It was an office romance.) Every time he made a brew, she felt her attraction for him wilt a little more. His nether regions had a habit of doing the same, although whether that was as a consequence of his tea consumption, or because he was just *that sort of guy*, she wasn't sure.

After Mr Camomile, Beth had become sensitised to certain nutritional habits. Low-fat fruit yoghurts, Dairylea cheese triangles and spritzers all reeked of a passionless existence. As for those people who took a tiny amount of margarine and spent ages spreading it evenly into all the corners of a piece of toast, well, there were support groups for that sort of thing, weren't there?

'Sandwich? They're Dairylea,' offered Marcia.

The door to Patric's office opened and he stepped out.

'Ah, Beth, would you like to come in?'

Beth followed him inside.

'Hello, sweetie, how are you?' Karen was sitting nursing a cup of coffee. Her face wore an expression of concern. Her eyes, however, glinted with malice. 'So good of you to find the time.'

Beth stretched her lips into a smile. She needed to process what was happening. Patric had asked to see her. Was that before or after Karen had got her bottom on his sofa? If they were here to talk about Valerie's hospitalisation, which surely they were, what had Karen already said?

'You know I'm always happy to see you, Karen,' Beth answered.

For a moment, Beth and Karen's eyes locked. There was a split second of naked hatred and then it was gone. Patric never even saw it.

'Well, Beth, I'm sure you know why we're here. Valerie is out of traction, and they now think the clot on her brain was just a doughnut stain on the X-ray. But we need to learn why this, um, accident happened,' said Patric.

'Well, Patric—' Beth was interrupted by Karen.

'As I told Patric, I was very supportive when you suggested using Sian.'

I suggested? thought Beth. What is she talking about?

Karen was still talking. 'I think it's so important to back directors, even relatively *inexperienced* ones . . .'

Patric nodded.

'Designers need such careful handling, and it's not your fault if you just don't have the experience to deal with, how shall I put it, an artistic temperament.' Here, Karen turned to Patric and smiled conspiratorially.

Patric spoke now. 'Anyway, Beth, I do have to put on record that this regrettable incident does constitute a serious blemish on your career. I hope you understand.'

Beth nodded glumly.

'Following that thing with the tortoise . . .'

'And the wall incident,' added Karen helpfully.

'Yes, that as well. You know the policy. Three strikes and you're out. This really is your last chance. We don't want to lose you, but . . .'

The message was clear. One more slip-up and Beth would be sacked.

But Patric wasn't finished. 'It's not all bad news, Beth. Karen has very kindly agreed to give you the benefit of her experience, which I'm sure you know is considerable. And I'm certain that with her supervision—'

Karen interrupted him again. 'Close supervision.'

'Yes, close supervision, we can avoid any further hiccups in the future. Karen feels, and I agree with her, that she needs to be a bit more hands-on.'

A wave of depression was sweeping over Beth. You had to hand it to Karen. She'd done Beth up like a kipper.

Karen was the essence of smugness. 'There are some things you can't delegate,' she purred. 'Liam Smith, for example. No luck there, I understand?'

'I've tried,' said Beth. 'I really have, but he is incredibly busy.'

'Well, perhaps I can use the benefit of my experience there too,' Karen oozed.

'See,' said Patric. 'This new arrangement is working already!'

Beth was ushered out. She had been hung, drawn and quartered and not even allowed a last word in her defence. If her position had been difficult before, now it was parlous.

'Oh, something I forgot to say.'

Richard was sitting on the edge of Chastity's bed. She was kneeling behind him with her arms wrapped round his shoulders, alternately blowing on and kissing his neck. Richard fumbled nervously with the buttons on his shirt. 'Well, I've been putting it off, actually. Um, don't know quite how to put this.'

Chastity sat up. 'What?'

'Beth wants you to come to dinner.'

Chastity was shocked. 'Why? She doesn't suspect, does she?'

'God, no!' responded Richard, standing up and tucking his shirt into his trousers. 'I mean, why would you think that?'

He had his back to Chastity and he had gone very pale.

Chastity crossed her arms over her chest and frowned. 'Well, it's a bit odd, isn't it? Her inviting me. Then again, maybe it would be good to meet her.'

Richard turned round and went even paler.

'Come here. Don't look so glum,' she said, putting her arms out towards him. 'It had to happen sooner or later. Maybe it's good. Maybe it's time, you know.'

Richard didn't move. 'Time for what?'

'Well, you're obviously not happy with her.'

Richard could hear his own heart beating in his ears.

'I mean, maybe you owe it to her to tell her. Or we could tell her together.'

Panic now gripped Richard. 'No, no. I never said . . .'

'You don't have to say. The fact that you're here says it all, don't you think?' Chastity was speaking gently, coaxingly. She got off the bed and walked over to Richard. She looked up at him. 'She doesn't appreciate you the way I do.'

Richard stepped round her and went to the bed to pick up his jacket. 'This dinner is a really, really bad idea. I'll put her off.'

'No, that's OK,' Chastity replied, following him.

'I'll stall her somehow.'

Chastity caught Richard's arm and pulled him round so he was facing her. 'OK, if you don't want me to say anything, fine. But I have to go. If I don't, it'll look *really* suspicious.'

'Well . . .' Richard was unsure.

'Don't worry,' said Chastity. 'She'll never know a thing.'

Chapter Ten

What do you wear to a dinner with a woman who might want to sleep with your husband? Beth surveyed her wardrobe and weighed up the options. She could do Cherie Blair Power Wife – trouser suit and a pashmina. But the last time Beth had seen Cherie on *News at Ten* she'd looked like Tony's mum, so maybe that wasn't a good idea. Perhaps she needed to be less subtle, slip into something short, tight and red, as a message to the Bimboid, as she'd secretly taken to calling Chastity: 'See, we do have sex!' But that felt demeaning. Besides, if this was to be a head-to-head confrontation, or more precisely a cleavage-to-cleavage one, Beth's nipples were a couple of feet lower than the Bimboid's. She didn't stand a chance trying to out-sexy her.

After much deliberation, Beth chose a pink silk dress with leopard-print straps – pretty with just a hint of Versace hooker – and pink kitten-heeled mules. This was an outfit dating from her pre-Stanley-with-sticky-fingers days. It felt weird to put it on now.

She walked closer to the full-length mirror and ran one hand through her hair. She'd had it cut specially at Tino 'n' Ray earlier in the day. Her stylist had been called Pedro and had his eyebrow pierced. She'd been tempted to leave then, but had held her nerve. She had asked for a Meg Ryan. It had looked a passable imitation in the salon. Now, however, instead of being fashionably tousled, it looked as if she'd had her hair done on a really bad student night.

No time to worry about that now. She could hear Stanley shouting from his playpen. A quick look at the tractor catalogue and he'd be ready for bed. Before Stanley, Beth had enjoyed a diverse mix of reading matter. Now this had shrunk to the latest models produced by JCB. How had this happened? It wasn't even as if Stanley had ever even seen a real hay baler, the Sainsbury's car park in Camden Town not being awash with agricultural vehicles. If only he had developed an interest in sofas, rugs and small electrical items. Then they could have spent many a happy hour poring over the IKEA catalogue. But no, it was tractors. Only tractors.

Beth walked downstairs and rounded the corner into the ground-floor playroom. Stanley was sitting in his playpen, laughing. He had managed to remove both his sleep suit and his nappy, tossed dismissively a good five feet away.

'Oh, Stanley, you are naughty,' sighed Beth, but she wasn't really angry.

Stanley jumped to his feet, grabbed his beaker of milk and did a triumphal jig. Beth picked him up. His bottom felt soft and warm against her forearm.

Drring. It was the door bell.

Damn, thought Beth. 'Richard!' she shouted upstairs.

Richard was in the bedroom. He'd been in the bedroom for forty-five minutes. Most of that time had been spent sitting with his head in his hands. How had he got himself into this? He was about to have dinner with his wife and his mistress. It was a nightmare come true. What if Chastity said anything? Or Beth guessed? Oh God!

Brring. The door bell rang again. Beth gave up on Richard and went to the door herself, holding Stanley. He wriggled and burbled happily, excited to see who was arriving. Beth felt only apprehension. This was like her driving test, only worse. When she'd taken her test, her clutch leg had shaken so much her knee had sounded like it was marking out a distress call in Morse code on the underside of the dashboard.

What was the Bimboid going to be like? Hopefully she'd be really stupid. Then, even if she had the body of a goddess, Beth could feel sorry for her. There is nothing more satisfying than being able to pity a pretty girl. If she was clever, or worse, clever and nice, then that would be just too depressing.

Beth breathed in as she opened the door. The Bimboid had her back to her. She was wearing a boob tube. A sequined boob tube. The only time Beth had ever worn a boob tube was when she was fifteen and it was the school disco. She'd leaned forward to pick up a cocktail stick of cheese and pineapple from a foil-covered orange and the front of her top had folded itself down, exposing her breasts to the whole of the upper fifth. Beth had been mortified, although, presumably, should the Bimboid perform a similar feat tonight, she wouldn't be that bothered.

The Bimboid's back was as smooth and taut as the fabric of a kite in a high wind. But things got better as Beth scanned downwards. She noted the Bimboid's jeans. They were bleached. A tasselled belt decorated the waistband.

Richard never understood it when Beth made assumptions about people based upon their clothing. He was forever ranting that you couldn't write someone off just because you didn't like their shirt. But it was only the female form of that traditional male sport – judge a man by his car. Beth couldn't have cared less what vehicle someone owned, but to Richard it was key.

When they'd gone to antenatal classes, about the only piece of information Richard appeared to have gleaned was what cars the other fathers drove. From hour upon hour of talk about epidurals and forceps, he'd came out moaning that he'd have to buy a Volvo. She didn't get it. To think he criticised her for being obsessed by pointless minutiae!

Now, Beth looked at the Bimboid in her sequins and her fussy belt and she thought to herself: What a total slapper! She found herself smiling, partly in amusement, but mostly in relief.

Had Chastity arrived wearing a power suit, something ethnic from Monsoon or even one of Issey Miyake's odder pieces, Beth would have been worried. But the way Chastity looked, well, she just wasn't Richard's type. Richard would never have an affair with a woman who wore sequins. He wouldn't even find her attractive. How could he? She was so, well, cheap.

Beth wanted to hug the Bimboid. Instead she greeted her warmly. 'You must be Chastity. I'm Beth, Richard's wife, and this is Stanley.'

Chastity turned round and Beth was struck by the two huge orbs of flesh rising above her sequined top. She tried not to stare, but they were humungous. They looked like a pair of pink bowling balls. Jesus. She's even got breast implants, thought Beth, incredulously. Now she definitely, absolutely, utterly, completely knew that Richard would not sleep with this woman. He hated boob jobs. In fact, when Beth had been a bit nervous about the state of her own cleavage after she'd stopped breast-feeding, Richard had told her he preferred a bit of natural sag.

Beth studied Chastity's face. Coloured mascara and that odd Essex-girl dark lip-liner and pale lipstick thing. Her hair was highlighted so much, you could have used the ends to scour saucepans. With each new tarty detail, the sense of relief flowed through Beth like Coca Cola up a straw. It wound its way through every vein and artery and pumped into every organ. Chastity was a tart, a floozie, a slapper. Beth grinned broadly.

'Do come in. It's *so* good to meet you,' she said, with genuine bonhomie.

Chastity didn't move. 'You've got, um ...' She was pointing in the general direction of Stanley.

'Yes,' said Beth. 'It's a baby.' Fantastic! She was stupid as well.

'Da, da, da,' Stanley babbled happily.

'No, he's, er – your skirt.' Chastity had a look of horror on her face.

Beth looked down. Stanley had tipped his beaker upside down. The lid was loose and milk was dribbling down her skirt.

'Da, da, da,' went Stanley delightedly, shaking the cup to release more milk.

'Stanley!' Beth exclaimed, holding him out from her body.

'Mama!' announced Stanley proudly.

Beth turned and began to jog towards the stairs. 'Sorry, do come in,' she shouted to Chastity as she went. 'I better sort this out. Richard's just upstairs.' Then she shouted: 'Richard! Our guest is here!'

Richard and Beth crossed on the stairs. 'Nice of you to make an appearance,' she said, sarcastically. 'I'm going to put Stanley down and get changed. Will you look after her?'

Richard nodded. He had already spotted Chastity at the bottom of the stairs. Oh God, this really was going to be a nightmare evening.

Two glasses of wine for Richard and a double vodka for Chastity later, he was nervy and slightly drunk. She seemed entirely unfazed.

'Just so we get our stories straight,' ordered Richard. 'We've had lunch, OK, but not dinner and obviously not anything else.'

'Will you just chill,' said Chastity, walking round the room. She picked up a blue and white china bowl. 'I like this. Where did you get it?' she asked.

Richard rushed over and took it out of Chastity's hands. 'Wedding present, I think,' he said. 'You are listening, aren't you? You're taking in what I'm saying? It's really important.'

'Yeah, yeah,' Chastity said, yawning and retrieving her cigarettes from her handbag. She opened the packet.

'No, no. You can't smoke,' Richard declared. 'Stanley, you know.'

Chastity put the cigarette back in the packet and yawned again. 'Get me another vodka then.'

'Do you really think you should? We don't want to get, um, tiddly and say the wrong thing, do we?'

'Just get me the fucking drink,' she hissed.

For Chastity, tonight wasn't exactly comfortable either. Meeting Beth had been fine. She seemed OK, although she really needed to do something with her hair. It looked terrible. Chastity actually found herself feeling sorry for Beth. It wasn't her fault if her body had gone a bit after the baby. However, having to watch Richard as he squirmed in case the truth came out was painful. It made Chastity feel cheap and him look pathetic.

Richard felt like he was ageing by the minute. He picked up Chastity's glass and went to the fridge to get the vodka. On balance, he decided it was better to have a pissed mistress than a pissed-*off* one.

He offered a silent prayer: Please God, if You let me get through this evening without something dreadful happening, I promise that I will never, ever see Chastity again.

Richard didn't know how other men managed it, having affairs, that is. He wasn't cut out for it. It was too bloody stressful.

'Everything OK?' asked Beth, looking at Chastity. She had reappeared in a pair of loose grey trousers and a cashmere polo. Her attempt at glamour having been effectively scotched by Stanley, she'd decided to be comfortable.

Chastity nodded. 'But I wouldn't mind another vodka.'

Richard's jaw clenched.

'Darling, aren't you going to get our guest another drink?' Beth asked, looking at Richard. He got to his feet and took Chastity's glass. 'Sorry, Chastity,' she said, before shouting over to Richard, 'I'll have a wine if you're going to the fridge.'

'Wine, yeah. Coming right up.' He poured her a large glass. On balance, he preferred the idea of a drunk wife to a sober, inquisitive one.

Beth sat down next to Chastity on the black leather sofa. 'Richard tells me you'd like to be a TV presenter,' she said. 'Any particular genre?'

Chastity looked blank. 'John who?'

Before Beth could explain, there was a ring at the door bell. She smiled. 'Oh, that must be Jack. Did I mention I'd invited him?' She addressed this to Richard, who looked shocked. 'Thought Chastity wouldn't want to play gooseberry with an *old married couple* like us.'

It had been Olivia's idea to invite Jack. She thought he and Chastity might hit it off.

Richard was silently seething. He didn't like Jack, possibly because the Australian was everything he wasn't. Jack was manly in an uncomplicated, old-fashioned way. He was capable and practical and he could carry a railway sleeper over his shoulder. Richard's skills were entirely cerebral. Had Richard and Jack been in the movie *Witness*, Jack would have built the house single-handed. Richard would have been stuck at the bottom, holding the bag of nails.

In the normal run of things, Richard's inability to so much as change a plug barely impinged on his life. Professionally, his wit and intelligence were more than adequate. Stick him in the same room as Jack, however, and this gap in his knowledge took on the status of a yawning chasm of incompetence. Richard secretly resented this vulnerability Jack engendered in him.

Beth brought Jack down to the basement. He and Richard nodded at one another as imperceptibly as possible. Then Beth introduced Jack to the Bimboid.

'This is Chastity, she's an, um . . .'

Beth's sentence hovered in mid-air. She's a what? A tart, a floozie? Richard intervened.

'A friend. She's a friend of ours.'

Beth looked at Richard as if to say 'A friend of *ours*?' and then went over to the kitchen to put the bottle of Aussie Chardonnay and six-pack of lager Jack had brought in the fridge and check the food.

She'd been in a quandary over what to cook. How to take the culinary high ground without it coming over as if she was the little woman at home, chained to the cooker. She wanted to be sexy Nigella rather than frumpy Delia. Plus, of course, she didn't want to spend the whole night in the kitchen. She wanted to watch things unfold between Jack and the Bimboid.

In the end she'd gone for a spinach and goat's cheese salad, followed by marinaded salmon. For pudding, it was a strawberry pavlova. That was another Olivia suggestion. 'It's only polite to give her something to take home, darling,' she'd declared. 'Cellulite!'

Beth took a jar of dressing from the fridge and walked across the kitchen shaking it. Everyone else was sat round the coffee table.

'So, Jack, you must, like, get invited to loads of celebrity parties,' the Bimboid was saying. 'Do you know lots of famous people?'

'Well . . .'

'Ooh, what's Valerie Chancellor like?' Chastity was squealing with excitement now. If the pitch of her voice rose any higher, half the dogs in the neighbourhood would arrive for dinner as well. 'I bet she's really nice, isn't she?'

Olivia had been right. The Bimboid had only to sniff the possibility of brushing shoulders with fame to be drooling all over Jack.

While not inured to Chastity's more obvious charms, Jack wasn't really part of the decision-making process in this encounter. He was like a rubber dinghy pitched over the side of a waterful and into rapids.

'Chastity wants to be a TV presenter,' Beth shouted over, as she tossed her salad.

The Bimboid leapt upon this. 'Do you think I have potential?' she purred to Jack.

'Well, we'd have to see you in front of a camera,' he replied.

'Ooh, I've been in front of a camera,' she said. 'The Alsatian was much more nervous than me.'

Beth choked on her wine. When she had stopped coughing, she managed to say: 'Supper's ready.' She walked over to the table with the salad and the others joined her. 'More vodka, Chastity, or are you going to swap to wine?' she asked.

'Vodka,' Chastity replied, with just a hint of a slur in her speech. Those double shots were taking their toll. Richard winced. How had he got himself into this?

Beth hadn't thought she was going to enjoy this evening, but it was all turning out rather well. Chastity and Jack seemed to be getting on famously. Only Richard was glum. Upstaged by an Aussie handyman!

On the outside, Richard was expressionless. He was shut down. It was the only way he could cope with the chaos going on inside his body. Fear gripped every one of his organs. He had a headache, stomach pains, felt hot and cold and clammy and his limbs ached. All at the same time.

The other emotion he felt was jealousy. As he gulped more and more wine, he tried to anaesthetise himself from the gnawing anger that he was feeling. He watched Chastity fawning all over Jack and he wanted to grab her and shake her. Why was she doing it? Perhaps she wanted to make him jealous. She couldn't really fancy Jack, could she?

Richard tried to claw back his position as alpha male by steering the conversation on to world affairs.

'What do you think of the Middle East situation, Jack?'

Chastity responded by going up a gear into flirting overdrive. She flicked her hair and fluttered her eyelashes. 'Ooh, Jack, is your . . . appetite always this big?'

Richard could hear a grating sound. It was his own teeth. He was grinding them.

'Are you OK, darling?' asked Beth with amusement.

'Fine,' Richard growled.

When it was time to leave, Richard somewhat tipsily offered to drive Chastity home.

'How kind of you, darling,' said Beth. 'But I think you might have had a touch too much Merlot. I'm sure Jack wouldn't mind sharing a cab, would you, Jack? Chastity is in your general direction.'

Jack nodded. 'No worries.'

Chastity and Jack climbed into a taxi and Beth waved them off. Richard stood on the doorstep and didn't speak. On the way back inside, Beth said: 'Well, I think that all went very well, don't you?'

'I'm just going to the study to check my e-mails,' Richard replied, tottering unsteadily upstairs.

Beth went to the kitchen to clear up. When that was done, she made her way to the bedroom. The bed was empty, but she was exhausted. She laid her head on the pillow and was asleep in a couple of minutes.

Downstairs, Richard was pacing up and down his office, his mobile clamped to his ear. 'I said don't make it obvious that you and me, you know. I didn't tell you to stick your tongue down his bloody throat . . . Well, that's what it looked like to me . . . I know . . . I know. She's my wife! What do you expect? . . . You know I can't do that . . . I didn't say that. It's just that, well, maybe tonight's showed it's time to call it a day . . . Don't take it like that . . . You don't have to shout . . . Look, there's no reason we couldn't still be friends, is there?'

When Richard got up to the bedroom, he stood in the doorway and looked at Beth, asleep in bed. She shifted in her sleep, turning on to her side to face him, pulling the duvet up under her chin. Richard slid in beside her so they were like spoons. He cupped her shoulder with his arm and thought how much he loved her and how close he'd come to losing sight of that.

Chastity took a long drag on her cigarette. She let some of the smoke seep out before sucking it back in again and deep down into her lungs. Then she blew it out with a furious hiss.

So he thought he could dump her, did he?

She picked a speck of tobacco off her tongue with her long fingernails and looked at it, before rolling it between her fingers and flicking it dismissively into the ashtray. Chastity wasn't accustomed to being dumped. She was the dumper, not the dumpee. Besides, she had too much invested in Richard to give him up so easily.

Chastity was a survivor. She'd had to be. Her background – single mum, multiple stepdads, sink estate – might not have equipped her with much of an education, but it had taught her to use what she had to get ahead. She knew she had power over men and that was why she'd become a lap dancer. But you don't see many forty-year-old lap dancers. It's a career with a cavort-by date. She needed a way out, and with Richard, she'd found it.

Richard was Chastity's escape route from lap dancing. But he was more than that. He was her ticket to a totally new life. He was her only hope. All the other men she'd ever been with had been slimeballs, but Richard was different. She wasn't in love with him. Chastity didn't know whether she was capable of loving anybody. But she was determined not to lose him.

Chapter Eleven

'Don't forget that the cleaner's coming today. I've left the money on the kitchen table,' Beth said, as she dashed up and down the hall, frantically scanning her surroundings. 'Now, where did I put my car keys?'

Richard held up the keys, jangling them. Stanley, who was standing at Richard's feet, made a grab for them. Richard pulled them away. 'I can cope, you know.'

Beth walked towards him to retrieve the keys. 'There's a load in the tumble dryer that needs to come out, and could you put the dishwasher on before you go to work. I've put an outfit out for Stanley. Could you make sure he doesn't splodge his breakfast down it. But if he does, and you have to change him, could you not put the orange jumper with the green trousers, like you did last time. He won't get asked round to any other children's houses dressed like that.'

'I thought it looked very good,' Richard said defensively, then, turning to Stanley, 'You liked it, didn't you?'

'For the sake of Stanley's social life, do the Baby Gap, darling,' Beth implored. Then she looked at her watch. 'Twenty-five past.

You need to drop him at nursery in an hour. My mother's picking him up and I should be back by eight.'

'Jesus! You'd think you'd never had an early start before! You'll be back tonight. Besides, I'm not a total imbecile, you know,' Richard said.

'I didn't say you were an imbecile!' Beth shot back.

'Well, you make me feel like one.'

Before Richard's affair with Chastity, his dissatisfaction had been vague and unfocused. Now that he'd ended it, however, he felt the lack of it. Life seemed mundane without the excitement and the flattery provided by their clandestine meetings. Unconsciously he'd started comparing Beth with Chastity. Chastity wouldn't criticise me. Chastity thinks I'm wonderful, he found himself thinking.

Richard knew it was ludicrous, but part of him wanted Beth to know about his affair so that she could appreciate the selfless act he had committed; so she could be suitably grateful. He resented Beth for being the reason he had made his big sacrifice, as if she had asked him to do it. He blamed her because that was easier than examining the reasons why he had got himself into the whole Chastity mess in the first place – boredom and jealousy.

For Beth's part, she could feel Richard's dissatisfaction, but she didn't have the energy or the time to pander to it. What had been a perfectly amiable start to the day was turning ugly. She knew she should stay and soothe Richard. But she was already late. Why did he always start a row when she was halfway out the door?

'Look, I haven't got time to deal with this right now,' she said. 'I'm late!'

'Fine,' announced Richard. 'You just go off then and leave *your child* and I'll stay here and load the dishwasher.'

'Don't act the bloody martyr. He's your child too. And you don't get an extra gold star for loading the dishwasher. It's part of the deal. The marriage deal, that is. Jesus! What do you expect for emptying the tumble dryer? A bloody OBE?'

Richard's lips pursed in annoyance. 'Just go. We'll be fine.'

Beth took a step towards Richard and kissed him gingerly on the lips, then bent down and planted another kiss on Stanley's cheek. 'Let's talk about this later,' she offered. 'I'll call you when I get there.'

Richard didn't answer her and she turned and hurtled up the hall, out of the front door into the waiting cab. Richard caught her just as it was pulling away from the kerb. She wound her window down, expecting an apology.

'You won't forget to pick up my new mobile, will you?' he said.

'As if I haven't got enough to do already.'

'You did offer.'

And it was true, she had. But she'd been in a better mood then.

Richard had dropped his current mobile in the street and it had been run over. Unless they actually wanted to paper their spare room with 'we called while you were out' cards from the delivery company, someone had to go to the depot to pick it up. It was only round the comer from Futura, so it wouldn't be that big a deal.

'All right, I won't forget,' she said.

Olivia lifted the silk dressing gown off her naked shoulders. It slid down her breasts and shoulder blades, traced the contour of her bottom and stomach, slithered down her long legs and came to a halt at her feet. She picked it up and hung it over the newel post at the bottom of the stairs in the hall. She fiddled with the folds. She wanted it to look like it had been flung there in a moment of wild abandon, so that took her a good ten minutes. Then she padded into the living room and switched on the hi-fi. Sadé warbled seductively in the background.

The kids were at her mother's, and a bottle of champagne in an ice bucket and two glasses sat on the coffee table. Everything was organised for a romantic lunch. The only thing left to arrange was herself. She climbed on to the sofa and practised lounging seductively. Then she dipped her hand into a bowl she had earlier placed on one of the arms. It was filled with rose petals. She sprinkled them over herself. A bit Jane Seymour, perhaps, but needs must.

If Colin didn't find danger seductive, then maybe good, old-fashioned romance would do the trick.

Everything was perfect. It was still perfect ten minutes later. And twenty. And forty. Where the hell was Colin? Olivia was about to put a jumper on, blow out the candles and stick something in the microwave when she heard his key rattle in the lock. She could hear his voice from the doorstep.

'No, it's fine. It's great to see you,' he was saying. 'I can always knock up a bit more linguine.'

Who was he talking to? Before she had time to ponder that, Olivia heard the door swing open.

'Are you sure your wife won't mind?' an unknown male voice asked.

A man! Colin was bringing a man she didn't know into their

house and she was stark naked on the living-room sofa. Olivia jumped up and looked for her dressing gown.

'Looks like the cleaner forgot to take this washing upstairs. Tell you what, you go through and I'll take this up. I'll just be a minute,' said Colin.

Her dressing gown had been in the hall, out of reach. Colin was now taking it upstairs, a million miles away.

Olivia heard the creak of the stairs as Colin went up, and another set of footsteps coming rapidly towards her. She made a dash for the double doors that led into the dining room. They wouldn't open. She pushed as hard as she could. Nothing. Then she remembered that Colin had taken delivery of a new set of saucepans this morning. She'd been annoyed because they'd cost an arm and a leg. And another arm as well. She'd told him to get the boxes as far out of the way as possible, so he'd put them in the dining room, up against the doors.

The footsteps were getting nearer and Olivia had to make a split-second decision. Bottom or breasts, which was least humiliating to reveal? If she stayed with her back to the room, her mystery guest would get a full view of her rear end. If she turned round, she reckoned she could cover her Brazilian wax with one hand, but her breasts would be pretty much on display. Bottom or breasts? Bottom or breasts?

When she'd been younger, Olivia would never just get out of bed with a boyfriend and walk across the room. She used to shuffle herself to the end of the bed, keeping her bottom away from her lover, and then do a full circuit of the room, hugging the walls with her buttocks. At no point was the man ever given a glimpse of her behind.

These days, she'd relaxed about her body. Still, when push came to shove – and this was one of those shove occasions – she'd still rather flash her breasts than her bottom. She turned round, put one hand down, one across and bent one leg. When her surprise guest entered the living room, she looked like a startled stork. Not half as startled as he looked, however.

'Um, I'm Olivia, Colin's wife,' she managed to say.

The man said nothing.

'You are?'

'Oh, sorry, I'm Nigel.' He put out his hand to shake hers, then withdrew it when he realised she was in no position to reciprocate.

'You couldn't hand me a cushion, could you?' said Olivia.

Nigel stepped forward and removed a brocade cushion from the sofa and handed it to Olivia.

'Thanks,' she said.

'Right, that's done,' Colin called as he came down the stairs. 'Spinach and ricotta with the linguine all right for you?'

Then he rounded the corner into the living room. 'Oh, Olivia? What are you doing here? Having a bath?'

'No, Colin, I'm not having a bath,' hissed Olivia. 'You know that dressing gown you just took up the stairs, you couldn't bring it back down, could you?'

Colin disappeared back upstairs and Olivia and Nigel were left together in awkward silence once again. Nigel was pleasant-looking, rather than handsome. His ash-blond hair was cut GI short. His skin looked scrubbed. His clothes were appalling, though. He was wearing some sort of surfboard shirt. Its short sleeves stood up in points from overzealous pressing, and, no, that couldn't be a crease in his jeans, could it? Nigel had taken the concept of grooming and really run with it.

Nigel had spotted the champagne and the rose petals.

'Well, Nigel,' said Olivia, trying to fill the awkward silence. 'How do you know Colin?'

'I'm your health visitor.'

Brilliant, thought Olivia. This is sure to go in some report or other. Olivia Timney, known to dance round living room naked. The children would be on the 'at risk' register before you could say unfit mother.

Colin reappeared and put the dressing gown over Olivia's shoulders. She turned round, slipped her arms in and tied the belt with a double bow. Shutting the stable door after the horse had bolted perhaps, but it was a relief anyway.

'You don't need to worry, you know, about, well, all this,' said Nigel.

'Oh, I'm not,' lied Olivia.

'Health visitors, we're a bit like doctors,' he said. 'Seen it all.'

'Yes, you have, haven't you?'

'No, no,' he stuttered, blushing. 'What I mean is, we are terribly discreet.'

'What, trust me, I'm a health visitor, sort of thing?'

'Exactly. You can trust me with anything.'

Valerie leaned her weight on one crutch. Olivia had done her best with it, spraying it silver and giving it a leopard-print cushioned top, but it still wasn't very glamorous having your leg in plaster. She looked bored. If she could have tapped her foot to display her annoyance without falling over, she would have done so.

To Valerie's right in the hall of a 1960s semi near Luton, Beth was on her knees in front of a door, speaking through the keyhole. 'Can't I come in for just a moment, Brenda?' she was saying. 'I'm sure we can get over this little problem.'

'It isn't a little problem. I hate him and I want a divorce,' Brenda shot back.

To Valerie's left, Saffron was also on her hands and knees, also talking into a keyhole.

'Now, Jeff, can't you just say a teeny-weeny sorry? It would mean so much to her,' Saffron pleaded.

'Why should I? Wish I'd never married her anyway.'

Saffron and Beth shuffled across the hall carpet to confer.

'She says she wants a divorce,' whispered Beth.

'Sounds like he agrees,' Saffron said.

'Oh, God. We've got an entire crew standing by to film a happy couple. I'm not saying they have to do a *Hart to Hart* and slaver all over each other, but is there any way they could just be in the same room together?'

'Shall we have another go?' asked Saffron, running a hand through her short hair to indicate she meant business.

Beth nodded.

'Now, I know you have had a tiny disagreement,' said Saffron.

There was a sniff from the other side of the door.

'But since we're all here, I was wondering if you could, just for half an hour or so, possibly stand to be in the same room together?'

'I wouldn't touch her with a barge pole.'

'You don't have to touch her. I promise.'

Beth was taking a break from wheedling and was talking to

174

Jack. 'So, what's the story with you and Chastity? You two seemed to be getting on very well the other night.'

'She's a bonzer Sheila, but, you know . . .'

'No, I don't. What happened after you left?'

Jack looked mischievous.

'My mouth's shut tighter than a croc—'

Beth interrupted him excitedly. She'd had an idea. 'Why don't you bring her to the transmission party? I'm sure she'd love to meet your *celebrity friends*.'

Officially, transmission parties are a way to thank staff and contributors who've worked on a show. A few warm bottles of house white and some curling sandwiches are the normal fare. Karen, however, had decided that the *On The House* transmission party was to be an extravaganza. She had insisted on hiring a room at achingly hip club Notting Hill Home, the invitations were fashioned from hand-tooled leather and everyone who was anyone in the world of TV had been invited. The florist's bill alone would have paid the wages of a runner for a year.

Karen had even managed to rustle up celebrity chef Justin Ellis to supervise the food. Justin hadn't actually cooked a meal since 1982. He was far too busy appearing on foodie game shows in a comedy apron. But his presence would add that little extra celebrity stardust to the event.

Beth had tried to work out why the party was so important to Karen. Was it a statement about her arrival – 'Hey, look at me. I'm in charge now!' – or was it to be the arena for something else? Beth shuddered at the thought of what Karen might be planning.

Richard was sitting in his office, reading an article in the newspaper about a gents' lavatory in Croydon that had just been listed by English Heritage. It had been converted out of an Anderson shelter and was quite the ugliest building he had ever seen. Then he looked up and surveyed his own surroundings. In his present mood, he could have been sat in Buckingham Palace and would still have thought it was a dump. He was depressed.

He picked up the running order for the show they'd be recording later in the day. It was a debate about the legalisation of cannabis. He'd already asked facilities to post extra non-smoking notices on the loos, but perhaps he should call catering and get them to lay on extra sandwiches anyway.

Richard couldn't summon any enthusiasm for the show. He was more interested in rehashing his argument with Beth. Why was it she always assumed he was bloody useless at everything, even looking after their son? She, Saint Beth, of course, could do the domestic equivalent of walk on water. It wasn't always like this. She hadn't thought he was crap when she met him. She'd thought he was clever and accomplished. Well, at least that was what she'd said. Under Beth's adoring gaze, he had felt supremely capable. He could have conquered the world. Now, she didn't let him go to the supermarket without a shopping list.

Richard was bewildered. He hadn't changed. He was still the same man, but all of a sudden his marriage had become a list of domestic duties he didn't perform, or if he did, not up to Beth's standard. He felt like a biscuit on a production line, only he was the one that was a bit misshapen, the one that wasn't good enough. Beth was the biscuit inspector in the white coat and hair net – not far off what she wore round the house these days –

and she had picked him off the conveyor belt and tossed him in the bin.

Since breaking it off with Chastity, Richard had done his best to settle back into monogamous married life, but it felt fake. He was carrying round a secret and it weighed heavily upon him. The affair had stirred up a whole range of emotions and he had nowhere to direct them. Obviously, he no longer had Chastity as a shoulder to cry on, or, more precisely, a bosom to whinge to, and the one person in the world he could usually talk to – Beth – was the one person he couldn't talk to about this.

Beth didn't suspect. He was sure of that. She kept going on about Chastity and Jack and how she'd brought them together. It was all Richard could do to stop from screaming when she started on that subject.

He'd done the right thing. He knew that. He'd given Chastity up, but for what? So Beth could tell him to unload the dishwasher and load the tumble dryer, or was it the other way round? Bollocks! It was all bollocks! Richard was working himself up into a state of righteous indignation. Except it wasn't really righteous. He had his address book open at C and he was looking for an excuse to call the last entry.

'Richard?' It was Doris, his secretary. She had no idea how to use a PC and guarded her manual typewriter like a pitbull terrier with a much-loved bone. Still, she had been at Channel 6 for ever, and no one else knew how to work the filing system.

Richard didn't turn around. 'Yes?'

'You've got a call from a woman. She won't leave her name.'

Richard stiffened in his chair. He felt a shiver of excitement, a frisson of wickedness. It had to be Chastity.

'Put her through and shut the door on the way out, Doris.'

Beth, Jack and Saffron were slumped side by side in Brenda and Jeff's hallway. They'd been there for four hours. Jeff and Brenda had refused to budge. Now Beth tried one more tack: bribery. She took a photo of Jack out of the folder at her feet, walked up the hall and pushed it under Brenda's door. It promptly came back.

'I want him to sign it,' said an irate voice from behind the door. 'Put to Brenda, B-R-E-N-D-A, with love.'

Jack shrugged, got to his feet and joined Beth. Then he took a pen out of his pocket, picked up the photo and, using his knee as a table, began to write. When he'd finished, he pushed the photo back under the door.

'There's no kiss,' declared Brenda.

'Well, if you come out, I'm sure Jack will give you a kiss *in person*, won't you, Jack?'

He looked doubtful.

The door swung open. 'I want a picture with him as well,' announced Brenda.

'I'm sure that can be arranged,' Beth answered in relieved tones.

At the same moment Jeff also emerged. He was clutching a handful of bank notes, Saffron having resorted to even more blatant bribery. He and Brenda stood on either side of Valerie in the living room. They needed to shoot it fast before the couple retreated again.

'Jeff and Brenda have been happily married for nine years,' said Valerie. 'Except they don't see eye to eye over the DIY, do you, Jeff?'

'You could say that.'

The fact that Jeff and Brenda were turned so far away from each other they looked like opposing figures on a weathervane – forecast, stormy – was a slight problem. Still, nothing that Tim, the cameraman, couldn't get over. 'If I can go a week without food and then shoot a charging elephant in the Kalahari, clinging to the branch of a tree while being struck by lightning, I reckon I can deal with these two,' he'd said. 'We'll do it all in singles and I'll cover it with cutaways of paint cans,' he assured Beth.

Ian, the sound man, had more of a problem. After every comment from Brenda, Jeff blew air through his teeth. Whenever Jeff spoke, Brenda sighed loudly. It reminded Beth of her antenatal class. All you needed were a couple of beanbags and some aromatherapy oil and you were there.

Richard had come to every one of those classes, even though she'd had to drag him. It wasn't that he was unexcited about the birth. Quite the opposite. At night, he'd gone to sleep resting a hand on Beth's tummy so he could feel the baby turn over. He'd bought a tiny pair of trainers and they'd argued over names. They'd been so happy. Now all they seemed to do was row.

Beth was suddenly aware of shouting.

'My dad was right about you. You're a useless, good for nothing–'

'Well, your sister is a much better shag than you, at least she was on the night before our wedding . . .'

'It's not as if the marriage is bad, exactly. It's just that sometimes I feel she doesn't care if I'm there or not.' Richard put his head in his hands. 'It's like she has a things-to-do list and I'm way down it, somewhere between pick up bin bags and change batteries in smoke alarms.'

They were sitting on the sofa in her living room. He'd arrived an hour ago, and so far all he'd done was talk about Beth. All Chastity had done was bide her time. She was only too happy to provide a sympathetic ear. She could involve the rest of her body later.

The white leather cushions squeaked as she moved across to sit closer to him. 'It must be awful for you. But you're so fantastic. She doesn't know what she's got,' she purred. 'You're handsome, intelligent . . .'

Richard let Chastity's flattery wash over him like the ripple of a silk sheet. Feeling sorry for himself eased his guilt about coming over to see her. Beth didn't care about him. He deserved a bit of fun. The longer Chastity went on, the more justified he felt, until by the end of it, he could have believed that an affair was not just allowable, it was a basic human right.

Richard laid his head on Chastity's lap and she stroked his hair. While adopting a concerned expression, inwardly she was smiling. She'd got Richard back and it had been easier than she'd thought. He'd practically come crawling on his hands and knees.

'When we first got married, the sex was fantastic, but now . . . Well, we're more like brother and sister, really . . .' Richard was saying. Chastity wasn't really listening. She was thinking how stupid wives were. Didn't they know they held all the cards, particularly if they had kids? All they had to do was give him a blow job once a week and they were laughing. But no, all those pathetic mumsy types in their flat shoes and unbrushed hair, well, they had only to pop a sprog and they let themselves go. No wonder she'd been able to lure Richard. Beth was only getting what she deserved.

Richard looked half-heartedly at his watch. 'I suppose I ought to get back to the office . . .'

'Do you have to?'

'Work to catch up on.' It was a pathetic attempt to make Chastity persuade him to stay, thereby further reducing his burden of guilt.

Chastity picked up the script perfectly.

'I know you're really busy, but don't you think you deserve an afternoon off? You look so tired. You work too hard, you know. Perhaps you ought to just have a lie-down next door. After all, you're the boss, aren't you? They can do without you for an hour or so, can't they?'

Richard shrugged. 'Well, maybe a nap, for five minutes . . .'

Siobhan stared at the rectangular box. She knew she had to do it, but she couldn't bring herself to. She undid one end and tipped out the plastic packet, then unfolded the paper with the instructions on it.

'Easy Test. The fast way to find out if you're pregnant,' it read. Siobhan studied the words. There was nothing easy about it.

She put the packet and the instructions back in the box. She put the box back in the bathroom cabinet and shut the door. She couldn't face this alone. She needed her friends around her. She needed Olivia and Beth.

Still, she couldn't put it off much longer. Then she had an idea. She'd do the test with Beth and Olivia at the transmission party! She could nip to the loo there. It wasn't ideal, but it was the best she could come up with, and even if the test was negative, she'd still need a bloody good drink just to get over the stress of thinking she was pregnant.

* * *

'Tomorrow night? Busy, I'm afraid,' Richard said, squinting in front
of the bathroom mirror and running his fingers through his hair,
trying to arrange it so it concealed the bald bits. 'This *On The
House* transmission party thing. I promised Beth.' He gave up with
his hair and walked back into the bedroom.

'Couldn't you unpromise her?' wheedled Chastity. 'Or, I tell you
what, couldn't you get me an invite? I'd love to meet Valerie
Chancellor.'

Chastity was naked, except for Richard's tie strung round her
neck. She let go of one end and pulled the other so it snaked
between her breasts. The lap-dancing training came in handy
sometimes. Richard's eyes flickered with desire. Then he pulled
himself together.

'Sorry, no can do. I don't control the guest list.'

'Oh, please.' Chastity lay back on the bed, spreading herself out,
then rolled over like a cat in front of a warm fire.

Richard shook his head.

'I suppose I could always ask Jack.'

'You wouldn't.'

'Well, if you can't get me in . . . There'd be nothing going on
between us.'

'I don't know.'

Chastity crawled to the end of the bed and put her arms out.
Richard walked towards her. She nuzzled his neck. 'The person I
really want to go with is you. At least if Jack takes me I'll be there
and we could sort of pretend that we're there together. You could
come round here first if you like.'

Richard liked the way Chastity felt pressed against him. 'Oh, all right,' he said. Then he looked at his watch. 'Oh, Jesus, I'm late. I promised Beth I'd cook her dinner tonight.'

Chastity smiled the sweetest of smiles. To have betrayed her annoyance at this psychological intrusion by Beth into her territory would have been to risk appearing neurotic. To get Richard, she needed to represent the easy, enjoyable, low-maintenance option compared to Beth's hysterical, shrewish one. 'Anything nice on the menu?' she asked.

Richard was oblivious to the clanger he had dropped. 'Thought I'd do some pasta. Beth likes pasta.'

Yes, thought Chastity. You can see it on her thighs.

Karen lifted her glass of champagne. 'To a new era for *On The House*,' she announced, before putting the glass to her lips and taking a self-satisfied sip.

'When are you going to announce it?' asked Patric.

'Oh, I think we should do it at the transmission party, don't you? Everyone will be there, so we can kill a great many birds with one stone, as it were.'

'And Valerie?'

'What about Valerie?'

'Don't you think she deserves to know before everyone else?'

'Don't you worry about that, sweetie. I know how to handle Valerie.'

'But . . .' Patric looked concerned.

'Darling, let's face it. Our audience profile is twenty-five to thirty-five. Valerie is forty-four. If we stick with her, the only ads we'll get will be for electric garage doors and incontinence pads.'

Karen caught sight of Patric's expression, which was one of awe.

'I know it sounds brutal, but there comes a time when even the most successful racehorse is carted off to the cat-food factory,' she explained. 'Let's just say the transmission party is Valerie's Whiskas moment.'

Richard walked to the table with the plates. 'It's ready,' he said. 'Sit down.'

Beth did as she was asked. 'It looks lovely.' Then she picked up her fork and spiked a ravioli. 'Mmm. Is that pecorino cheese?'

'Yes,' said Richard. 'Got it from a special deli in Soho. That's why I was late back. Had to make a huge detour. Sorry about that.'

'Oh, it doesn't matter. I think it's rather romantic to eat dinner at midnight. Sort of reminds me of when we were first together.'

For Richard, this dinner was an attempt to justify his restarting of his affair with Chastity. According to his logic, if he was really, really nice to Beth then the affair wasn't doing any damage to their marriage; in fact it was actually helping it. Not that it was as cold and calculated as that. The sheer guilt of sleeping with Chastity made him want to beg Beth's forgiveness. Of course he couldn't do that, so instead he laid his dinner before her like an offering in front of a statue of a Hindu goddess.

Beth knew nothing of this. She was just relieved that the atmosphere of recent weeks appeared to have passed. She read Richard's cooking as a sign that he was sorry for their row. That was all.

After dinner, Beth went to bed. Richard insisted that she leave him to do the clearing up. He also wanted to get all the bits for the new phone Beth had picked up for him out of the box, so it would be up and running in the morning. When he appeared in the bedroom, he paused in the doorway and looked at Beth, illuminated by the bedside lamp. Her eyes were closed. He felt a pang of conscience. He closed the door and tiptoed round the bed, trying not to wake her.

'I'm not asleep,' Beth whispered, startling Richard, so that he stubbed his toe on the blanket box at the foot of the bed.

'Shit!' he exclaimed, hopping round to sit on the edge of the mattress.

Beth sat up and rolled towards him. 'Are you OK? I'm sorry, let me see.' He swung his whole body on to the bed and she took his foot in her hands, peeling off his shoe and sock.

'Shall I kiss it better?' she asked softly.

Richard nodded and closed his eyes. His toe was throbbing, but it was soon soothed by the sensation of Beth's lips against his skin. She began moving them up his foot, and then did a circle of his ankle. It felt good, but then the guilt returned. Here she was being so tender and sweet, but it was she who needed to be made a fuss of. She was his wife and he'd taken her for granted.

Richard sat up, bent forward and took Beth by the shoulders. Gently he pulled her towards him. He looked deep into her eyes in the half-darkness. There was so much he wanted to tell her. He wanted to explain and say sorry and tell her it would never happen again. The words were squashed up inside him like jelly beans in a jar. He wanted to tip it over and let them all tumble out, but he knew he couldn't. So he kissed her instead.

By some miracle, Beth and Richard both stayed awake and Stanley stayed asleep, so that, for the first time in a very long while, they actually made love. They didn't have sex. They made love. Afterwards, they lay curled up in each other's arms. Richard fell asleep immediately, but Beth lay awake. She was thinking how wonderful and simple life could be. Never mind all the crap at work. Here she was, lying next to the man she loved, and that was all that mattered.

Chapter Twelve

Beth was late. Late and furious. Richard had agreed to meet her at home so they could change before they went to the transmission party. She wanted his opinion on her outfit. Well, she didn't really. This was a ruse so she could supervise his own choice of clothing just in case he went for something disgusting. After all, they were going to be in the company of her friends.

Beth had only once asked Richard's opinion on an item she was wearing. This was long, long ago. She'd been trying on shoes in a shop and he'd uttered the immortal line: 'As long as they're comfortable.' The shoes in question were so high you got altitude sickness. They didn't have a hope in hell of being comfortable.

Still, as Olivia always said, choosing a pair of shoes was a trade-off between how they looked and how they felt. Before putting tonight's pair on, Beth had had to do quite a complex bit of mental arithmetic. Length of wear (including sitting/standing and walking time) plus degree of painfulness, minus how gorgeous she wanted to be. Tonight she had settled on fabulous but semi-crippling. She'd be having a few glasses of wine and, in the shoe equation, alcohol halved the painfulness quotient.

Beth looked at her watch. Seven p.m. No Richard. She tried his mobile. It was turned off. She'd have to go without him.

Immediately, she wished she hadn't worn the heels. Tim, the cameraman, had told her Notting Hill Home was 'just round the corner' from the tube. But coming from a man for whom a nice weekend away meant parachuting into deepest Alaska under cover of darkness, traversing a glacier in bare feet and then building an igloo, it wasn't surprising if his notion of ease and distance was a bit off. Even had it not been Tim but another man who'd told her it was 'just round the corner', Beth should have been suspicious, boy miles and girl miles bearing no relation to each other when four-inch stilettos were involved.

Beth staggered the last fifty yards and rang the bell. The door opened and she was faced with a very tall flight of stairs. By the time she got to the top, she half expected a member of the St John's Ambulance to step forward with a silver foil blanket and a sucrose tablet. Instead she was handed a glass of champagne.

She surveyed the crowd. It was an amazing turn-out. Karen had certainly done a good job. In the corner, Beth could see Valerie, not with Neville of course. She'd left him at home with Fluffy the cat and his sandwich toaster. Valerie was talking to Karen; well, fawning more like. She kept trying to tempt Karen to nibbles off a tray, but Karen was more interested in talking to Jack. She had her hand on Jack's shoulder, and whatever he was saying, she clearly found it hilarious.

Next to the bar were TV presenter Oona Kirkpatrick (better known for her long-running affair with a minicab driver than for her show) in a too-tight pink dress – she looked like a glittery pork sausage. Oona was notorious on the party circuit for her sharp tongue and enthusiasm for canapés. No bash was complete without her. She was talking to Serena Tiverton and Lucas Lieberman. Serena had a new wig and Lucas's tan was even darker than usual. Business was obviously good. Then there were a couple of people from *Big Sister*. It had been at least a week since their release and Beth, like everyone else, had already forgotten their names. Marcia was hovering on the periphery of this group, looking like a cod in a trout stream.

Celebrity gardener Bill Patterson was sipping a pint of beer with Hamish. The two had once worked together, resulting in an incident in Hove when Hamish accidentally hit Bill over the head with a shovel. After this, Bill's presenting style had moved from laid-back to semi-comatose. Still, the viewers didn't seem to have noticed. Patric was standing nearby talking to Anastassia. Or rather, she was talking; he was listening.

As Beth looked round the room, she was struck by the decor. It looked like someone needed to put a Hoover round. What appeared to be dirty clothes were strewn about. The carpet was littered with plates of half-eaten food, empty coffee cups and brimming ashtrays. The walls were decorated with posters of heavy rock and rap bands and satanic symbols. Beth was just squinting at a picture of a man with multiple piercings when Olivia appeared at her shoulder.

'Felicity's done her usual, I see,' Olivia announced.

Felicity Harmswerth-Gore was a fashionable young artist who specialised in appearing on TV talk shows, including *Smart Talk*, and occasionally made the time to create shocking installations. So it was she who was responsible for their awful surroundings.

'The dirty clothes and posters and stuff. It's supposed to be a recreation of a teenager's bedroom,' explained Olivia.

'I just thought . . .'

'Yeah, that it needed clearing up. Well, it cost fifty K, which means that if Mrs Mop does get her Marigolds on that –' Olivia indicated an ashtray and a half-eaten packet of crisps – 'that's a couple of grand down the Swanee.'

So, Karen had spent £50,000 on a pile of old rubbish. Literally. Well, it made a change from talking it.

Beth and Olivia spotted Siobhan at the far end of the room. They picked their way through the crowd.

'Blimey! Have you seen Karen and Jack?' asked Olivia when they reached Siobhan. 'I thought he was with Chastity now.'

'Oh, that wouldn't bother Karen,' said Beth. 'She's like a shark circling a minnow. And it's not often you can call Jack a minnow, sexually speaking.'

Siobhan shifted uncomfortably. 'He can't possibly fancy her. I mean . . .'

'Come on, Siobhan, Jack would fancy a coat rack if it had breasts,' said Olivia.

'Is Chastity here?' asked Beth.

'No, she'll make her grand entrance later, I dare say. I'm sure she'll come to say hello.'

'She's all right, you know. Just a bit dim,' said Beth.

A waiter arrived with a tray of food. Beth, Siobhan and Olivia stared at it in amazement. Slices of what looked like white Mother's Pride had been cut into quarters and smothered in something bright orange and slimy.

'That's not . . .?' asked Beth.

'Yeah, tinned spaghetti,' confirmed Olivia. 'Justin Ellis is doing retro teen food this evening. You just missed a tray of crispy pancakes, and I'm sure I saw some Wagon Wheel-type things over there. Actually,' she confided, 'it's a wonder there's any food at all. Apparently Justin's on another one of his diets, and you know how foul he is when he's counting calories.'

Siobhan nodded. 'I heard that the last time he was fighting the flab, he tried to strangle one of the contributors on *Quick Cuisine* because her chiffonade of lettuce wasn't fine enough. He had to be held down while someone forced a Mars bar into his mouth until the sugar kicked in.'

There was the sound of a spoon ringing on the side of a wine glass. It was Karen. 'If you'd all like to go through to the other room, *On The House* is just about to start.' The party was built round the transmission of the first programme of the new series. Guests dutifully filed into a room in which a video screen had been installed.

Beth and Olivia started to follow the crowd, but Siobhan held them back.

'Do you mind if we give the show a miss, at least the first bit?' she asked anxiously.

Olivia and Beth both looked surprised, but followed Siobhan towards the Ladies'. On the way, Olivia asked Beth where Richard was.

'Don't ask me. He was supposed to meet me at home, but he didn't show up. Where's Colin?'

'He was discussing sausage technique – to prick or not to prick – with Justin the last time I looked.'

'So, prick or not?'

'Justin? He's not too bad, really, in a celebrity-chef sort of way.'

'No, the sausages. Do we prick or not?'

'God knows. When Colin starts going on about food, I glaze over.'

The ladies' loo at Notting Hill Home was covered in white mosaic tiles. The centre of the room was dominated by a huge circular hand basin. There were no obvious taps and it was not unusual to see desperate females waving their hands wildly in the vicinity of the basin, hoping to trigger some invisible mechanism.

Regulars who could afford the £3,000 a year membership fee and were judged hip enough to be invited to join went though a secret initiation rite. Never mind swearing allegiance or having a tattoo; female members of Notting Hill Home were shown the mystery of the hand basin – a foot pedal underneath.

When Beth, Siobhan and Olivia went into the loo, there was indeed one woman directing traffic over the basin. Olivia, who was a member, took pity on her and gave her a free pedal initiation. Once she'd gone, Olivia turned to Siobhan.

'OK, what's going on?'

Siobhan pulled out the rectangular box she'd been carrying around in her handbag for three days.

'You're not, are you?' said Beth, aghast.

'Well, I don't know. That's why I bought this,' answered Siobhan, shaking the box. 'Only I couldn't bear to do it on my own. So I thought . . .'

'Right. Best to get it over with,' said Olivia firmly. 'We'll wait here.'

Siobhan went into a cubicle. They could hear the *On The House* theme music coming from next door. Inside their perfect white space, however, it was eerily quiet. Ten minutes passed, and not a sound came from Siobhan. Finally, Beth knocked on the door.

'Are you all right?'

Siobhan swung the door open and stepped out. She was holding a biro-sized piece of plastic. Olivia and Beth immediately clustered round her. There were two windows. Both had blue lines in them.

'Does that mean what I think it means?' said Beth.

'I've done enough of these to know. It's positive. You're pregnant,' confirmed Olivia.

Siobhan didn't react. Her face was waxy, her eyes blank. The sound of a power drill drifted through the wall.

'There is an obvious question we need to ask here,' said Olivia. 'Not to put too fine a point on it, who's the father?'

Siobhan just shook her head.

Brrng, Brrng.

Beth and Olivia both put their handbags up to their ears.

'Sorry, it's mine,' said Beth, fishing her phone out and stepping away from her friends. It was Richard.

'Where are you?'

'I'm on my way. I got caught up at work. You know how it is.'

'Look. I can't really talk now. Just get here.'

'Fine. I'll see you in twenty minutes.'

Beth was about to put the phone back in her handbag when she heard something. It was Richard's voice. The buttons on his new mobile were different from those he was used to. The red, call end, and green, call start, ones were reversed. He must have pressed the wrong button. Instead of ending the call, he was still on the line. Beth put the phone back to her ear to alert him to his mistake.

'Richard, Richard. Your phone . . .' He couldn't hear her. It was obviously in his pocket.

'We really should be making a move, you know,' he was saying. 'Can't believe Crocodile Dundee got you an invite, just like that. Are you sure you didn't promise him anything in return?'

'How many times do I have to tell you? I'm not interested in him,' said a female voice. 'Come back to bed and I'll prove it.'

'Oh, Chastity . . .'

Beth was stunned. Richard and Chastity . . .

'I'd love to, but the wife, you know,' Richard continued.

The wife? Beth's shock turned to indignation.

'Her indoors giving you grief, is she?'

Her indoors? How dare she! If Richard found *her indoors* such a pain, why had he cooked her dinner last night? Jesus, they'd had sex last night. Great sex. The best sex they'd had in ages. They'd talked, laughed, had fun and then HAD GREAT SEX!

'Well,' said Richard, 'maybe I could be a bit late . . .'

There was a rustling then a dull thud; a jacket was being taken off and thrown on a chair. Then there were footsteps and a door slamming.

Beth put her phone back in her handbag and walked over to the others. She was on automatic pilot, her brain struggling to catch up with what she had just heard.

'What?' said Olivia, the only one of the three of them to be fully *compos mentis*. 'What?'

Suddenly the door was pushed open. It was Saffron. 'The show's over. Karen's making a speech and she wants us all to be there.'

Nobody moved. Saffron shrugged and left.

Beth looked at Olivia. She had a choice. Crumble into little pieces right here in the ladies' loo, or pull herself together, even for just a few minutes. Beth, being Beth, chose the latter. She'd decide what to do later. For now, she just had to get through the next ten minutes or so.

By the time they had joined the throng next door, Karen was already well into her speech.

'At *On The House*, we like to embrace the new,' she was saying. 'Push the envelope of home and garden design, if you like.'

Beth and Siobhan, both staring blankly ahead, barely heard her. Only Olivia was in a state to take in what was about to happen.

'Well, I am pleased to announce that we are about to enter a new and exciting phase,' continued Karen. She paused for effect and there was a murmur among the crowd.

'Do come in, Liam.'

Liam Smith stepped from a shadowy corner. He was wearing a highwayman's cape, jeans and a blue baseball T-shirt. His mohican had also been dyed blue and fashioned into a wave. All he needed was a miniature surfer anchored to his scalp and he could have been wearing an ad for Blue Stratos on his head. He smiled and waved regally at the crowd.

Olivia looked at Beth. 'How did she do it?' she whispered.

Beth just shook her head.

'Bribery? Black magic?' asked Olivia. 'I wouldn't put anything past her.'

'Liam will be joining us as presenter,' continued Karen. 'Which is fabulous news.'

There was a ripple of applause, followed by a bloodcurdling scream. It was Valerie. She had one hand raised over her head, holding a plastic fork at a menacing angle, and she was walking purposefully towards Karen.

'You bitch!' she shrieked.

As she lunged for Karen, it was only the swift action of Hamish and Bill Patterson that averted disaster. Hamish pulled fencing twine from his pocket, while Bill, in a show of speed that amazed onlookers, leapt forward and held Valerie down. Hamish then disarmed her and tied her hands behind her back.

An ambulance was called, and Valerie was carried out of the party on a stretcher.

'Fencing twine! Not the fencing twine!' she was bellowing as she was ferried to the nearest secure psychiatric unit.

Beth went to the bar. 'I think we all need a drink,' she said to Olivia and Siobhan. When she turned round, she saw that someone was working his way through the throng to join them. It was Richard. Beth wobbled on her high heels. He smiled and waved at her. For a moment, she thought she must have imagined the phone call. He wouldn't really get out of his mistress's bed and come here and smile and wave as if nothing had happened, would he?

But she hadn't imagined it. She knew what she'd heard. Something inside her began to harden. Seeing Richard snapped her out of her torpor. She walked towards him. Her expression must have warned him something wasn't right, because when she reached him he said: 'What's up?'

'You bastard.'

'What?'

'You total bastard.'

Beth could see Richard's panic now. He wasn't sure if she knew and he didn't want to drop himself in it, but he was scared.

'I said, you total bastard.'

At that moment she felt a tap on her shoulder.

'G'day, Beth.'

It was Jack. Hanging on to his arm like a cheap identity bracelet was Chastity, who'd arrived late but was now determined to claim her place on the celebrity A-list by association.

'Hi, Beth,' she cooed, before turning to Richard. 'How are you?'

'Well, you should know, since you've just got out of bed with him,' said Beth. 'Shame *the wife* had to spoil your fun,' she hissed. '*Her indoors* cramping your style tonight, Chastity?'

The room had fallen silent. All eyes were now on the little scene unfolding between Beth, Richard and Chastity.

Jack looked confused. 'What's going on?'

'You really should learn how to use your new mobile, Richard. You didn't switch it off after you called me. I heard everything,' spat Beth.

Chastity removed her arm from Jack's and put her hand on Richard's shoulder. Richard looked panicked, as if he'd missed his stop on the train and was hammering on the door as it pulled out of the station. And in a way, he was. The infidelity express was gathering speed and he was hurtling towards disaster.

'Richard and I are in love,' declared Chastity. 'We wanted to tell you, but—'

'Beth, I can explain . . .' begged Richard.

'Oh, please, spare me,' Beth said with contempt.

'Look, let's just go somewhere and talk. You and me,' pleaded Richard.

Chastity had her hand clamped on his shoulder. She wasn't

going anywhere. 'There's nothing to talk about. We're in love, aren't we, Richard? Just tell her.'

Beth's gaze fell upon Chastity's shoes. They were red and open-toed. Something about the shoes pushed her over the edge.

'That you would have an affair is pretty unbelievable,' she exploded. 'But to sleep with a woman with red shoes! I really can't believe that.'

Richard looked nonplussed. 'What have her shoes got to do with it?'

'What's worse,' continued Beth, 'is that I can't believe that I married a man who would sleep with a woman who wears red shoes!'

'Well, she wasn't wearing them at the time.'

'You're not helping, Richard,' said Olivia.

Beth had forgotten that Olivia, Siobhan and Jack were there, so caught up in her rage had she become. Richard also suddenly became acutely aware of his audience.

'Look, I'm sorry, Beth. If we could just go somewhere . . .'

She shook her head.

'It was stupid. It didn't mean anything,' Richard begged.

'Hang on a minute,' said a miffed Chastity.

Like a sleeping giant awakened, Jack stepped forward.

'So she's sleeping with your husband?' he said to Beth, who nodded.

Jack hit Richard hard in the face. There was a gasp from the crowd as he fell backwards against a table with a tray of slices of Arctic Roll on it. The sponge offered a meagre form of cushioning as his head crashed to the ground. For a moment there was an eerie silence, broken by Jack.

'Fancy getting out of here, Beth?'

'Yes, I would actually.'

Jack put out his arm. Beth hooked hers through it, and with a flourish they turned and walked to the door.

'Beth, Beth, I'm sorry . . .' she heard Richard pleading as she left. He was struggling to get to his feet. 'Can't we just talk about this?'

Then he groaned, as Chastity aimed a pointy red toe at his testicles.

The sunlight cut through the Venetian blinds like a stack of razor blades. Beth's head hurt and her mouth didn't seem to be working properly. Her tongue felt twice its normal size. She could hear her own breathing ricocheting around inside her skull. She screwed her eyes up tighter and rolled over. She felt an arm land across her waist.

'Don't even think about it. I feel like death,' she hissed.

'No worries.'

For a moment she wondered why Richard appeared to have become Australian. Then she opened one eye very slowly. A furry blond forearm was resting on top of the duvet across her. She took the sight in slowly, then began to turn her head. She could see a tanned shoulder, then a luxuriance of rumpled blond hair.

Beth said nothing, but inside her rockets of nuclear intensity were going off. Jack. She was in bed with Jack. The events of last night came back to her, but hugely speeded up, as if she was skipping the trailers at the start of a rented video. The mobile phone call; the row with Richard; Chastity; storming off; and then . . . What? She couldn't remember anything after that.

Beth took another surreptitious look at Jack. He had fallen

asleep again. She was in bed with him, but maybe they hadn't actually done anything. Maybe they'd just passed out. The bad news was that he appeared to be naked, from the waist up anyway. Dare she? She had to. Beth gingerly lifted the duvet and peered underneath. Dear God! He wasn't wearing any pants. She was in bed with Jack and HE WASN'T WEARING ANY PANTS.

The thudding in her ears, from a mix of panic and hangover, was getting louder. She sat up and felt dizzy, so immediately lay back down again. OK, OK, so Jack was starkers, but she was still in with a chance that good sense or total drunkenness had prevailed. She lifted the duvet again and this time looked down at herself. She wasn't wearing any pants either.

I AM IN BED WITH JACK AND NEITHER OF US IS WEARING ANY PANTS.

The odds that they had played Travel Scrabble last night didn't look too good.

Chapter Thirteen

Beth ran herself a deep, hot bath and slid into it like an exhausted eel. She rested her head against the cool white enamel and basked in the soothing water, trying to process all that had happened over the last twenty-four hours. Everything had changed, so why were her surroundings so entirely unaltered? Same black-and-white tiled floor, same chrome taps on the sink, same two toothbrushes in the mug on the glass shelf.

Part of Beth wished she hadn't overheard Richard's conversation with Chastity. OK, her marriage might have been in a crisis, but she wouldn't have had to deal with the aftermath of that. Another portion of her was livid that she hadn't known sooner. How long had it been going on? How many other people knew? Perhaps everybody. She felt such a fool. She shivered, despite the hot water.

Beth surveyed the mounds of white flesh sticking out of the water. Even lying down, her tummy wasn't flat. Her bosoms had made a rush for cover, cowering in her armpits. She had Henry VIII's calves.

All the times Richard had made love to her and told her she was beautiful, had he been lying? Had he been secretly, coldly appraising her body, like a farmer grading livestock? Not bad haunches but has run to fat in places. And what about the Bimboid? How could Beth compete with that?

Beth glanced up at the metal clock on the wall facing the sink. Eight thirty. Her mother would be here in fifteen minutes with Stanley. Then she had to take him to nursery. It was the cleaner's morning as well. Oh God. She had an audience to survey the car crash that was her marriage. What was she going to say? It was bad enough being humiliated, without having to rehash it as if it was a funny anecdote at a dinner party.

Perhaps she should say nothing at all. She could behave like one of those middle-aged middle managers who is downsized but doesn't tell his wife. He continues going out in the morning in his Marks & Spencer suits and sits in the park to eat his cheese and pickle sandwiches. She could lay a place for Richard at the breakfast table, scatter cornflakes around and make it look like he'd been there.

But why should she? It was Richard who was in the wrong. He'd been shagging some topless tart. Beth had a sudden twinge of guilt – Jack. But that was a mistake, and besides, it was Richard who'd broken his wedding vows first.

Beth had a flashback to her wedding. She could smell the lilies mixed with the aroma of damp leather. It had rained all day and everyone's shoes were wet in the church. She'd had to hold a newspaper over her head when she got out of the car. Some of the newsprint had come off on her fingers and she'd put a mark on her dress. None of it had mattered, though. Richard had looked so handsome in his suit. He'd squeezed her hand when she got her vows wrong. She'd thought they'd be together for ever. But now the foundation on which she and Richard had married and had Stanley had crumbled. She was scrambling across a whole new terrain.

According to Olivia, the tragedy of modern marriage was that it was based on a mismatch of expectations. Men got hitched so they could have regular rumpy pumpy and women tied the knot so they could wear old track pants round the house. Men wanted hot sex; women wanted hot pizza. To achieve some sort of level ground, both parties colluded in an elaborate series of white lies. She said: 'Yes, darling, of course I find you as sexy as the first day I met you. No, I would not like to spend the night with George Clooney.' He said: 'Of course you don't need to wear make-up to go to the supermarket. And, no, I haven't noticed your stretch marks.'

Beth considered her own marriage. As the years had gone on, the white lies had become stretched as thin as spun sugar. And now they'd been shattered by a single mispressed button on a mobile phone. Beth felt cold. She wanted desperately to hug Stanley. Feel his plump hands patting her on the shoulder when she brought him downstairs for breakfast, or the way his head rested in the nape of her neck as she carried him up to bed. She looked at the clock. Better get a move on. He'd be here in five minutes.

Once dressed, Beth went to the kitchen to make herself a coffee. The answerphone light was flashing. It must have rung while she was in the bath. Richard calling to apologise? Not that she'd accept. It would take a hell of a lot more than one phone call to put this right. Still, they were a family. She had Stanley to think about. Did she really want to bring him up as a single parent? She pressed the button.

'Hi, Beth, it's Jack. Great night last night. Fancy a few tinnies later on?'

Oh God, what was she going to do about Jack?

Siobhan sat on her bed. She stroked the fur throw methodically, as if it was a cat. She had once had a cat, but she was out so much, Fred had moved out, decamped to live with an old lady called Iris up the road. Iris fed him chicken livers and bought him a special cushion, which she positioned directly in front of a gas fire that glowed fourteen hours a day. Siobhan hadn't stood a chance.

She took the pregnancy tester out of the pocket of her jeans and looked at it again. Those two blue lines were still there. She was trying to stay calm, but failing. She was pregnant and she didn't know who the father was. 'OK, let's consider the evidence,' she murmured to herself.

Darren: young, therefore likely to be very fertile. Also energetic. A lot of sex in a short space of time. However, used condoms and no mishaps as far as she was aware. Odds on him being the father? Slim.

Kyle: also young. Sperm probably didn't just swim towards the ovum, they did one of those trick dives on the way. Still, they'd only spent the one night together and again they'd used condoms. Could he be the father? Very unlikely.

Simon: at forty-four, Simon's sperm would have needed a lilo over long distances. However, they didn't always use condoms. They'd got lazy. The last time they'd slept together, well, Siobhan hadn't planned it and they'd got carried away and . . . Oh Jesus, it was Simon, it had to be.

On paper, Simon was the worst option of the three. He was

married. He already had three children. Inside, though, Siobhan was relieved that it was him. The thought of abortion fluttered like a feather in the wind across her thoughts. It settled for a micro-second, but then was gone. She wanted Simon's baby. Besides, if she was pregnant with his child, he'd have to leave Elaine, wouldn't he? Maybe it was all for the best after all.

Siobhan picked up the phone and dialled carefully. Simon didn't really like her calling him on his mobile, just in case Elaine picked it up. She had once. Siobhan didn't know what she had expected, but Elaine's voice had sounded sort of normal. If she'd met her in the queue at Café Café, she'd probably have had a chat with her. Siobhan was so panicked by this notion, she'd slammed the phone down.

'Hello.'

Siobhan relaxed. It was Simon. Just hearing his voice quieted all her doubts.

He was apologetic and sounded pleased to hear from her. 'Sorry I haven't been in touch. It's been murder here. I'd love to see you, though.'

'Actually, I need to talk to you.'

'Can't talk now, I'm afraid. I could come round to your place tomorrow night.'

'Do you mind if we go out? Dinner or something?'

'All right. Where?'

'Oh, I don't know. Somewhere quiet, off the beaten track, you know.'

'I'll find somewhere. I tell you what, I'll surprise you.'

Karen popped her head round her office door. Her hair looked even more annoyingly flicky and girlie than usual. Her Barbie-sized T-shirt featured a heart with the words '2 Kute'. Beth grimaced inwardly.

'Ah, Beth, we did wonder whether you'd manage to make it in today. Last night was a bit . . .' she paused for effect '. . . difficult for you, wasn't it?'

'I'm fine,' said Beth.

'Well, if you're sure, sweetie.' Then she lifted her voice and addressed everyone else in the office. 'Guys, could you all come in for a bit of a pow-wow?'

Beth put down her bag, slipped off her coat and began to plod towards Karen's office with all the enthusiasm of Mary Queen of Scots on her way to her own beheading. It was 10.30 a.m. and that meant the ratings for last night's show would be in. Beth had a bad feeling. When she reached Karen's office, Liam and Jack were already inside. Beth took up position leaning against a glass wall as far as possible from Jack and avoided his eye. Nothing like dealing with a problem by not dealing with it.

'Now that we're all here,' announced Karen, 'I've got last night's figures.'

She began to read from a notepad in front of her. 'Average audience three and a half million. Peaked at four. Share fourteen point five per cent. Apparently, we inherited well, then they all switched over to watch the climax of the darts.'

Beth wasn't aware darts had a climax. Still, she said nothing. There was silence in the room. Beth knew that Anastassia Frink wanted nine million. How would she react to four? At best, *On The House* would be banished to the twilight zone of Sunday night at 10.40. At worst, they'd pull it completely. Either way, it didn't look good for a recommission.

Jack punctured the atmosphere. 'Four million? That's better than a bite on the bum from an angry croc,' he said hopefully.

No one spoke. The truth was, four million wasn't good. Hell, *Guess That Hymn!* had done four and a half.

Karen looked up from her notepad. 'Any comments?'

Everyone had their heads down.

This is what it must have been like to be a Tommy in WWI when they asked for a volunteer to go over the top and single-handedly tackle a sniper, thought Beth, before feeling the cold draught of Karen's gaze upon her.

'Beth, perhaps you could give us the benefit of your experience in the area of makeover television.'

'Um, well . . .'

'Oh yes, you don't have any experience, do you, Beth? Luckily, I have.'

Karen then launched into an assassination of the show. Some bits were too slow. Others were too fast. There either wasn't enough information in it, or it was repetitive. It lacked warmth, authority and glamour. It was basically all a load of rubbish, they were all morons and Karen, aka Wonderwoman – she clearly saw herself in Lynda Carter's headband – was the only one who could save the day.

Poor ratings for the first show of a series are bad news, but there could still be a happy ending, Karen reminded them. Anastassia Frink wouldn't be making the decision whether to recommission or kill off the show until halfway through the run. Having Liam on board was a start, said Karen. Liam smiled at that. Wholesale re-editing, some reshooting and a 'change of emphasis' might yet retrieve the situation.

'There are going to be big changes, very big changes indeed,' declared Karen.

Marylebone station was crowded with commuters. Siobhan felt out of place in her satin sandals and pink raw-silk coat. She was jigging from foot to foot. She was excited, but nervous. She liked surprises. She just hoped Simon did. How would he take the news?

'I've got the tickets. Platform three. Shall we go?' Simon gave her elbow a discreet squeeze. He never kissed her in public, just in case someone saw. Simon set off for the ticket barrier.

Siobhan had trouble keeping up with his long stride.

'Where are we going?' she asked.

'Stratford.'

'East London?'

'No. Upon Avon. Why else would I tell you to bring a tooth-brush? You did bring one, didn't you?'

Siobhan nodded. 'Yes, but . . .'

Simon lifted his bag up so Siobhan could see it. 'Elaine thinks I'm in Brussels, so I don't have to be back till tomorrow night.' He smiled naughtily.

'OK, where are we actually going in Stratford-*upon-Avon*? Have you booked us tickets for some Shakespeare?' Siobhan was getting excited. She risked a gentle arm on his shoulder. She wanted to give him a big hug, but she didn't. 'It's not *Romeo and Juliet*, is it?'

Simon looked enigmatic.

'What's the hotel like? Has it got a four-poster? And dinner? Is it candlelit and all that? Oh, Simon, you're so romantic.'

They were boarding the train now. Simon let Siobhan go first.

'It's a surprise, remember.'

The train pulled out of the station and Siobhan surveyed the grubby housing estates of Kilburn, their backs turned on the train as if in a huff. It was good to be getting out of London. What more perfect setting to tell Simon about the baby than over a romantic meal after some Shakespeare?

'Dada,' babbled Stanley happily. 'Dada.'

'He's not here, darling,' Beth found herself saying. And for the first time it really sank in that he wasn't.

They were in the bathroom. Beth had run the water and Stanley was now throwing things in. Normally, Beth would have put a limit on his bath toys, but tonight she didn't care. Soon, every inch of the surface of the water was covered with brightly coloured bobbing plastic.

Beth watched as Stanley stamped back and forth picking up more toys and tossing them over the side of the bath. He was like a woman in hurry, shopping in a familiar supermarket, throwing things into her trolley as she raced round. Stanley had a job to do and he didn't waste time dithering. He just got on with it. For Beth, it was a heartbreaking sight. Stanley had absolutely no idea that their whole world had collapsed. She didn't want him to be trau-matised, but for him so be so unfazed magnified her feeling of loneliness. She was the holder of a terrible secret – your father has left us – and it felt oppressive.

Beth lifted Stanley into the water. He began driving one of his cars up the side of the bath, then letting it go so it fell backwards. He was making 'brrm, brrm' noises. Beth wanted to stand up, run round the room and scream: 'Your father is shagging a floozie!' but she didn't dare leave him in case he slipped, hit his head and drowned. Her marriage was over, and yet for Beth, nothing had changed. Here she was, as she had been most nights since Stanley's birth, bathing him and worrying that he might slide under the water.

She reached into the bath and pulled out the plug. 'Bye bye, water,' she said.

Stanley waved enthusiastically and looked up at Beth. She took hold of him under his arms and lifted him out. Then she wrapped a towel round him and sat him on her knee on the floor. She handed him a toy car to hold and patted at his wet hair with the edge of the towel. Richard hadn't so much ripped Beth's life to shreds as frozen it. It was frozen at the moment she heard that phone call. This was how it would be from now on. Just her and Stanley. Meanwhile, Richard had swanned off to start a new life in a new house with a new woman. Maybe he'd even have a new baby. The thought horrified her.

She hugged Stanley close. No baby could ever be as precious as this one. Anyway, if the Bimboid gave birth, she'd probably have one of those really ugly sprogs. Good-looking women – not that Chastity was that good-looking – always had weird babies with big heads or lots of hair.

Brrng, brrng.

Beth let the phone ring. Jesus! Not Jack again. Couldn't he take a hint? In the bedroom, she heard the answerphone kick in. She panicked. She'd forgotten that it was Richard who'd recorded the message.

'You've reached Richard, Beth and Stanley Davies . . .' went the recording. It felt like hearing a ghost, the voice of someone who'd died.

'Dada,' said Stanley excitedly.

Richard's disembodied voice poured out of the machine. The house was filling up with it. Like smoke, it billowed from room to room, working its way into every nook, cranny and corner. Beth was choked by it. She felt sick and invaded.

Finally, she heard the beep. Thank God. However, her torture wasn't over. It was Richard, leaving a message.

'Hi, Beth, if you're there, will you pick up? I think we need to talk,' he said, nervously. 'Beth? . . . Beth? . . . Please, Beth. Can't we at least talk about this?'

Beth listened with horrified fascination. Here was the man who had betrayed her and he was now begging her to talk to him. Well, she wouldn't. She didn't have much power left, but she could do that.

'Look, I know you're there. I'm not going away. I'll just keep talking until you pick up . . .' Beth ignored him. He could talk as long as he liked, she wasn't— The line went dead. He'd put the phone down. Beth looked at the clock. Eight seconds. That was how long he'd waited. Eight seconds. That was all she'd been worth. She had thought her mood couldn't get any more dejected, but she'd just gone down another level of misery.

Stanley was oblivious. He squirmed, broke free and ran off, pausing at the door to turn and laugh. Then he disappeared into the bedroom. Beth walked to the door. Stanley was on the bed, snuggled into the pillows. Beth had been dreading sleeping alone. Still, she'd read all those books that said that if you let your baby sleep with you, you were making A Rod For Your Own Back, that most heinous of parental crimes. She looked at Stanley.

'Mama?' he said, questioningly. Then he held his arms out to her.

'OK, OK, but just for tonight,' Beth said, as much to herself as Stanley.

'Ye Olde Shakespearean Banqueting Hall', read the sign. It was suspended from a wrought-iron bracket, fixed to the wall. The bracket's fancy design was a style known in the makeover trade as B & Q Tudor. The sign was creaking as it swung in the wind. Beneath it, a morose-looking youth in a ruff, puffy shorts and shoulder-length curtains of red hair, centre-parted so severely it looked like a section of a crop circle, was slouching. He grunted as he grimly shoved flyers into people's hands.

Siobhan took a leaflet. 'Deluxe Elizabethan pig roast tonite! Genuine pig on a spit! Live entertainment! Free tankard of mead with every banquet meal! (Offer limited to one per person.)'

She looked at the sign, the youth, the piece of paper she was holding and then at Simon. 'Tell me you're not serious?'

Simon was bemused. He squinted his grey eyes. 'Yes, why?'

'Do you need a list? Well, let's start with the fact it's a pig roast. Who do you know who goes out for a romantic dinner and chooses a pig roast? I mean, are we having a relationship here or appearing in a reality TV re-inactment of village life in the Middle Ages?'

'But you like pork.'

'Yes, but not with the head on and a sodding great skewer shoved up its bottom.' Siobhan saw that Simon was hurt, so dropped her voice. 'Look, I'm just disappointed. I thought we were going to have a nice quiet dinner. Still, I suppose the play will be nice.'

'What play?'

'*Romeo and Juliet.*'

'We're not going to see *Romeo and Juliet.*'

'But I thought . . .'

'Look,' he said, pointing to the flyer. 'There's entertainment here.'

Siobhan was speechless. Simon had brought her all the way to Warwickshire so she could have the Elizabethan equivalent of a Happy Meal.

'I thought you'd be pleased,' he said. 'You said you wanted something a bit off the beaten track.'

A thought suddenly occurred to Siobhan. She turned to Simon accusingly. 'Nothing to do with *you* not wanting to run into anyone you know? Take her to a really crap restaurant and you can be pretty damn sure that you won't get found out?'

Simon looked embarrassed. 'Well, you said you wanted to talk to me and I didn't want us to get interrupted.'

Siobhan's mouth dropped open. She couldn't believe he'd just admitted it.

Simon realised his mistake. 'When I say interrupted, I mean, by anyone, not just someone who I might know. I mean . . .'

Siobhan spun round and began to walk away. Simon ran after her.

'Siobhan, Siobhan, I'm sorry. I've said the wrong thing. I love you.' He repeated the last bit with increasing desperation. 'I love you. I love you.'

Siobhan stopped. She turned and looked at Simon. His face registered real distress. He did love her. Moreover, she loved him and she was carrying his child. He had caught up with her now. He put his arms around her and she buried her head in his neck.

'I am so sorry. I've made a mess of this evening. Can we start again?' Simon whispered in her ear.

She pulled away so her face was a few inches from his. 'Give me a kiss and I'll think about it.'

They kissed, then walked back to the restaurant.

'It might be fun,' said Simon.

Siobhan gave him a look.

'Well, we're here now,' he said, rushing her inside before she could change her mind.

The corridor leading to the banqueting hall was clad in boot-polish-brown wood panelling. The only lighting was provided by a row of faux flaming torches bolted to the wall – actually shards of polyester lining fabric with a fan heater fixed underneath delivering a half-hearted flutter to simulate a flame.

Great, thought Siobhan. Lighting courtesy of Hammer House of Horror.

Siobhan deposited her coat in the cloakroom. She was given a 'silver ducat', actually made of plastic, with a number on it. As she was leaving, she heard a voice. It was the cloakroom attendant, a short, round woman in a wimple.

'You forgot your hat.'

'I didn't bring a hat.'

'No, you wear one for dinner.'

Siobhan looked down and saw Wimple Woman was holding a tall, cone-shaped affair with bits of chiffon coming out of the top like tattered seaweed.

'Oh, I think I'll give that a miss, thanks.'

'No. You have to wear it. It's the rules.'

The hat was shoved into Siobhan's hands, but she was damned

if she was going to put it on. She tucked it under her arm and went to find Simon. He was wearing a velvet tam o' shanter. It was trimmed with fake pearls, most of which had peeled down to the milky plastic beneath.

Simon saw her expression. 'Look, why don't we have a drink?' he said quickly.

There was nothing Siobhan would have liked more at this moment than a large glass of wine, except forty Marlboro Lights, of course. But she'd given those up too.

Simon had spotted an overweight girl wearing a wench outfit holding a tray. He pushed Siobhan towards her. Close up, her white muslin shirt, which exploded out of a burgundy velvet corset, was having trouble containing her breasts. They were white and doughy and started somewhere under her chin. The brown dirndl skirt didn't help matters. This was what Nell Gwyn would have looked like after a few too many McFlurries.

'One of those, please,' Simon said, pointing to a pewter-effect tankard. 'And?' He looked at Siobhan.

'Diet Coke,' she said.

The waitress sighed. Boredom rolled off her like mist in the Highlands. 'No Diet Coke.'

'Oh well, what about an Aqua Libra?'

Nell Gwyn couldn't have been less helpful if Siobhan had asked for yak's milk. 'We've only got mead.'

Siobhan realised she wasn't going to get anywhere. She took a tankard of mead and sniffed suspiciously. It smelled sort of oaty, as if someone had mixed Ready Brek into a pint of Stella Artois.

'It's OK, after the first couple of sips. Then you don't notice the aftertaste,' said Simon.

Siobhan decided not to risk it. She clutched her tankard and looked around. The room was large and square. A single row of wooden tables placed end to end ran round three sides. The fourth was dominated by a huge pig with an orange in its mouth being turned on an electric spit on wheels. A trough sat underneath the pig to catch the fat as it ran off so that it formed a pool of congealing lard. Siobhan felt sick. In the centre of the room was a raised platform.

The place was already heaving. As far as Siobhan could see, there didn't seem to be any other couples. Everyone else was part of one big group or another. Most were already the worse for wear, some of the men having swapped their Henry VIII hats for the women's conical affairs. Out of the corner of her eye she watched as one woman removed her black lacy bra through the sleeve of her white blouse and waved it in the air to riotous applause from her gang.

'Oh God, we have descended into office party hell,' she hissed at Simon.

'Don't be so negative. Have some mead.'

'I don't want any bloody mead.'

'Well, I'll have yours then.' He took her tankard and began to gulp it down.

The pig was wheeled off to be carved and a man in a red and green tunic that had been run up by someone with the skill of a ham-fisted toad appeared on the stage. He was also sporting green tights, shoes with bells on and a hat with points.

That'll be the jester, then, thought Siobhan.

'Would all ye olde Elizabethan revellers take your seats for dinner, please,' he said. 'The young ones can park their bums as well.'

216

This went down a storm with the audience, who did an Elizabethan Mexican wave with their tankards. Siobhan and Simon took the only spare seats left.

'Let ye fun begin!' bellowed the jester.

'Let's not,' Siobhan whispered under her breath with a desperate fervour.

'OK, let's see who we've got in tonight,' continued the jester. 'Where are the crazy guys from the BT call centre in Walsall?'

Cue much foot-stamping and whooping from one corner.

'And the Littlewoods catalogue crew?'

Cue even louder stamping and whooping from another.

It transpired that to Simon and Siobhan's left they had a group of McVities biscuit packers – Rich Tea division – celebrating record sales. To their right, Guinness Breweries were on a jolly to mark someone called Brian's birthday. Brian was easily recognisable. He was the one wearing a black lace bra over his shirt.

While all this was going on, a dozen more depressed teenagers in dirndl skirts appeared and began plonking plates down in front of the diners. Siobhan tried a bit of her pork. It had the consistency of bicycle inner tube and smelt a bit like one too.

Now she felt really sick. Pushing her plate away from her, she leaned towards Simon. If she didn't do it now, she never would.

'You know I said I wanted to talk to you?'

'Yes.' Simon was tucking into his dinner, apparently unworried by the mountain-bike aroma. 'You should try the roast potatoes. They're not bad.'

'Perhaps you'd like to pop into the kitchen for the recipe,' said Siobhan sarcastically. She was frustrated. This wasn't the way this evening was supposed to be.

Simon put down his knife and fork. 'Sorry, what did you want to talk about?'

At that moment the jester leapt back on to the stage.

'Right, time for a little music. I take it you all know "The Twelve Days of Christmas"?'

There was general shouting.

'OK, well we're going to go round and everyone's going to do a line each. We'll start over here.' He pointed at one especially inebriated group in the corner. 'Railtrack Midlands Branch. You're gonna do partridge in a pear tree.' Then he pointed at the people next to them. 'Coventry City Cleansing Department. You're ten lords a-leaping.' And on he went, working his way round the room.

Siobhan slunk as far down in her seat as she could. It wasn't far enough. 'You two young lovers over there,' the jester said, pointing directly at Simon and Siobhan. 'You're going to have to give it some welly. You're two turtle doves.'

Siobhan shook her head. 'No, really, I don't sing, do we, Simon?'

The jester simply shouted, 'Can't hear you!' with his hand cupped to his ear, and moved on.

Five minutes later, the torture had begun and 'The Twelve Days of Christmas' was in full swing.

'Four calling birds,' bellowed East Midlands Airport Security, all forty of them standing and swaying.

'Three French hens,' yelled twenty-five members of Edgbaston Golf Club.

All eyes shifted in Simon and Siobhan's direction.

'Come on,' shouted the jester.

Siobhan looked at Simon imploringly.

There was a rhythmic banging of stainless-steel cutlery on wooden tabletops. Simon shrugged his shoulders and got to his feet. Siobhan followed. She could feel herself shrivelling with embarrassment, like a cake dropping when you open the oven door during cooking.

'Two turtle doves,' they sang, their voices sounding pathetic and weedy next to the group bellows that had preceded them.

'And a partri-i-idge in a pear tree!' The room had already moved on. Siobhan sat back down with relief.

'Thank God that's over,' she hissed at Simon.

But it wasn't. They did 'The Twelve Days of Christmas' twelve times. On each occasion, Siobhan and Simon had to get up and sing 'Two turtle doves' again. A pair of semi-sober people in a room full of paralytic office workers. When it did finally come to an end and Ye Olde Crème Brulée was served, Siobhan was exhausted.

'Look, I really have got to talk to you,' she said.

'I know. I am so sorry. This evening has been a disaster, hasn't it?'

'Well, it's certainly been different,' and for the first time that evening, Simon and Siobhan shared a smile.

He took her hand. 'You do know how much I love you, don't you? I couldn't bear it if we broke up again.'

'I love you too, that's why I need to tell you something.'

Siobhan was interrupted by the jester again. That man was getting really irritating.

'Now we have a rule here at Ye Olde Shakespearean Banqueting Hall,' he was saying. 'You have to wear your hat.'

Siobhan was trying to have the most important conversation of her life and this guy was going on about hats! If she didn't say it now, she'd lose her nerve. She ploughed on.

'I'm pregnant.'

There was no reaction from Simon. He was watching the stage.

'Simon, did you hear what I said?'

'Er, can you hang on a sec?'

'No, I can't!' said a furious Siobhan. 'Are you listening?'

Up on the stage, the jester was shouting, 'There is one naughty wench here tonight who isn't wearing her hat.'

Siobhan touched Simon's chin. He turned back to face her, and this time she had his full attention.

'Simon, I'm pregnant.'

Suddenly there was a deafening thumping of feet, spoons and tankards. Siobhan had three hundred pairs of eyes all focused on her. The only eyes she was interested in were Simon's. He was looking right through her. His face was etched with shock. He seemed unable to speak.

'So what do you think?' offered Siobhan, desperate to break the awful awkward atmosphere that was settling between them.

Before Simon could answer, a chorus broke out.

'Naughty wench, naughty wench, naughty wench . . .'

'And what do we do to naughty wenches?' shrieked the jester gleefully.

'Stocks, stocks, stocks,' roared the audience.

Siobhan glanced at the stage. A set of wooden stocks had been set up next to the jester. She looked back at Simon. Suddenly, two burly men in ruffs took hold of her under her arms and picked her up. Her feet brushed the chiffon of her hat where she had shoved it under the table as she was swept up and over it. They carried her to the stage. Siobhan kept shouting, 'I'm pregnant,' but no one could hear her above the mêlée.

Once she was in the stocks, members of the audience were invited to pelt her with wet sponges. She kept her eyes closed as soggy bits of foam hit her face, neck and arms. The water ran off the end of her nose and down in between her fingers. It felt clammy and cold. When at last the ordeal was over, she walked from the stage back to her seat, patting herself with a towel.

The jester urged the crowd to 'Give a big hand to such a game girl.'

Siobhan just wanted to sit down. Back at her table, however, Simon was nowhere to be seen. His seat was empty, his food unfinished. Then she noticed some money folded neatly under her tankard. She counted it. There was £50. There was also a napkin with something written on it.

'Can't deal with this now. I'll call you. Enjoy the hotel. It's all paid for, plus see money for cab. Simon.'

Siobhan took a big gulp of mead. Next to her they were flicking Ye Olde Crème Brulée at each other and laughing. A single tear ran down her cheek.

Chapter Fourteen

Olivia was incredulous. 'So he just left you there? Walked out and abandoned you?'

Siobhan nodded.

'What a complete shit.'

'Well, I know that's how it sounds, but it was a lot to handle and he did leave me money for a taxi and—'

'Siobhan, let's get real here. First he takes you to an Elizabethan theme restaurant...' Olivia shuddered as she said the words. 'Please tell me there wasn't a strolling minstrel.'

Siobhan shrugged.

'Oh God, it gets worse. Anyway, not only did he take you to this hideous place, he sodded off and left you there. I mean, if someone was looking for a definition of a shit, that would pretty much be it, wouldn't it?'

They were sitting in Beth's kitchen, round the table. Siobhan was crouched forward, her elbows resting on the glass top. Olivia was also sitting forward to make her point.

Beth joined them. 'It's OK. He's gone back down now, but I think he misses Richard.' She took a sip of her wine and sat down.

'We'll get to Shit Number Two in a minute,' said Olivia. 'For the moment, though, I think we've got our hands full with Biggles.'

Even Siobhan smiled at that.

'So what are you going to do?' asked Beth.

'I don't know. I called his office today and they told me he's doing a long haul. Australia via Singapore. He's away till Friday.'

'But what do you want to do?' said Olivia.

'I don't know. I need to talk to him.'

'What if he doesn't want the baby?' said Beth gently.

Siobhan twisted her hands in agitation.

Beth carried on. 'I mean, you have to admit that the signs so far are not terribly positive, are they?'

'I know he loves me. He might just need a bit of time to get used to the idea.'

Siobhan took a sip of water and sat back in her seat. Olivia and Beth raised their eyebrows. Then Olivia also sat back, turning her body towards Beth and announcing: 'Right, next on the agenda of the All Men Are Bastards Club is—'

'But Colin's not a bastard. You've done OK, second time around I mean,' said Beth.

Olivia considered the matter for a moment. 'All right. Next on the agenda of the All Men Except Colin Are Bastards Club is Richard, who shall henceforth be known as the Bimboid Shagger. Have you spoken to him yet?'

'He rang last night, but I didn't pick up.'

'Not quite pouring paint over his Porsche, but it's a start,' declared Olivia.

'He hasn't got a Porsche. He's got a Vauxhall Astra,' protested Beth.

'You know what I mean.'

'Do you know where he's living?' asked Siobhan.

'You mean, is he with her?' asked Beth.

Siobhan nodded.

'Haven't a clue and part of me doesn't give a stuff. He could have jumped off a cliff for all I care. But then another part of me thinks he should be with her, that she should be the love of his life, for all the bloody havoc she's caused. If it's just a silly fling, then how important could our relationship have been to him to risk it for that? And then another part of me wants him to come crawling back on his hands and knees, begging me to forgive him, and it's like it never happened and we live happily ever after. Most of me just wants to kill him.'

'If it was me,' said Siobhan, 'I'd be desperate for an explanation. Do you want to talk to him?'

There was silence. Beth was thinking. 'You know, I don't know. I want to find out what happened. I mean, I thought we were OK and then he goes and does this. I suppose I want him to say we were OK, so I don't think I am going mad. You know, when I first suspected something, he made me think I was crazy and I believed him! And to think, all the time . . .'

'I know, but there is Stanley to sort out,' Siobhan said.

'Are you going to let Richard see him?' asked Olivia.

'Not if I can help it. I mean, why should I? He doesn't deserve it. If *she* goes within ten feet of my child I'll rip her legs off.'

'If Colin ever left me for another woman,' said Olivia, 'I'd want to gouge her eyes out with the heel of my shoe.'

'You don't think *Colin* would ever have an affair, do you?' asked Siobhan.

'God, no. He'd need a sex drive for that.'

'So are things still quiet on that front?' wondered Beth.

'Totally dead below the waist, darling. Actually, he's agreed to come to sex therapy with me. Had to twist his arm, but we're booked in for a tantric workshop.'

'Jesus, I've read about tantric sex, but what actually goes on at a tantric workshop?' asked an incredulous Siobhan.

'I don't know, but I had to go and buy some weights, and I'm not talking about dumb-bells.'

'Oh my God! I've read about those too. The French are mad for them,' Siobhan squealed.

'Mad for what?' asked Beth.

'Let's just say you suspend the weight from *inside yourself*, and then hold it there for as long as possible.'

'You don't mean . . .?' Beth's eyes were like saucers.

'Yup, half a dozen sessions and I should be able to pull a truck with my pelvic floor muscles.'

'I knew there was a reason I should have done those exercises after Stanley. When the car broke down, I could have towed it home myself.'

'This whole childbirth thing is beginning to scare me,' said Siobhan.

'Don't think of it as giving birth. You're just going for the burn,' Olivia said, laughing.

When things had quietened down, Beth looked serious. 'You know what really gets up my nose?' she asked.

The others shook their heads.

'Those shoes. The red shoes. They sum her up. She's so cheap. His lack of taste is *so* insulting. I know it's a bit petty, but if he'd just chosen a woman I could respect. I wouldn't have been happy, obviously, but at least I wouldn't have felt so crap by association. Richard sleeping with her, well, it's like being knocked off the top of the singles chart by "The Birdie Song". I want to run down the street shouting: "I am better than that!" '

'Unfortunately, having an affair is not like choosing a sofa, Beth. Taste doesn't come into it,' announced Olivia.

'She probably looks terrible first thing in the morning,' offered Siobhan.

'Well, from what I saw, she's got a very short neck. Short and flabby. Sort of hippo-like,' added Olivia.

The three of them laughed again. They laughed so long and so loud they didn't hear the phone. By the time they had calmed down, it had clicked into answerphone.

'G'day, Beth.'

Beth mouthed the word 'Jack' then shook her head in exasperation. 'Why did I do it?' She put her head in her hands.

'Revenge sex. Never a good idea,' declared Olivia.

'I don't know whether I actually had sex with him,' Beth reminded them.

'You were *sans* underwear,' Olivia pointed out. 'Anyway, if you didn't, are you going to? And if you did, are you going back for more?'

'God, no. The last thing I need is another man in my life. I already feel like I'm walking through a fog of testosterone. Anyway, I don't think he's that keen, really. The phone calls are just him being polite.'

Olivia rested her chin on her hand, thoughtfully. 'In normal circumstances I'd say you were talking rubbish. No man ever calls to be polite. Actually, most men never call at all. Still, in this case, Jack must have an agenda. The two of you do have to work together. He's probably shitting himself in case you go weird on him.'

'Do you think I ought to call him back?'

'No, don't bother,' replied Olivia. 'This is Jack we're talking about, remember. He's got the skin of a rhinoceros. Anyway, I think he might have his hands full pretty soon. Remember Karen at the party? She was practically drooling.'

'At least it would get him off my back.'

'Was that the first or the second time you did it?' asked Olivia.

'I told you . . .'

'I know, I know.'

'You two talk about men as if they had no feelings,' chastised Siobhan. 'Jack's not that bad. He can be quite sensitive underneath, you know.'

'Oh God, you're not getting a thing for Jack, are you?' asked Olivia. 'Is there no lost cause you won't go for?'

'No, no, don't be silly. I'm just saying . . .'

'Well, I reckon the sooner Jack shags Karen the better,' said Beth. 'It might give her something other than making my life a misery to think about.'

'I doubt it,' said Olivia. 'Anyway, pour me another wine. I've got a present for you.' Then she reached down into her handbag and pulled out a CD. 'Do you want to put on "I Will Survive" or shall I?'

Liam ran a hand over the exquisite art deco walnut veneer. The colour was as deliciously warm as caramel. The surface was so smooth, he could see his reflection in it. He tweaked his mohican and pouted, pulling the collar of his black leather jacket (with vicious-looking silver studs) up so he could peer seductively over the top. Satisfied at his own gorgeousness, he stepped back.

'Not bad, not bad at all,' he said, giving the art deco dressing table another long look. 'But how did you know I'd had my eye on it?'

Karen smiled enigmatically. 'I have my sources. Anyway, it got you on the show, didn't it?'

'Yes, it did.'

Liam couldn't keep his eyes off the glossy walnut. He drank in the voluptuous curve of the bow front and thrilled at the gleam of the chrome trim. Then he stepped forward and began sliding the drawers in and out. He sighed with pleasure.

'And they can deliver it on Thursday, you say?'

Karen nodded.

'Well, it really is very generous of you,' he cooed.

'Don't worry about it. Had to sack a director and cancel the cab account for six months to pay for it. Plus, that couple in Llanelli who wanted a wall-to-wall hundred per cent wool Wilton will have to make do with nylon carpet tiles. But, hey, you're worth it, Liam.'

Liam wasn't listening. He was kneeling down. His head rested against the glass top of the cabinet and he was stroking one of the legs. He was a man in love.

Beth was sitting at the kitchen table. Olivia and Siobhan had gone. Stanley was asleep upstairs and the house was quiet.

Beth had put Stanley into his own bed tonight. She hadn't

wanted to. Lying awake at night was almost bearable if she had Stanley's little sleeping face to look at. Still, she had to be firm. Not with him, with herself. She didn't really want to become one of those clingy single mums who had sons instead of boyfriends. She didn't want Stanley to be tucking his shirt into his pants and still living at home when he was forty-two.

Stanley had protested. Still, she bribed him with his favourite toy and he settled in the end. Unfortunately, his favourite toy was a metal wastepaper bin. Beth had left him lying on his back with his arms wrapped round the metal cylinder as if he was Leonardo DiCaprio and the bin was Kate Winslet.

Beth felt cold. The chill went right into her bones. She got up to turn the thermostat up. Tomorrow she was going to Southampton. It was Liam's first bit of filming for *On The House* and the pressure was on. Karen had announced that she would be paying a royal visit to the location.

Having to sit across from Karen at meetings in the office was bad enough, but this would be a whole day with her. Beth was dreading it. She'd have to put on a brave face, keep a stiff upper lip and other such wartime clichés. It was as if Richard had dropped a big bomb on her life. And, like those houses attacked in the Blitz where, through the rubble, you could still see wallpaper, a big hole had been ripped in Beth's former existence. Past the torn and tattered edges, you could catch heartbreaking glimpses of what had been.

Beth put down her coffee mug and picked up two pieces of paper laid out in front of her. They were theatre tickets. She'd ordered them a month ago when she thought she was happily married. She ran her finger along the edge of the tickets. Then, very slowly she began to rip. The sound was satisfying. Four pieces, eight, sixteen; she carried on tearing until she had a little pile in front of her. A funeral pyre for her marriage.

Drring. It was the door bell.

Beth rolled her head back and screwed up her eyes. 'Go away,' she hissed. 'Whoever you are, just go away and leave me alone.' She felt tears prick the corner of her eyes. Didn't she deserve to be allowed to be depressed in peace?

Drrring. The bell went again. They weren't going away. Beth would have to answer it. She pushed her chair back from the table. It made an awful scraping noise against the laminate. The floor was a bit scratched anyway. Stanley and his building bricks. She'd meant to have it replaced, but there was no point now. They'd have to sell the house when they got divorced anyway. Richard and Chastity would move into a swishy loft apartment with expensive radiators. They'd buy Stanley a puppy and he'd leave her too. Beth would end up alone in a damp bedsit in Peckham and she'd have to buy her shampoo in multi-packs from Kwik Save. She'd be a broken woman.

As Beth walked up the hall, she could see the shadow of a figure through the stained-glass panel. It was distorted, but the height and rough outline told her it was male. If it was the local MP, someone doing a survey or anyone selling tea towels she would not be responsible for her actions. Then a horrifying thought struck her. What if it was Jack? Beth toyed with turning round, but he'd have seen her by now. Better brave it out.

She opened the door. Richard was standing awkwardly on the doorstep. His head was down and his shoulders were hunched. He was clearly bracing himself. What for? Did he think she'd attack him? Perhaps he was afraid Jack might be lurking, ready to finish the job he'd started.

Richard didn't move. Beth stared at him. She was annoyed. He looked bad – tired, nasty eye bags, a spot coming up on his chin – but not bad enough. She wanted proof that he'd lain awake every night since the party, tossing and turning, racked with guilt. A consumptive pallor, a nervous twitch, a limp and a rasping cough. That sort of thing. Instead, beyond looking a tad rough, he appeared exactly the same as the last time she'd seen him on this doorstep. It had been the morning of the party. He'd been leaving for work and she'd chased him down the hall and called him back from the car because he'd forgotten his mobile. What if she hadn't caught him? What if he hadn't pressed the wrong button? What if . . .

Richard coughed with a distinct lack of a rasp. 'Um . . .'

'Why didn't you use your key?'

'Well, you know, I thought you might think it was a bit, um, presumptuous.'

Beth was staggered. 'Presumptuous! I'll tell you what's presumptuous! Shagging some bimbo behind my back. That's fucking presumptuous!'

Richard looked round nervously. A couple were walking past on the opposite side of the road. Susan and Derek from number 37. She was a school nurse and he worked for a company that made widgets. Beth had yet to establish what these widgets were, but then that wasn't surprising, as the two couples only enjoyed a bottle-bank acquaintance.

When it comes to neighbours, there are grades of intimacy. The lowest is windscreen-scraper diplomacy. This is when you never meet except when you're both out clearing frost off the car first thing. Conversation is limited to 'Bit nippy, isn't it?' The next level up is bottle-bank bonhomie. You haven't been to each other's houses, but you have had a bit of a chat. The talking is invariably a pathetic attempt on both your parts to conceal the fact that you are each disposing of enough empty bottles to stock a branch of Majestic Wine Warehouses.

Go to the other end of the mateyness scale and you're talking car key parties, but they didn't do that sort of thing in Islington. Or so Beth hoped. The notion of Derek in leather chaps and Susan in an apron, brandishing a novelty vibrator, was too much to bear.

Derek and Susan were peering curiously at Beth and Richard. 'Just off to the bottle bank,' shouted Derek, swinging a plastic bag jauntily until the glass clinked together inside. 'Got to do your bit for the planet.'

'Yeah, um, global warming and all that,' said Richard, smiling weakly. 'Very good.' He turned back to Beth and whispered urgently, 'Can we go inside?'

'Don't want me making a scene in public?' Beth hissed back. Forget global warming, she could feel her own temperature rising dangerously.

Derek and Susan were walking away, but were still within earshot.

'He's been shagging some tart who takes her clothes off for a living,' Beth shouted.

Derek and Susan stopped and turned.

'Sorry? Didn't quite catch that,' said Derek.

'Please, Beth,' Richard whispered, giving her an imploring look.

Beth knew that, given the choice between having a row with their other half in private and doing so in public, most men are in a quandary. In private, he thinks, she's liable to go completely off the deep end. There will be tears and recriminations and then possibly they'll end up in bed together. This, in one sense, he regards as a bonus, except that it means he'll have to go through the whole emotional scene again afterwards, when he doesn't call her. Should he go for the public option, he's on neutral ground. He hopes this will make her behaviour a little more stable. That's why so many blokes dump their girlfriends in bars or restaurants. However, should she decide to make a scene, he faces the distinct possibility of public humiliation. Plus, in a bar or restaurant, she has access to alcohol, which is a dangerous unknown factor to stir into the scenario.

Richard had selected the doorstep as a compromise option. Now things were turning nasty, and he needed to switch the location to indoors so as to avoid being called a bastard in front of a man he might or might not meet at the paper shop in the near future. Beth, however, was in no mood to ease his discomfort.

'I said,' she bellowed, 'Richard's been shagging a stripper.'

'Lap dancer,' corrected Richard.

Beth gave him a furious look. 'I think we're at the point when we can call a spade a spade, which is, by the way, what she looks like she puts her make-up on with!'

Richard winced. 'I came to talk,' he said, in an I'm-going-to-be-really-reasonable voice.

This just wound Beth up even more. 'Oh, you want to talk now, do you?' she spat. 'Shame you didn't just talk to your tart, isn't it? Shame you had to sleep with her!'

Derek and Susan exchanged a look that said: 'Oops, walked in on a domestic,' and resumed their journey. Their heads were set rigidly ahead as if walking past an especially pathetic-looking *Big Issue* seller.

'Look, I'm sorry, OK. I'll go, but I thought we ought to talk,' said Richard. 'But if you don't want to . . .'

Beth looked at him. His cheeks were flushed. He'd bitten his lip and there was a thin red line where it had been bleeding. He did look genuinely upset. She was exhausted from shouting anyway.

'OK, OK,' she sighed. 'It's just . . . Well, let's go in.'

Beth went in first and Richard followed her down into the basement, towards the kitchen.

'D'you want a glass of wine?' she asked.

Richard nodded, and while Beth went to the fridge to get the bottle, he sat down. When she turned, he was playing nervously with the ripped-up theatre tickets.

'What's this?' he asked quietly.

'Nothing,' she said, leaning over and sweeping them quickly into the palm of her hand, before putting them in the bin. 'Anyway, you said we should talk.'

'Um, yes,' said Richard hesitantly, clearly aware that he was on very dodgy ground. 'I know you probably don't believe me, but I'm sorry.'

Beth said nothing.

'It didn't mean anything.' He was looking down, tracing greasy lines with his finger on the glass top of the table. 'It was just, um, sex. Not love. I'm not in love with her, whatever she said.'

Beth resisted the urge to throw her glass of wine in his face. She might need the alcohol later.

'Where are you living?'

Richard didn't answer.

'So you're with her, then?'

He shrugged.

Beth decided to leave Richard's living arrangements for the time being. She had something more pressing on her mind.

'Tell me something. Honestly.'

'Yes.'

'The last time we slept together, the night before the party . . .'

'Yes.'

'It was good, wasn't it?'

'Yes, yes. It was great.'

'But had you already slept with *her* that day?'

Richard looked ashamed. 'Yes, but I can explain . . .'

Beth shuddered. She wrapped her arms round herself as if to prevent bits of her falling off. She felt as though her whole body was disintegrating and, like the theatre tickets, there'd just be a little pile of her left on the floor. 'Oh my God,' she said. 'How could you?'

Richard said nothing. Just looked down.

'How could you sleep with her and then come home and sleep with me? I mean, I thought men who had affairs went off sex with their wives. But we had brilliant sex that night. The best ever.'

Richard looked up at her anxiously. 'Yes, it was great.'

'So?'

'Does it really matter? Can't we just put it behind us?'

'No. It does matter to me. Just give me a straight answer. I deserve that much, don't I?'

Richard was still trying to deflect Beth. 'I really don't think it will do you, us, any good. Let's just—'

Beth's face started to turn pink with anger. Richard spotted the danger of a revisit to the hysteria and realised he had no choice. He'd have to answer her. 'All right. I thought . . .' Richard's words were tumbling out as if he believed that if he said it fast enough it wouldn't count '. . . after I'd slept with Chas . . . with her, I mean, if I also, you know . . .'

'Had sex with me,' prompted Beth.

'I was going to say made love to you, because that's what it was. Anyway, making love to you sort of cancelled out the sex with her.'

Beth was stunned. She was standing over Richard, who was cowering in a chair at the table. 'Cancelled it out? Like tit for tat, or should that be tit for tit?'

Richard braced himself for the onslaught, but Beth was quiet. She was thinking about her childhood. In winter, if she woke up to snow, she used to rush downstairs to be the first to walk on it. Then she'd retrace her steps backwards, placing her feet in her earlier footprints, so as to leave only one set. Richard hadn't made love to her that night. He'd merely placed his feet in his earlier footsteps, so as to leave only one set of prints.

Beth began to walk across the kitchen. She was calm. 'I'd like you to go now,' she said.

Richard was confused. 'You said you wanted me to be honest. And I've been honest . . .'

'Just go.'

'But what about Stanley?'

'He's asleep.'

'Can't I just pop up and see him?'

'No.'

'Just for a moment?'

Beth was at the bottom of the stairs now. Richard stumbled towards her.

'You didn't think about him when you were shagging *her*, did you? You can't turn around now and start being father of the bloody year. You lost the right to even breathe the same air as him the moment you fucked around.'

Richard began to walk up the stairs, followed by Beth. When they got to the front door, he turned round.

'I'll come back tomorrow. When you've had time to calm . . . I mean, when, well, you know.'

Beth opened the front door. 'I am perfectly calm. I just want you to go.'

'We can get past this, you know. She doesn't mean anything to me. I love you,' Richard begged. He reached out to take Beth's hand. She snapped it back. 'I made a mistake, but I can make it right, I know I can.'

Richard was on the doorstep. It was drizzling.

'Have you got a coat?' she asked.

'Oh, that's all right, Chastity's waiting round the corner with the car . . .' As the words came out of his mouth, the regret followed as fast as the surf off the back of a speedboat. 'I mean, well, you know . . .'

So, not only was he living with the Bimboid, she'd actually given him a lift round here tonight. Beth couldn't believe Richard's gall. Here he was telling her that he loved her, and all the while his mistress had the engine running round the corner.

Richard was gabbling furiously, as if attempting to bail out a sinking rubber dinghy. Only with every word, the boat became less seaworthy.

'She offered to drive me and the weather was terrible and . . .'

Beth looked at her husband. His jumper was sticking to him in the drizzle. 'Fuck off, Richard,' she said as she slammed the door in his face.

Marcia got a hankie out of her pocket. 'It'll be OK,' she said soothingly. 'You're sure to get another job really, really soon.'

Marcia was standing next to Ros's desk. Ros was a director on *On The House*, or she had been until Karen had bought Liam his art deco dressing table, thereby necessitating her sacking of Ros five minutes ago. It had taken Karen, oh, about forty-five seconds to sack Ros. She'd called her in, told her her services were no longer required and instructed her to shut the door on the way out.

'I don't understand,' Ros said, taking the hanky and blowing her nose loudly. 'I thought things were going really well, and now this.'

Marcia eyed the cardboard box sitting on the desk beside them. 'Shall we organise your things?' she suggested gently. 'It's amazing how much stuff you collect, isn't it?'

Ros pulled open a drawer and began emptying the contents into the box. Marcia picked up a picture frame containing snaps of Ros's two small children and went to put that in the box too. Ros snatched it from her, hugged it to her chest and burst into more loud tears.

'My ex hasn't paid maintenance in three years. How am I going to cope?' she wailed.

'Something will turn up,' Marcia said unconvincingly. She had to get Ros out within the hour. Those were Karen's orders. She didn't like to rush Ros, in fact, she didn't like anything about this little scene, but she thought it was better she did it than Ros be stood over by Karen.

Marcia picked up the now full box and handed it to Ros, who was still snivelling.

'Are you going to be all right?' she asked.

Ros nodded and began the long walk down between the desks to the exit.

Marcia watched her go. Out of the corner of her eye, she saw Karen pop her head out of the office. Not a flicker of emotion passed across her face. Here was a woman for whom anyone was dispensable. Marcia made a conscious decision never to forget that.

Colin cast Olivia an appalled glance.

'He's not really going to—' he whispered, before being interrupted. A length of cotton fabric had landed on the ground.

'Oh God,' Colin wailed.

Standing about three feet in front of them was a small, brown, sinewy fifty-something man. He looked like a very thin, very tanned garden gnome – if the garden gnome had lived in Thailand and spent a lot of time on the beach in a sarong. His name was Teo. Together with his 'life partner' Ayesha (her real name was Marion) – not Thai, and somewhat larger than Teo; her thighs looked in danger of crushing all the life out of him – he was about to demonstrate the wonders of tantric sex. Not that Teo seemed to need any further stimulation. He was in attack position already.

'I was looking for somewhere to hang my coat,' giggled Olivia, still clutching her mac on her knee.

Olivia was trying to lighten Colin's mood, which was turning more murderous by the minute. She had to admit that it wasn't quite what she had expected. She had thought there'd be someone with a whiteboard and a jumbo magic marker. It hadn't actually occurred to her that she'd booked them in for the sort of night that normally means walking through a neon-lit doorway and down a very steep set of stairs in Soho.

Colin rolled his eyes. 'If she does anything with ping-pong balls, I'm going,' he hissed.

Olivia nodded. 'OK, OK. Just give it a chance.'

Olivia was at the end of the line. She didn't know what else to do. She'd tried open-air sex, S & M, and naked romance on the sofa, and everything had failed. Colin's loins were about as warm as a day-old bag of chips. She now hoped they might be reheated by the Tantra, the microwave of love.

Teo had lain down on a hastily erected wallpaper table. Ayesha, wearing a Japanese silk kimono with birds of paradise embroidered on it, stood over him, like a magician about to saw him in half.

Colin was wearing a look that said: 'Please God, don't let her take her clothes off too.'

'At the core of the tantric principle is the belief in nurturing the spirit,' announced Ayesha gravely. Her attentions appeared to have begun further down, however. Her right hand was now making movements not unlike those used to knead bread. Teo was moaning softly.

Colin was moaning too, only his were not moans of ecstasy. He didn't want to be here. Olivia had forced him into it. Now he was in someone else's horrible living room looking at an overweight woman giving her dwarfish other half a hand job. It was horrific. Did the Royal Borough of Kensington and Chelsea know about the goings-on at number 3 Coleridge Square?

'Tantric love is never-ending,' continued Ayesha, her tone even and hypnotic. 'The sexual act can go on for up to twelve hours.'

Colin's eyes watered. Twelve hours! She had to be kidding.

Olivia, too, was a bit shocked at this comment. Didn't these tantric people have shopping to do?

Colin was beginning to feel like this evening was never-ending too. Just when he thought it couldn't get any worse, Ayesha went up a gear.

'Since we only have two hours, we will move things on,' she explained. 'Let's assume your chi is aligned and your chakras are in harmony; now you can progress to the next stage.' With that, she reached for the tie to her kimono.

Colin leapt to his feet. It was more than embarrassment. It was terror. As he fled, he shrieked, 'Must dash. Got a leg of lamb in the oven.'

Chapter Fifteen

'OK, we'll do a one-two combination, so lead with the left then go in hard with the right.'

Karen nodded and began hopping from foot to foot. She was wearing a pink vest and matching three-quarter-length leggings. Her hands were buried in enormous red boxing gloves. A head guard protected her temples, cheeks and chin.

Terry, a good foot taller and at least the same amount wider, hadn't bothered with the head guard. As the former London regional heavyweight champion, he reckoned he was pretty safe. Terry now made his living jogging gently round the ring while angry, stressed-out and largely hysterical executive women scampered after him trying to punch him and failing.

For women like Karen, sparring with Terry was the perfect exercise. With every punch, they wrought revenge on every man who had ever been unfaithful, refused to commit, or any other of the litany of standard male crimes. An hour with Terry and you burned calories and achieved catharsis in one go!

Karen danced around. She thought about the men who had mistreated her. It wasn't a long list, largely because she hadn't had that many boyfriends. Work had always come first, or maybe it was because she wasn't good at relationships that she had always buried herself in work. She didn't know. To have found out would have required a level of self-examination that Karen wasn't willing to embark upon. Her whole life was devoted to avoiding going too deep for fear of what might lurk.

Still, that didn't mean she was incapable of love. Indeed, she fell in love easily. When she did, she was clingy, demanding, needy, all the qualities she despised in others and coincidentally just the ones to make a man run in the opposite direction. But then she didn't choose the sort of men who might stick around anyway. That way, when they behaved badly she wouldn't be disappointed. No wonder her latest crush was on Jack.

Karen would see Jack tomorrow. She felt a tingle of excitement. She wasn't really interested in the shoot, but it gave her a chance to move things on with him. At the transmission party, he'd played hard to get, but she was going to redouble her efforts.

Even while thinking about Jack, Karen couldn't switch off completely. She aimed a left at Terry and missed. She'd put so much determination behind it, however, that she almost overbalanced. She recovered herself and landed a glancing right to his shoulder.

'Good,' Terry said absent-mindedly and just a tad patronisingly. He hated these ridiculous middle-class females in their cute little outfits, but he had no choice. He owed forty thousand in back taxes and had the CSA on his back.

Karen was furious with herself for missing her punch. She circled aggressively. The idea of these sessions wasn't to actually obliterate your partner, just to get a bit of a work-out, but Karen hadn't quite absorbed that point. That would have been like asking a lion to go easy on the antelope.

Just when Terry wasn't paying attention, Karen caught him with a left to the cheek, followed by a vicious right upper-cut to the jaw. She added a left hook to the kidneys and he went down like a condemned sixties tower block. Karen looked down at him with barely disguised pity.

Jack didn't stand a chance.

Liam studied the patch of damp on the ceiling. One tweed-clad arm was wrapped round his waist. The leather-patched elbow of the other arm was resting on it, his fingers fiddling with the pearl choker round his neck. He was an interesting sight, his mohican contrasting fetchingly with his country squire outfit. It was an effect the Queen Mum might have achieved if she'd hung about on the King's Road in 1976.

Liam waved his hand in the general direction of the brown stain. 'It's very . . .' he paused, searching for the right word '. . . real, isn't it?'

'Well, yes, our tag line is "The *Really* Good Homes Show",' said Beth.

'Yes, but I didn't think the homes I'd be redesigning would be *really* real, if you see what I mean. I thought they'd be . . .'

'Fake?'

'Yes, I mean no. Not exactly fake. Sort of faux. You know, some duchess on her uppers. Fabulous country pile, great proportions, nice touch of period detail, but the carpet's a bit of a nightmare. We spend thirty grand on a gorgeous Aubusson and a couple of chaise-longues and I hang some Chinese silk on the walls.'

'Sorry, Liam. No budget for Chinese silk. Will calico do?'

Liam grimaced.

'Cheer up, Liam. You've got five grand to spend on this kitchen.'

'Darling, I can spend that in Conran in ten minutes.'

Their conversation ended abruptly because Liam's mobile rang.

'Hi, how's it going? . . . *The Best Days of Your Life*? But I don't think I've ever met a Bill Patterson. Who is he? . . . A gardener? Doesn't ring any bells . . . Oh, he did mine, did he? . . . Did he say anything nice? . . . Well, if he did the business for me when I got my big blue book, I suppose I'd better return the favour. Can they bike over a CV and an amusing anecdote? . . . Fine, now what about that Italian tile company sponsorship . . .'

Beth walked away. She wasn't really in the mood to deal with Liam. Unlike Valerie, who had been evil, Liam's heart was more or less in the right place. It was just that the rest of him existed in a different solar system to most of humankind. Asking him to tart up the kitchen of a 1930s mock-Tudor semi in Southampton was like expecting Anne Robinson to buy a card with a kitten poking out of a wellington boot on it. It was behaviour that was entirely beyond their frame of reference.

She walked into the hall and saw Jeanine sitting slumped in a corner. Jeanine was the production manager of *On The House*. It was her job to be everybody's mummy. She made sure staff got on the right train or into the correct car to get to the shoot. Then she was responsible for everything from ensuring there were plenty of biscuits for tea to checking there was enough film stock for the cameras. Most difficult of all, she oversaw the budget.

In Beth's experience, production managers started out as

relatively normal people. However, the weight of responsibility meant that, in a few short years, most developed eczema, asthma, stammers or other such tics. The last production manager at *On The House* had been discovered rocking in a corner after the Sian Jones concrete débâcle. She had been moved on to less arduous duties in news, arranging clandestine filming in the more inaccessible caves of Afghanistan.

Jeanine was new. In her early forties, she had seemed sort of sane. However, coping with Liam's outrageous demands – he had already insisted she order a seventeenth-century marble fountain, a pair of bronze obelisks and a Bauhaus patio recliner for a forth-coming garden makeover – was already taking its toll. Jeanine had gained about twenty pounds and her obsessive/compulsive consumption of doughnuts was becoming alarming.

'OK?' asked Beth.

Jeanine mumbled something. It was difficult to understand her as she was munching on a Cadbury's mini roll. Beth was about to attempt to prise the cake away from her, for her own good, when she heard Jack's familiar strangled vowels coming out of the front sitting room. She'd managed to avoid him since their night of drunken passion. She tried to dart into the dining room, but it was too late. He'd seen her. He gave her a broad smile.

'G'day, Beth. I'm as glad to see you as—'

Beth interrupted him. 'Look, Jack, I think we need to clear something up.'

She gestured for them to go into the sitting room, then closed the door and turned to face him. 'You're a very nice man and everything, but you know, but when we, er, you know, *ended up in bed together*, it was a mistake.'

Jack smiled and walked towards her. 'Oh, come on, don't say that.'

Beth's whole body tensed. 'I just think we should forget about it, OK?'

Jack put an arm round Beth's shoulder. 'You don't really mean that.'

'I do,' said Beth vehemently, shrugging him off. 'I tell you what. There's an attractive single mum up the road. Number twenty-two.'

'Well . . .' Jack was wavering. He removed his arm from Beth's shoulder.

Beth continued. 'Why don't you take half an hour off and go and give her a hand with some shelves or something?'

Jack brightened. 'Ripper!'

It was Beth's chance to escape. She walked hurriedly to the door, opened it and stepped out. Saffron was standing in the hall. Both of them jumped.

'Oh, hi,' said Saffron. 'You seen Liam at all?'

'He's in there,' said Beth, pointing to the living room and trying not to appear flustered.

Saffron squeezed past Beth who walked off to take refuge in the kitchen. She shut the door and lay back against it. She tipped her head up so she was staring at the artex ceiling. The swirls were therapeutic in a completely horrible way. She was relieved. Hopefully, that would be the last she'd hear of the Jack business.

There were a lot of variables in Beth's life right now, but she was certain of one thing. She looked upon the opportunity of spending another night with Jack with all the relish of Stanley presented with a plate of spinach. The difference was that she was polite enough not to make a disgusted you-are-trying-to-kill-me face, in front of Jack at least.

There were footsteps outside, then voices next door. Beth strained to hear. Karen was talking to Jack.

'So, Jack, you're looking very attractive today. Is that a new tool belt?' she purred.

'Er, no,' said Jack cautiously.

'It looks very good on you.'

Jack sort of grunted. Karen in full killer bimbo mode was obviously a bit much even for him.

There were rustling and clinking sounds.

'Ooh, Jack. Is that a lump hammer or are you just pleased to see me?'

Blimey, Karen wasn't wasting any time.

There was a sharp intake of breath, followed by a high-pitched squeal of the sort pigs make when they know they're about to be taken to the bacon factory.

'Ooh, Jack.'

'Hang on, Karen. You're coming on stronger than a dingo in heat!' exclaimed Jack.

There was more rustling, or was that grappling?

'Karen!' Jack's voice was muffled, but panicky.

'Oh, you're such a tease, Jack.'

There was more rustling, then a crash as if a person, or perhaps two, had collided with a table.

'You're so big and strong, Jack, but maybe you're right. We should save this till later. I'm staying over tonight at the hotel. We could have a drink with the crew and then slip away. You just make sure your power screwdriver is fully charged.'

Beth smiled to herself. It looked like Karen would be off her back for a while.

* * *

Siobhan stared at the envelope. It was Simon's handwriting. The postmark said Esher, so he must have posted it from home before he went to Australia. She sat down on the bottom step of the stairs and ripped open the envelope. Inside, she found one sheet of A4 paper folded into three. She unfurled it and began reading.

> Dear Siobhan,
> You probably hate me after the way our night in
> Stratford ended, and I wouldn't blame you. The thing
> is, I really did need time to think. When you told me
> your news I was shocked. I'd never seen you as the
> maternal type and, well, you know my situation.
>   Obviously, it is your decision what to do, but I have
> to be honest. I don't feel that, at the moment, I am in
> a position to be really involved. I have my hands full
> at home.
>   Elaine is pregnant. I meant to tell you in Stratford,
> but it didn't seem the right time. Anyway, I will
> always remember the special times we have shared.
> You are a wonderful woman and you deserve
> someone so much better than me.
> Love,
> Simon
> P.S. If you need any money, let me know.

The bar of the Budget Inn, Southampton, was full. The Budget chain of hotels were offering a special wedding package, of which a large and raucous party appeared to have taken advantage. Either that or the bride, wearing a dress with a skirt so hugely lamp-shadesque it could have housed several homeless families, was actually a man in drag rehearsing for the part of Widow Twanky.

'Let's just pray no one lights a match near that lace,' whispered Olivia to Beth, raising an eyebrow. She'd arrived earlier in the evening with a selection of garments for Liam to try on. Liam was with them, up at the bar, attempting to explain to a blank-looking barmaid how to mix a martini.

'Vermouth, dry vermouth . . . No, not Vim-to, Ver-mouth. V-E-R-M-O-U-T-H.' In the end, he gave up and ordered a glass of warm Liebfraumilch. They looked for a place to sit.

Occupying one set of sofas were the crew, Tim the cameraman, Saffron, Jeanine and Ian, the sound man. Ian wasn't speaking, but that wasn't unusual for a sound recordist. They spent so much time wearing headphones and listening out for low-flying aircraft, distantly barking dogs and the whirring of fridge freezers, if they did speak it was in a frequency only bats could hear.

Jack had already gone up to bed, which also wasn't unusual, except that for once it was his own.

Jeanine was working her way through four rounds of sandwiches and a plate of chips. Liam had insisted that they have a rare 1930s Aga so big and heavy they'd already had to remove one wall of the kitchen to get it in, and reinforce the floor. The Southampton shoot was therefore over budget by £23,000. And that was only so far.

Beth, Olivia and Liam sat down on the remaining antiqued leather Chesterfield sofa.

'Not so much distressed as suicidal,' was Liam's verdict.

Olivia and Liam were getting on famously. In large part, Olivia was simply relieved not to have to work with Valerie any more.

However, in Liam she had found someone who was an even more inveterate shopper than herself. Beth listened to them comparing designer purchases.

Karen was sat, or rather slumped, on a paisley pouffe. She was addressing Jeanine and Saffron: 'As I said to Alan Yentob, sweetie, reality television is all very well, but there are only so many salt-of-the-earth cabaret singers one can pluck from obscurity.' Karen burped loudly. 'Obscurity's not as crowded as it was,' she slurred.

Suddenly, she looked round and frowned. 'Where's Jack?'

'He went to bed,' said Saffron. 'Tired, you know.'

'Tired, oh yes, I forgot. I'm feeling rather TIRED myself. I think I'll go to BED too.' Karen smiled woozily and got, unsteadily, to her feet. 'Yes, yes, time for me to go to BED too!'

As she lurched off towards the front desk to pick up her key, the team breathed a collective sigh of relief. Liam was now working the room, signing napkins and posing for pictures with the bride in the massive frock.

'Karen's been hitting it a bit hard tonight, hasn't she?' whispered Olivia.

'Yeah, she's working up to a night of passion with Jack,' said Beth.

'Is she? How do you know?'

'I overheard her.'

'Makes you almost feel sorry for him' exclaimed Olivia, and they both smiled.

Half an hour later, Beth and Olivia decided to call it a night. Beth left Olivia on the second floor and pressed the button in the lift for the fourth for herself. When she stepped out, she caught sight of her reflection in a mirror opposite. She had no make-up on, and the layers of knitwear she had donned to keep out the damp of the semi made her look like she was wearing a Hollywood fat suit.

Ding. The other lift arrived.

Beth turned round hastily, embarrassed at the thought of being caught studying herself in the mirror. The doors of the other lift slid open slowly. Inside, a woman lay slumped on the floor. She was naked except for a pink bra and knickers, black stockings and a tool belt slung around her hips. The woman's face was turned away and there was hair over it. Beth put one foot into the lift to stop the doors closing again and looked closer. Blimey, it was Karen. She appeared to have passed out. Then she stirred. Beth jumped backwards in horror. Before she knew what was happening, the doors slid closed.

Beth hammered at the call buttons frantically, but the lift was already moving. It was going up. She pushed open the door to the emergency stairs and hared up them. In her haste, she didn't stop to think why she was doing this. If she had, maybe she'd have turned around and left Karen to her ignominy. But she was on automatic pilot.

Luckily, the lift was old and slow. When Beth got up to the next floor, it hadn't arrived. She pressed the call button. The doors opened and Beth was presented once more with the vision of a semi-naked Karen. Her body was as thin and fatless as a cheap boiling chicken. Beth reached in to pull her out. However, though there might not have been much flab on her, in her unconscious state, she weighed a ton. Beth couldn't lift her.

She looked round frantically for some help. She thought about pressing the lift alarm, but that would have meant who knows how many male security guards arriving on the scene. However much she hated Karen, she couldn't do that. Instead, she tried waking her up.

'Karen, Karen!' she shouted.

Nothing.

She would have to try something else. She slapped Karen's face. At first she was gentle. Then she used more and more force, stepping back and hurling her whole body forward as if attempting to hit a rounders ball. She had to admit it felt quite satisfying.

'Wha' you doing t' me?'

Beth flushed with guilt. Karen was coming round.

'Oh, thank God, Karen. You've got to wake up.'

'No, no, I go to bye-byes,' burbled Karen.

There was a frantic beeping sound. Someone on another floor was getting tired of waiting for the lift and was trying to get it moving. Beth reached under Karen's armpits and, with an almighty effort, hauled her to her feet, then managed to get her to stagger out. The lift doors slammed shut.

'What's your room number?' said Beth urgently.

'Dunno,' answered Karen, beginning to slide down the wall.

Beth spotted the key in Karen's tool belt. With one arm round her waist to prop her up, she used the other hand to retrieve it. The brass fob read '502'.

'This floor,' Beth muttered to herself, before raising her voice. 'Now you're going to have to help me. Walk, Karen.'

Beth and Karen shuffled down seemingly interminable corridors. Finally they got to 502, Beth turned the key in the lock, pushed open the door and the pair of them fell inside.

'Ow!' said Karen, the pain bringing her to her senses slightly.

Beth attempted to scramble to her feet, but the static electricity coming off the acrylic hotel carpet had her pinned to the floor by her clothing. Maybe she'd never be able to free herself and she'd die here, like an old person in a house too big for them, with children that never visited. They'd find her body weeks later, surrounded by cats.

'Fancy a little dwinkee?'

In a recovery nothing short of biblical, Karen was on her feet and rifling through her mini bar. Lack of clothing had made assuming a vertical position somewhat easier for Karen than it was for Beth.

'We've got, hic, Scotch, hic, vodka and, hic, gin.'

Now Beth was standing too. 'I think you've had enough. And I really should go to bed.'

Karen grabbed two handfuls of Beth's jumper. 'You can't go to bed now.' Suddenly she didn't sound drunk. Mad, yes, but drunk, no. 'Don't leave me. Please don't leave me.'

Beth felt embarrassed. She reminded herself that she didn't like Karen. But then she looked at her, desperate and pathetic in her pink underwear and tool belt.

'Please, please have a drink with me. I don't want to be alone.'

Beth relented. 'Maybe just a quick one, then.'

Karen poured Beth a gin and tonic and herself straight whisky and they sat on the bed. For a couple of minutes neither of them said anything. The atmosphere was awkward.

Then Karen broke the silence. 'I have hated myself for the majority of my adult life,' she said.

Beth was flummoxed. What was the correct response to a statement like that?

No response proved to be necessary. There followed a mono-
logue from Karen on everything that was wrong with her life, to
which Beth simply added an occasional nod or shake of the head.
The gist of things was that Karen didn't have a man, didn't have
children and everybody hated her. When it came to the last bit,
Beth was tempted to nod rather too vigorously, but she didn't. She
put an arm round Karen's bare shoulder and pulled a tissue out of
her trouser pocket when Karen began to cry.

Of all the things Beth might have imagined she would be doing
on a Saturday night, sitting in a hotel room with Karen in her
underwear, listening to her say her life was crap, was about the
last option she would ever have expected. And yet it felt good.
Well, not good exactly. The feeling was more of relief. Karen was
human after all. Beth's animosity began to fade and she actually
began to feel sorry for her.

OK, so maybe Richard had left her, maybe he had moved in
with a bimbo stripper with plastic breasts and no stretch marks,
but at least Beth wasn't reduced to crying on the shoulder of
someone she hardly knew. Beth had Olivia and Siobhan. She
thought how lonely it must be to be like Karen, to have no one to
talk to.

'You know the worst of it?' said Karen, crying even harder. 'I
went to Jack's room tonight and he knocked me back. I mean, he
turned me down. I threw myself at him and he ran a mile. How
pathetic does that make me?'

'You're not pathetic,' cooed Beth, as alarm bells went off in her
brain. Probably not a good idea to mention that Jack hadn't
knocked *her* back and that they'd actually ended up in bed
together. 'You're really, really not pathetic.'

'Oh yes I am. He'll sleep with anything with a pulse!'

'Well, not anything,' said Beth, secretly annoyed.

'Oh, he's famous for it. I haven't had sex in two years and I thought at least I'd get a shag out of Jack.'

'I'm sure it's all for the best. You don't want to get involved with Jack,' Beth said with feeling.

'I suppose you're right. But you won't tell anyone, will you?'

Beth shook her head.

'Promise?'

'Yes.'

Ten minutes later, Karen had pulled herself together enough for Beth to be able to leave. As Karen walked her to the door, she touched Beth's arm.

'Thanks.'

'Don't mention it.'

Beth waited for the lift back to her floor. Maybe Karen wasn't so bad after all.

Siobhan had read and reread Simon's letter and it still hadn't sunk in. He was ending it. He was offering her money. He wanted her to have an abortion. He wanted her to kill their child, so he could play happy families with Elaine. Siobhan couldn't believe it. He couldn't be that cruel. But there it was in black and white. He was ending their relationship and going on with Elaine as if nothing had ever happened.

Siobhan sat on the stairs for a long time, staring blankly ahead, trying not to believe what was staring her in the face. When the chips were down, Simon had chosen his wife over her. But she couldn't accept it. She knew him too well. As he said, they'd shared special times. He loved her, he'd said he loved her. He was only staying with Elaine out of duty and a sense of responsibility to the children.

Even with the proof in her hand, Siobhan clung to the hope that there might still be a happy ending. She had too much invested in Simon to walk away or allow him to do so without a fight. Siobhan had one last desperate card to play.

Chapter Sixteen

Twenty . . . twenty-two . . . twenty four . . .

Siobhan stopped. She stared down at her piece of paper. It said '24 Larksmead Avenue, Esher, Surrey.' She looked again at the number on the gate. This was where Simon lived. Correction. This was where Simon and Elaine and their three children and *one on the way* lived. Siobhan bit her lip and gradually moved her gaze upwards. It was too much to take in all at once. She needed to process the information in bits.

The first thing she noticed was the window box. Where she lived, the flats were all rented. The window boxes, if there were any, consisted of a few straggly strands of ivy, brown at the edges, and maybe some half-dead geraniums. This window box sprouted well-cared-for pink and orange pansies. This was very definitely an owner-occupier window box.

Siobhan moved her gaze to the right. The front door. This was the door Simon stepped out of when he wasn't in Singapore, New York, Sydney, or wherever he told Elaine he was when he was with Siobhan. The door was dark green. There were scuff marks at the bottom. The legacy of children's bikes, a pushchair perhaps?

Siobhan's stomach turned over. Such a stark reminder of Simon's other life, his legitimate life, jolted her. She couldn't do this. She couldn't face the woman she and Simon had deceived for the last four years. And what if it wasn't Elaine who answered the door, but one of the children instead? She'd just crumble.

Elaine and the children had buzzed round her relationship with Simon like gnats at twilight. Sometimes, as Simon had been getting dressed at her place, Siobhan had caught a troubled look. He'd tried to hide it by keeping his back to her, but he'd been quiet. He was in transition, preparing to move from her sphere into Elaine's. Simon was like a diver who has to go into a compression chamber before being able to walk on dry land. Elaine was Simon's terra firma. Siobhan existed only if refracted through guilt.

Siobhan had looked inside his wallet once. There'd been a picture of Elaine and the children. No picture of her. That hurt more than anything. More than the times he stood her up because one of the children was ill. More than the Christmases and New Year's Eves she'd spent on her own. More than the sad little collection of birthday presents she'd given him which he'd left at her place because he couldn't take them home. Siobhan was invisible.

But she wasn't willing to be invisible any more. She had to meet Elaine, not just for herself, but for Elaine too. She should know what sort of man she was married to. It was Siobhan's duty to reveal his deception. If she was in Elaine's position, wouldn't she want to know? Of course. They say the wife's always the last to know. Well, not this time.

The front door opened. Siobhan ducked down behind a parked

car. Her grey cashmere coat dragged in the gutter. Damn. She'd just had it dry-cleaned. Still, she had more important things to think about. She peeked round the bonnet and gasped. The woman from Simon's wallet was pushing a pram out of the door. Simon had said she was pregnant, but this woman was huge. At least seven months. And yet he'd called Siobhan and asked to see her again.

She watched as Elaine bumped a pushchair down the front steps. Inside was a little boy of about two. That must be Josh, she thought.

Simon had been so excited when Josh had cut his first tooth. He'd told Siobhan all about it. She'd shared his first solid food, his first steps, the time he'd fallen off the sofa and had to go to hospital. Looking at Josh now, though, Siobhan realised that she hadn't shared any of it. He was a stranger. He wriggled in his pushchair, looked up at his mother and smiled. Siobhan felt utterly excluded.

Looking at Josh had allowed Siobhan not to look at Elaine's face. But there was no avoiding it any longer. Siobhan studied her carefully. Simon had said she was thirty-five, but she looked older, or maybe that was what three kids did to you. Siobhan laid a hand on her own stomach and wondered what she'd look like by eight months. A dog's breakfast probably.

Now, there are certain times when it is imperative a woman looks her best. A school reunion, attempting to get a flight upgrade and going to your ex's wedding are all occasions when it is wise not to attempt the natural look. Being watched by the woman your husband has been having an affair with for four years and who is currently pregnant with his baby tops all of these.

Siobhan wanted to rush over and say: 'Your husband's mistress is watching you. Go back inside and put some make-up on,' except, of course, she was her husband's mistress, so that was a non-starter. Instead, she spied on Elaine from behind a parked car, like some sort of mad stalker.

Elaine left the pushchair at the bottom of the steps and struggled back up them.

'Hannah, Emily, come on!' she shouted through the open door. 'If you don't come now I'm going without you!'

Eleven-year-old Hannah, and Emily, seven, tumbled out of the house. With them came a flood of memories for Siobhan. The time Hannah had played the recorder in the school concert and Simon had had to listen to 'Clair de Lune' for weeks beforehand; Emily winning the egg and spoon race at the summer fête. Now she watched the two of them coming down the steps and felt nothing. There was no connection between them and her. It had all been in her head.

'Tell her, Mum. She's been nicking my nail varnish again,' whined Hannah.

'No I haven't,' snapped Emily.

'Oh, do stop it, both of you,' said Elaine in exasperation.

Siobhan watched as Elaine began to push Josh down the street, while Hannah and Emily trailed behind, bickering. At any moment she could have stepped out and introduced herself. 'Hello, you don't know me, but . . .' She didn't. She just watched as they got further and further away.

Then she sat down on the kerb, her back against one of the front wheels of an Audi estate. A dark stain spread up from the hem of her coat where it was dangling in a puddle. Four years' worth of frustration and shame, wasted nights and lonely birthdays welled up inside her. She took her fists and drummed them on her knees until they hurt.

All that stuff she'd told herself on the way here about it being in Elaine's interests to know that her husband had been unfaithful crumbled to ashes in the face of the picture of domestic normality she'd just witnessed. Maybe if Elaine and the children had been more perfect, more like something out of a Boden catalogue, Siobhan might have felt the need to prick the bubble. Jealousy would have overcome good sense.

However, seeing the the kids arguing and their mother with her shattered expression, Siobhan didn't feel jealous. She felt ashamed. Elaine was no longer a ghost. She was real. Her children were real and so was her pregnancy. Frankly, she had more than enough on her plate already without Siobhan squeezing poison on to it like ketchup.

And yet it wasn't pity that held Siobhan back. It wasn't a sudden burst of sisterhood either. It was the realisation that she didn't belong in the scene she was watching. In a moment of absolute clarity, Siobhan knew that she would never tell Elaine about her and Simon, or the baby.

'Do you want a drink?' asked Colin, sounding rattled and rifling through the contents of the Indian sideboard. 'Vodka, whisky. There's some of that weird melon-tasting stuff we got duty-free in Athens that time. If it hasn't gone off . . .'

'I don't want a bloody drink. I want to know what's been going on,' spat Olivia.

She was standing in the middle of the living room waving a pair of gold and purple printed men's briefs like a matador brandishing his cape. Colin was cowering. He appeared to be trying to work out if he could fit inside the sideboard and shut the door behind him.

'Look, Colin. I know these aren't yours. I would never purchase such a crime against good taste. So they must belong to someone else, which raises the obvious question: what is some other bloke doing taking his pants off in my house? I always wondered what you did in the afternoons. Have you been having secret wife-swapping parties while I'm at work? If I talk to the neighbours will they tell me it's all back to yours after *Neighbours* for some bruschetta and a bunk up?'

'No, no . . .'

'After all the trouble I've gone to to inject some passion back into our marriage and you've been staging orgies behind my back. Shit! I'm married to Cynthia Payne!'

'Don't be ridiculous. I'm telling you, the pants are mine,' Colin announced defiantly, his voice muffled by the wood of the cupboard.

'And I'm telling you they can't be. I know your wardrobe intimately and I've never seen them before. So whose are they? Perhaps I should take a picture of them, make up some posters to stick on trees like they do for missing cats. "Have you seen these pants? Phone 0207 . . ." '

'You have to believe me,' Colin insisted, still rifling through the sideboard. 'They belong to me.'

Olivia was exasperated. 'OK. Let's suppose they are yours. I didn't buy them for you, so who did?'

Colin straightened up. 'No one. I bought them myself.'

This comment merely fuelled Olivia's suspicions. Aside from

teenage boys, who occasionally splash out on Saturday-night specials in the hope their contents might get an airing in female company, no man buys his own underwear. The male of the species moves seamlessly from having his mother buy his smalls to leaving that to his girlfriend/wife. Actually, some of them never made the shift, their mums still passing them pants parcels at Christmas.

She set a trap for Colin. 'So,' Olivia said calmly, 'when you bought these pants, did they look any better in the changing room mirror than they do now?'

Colin looked embarrassed. He coughed. 'They looked, you know, OK.'

Olivia had him bang to rights now. She knew that while no woman would dream of buying a bra without examining herself from all angles first, men never tried underwear on before they bought it. That went for swimwear too. How else could you account for the number of pot-bellied Germans who hit the beach wearing weenie wrapper thongs? They certainly didn't study the side view before buying. Colin was definitely lying.

'OK, who is she?'

'Who?'

'The woman who bought you these abominations?'

Olivia threw the pants at Colin. They landed on his head, draping themselves over his glasses. He removed them, but said nothing.

Still, Olivia was determined to get an answer. 'Who is the tart you're having sex with?' she bellowed. 'I have a right to know!'

Colin registered Olivia's determined expression and her ramrod posture. He crumbled.

'OK, OK, they're not mine,' he said.

'You can't have it both ways, Colin. Either they're yours or they're not.'

'They're not.'

Olivia waited.

'They're Nigel's,' said Colin, pushing his glasses back up his nose nervously.

Olivia thought for a moment, then shock swept across her face. 'Health visitor Nigel?'

'Yes.'

'But . . .'

'We're in love.'

Olivia frowned. Was Colin saying what she thought he was saying?

Colin cleared his throat. 'Yes, I'm gay.'

Beth dumped her coat on the back of her chair and began flicking though a pile of post on her desk. She had five minutes before she had to be in Karen's office. She hadn't seen Karen since the two of them had shared their mini-bar bonding session. Karen had come back early from the shoot, leaving Beth to handle the last couple of days and the reveal.

It had all gone rather well. Liam had been persuaded to swap his antique Aga for something from IKEA. The contributor had burst into tears. Fortunately, they were tears of joy. For the heart-warming finale, a group of local Brownies had arrived clutching a cake they'd made in the shape of a saw. They'd even managed to hide the one with acne behind a large pot plant.

All in all, Beth was feeling pleased with herself. Professionally, at least, things were coming right at last. The only potential cloud on the horizon was the ratings. Beth looked at her watch: 10.58. The overnights would be in for last night's *On The House*. She touched the simulated wood of her desk as she skirted it and headed for Karen's office.

Most of the team were already assembled. Liam was lounging on one end of the sofa in a fur gilet and a kilt, stroking the top of his mohican, which had been redyed peacock blue. Saffron was next to him in something baggy. They looked like bizarre bookends.

Someone had brought in some plastic chairs from the main office. Beth took a free one next to Olivia.

'How was the shoot?' whispered Olivia.

'Eventful. What about your weekend?'

'Snap.'

Olivia and Beth raised eyebrows at each other.

'Let's have a coffee after,' said Beth. 'You seen Siobhan?'

At that moment, Siobhan rushed in, shrugging off her coat as she did so.

'You know you've got a stain on that, don't you?' Olivia pointed out.

Siobhan sighed. 'Yeah, well, that's what comes of stalking your boyfriend's wife.'

Before she could explain, Karen appeared in the doorway to the office.

'Right, guys, let's get started, shall we?'

Beth smiled at Karen and gave her a little wave. It's amazing how a thing like discovering someone slumped unconscious in a lift wearing only their underwear can make you warm to them.

Beth wasn't scared of Karen any more. She couldn't even remember why she had been.

'First up, the overnights,' announced Karen, apparently oblivious to Beth's greeting.

Everyone in the room held their breath.

'Better, but not good enough. Four point five, peaking at four point eight, twenty-one per cent share.' Karen left a dramatic silence. 'However, I have every hope that things will now improve.' There was another pause for effect. 'You may have noticed that Jack is not here.'

Beth looked round the room. She hadn't noticed Jack's absence, but Karen was right. He wasn't here. Beth was suddenly aware that Karen was looking at her. Beth smiled again, but Karen didn't smile back. There was a strange look in her eyes. The hairs on the back of Beth's neck prickled.

'Jack is no longer with *On The House*,' announced Karen.

Beth was confused. When she'd seen Jack yesterday, he hadn't mentioned anything about leaving.

'It was felt that he had got rather too close to a *certain member of staff*,' continued Karen, now staring directly at Beth, her eyes like lasers. 'His work and the show were suffering as a result.'

So, Karen had got rid of Jack because he was cosying up to a member of staff, but who?

Karen was still staring, Beth realised. Oh my God. She means me! Karen knew about her and Jack. Beth felt a hot red flush spreading down her neck. How had she found out? The only other people who knew were Siobhan and Olivia. And she'd sworn them to secrecy.

Beth rewound the events of the last forty-eight hours. Karen had definitely not known when she and Beth had been in her room emptying the mini-bar. She was so drunk, she would have let something slip. It had to have been since then. Beth knew neither Olivia nor Siobhan would have said anything. This only left Jack. Had he called Karen over the weekend to confess? It didn't add up.

Karen was smiling, but her grin had more than a touch of the reptilian about it. It was as if Friday night had never happened. Maybe if Beth had a chat with her after the meeting, she could clear things up. She could explain that what had happened between her and Jack had meant nothing, and she'd been really drunk and . . .

Karen was speaking. 'However, we have a very exciting replacement for Jack.'

Beth, Siobhan and Olivia exchanged puzzled glances.

'As you all know, I like breaking new ground. So I have decided that what *On The House* needs is not a new handyman, but a handy*woman*.'

A woman? thought Beth. Actually, that wasn't a bad idea.

Karen continued: 'I'd like to introduce you to Linda Watson.' She leaned round the corner out of her office. 'Would you like to come in, sweetie?'

'Have you heard of her?' Olivia whispered to Beth, who shook her head. Siobhan did the same. There was a murmur as the whole room craned their heads round to see who Karen was referring to.

'I believe you already know each other, Beth,' Karen said, wearing a smile of pure evil.

A figure appeared in the doorway.

Beth gasped. 'Chastity!'

'It's Linda now. That's my real name. Karen thought it sounded better, didn't you, Karen?' Chastity announced. She was wearing a very short skirt and a smirk.

Beth felt sick.

Karen was enjoying herself. 'We got chatting at the transmission party, didn't we, Linda? I think you'd left by then, Beth. With Jack.'

Beth cringed. Chastity's arrival was no accident. This was Karen's revenge for her and Jack.

'Linda doesn't know that much about DIY, but she's very keen, aren't you, sweetie?'

Chastity nodded.

'So I'm sure we'll all make an effort to help her out, won't we?'

There was a lukewarm mumble of agreement from around the room.

Beth felt as though she was suffocating. Her face was hot, but her hands and feet were freezing cold. Only forty-eight hours ago, she and Karen had been sitting on her hotel bed. Beth had put her arm round Karen's shoulders and she'd cried. She'd been vulnerable and frightened. Now she had turned back into Cruella De Vil. What Beth was now watching wasn't just an about-turn, it was the psychological equivalent of one of those triple salchow thingies Jane Torville used to do to Ravel's *Bolero*.

Karen hadn't finished. 'I've got one more teeny-weeny announcement to make,' she said, turning to Saffron. 'As you know, we had to let Ros go. Well, I've decided to promote Saffron to director level, strictly on a trial basis. And she's very gamely agreed to have a go, haven't you, Saffron?'

Saffron nodded energetically.

Karen continued: 'I feel Saffron's talents have been overlooked up to now. Her *communication skills*, in particular, are excellent. Well done, Saffron.'

There was a ripple of applause. Liam leaned towards Saffron and planted a kiss on her cheek. She smiled, but it was an uncomfortable smile. Her eyes darted sideways towards Beth. Then she looked away quickly.

Suddenly, Beth remembered her conversation with Jack in Southampton, the one where she'd told him they should just forget about ending up in bed together. Who'd been outside the door when she came out? Saffron. She must have heard everything, then told Karen. The promotion was her thirty pieces of silver.

Karen signalled that the meeting was over and everyone began to file out of her office. Beth headed back to her desk. Siobhan and Olivia were already there, waiting for her.

'I'm so sorry,' said Siobhan.

'What a complete bitch,' said Olivia.

Before Beth could agree, her phone started to ring. It was Marcia, asking her to 'pop in' to see Patric. That was all she needed, an audience with the boss.

Beth had to walk past Karen's office to get to Patric's. Through the open door, she could hear Karen speaking.

'You and Richard really must come to dinner.'

'Yeah, great, or we could go out. Sionara Gdansk is fab. Richard and I are practically regulars.'

When Beth got to Patric's office, Marcia had the sort of expression one of the more kind-hearted tricoteuses might have worn just before some aristo's head rolled into the basket. As she showed Beth in, she pressed a piece of paper into her hand.

'Call me if you ever need anything,' she said.

Beth stuffed the paper in her bag. Patric was standing with his back to Beth, looking out of the window. There was to be no flirting at this meeting.

'I'll get straight to the point,' he said, without turning round. 'Reports of the events of the weekend have reached me and, I must say, I am very disappointed.'

'What events?' said Beth.

'Oh, really, Beth. There's no point being obtuse. I know everything.'

'I don't know what you're talking about,' stuttered Beth.

Patric turned round. His jaw was tight. 'I'm talking about propositioning on-screen talent and then being found unconscious and only partially clothed in a lift, Beth. Does that jog your memory now?'

'You don't understand . . .'

'Oh, but I do. Karen has explained everything to me: the fact that your husband left you for a younger woman, a rather talented one, I hear, and that you threw yourself at Jack in some pathetic attempt to boost a damaged ego. I must say, you're very lucky to have a friend like Karen. She lobbied very hard on your behalf, but I really can't have someone at Futura who is so obviously lacking in judgement.'

Beth was desperate. 'No, it wasn't me.'

'Oh, really, Beth,' Patric drawled sarcastically.

'No, it was Karen. She threw herself at Jack and then got drunk and passed out in the lift in her underwear. Just ask him, Jack, I mean.'

'So this is how you thank Karen for being a good Samaritan to you. If it hadn't been for her rescuing you from that lift, who knows what would have happened.'

Beth could see her situation was hopeless. She stared down at the floor.

'As you know, Beth, you have already had two warnings, so I'm afraid this is goodbye. I think it's better you leave immediately, so as not to disrupt the rest of the team. Marcia will arrange for someone to clear your desk.'

Beth had been in Patric's office for exactly two minutes and forty seconds.

The match made a wonderfully satisfying rasp as it was dragged along the side of the packet. A flame burst into life. Siobhan dropped the match into the waste-paper bin. The shiny paper blistered and blackened, Simon's familiar features first warping, then disappearing into ash. Siobhan stood, warming her bitter heart over the blaze and watching as four years of her life went up in smoke.

'Exactly how do we do this?' asked Olivia. 'I mean, it's not every day my husband introduces me to his lover.' Her tone was exasperated, but also aggressive. Tonight was not part of Olivia's life plan. But then, that included lots of trips on yachts with rich and attentive men, and that bit hadn't worked out either.

Colin and Nigel exchanged nervous sideways glances. Nigel hadn't wanted to come, but Colin had said they'd have to do it some time, so why not get it over with. They both knew Olivia was on a knife edge.

'I think we should all sit down for a start,' said Colin.

Olivia chose an armchair and Colin and Nigel walked over to the sofa and sat down next to each other. Nigel was wearing another of his awful shirts pressed to within an inch of its life. This one featured Popeye. Oh dear, thought Olivia, she'd have to take him in hand. She couldn't have her husband, estranged or not, being seen in the vicinity of a shirt like that.

'Do you iron your own shirts, Nigel?' she asked mischievously.

'Yes, why?' asked Nigel innocently.

Colin gave her a look that said: 'Stop it!'

'You do a very thorough job,' said Olivia.

Olivia noticed their thighs were touching. They had that physical ease, that lack of barriers that only comes from great sex. She felt a rush of jealousy.

Nigel broke the silence. 'I'd just like to say how good of you it is to invite me round.'

'Yes, it is good of me, isn't it? Good old Olivia. She won't mind if her husband shags another bloke.'

'Olivia!' exclaimed Colin. 'We said we were going to be civilised about this.'

'Yeah, well,' answered Olivia, 'maybe I lied.' She looked straight at Nigel, who squirmed.

'Oh, come on, Olivia. Nigel didn't have to come tonight, you know.'

'No, you two could have continued sleeping together behind my back, couldn't you?'

'Well, if you're going to be like this, there's no point, is there?' said Colin. 'Come on, Nigel.'

Colin and Nigel got to their feet and began to walk to the door. Olivia realised she had no choice. She might as well talk to them.

She'd lost Colin. Seeing him and Nigel together, that was clear. They were a couple. She'd treated Nigel as the interloper when it was she who was now the cuckoo in the nest.

'OK, don't go,' she said. 'Let's try and find a way through this mess.'

Stanley's plump hand touched Beth's cheek, patting at the tears that were rolling down it. 'Baa,' he said 'Baa.' This was Stanley's new word. It was meant to be applied to those of a woolly and four-legged persuasion, but was now intended as a more general maternal tonic. Yesterday, when he'd said it for the first time, Beth had laughed and laughed. Now Stanley wanted to cheer her up and this was the only way he knew how.

Beth kissed the top of Stanley's head, but couldn't stop the sobs. They shook her whole body like a series of wet earthquakes. She looked around her. The kitchen was a tip. Toys littered the floor. Plates were piled in the sink. She'd run out of dishwasher tablets three days ago and had simply moved on from the normal crockery to the dinner party stuff they'd had as a wedding present and had hardly ever used.

For a week, Beth had hibernated at home with Stanley. She'd put the answerphone on and had ignored the doorbell. The high point of her day was sitting down with Stanley in front of the microwave, switching it on and watching the little plate inside go round and round. She no longer bothered to get dressed, just swapped one old T-shirt for another, although not the Paul Weller one, obviously.

Self-pity was Beth's full-time occupation now. That and eating. She was gradually working her way through the contents of the freezer, starting with the gateaux and ice-cream. It didn't matter how fat her thighs got now, as she was never going to sleep with any man ever, ever again. She would have become a lesbian, but she couldn't stand Tracy Chapman.

Three weeks ago, Beth had had it all. Well, not exactly all, but close enough. Now what did she have? She'd been traded in for a younger model. Worse, she had lost her job as well. She'd been doubly betrayed. The weird thing was, of the two betrayals, Karen's had hit her harder. Partly this was because it gave her time to think about Richard. When she'd been working, she'd been too busy to dwell on things. Now, Richard's affair went round in her head like that plate in the microwave.

Beth kept trying to work out why. Why had he done it? Was it her? Was he bored with her? Maybe he was just having the common or garden male mid-life crisis. The next time she saw him he'd be wearing a leather jacket and driving a red sports car.

She looked at Stanley. His eyes stared deep into hers. His gaze was unflinching, his love utterly unconditional. Had Richard ever loved her like that, or had he just stuck with her until someone better came along?

All the special memories Beth had of her time with Richard were now tainted with doubt. Her entire value system was in chaos. It was as if she had suffered a blow to the head and her balance had gone. She was staggering around, trying to grab on to things to keep her upright, but she couldn't find anything concrete. She searched her relationship with Richard for words and incidents that might anchor her, but she was now so punch-drunk that she couldn't even get her bearings.

Brring. It was the door bell. Beth ignored it.

Brring. Brring.

There was a rattle as the letterbox opened.

'Beth, we know you're in there. Answer the door.' It was Siobhan's voice.

'Come on, darling, enough is enough.' Olivia was with her.

'Da, da, da,' shouted Stanley excitedly.

'Sssh,' said Beth.

Stanley wriggled, trying to get free.

'We're worried about you,' implored Siobhan. 'Just let us know you're all right.'

'It's been a week. If you were a hostage, they'd have sent in a doctor and a couple of family-sized pizzas by now,' shouted Olivia.

With an arch of his back, Stanley slipped off Beth's knee and made a dash for the door that Linford Christie in his prime would have been proud of.

'Stanley! Come back!' Beth shouted as she ran up the hall after him.

He giggled and ran faster.

A pair of eyes were staring through the letterbox.

'Thank God. We thought you might be lying in a heap at the bottom of the stairs with a broken hip,' said Olivia. 'I was about to order you one of those bath hoists and a blue rinse. Now for God's sake, let us in.'

Beth led the way back into the kitchen.

Olivia surveyed the scene. 'What is this, revenge sluttishness? You think Richard will take one look at the grime and be overcome with remorse?'

Beth crossed her arms protectively over her chest. 'It's my

house. Anyway, I've never seen you so much as pick up a J-Cloth. Colin does it all.'

'Colin's been a bit busy picking up something else lately, actually.'

Beth didn't hear. She was concentrating on the mess. Maybe the place could do with a bit of a tidy-up.

Olivia picked up an empty strawberry cheesecake box. 'What's this?'

Beth snatched it from her. 'I don't care how fat I get, since I have no intention of going out ever again.'

Siobhan began filling the sink with hot water. 'Look, we'll help you clear up,' she said.

'I'm fine,' Beth insisted.

Olivia sat down at the table and pulled Stanley on to her knee. 'Remember, I've been where you are. When James had his affair, I wanted to brick myself into the house. Well, actually, I wanted to brick him and Allyson With a Y into the house. Shutting yourself away for a while is only natural, but you can't stay here for ever.'

Something clicked in Beth's brain. She opened her mouth and a torrent of words flew out. 'Yes I can. I can stay here for ever. I'm going to stay here for ever. I don't want to go out. I don't want to see anybody. I don't want to do anything. I just want to stay here. Just me and Stanley. Here alone. FOR EVER!'

'There was a film about that, Beth. It was called *Psycho* and I don't think the son in question was that well adjusted, actually,' said Olivia.

Siobhan looked up from the washing-up. 'I know you're devastated, but at some point you are going to have to face the world, Beth,' she said gently. 'For Stanley's sake as much as for your own.'

'No I'm not. I'm going to be like one of those Americans who stockpile corned beef and automatic weaponry and barricade themselves into their log cabin and NEVER COME OUT.'

'That's in the Appalachians,' said Olivia. 'This is Islington. I don't think you can get an Uzi with your pint of semi-skimmed from the milkman.'

Beth started to cry. She was exhausted. 'I just want to be left alone. Why can't you leave me alone?' she sobbed.

Siobhan turned from the sink and, with the washing-up froth still on her hands, walked over to Beth and hugged her.

Olivia stood up and carried Stanley over to Beth. 'I know,' she said, 'but if you don't let the cleaner in soon, the carpet will walk out and leave you as well.'

Beth laughed weakly.

'Look, I've had an idea,' said Olivia. 'We could all do with a break. How do you fancy a little holiday?'

Chapter Seventeen

The road skittered up the mountain in an uneven zigzag. At the bottom, a few scrubby trees huddled together. Further up, green was scarce. To prevent landslides, the rock face was swathed in chicken wire like old ladies' hair nets. Especially precarious stretches of mountainside were shored up by sections of dry-stone wall, soaring up twenty or thirty metres.

'Shame they don't make bras like that,' said Beth.

Siobhan smiled and wound down the window of the taxi. They breathed in the Sicilian air. It was warm and heavy, with just a whiff of sulphur from Mount Etna, which glowed a gentle red in the distance.

'This was a really good idea,' said Siobhan.

'Yeah,' said Beth.

They spent the rest of the journey in silence, apart from Stanley's babbling. 'Mama, dada, baba,' he chanted. As the afternoon light faded to evening, the landscape turned from gold to a deep olive green, tinged with terracotta. Shadows settled on the hills, giving them a chiselled appearance. Beth and Siobhan sat back in their seats and let the Italian landscape wash over them.

By the time they reached Castelmola, at the top, it was dark. It was easy to pick out the house. With no street lamps, the light from the windows poured out like luminescent golden syrup into the inky night.

Olivia was standing in front of the open door when they pulled up. She smiled and they all hugged. 'Come in. Colin's cooked some sort of stew,' she said, before showing Beth to one of the upstairs bedrooms, so she could put a slumbering Stanley down.

When Beth rejoined the others, they were in the sitting room at the back of the house. She sank into a soft brocade sofa. 'Your friend really doesn't mind us borrowing this?' she asked.

Olivia shook her head. 'Got another place in Majorca. Next door to Michael Douglas and Catherine Zeta Jones. They only come here to get a break from the paparazzi.' She handed Beth a glass of wine.

'I think we should have a toast, don't you?' announced Beth. 'To good friends, good wine and . . .'

Siobhan glumly indicated her chaste glass of water.

'Oh, right, maybe not to good wine, then.'

'What about to life, love and . . .' said Siobhan.

'Jesus, Siobhan. You are one of life's optimists, aren't you?' Olivia exclaimed in astonishment.

Siobhan blushed.

'Well, I'm gasping for a drink, so we've got to make some sort of toast,' said Beth. 'I know. To marriage as an outdated institution!' Then she looked at Olivia. 'Oh, damn. Tend to forget not all husbands are duplicitous little worms.'

'Well, now you come to mention it . . .' said Olivia.

At that moment, Colin emerged from the kitchen. He was

wearing a swirly-patterned shirt that should surely have come with the sort of warning TV channels give to epileptics before a programme featuring strobing lights. He was pink-cheeked from the heat of the stove.

With Colin was a man neither Siobhan nor Beth recognised. He looked clean, scrubbed almost. He was tall, with very precisely cut blond hair and an even more horrible shirt than Colin's. Was this bad clothing thing catching?

'You know Colin, of course, but I don't think you've met Nigel.' Olivia paused. 'Nigel is Colin's boyfriend. Now, what was it you were saying, Beth?'

'Action!' shouted Saffron.

Chastity picked up her hand saw and applied it to a banister. 'When you're using a saw, my top tip is to rub the end with candle wax to get a smoother cut,' she announced. She pushed the saw back and forth. There was squeaking but no cutting. She shook the saw in disgust. 'This thing isn't working!' she exclaimed.

'It might help if you held it the right way up,' said Saffron, sighing. 'Shall we go for another? Take Forty-two.'

With the dinner plates cleared away, Colin and Nigel excused themselves. Seth had had a nightmare and they'd gone to read him another bedtime story.

'One good thing about having a husband who's shagging the health visitor, you get a built-in grade-A baby-sitter,' said Olivia, moving over to the coffee table. Colin had laid out a bottle of grappa and some glasses. She began to pour.

'This Nigel,' said Siobhan, waving away the grappa and sticking to her cup of coffee. 'He's not the same health visitor . . .?'

'Yup.'

'Oh, God. The one who saw you naked?'

'Oh, yes. Having crossed the Rubicon of my bare breasts, Nigel clearly felt becoming bosom buddies with my husband was the natural next step.'

Beth put a hand on Olivia's arm. 'Why the hell didn't you tell us this was going on?'

Olivia looked serious. 'First, I didn't know. Then, you both had your own problems.'

'Yeah, but, Jesus, Olivia,' said Beth. 'You shouldn't have had to cope with it on your own. It is your turn to need help occasionally, you know.'

Olivia smiled weakly. 'OK.'

'Can I ask a question?' said Siobhan tentatively.

Olivia nodded.

'How does it feel when your husband turns gay? I mean, is it better or worse than if he'd gone off with another woman?'

Olivia took a long sip from her drink. 'To tell you the truth, when he told me, I was relieved.'

'Relieved!' said Siobhan and Beth together.

'Yeah. The sex thing had never really worked. I was flogging a dead horse, well, flogging something, on occasion anyway.'

'But you managed to have four children!' gasped Siobhan.

'Yeah, well let's just say we must both be incredibly fertile. What I mean is, the spark was never really there. Now at least I know it wasn't me.'

'Aren't you worried about, you know, HIV?' said Siobhan.

'He said they practised safe sex,' Olivia answered.

'What does that mean?' asked Beth.

'I didn't want him to draw me a diagram of what they'd been up to. But I believe him. Colin may be many things, including gay apparently, but he is not reckless. He'd never put me or the children at risk.'

The three of them were quiet for a moment. They looked out of the window into the blackness beyond. A dog barked and somewhere across the valley a pair of car headlamps made jerky progress up a steep slope.

'You know, to be honest, I always had my doubts about Colin. His trainers were too clean,' mused Olivia.

'What?' said Beth.

'You know. He was too pristine, finicky almost. But I ignored it. It suited me. After James, the last thing I wanted was another red-blooded male.'

'So you chose a pink one instead,' said Beth.

Olivia smiled. 'In a way, yeah.'

She picked up the bottle of grappa, pouring more for herself and Beth. 'This is a terrible admission to make, but I never really loved him. And he knew that. I liked him, of course, but I never loved him. I used him. I was on the rebound. I wanted someone safe, so I settled for Colin. I'm not proud of it, but I did.'

'But you seemed so good together,' said Siobhan.

'Yeah, and we were. But there was always something missing. I blame myself. I should probably never have married him. It was a cowardly thing to do. If I'd been braver, I'd have found myself someone I really did love. But that would have meant risking myself, starting again, and I didn't have the courage to do it.'

Olivia took a sip of her drink. Her voice had dropped almost to a whisper. 'I was thirty-one. I was afraid I'd end up in a flat on my own with a cat . . .'

Siobhan winced, thinking of Fred, her cat who had gone walkabout.

'. . . and the complete boxed set of *Friends* videos,' continued Olivia.

Siobhan winced again, visualising her own video collection.

'I wanted to be married. I wanted kids. Colin was the easy option and I took it. Him, I mean.'

'No marriage is ever easy,' said Beth, sadly.

'No, but I think it was harder for Colin. How do you imagine it feels to know you are someone's fallback position? Colin knew how I felt. We didn't talk about it. But he knew.'

'But weren't you his fallback position as well, while he worked up the nerve to admit to himself and everyone else that he was gay?'

'Yeah, I suppose I was. God! What a recipe for disaster! It's amazing we lasted as long as we did.'

Beth thought for a moment. 'What if things had been reversed and it was you who'd been secretly gay?' she asked.

'I'd have hung on in there for the sake of the children, probably never acted on my feelings,' said Olivia. 'But men, even nice ones like Colin, are different, aren't they? Sex is so central to everything. It isn't even a question of self-sacrifice for them. It's about identity. I'm lucky in a way that Colin did come out to me. If he hadn't, he'd probably have been doing dodgy things on Hampstead Heath without me knowing.'

Beth and Olivia sat back on the sofa. The grappa was beginning to have an effect. Olivia felt calm. Talking about things had helped her to sort them out in her mind.

'What I can't get my head round, though,' said Siobhan, 'is why you've let him, Nigel that is, move in.'

'It's self-interest, really. If I didn't, then Colin would have to move out and then where would I be with the children? That sounds really callous, I know. But it's true. I'm not saying that it's easy. It feels odd having someone new in the house. I suppose it's a bit like having an au pair.'

'That your husband is sleeping with,' said Beth.

'As I said, it's a bit like having an au pair,' laughed Olivia.

The others laughed too.

'You know, I'm not laying out my life as any kind of blueprint to anyone else. For the moment, we're sort of making it up as we go along, muddling through. Isn't that what everyone does in the end?'

'Not Richard,' said Beth glumly. 'If he'd been prepared to muddle through, we'd still be together. But no, he had to go off and have an affair. Do you think men are genetically programmed to be unfaithful? I mean, just look at the three of us. We've all been messed about, in one way or another, by a man who can't keep his trousers on.'

'Affairs are like hobbies,' announced Olivia. 'Women are too busy for either. We've got dry-cleaning to pick up, roots that need doing. Important stuff. Men have got time to fill. So, if he isn't fiddling about with model trains or dressing up as Oliver Cromwell at the weekend, he's probably shagging Debbie in accounts.'

Siobhan cradled her cup of coffee. 'It's so depressing. Aren't there any men you can trust?'

'I think they wear tank tops and are called Derek,' said Beth.

'But that makes it sound like only unattractive men are faithful,' said Siobhan.

'Oh, no,' argued Olivia. 'The uglier the man, the more of a shagmonster he's likely to be. He's got something to prove. You know you always see those complete gargoyles in *Bravo!* with some bit of fluff of a third wife and people assume he got her because of his money?'

Siobhan and Beth nodded.

'He didn't. He got her because he's good in bed. Let's face it, she's not there for the view, is she? He tries harder between the sheets. Trouble is, Mr Ugly wants everyone to know he's good in bed, so he shags anything in a skirt, hence wives number one and two getting pissed off and divorcing him.'

Beth took a gulp of her grappa. 'I suppose I'm going to get divorced now. God! I wish if Richard had been unhappy he'd said something. But that would have been mature, wouldn't it? He's behaving like one of those spotty youths who packs your shopping in Sainsbury's—'

'And puts the eggs on the bottom?' Olivia interjected.

'Yeah, one of those teenage boys. I suppose it's my fault really. I expected, or at least hoped, that Richard would progress emotionally beyond the age of fifteen, which I now know no man ever does. But you know what *really* pisses me off?'

Siobhan and Olivia shook their heads.

'It's not the lying and the cheating – well, it is – but what I *really* resent is what his behaviour has turned me into. I am the Wronged Wife and there's a script for that, isn't there? Either I've got to lose six stone, get a new haircut, or I've got to be stoic and keep the bloody home fires burning while he gets this crisis he's having out of his system. Then I'm supposed to take him back and make a go of things.'

'So which is it going to be?' asked Siobhan.

'Dunno. Stoic takes less effort.'

'Does he know you're here?' asked Siobhan.

'No, and I have no intention of telling him. Let's see how he likes being in the dark.'

Olivia looked at Siobhan and pointed to the coffee pot.

Siobhan shook her head. 'Having trouble sleeping as it is.'

Beth leaned forward. 'Simon?'

'No, the baby actually. I didn't tell you I had a scan yesterday.'

'And?' said Beth.

'I'm a bit more pregnant than I thought.'

'How much more?' said Beth, suspiciously.

'A lot more.'

'Well, don't keep us in suspense. Do I rig up some stirrups in the kitchen or not?' asked Olivia.

'I'm six months.'

'Six months!' gasped Beth.

'Well, I suppose that scotches any doubt about who the father is. It has to be Simon.'

Siobhan nodded.

'I looked like the back of a bus at six months,' said Beth.

'I looked like the back, the front and the sides,' added Olivia.

'You really think it's not showing?' asked Siobhan, pulling up her jumper and smoothing a hand over her gently rounded stomach.

'No!' shouted Olivia.

'Lucky cow!' laughed Beth.

Olivia looked serious. 'So, what about Simon?'

Siobhan shook her head. 'It's finished.'

'We've heard that before,' Beth said gently.

'I know, but this time I really do mean it. After that letter, and then seeing Elaine, it made me realise what a—'

'Bastard he is?' suggested Olivia.

'I was going to say, well, what a weak man he is.'

'Weak men are far more dangerous than bastards,' announced Olivia. 'At least with a bastard, you know where you stand – at the end of the very long line of other women he's sleeping with, usually. Weak men are so afraid of hurting anyone, so terrified of confrontation, they dither and end up slicing everyone to shreds.'

There was silence, then Olivia laughed. 'You know what? I've just realised something. I'm such an expert on men, and yet I managed to marry a gay one!'

'Yeah, well, maybe you've got it right after all,' declared Beth. 'When you get divorced, you're not so much losing a husband as gaining someone to go cushion-shopping with.'

Simon stared straight ahead, trying to cut out the noise coming from the back of the car.

'Mummy, Mummy, she hit me,' wailed Emily.

'No I didn't. Anyway, you hit me first,' squealed Hannah.

'Waah,' went Josh.

'Be quiet, all of you. You're upsetting the baby,' said Elaine firmly.

Elaine was sitting beside Simon, but Simon was barely aware of her. He was trapped inside a bubble of his own thoughts. He was thinking about Siobhan. That had been a close one. He'd definitely got himself in too deep there. Good to have laid his cards on the table when he did, before anyone got hurt. Ending it was the best thing all round, really.

Simon repeated this to himself silently, but none of it took away the sadness that had settled on him like a cloud from the moment he wrote that letter. He felt bereft without Siobhan. He knew he shouldn't feel like this. Here he was with his wife next to him, his good, honest, kind, loving wife. But the truth was, she wasn't enough.

The car in front crept forward a foot or so. Simon eased his foot off the clutch and slid into the space.

'I spy with my little eye,' Elaine was saying, 'something beginning with . . .'

Simon tried to pull himself together. He knew he and Siobhan were finished. Siobhan's pregnancy had seen to that. Were he to go back now, he'd have to leave Elaine, and he could never do that. No, from now on, he was going to be a better husband to Elaine. A better man. No more complications. The new baby marked a new phase.

'Lamp!' shouted Emily.

'No,' said Elaine.

'Lollipop!' shouted Hannah.

'Lollipop, what lollipop?' laughed Elaine. 'No.'

'I know, I know,' shrieked Emily. 'Line, white line!'

'Yes. Well done. Give that girl a gold star!'

Simon looked over at Elaine and smiled. As he did so, his eyes strayed over her shoulder and caught those of the driver in the next car. She was young, twenty-two, twenty-three, with an upturned nose and blonde hair cut in a bob. She smiled back.

* * *

Siobhan lay on a sunlounger on the terrace. Her bare legs dangled over the edge. It was so hot, she could feel the heat reflecting off the terracotta tiles on to the soles of her feet. She looked up into the sky and squinted. It was a vivid blue. When she looked back down again, she had spots in front of her eyes.

'Aunty Siobhan! Aunty Siobhan! Look at me!'

It was Seth. He was poised to jump into the pool. Siobhan did as instructed and Seth flung himself into the water.

'Very good!' said Siobhan, when Seth's head had bobbed to the surface. He beamed with pride. Siobhan watched him splash his way to the edge. He was so determined and so full of energy, it tired her out just to look at him. Siobhan tried to imagine what it would be like to have a child like him full-time, not just for an hour or two.

From a practical standpoint, she was in a fix. She was pregnant and on her own. A few months down the line and she'd be coping with a newborn baby without anyone else to help share the load. What if the baby had colic, or didn't sleep, or was born with one of those life-threatening hole in the heart things? How would she manage alone? Siobhan was also embarrassed. She'd been such a fool. Getting pregnant by a married man, it was so pathetic. This certainly wasn't how she'd envisaged having her first child. She'd wanted at least to be with the father. Maybe not married, but certainly together.

Some people would think she was being selfish, bringing a child into the world without a dad. And, to be honest, deep down Siobhan was rather relishing the chance to have an exclusive relationship with her baby. This was one person with whom she could plan a future. But her overwhelming emotion was fear. She watched Seth pad along the side of the pool, his tiny wet feet leaving perfect prints on the dry clay tiles, and she was overwhelmed by the responsibility that lay ahead.

Siobhan looked down at her laptop.

'You have one new message,' it informed her.

She sighed. Not Karen again! From the moment she'd touched down in Sicily, Karen's demands had been making Siobhan's life a misery. Without much enthusiasm, she began tapping keys and moving the mouse. She cupped her hand round the screen to cut out the sunlight so she could read the message. It wasn't from Karen after all; the sender was, of all people, Jack! Siobhan hadn't seen or spoken to him since he'd been sacked by Karen. So why was he e-mailing her now? She double-clicked on his message and waited for it to come up in full on the screen.

'hiya blondie, how r u? something has come back and bitten me on the bum. need yr help. jack.'

Jack in trouble? He was one of life's natural survivors. Siobhan was intrigued.

'Do all the men in Sicily look like Antonio Banderas, or am I just desperate?' said Olivia.

'You're just desperate,' chorused Siobhan and Beth, then giggled.

The three of them were sitting at a pavement café five minutes' walk from the villa. Colin and Nigel had stayed behind to babysit. As Olivia had said: 'What's the point of having an unfaithful husband if you can't take advantage of him occasionally?'

The café was tucked into one corner of a pretty cobbled square. Half a dozen tables were crowded together, their paper cloths fluttering wildly in the breeze. On one side, over a low wall, was a sheer drop all the way down to Taormina below. On the other, they had a view of a castle clinging to the craggy mountain above. The café was busy with a mix of tourists taking a break in the steep climb to the castle, and locals enjoying a late breakfast of coffee and sweet cake.

Tiny, open-backed trucks, some loaded with fruit and vegetables, others with crates of empty bottles or cartons of cigarettes, criss-crossed the square. Powered by motorcycle engines, their bulbous cabs and high-pitched whine made them seem like frenetic bluebottles. Other traffic consisted mainly of Vespas, roaring past at regular intervals, bearing young, darkly handsome men with bare ankles and wrap-around sunglasses.

Beth finished the last of her strawberry granita, scraping her spoon round the bottom of the bowl. 'Mmm. It would be nice if we could just stay here, wouldn't it?'

'What?' said Olivia. 'You mean live a life of unalloyed pleasure, lounging about, sipping something cool and having oil rubbed into our backs by gorgeous young men on Vespas?'

'I think the tyres might leave a bit of a mark,' said Siobhan. 'Besides, there is the little matter of having to earn a living.'

'Yeah, there is that, I suppose,' said Beth. 'At least you two have got jobs.'

'Yeah, working with Karen!' exclaimed Siobhan.

Beth grimaced. Siobhan had a point. Karen on a daily basis Beth was spared. A welcome state of affairs in one sense, it was also a luxury. She had bills to pay and no way at the moment of doing it.

'I know I'm supposed to be really karmic and say what goes around comes around, but actually, I'd like to see Karen burn in hell. When I think how I listened to her in her hotel room that night, droning on about how terrible her life was, I want to scream. I mean, I actually believed her!'

'But don't you see?' said Olivia. 'She was telling the truth.'

Beth frowned.

'That's the whole problem,' explained Olivia. 'Karen didn't sack you because you slept with Jack, although that probably didn't help. You got the boot because you discovered a chink in her armour. Once she'd sobered up, she was mortified that you'd seen past the mask. You paid the price for that.'

Beth sighed. As she did so, she gazed down the mountain and into the distance. She could just about glimpse the sea. It was silver and gently rippled, like pleated kitchen foil. Were it not for the motorbikes, the delivery vans and a couple of policemen who, having used a tape measure to calculate the exact square footage the café tables were occupying, were now arguing with the owner, the scene would have been entirely peaceful.

'What I've got to do is get a job,' said Beth, turning back to the others. 'Any ideas?'

Neither Olivia nor Siobhan answered. Siobhan was watching Olivia, who was staring, transfixed, and it wasn't by the scenery. A waiter was walking towards them. He was in his mid twenties, medium height, slim and with a mop of shiny dark hair. He moved with that peculiarly Italian brand of machismo that makes even an apron look sexy.

As the waiter approached the table, he and Olivia locked eyes.

'Signora?' He said it slowly, flirtatiously.

Olivia, normally the picture of confidence, was slightly flustered. '*Delicioso*,' she stuttered to the waiter. '*Grazie mille.*'

'*Prego*,' he said, picking up the dishes. 'You Eenglish?'

'Yes,' answered Olivia.

'Sween-don. You know Sween-don? I have seester there.'

'Well, I can't say I know Swindon well. A lot of roundabouts, I think,' Olivia said, smiling.

'Roundabouts, what ees roundabouts?'

'They're sort of . . .'

Olivia and the waiter, who introduced himself as Gianni, talked for five minutes or so. The café's customers had thinned out, but neither he nor Olivia seemed to notice. It was lucky no one wanted a coffee. If they had, they'd have had to use a klaxon to get his attention. He was completely focused on Olivia.

Siobhan and Beth felt awkward.

Siobhan got up from the table. 'Look, I'll see you later,' she said. 'Got to buy postcards. You know.'

Beth followed Siobhan's lead. 'Yeah, see you later.'

Olivia nodded vaguely. 'Right, fine.'

Siobhan and Beth took refuge across the road, among the racks of postcards outside a shop selling lace headscarves, brightly painted crockery and other tourist trinkets. They peered over at Olivia, still in animated conversation with Gianni.

'They've been talking nonstop for ages. Considering his English is about as fluent as my Serbo-Croat, that's pretty good going,' said Siobhan.

'Just goes to prove the language of love really is universal,' smiled Beth.

'I don't want to get preachy, but, you know, she is a mother. Shouldn't she be . . .'

'What, at home knitting? Or maybe whipping up something from the Annabel Karmel meal planner? Jesus, Siobhan, just because you give birth doesn't mean you turn into Mary Archer.'

'I know. I just . . .'

'Look, having a baby is a bit like losing loads of weight. You feel the same, but everyone else treats you completely differently, which is incredibly frustrating because, basically, you are the same woman, just with bigger eye bags.'

Gianni and Olivia walked over to a scooter parked round the side of the restaurant. He'd taken off his apron and slipped his arms into a light cotton bomber jacket. He swung his leg over the scooter and got on. Olivia climbed on behind him and put her arms round his waist. He started the engine and they disappeared, at speed, up a narrow windy street.

Siobhan and Beth watched them go. 'He is a bit, you know, young, isn't he?'

'That's rich coming from a woman whose last two boyfriends were practically still in the womb!' declared Beth.

'All right, but this is what, exactly? A holiday romance? I mean, it's what you do when you're seventeen.'

'Yeah, well, maybe Olivia needs to have a bit of a delayed teenage right now. I reckon she deserves it.'

Siobhan nodded. 'You don't really want any postcards, do you?'

'No. Well, not unless I send one to Richard. "Wish you were here." ' She wrinkled her nose. 'I don't think so.'

Beth and Siobhan began to walk slowly through the square. Halfway across, there was the sound of grinding gears. A shiny Mercedes shot round the corner. It was going at speed on the wrong side of the road. They jumped back. The car didn't stop. As it roared past, a man inside shouted: 'Look out!'

'You wanna drive?' screeched the woman beside him. 'Or maybe you're too stressed to do that either!' The faintest hint of an Essex twang lingered in the air.

Chapter Eighteen

Richard was sitting on the edge of the bed, hunched forward. 'I'm sorry,' he whispered dejectedly. 'Usually, you know, I'm, um, fine. It's just . . .'

'I know, I know,' sighed Chastity, who was lying on her back on the bed. 'You're under stress. Well, so am I.'

'I know. I'm sorry.'

'For God's sake. Just stop saying sorry!'

'Sorry.'

Chastity groaned and rolled on to her front, reaching for the remote to switch on the hotel TV. She flicked channels. There was a game show featuring a male anchor with too much tan and not enough hair flirting with a pair of much younger women. The alternatives were twenty-four-hour Euro news, kids' cartoons and a music channel. She went for the music station. En Vogue burbled in the background.

Richard turned round. 'I know I'm not much fun at the moment,' he said.

'You can say that again,' muttered Chastity.

'What?'

'Nothing.'

'I've lost my home, my family. Everything really.'

'Thanks,' said Chastity drily.

'No, I mean, I know I've got you, but it all happened so fast. If I'd had more time to explain to Beth, maybe she would have taken it a bit better. We could have at least stayed friends, for Stanley's sake . . .'

At the mention of Stanley, Chastity's eyes glazed over.

'I really do miss him,' continued Richard. 'If only I could see him. I don't understand it. I've left loads of messages and Beth doesn't call me back. I mean, I am still Stanley's dad. I wonder what he's doing now. Probably playing with his toys, or maybe looking at his tractor catalogue. Did I tell you about the tractor catalogue?' Richard's eyes were tearful. 'Maybe Beth's reading that to him now. She is a good mother. You've got to give her that.'

'Look, there's no use going on about it, is there?' snapped Chastity. 'You talk as if she was the Virgin Mary or something. If she was so great, how come you jumped into bed with me?'

'I don't know,' said Richard. And he really didn't.

One minute, Richard had been a respectable married man with a baby. The next he was living with a woman he barely knew. His wife wasn't talking to him. His parents, her parents and most of their friends weren't talking to him either. Richard tried to pinpoint the exact moment when he'd made the decision to become a social pariah, but he couldn't. To the best of his recollection, he had never decided to alter the course of his life in this way.

Yes, he'd been unhappy with Beth – well, maybe unhappy was too big a word. He'd been dissatisfied. But he'd never asked for this. Had there been a fork in the road which had said 'Happy and

Socially Acceptable Married Man' to the left and 'Ridiculous Middle-Aged Cliché and Adulterer' to the right, he would have veered left immediately. Somehow, however, he'd ended up here, and it wasn't a place he wanted to be.

Richard knew he'd made his bed and now he had to lie in it. And that was about all he did do. He tried to fool himself and Chastity, pretend he was happy, but his body exposed his dishonesty. He and Chastity hadn't had sex since the night of the party. His nether regions had as much spark as a broken cigarette lighter. They'd come away in the hope that some sun and sea might put the relationship back on track. There was no sign of that happening as yet. What should have been a romantic break was fast turning into a hellish week. Being together twenty-four hours a day, the differences between them were opening up into a chasm. Richard was glum and guilty. Chastity was shrill, impatient and resentful.

Richard put a hand to his brow. 'You know, maybe I'm coming down with something. I feel a bit clogged up and I've got a headache and—'

At this, Chastity snapped. 'If you want Florence fucking Nightingale, go back to your wife,' she stormed. 'We came on holiday to have some fun and all you've done since we got here is whinge. Well, I'm sick of it. I'm going to the beach. We've come all the way here and the least I'm going back with is a tan!'

She got off the bed, stomped into the bathroom and slammed the door. When she came back out, she had on a large straw sun hat and a gold-printed sarong over her gold bikini. She picked up a set of car keys from the desk.

'You coming then?' she asked, jangling the keys irritably.

'Er, no. I left this number on Beth's answerphone. Better wait here in case she calls,' he said.

'Jesus, if you didn't want to come on holiday, why didn't you just stay at home? I hate this place anyway. I wanted to go to Florida. It was your idea to come to fucking Sicily!'

Patric held the phone away from his ear.

'Since when was a tarantula spider a ratings winner?' bellowed Anastassia. 'The Andrex puppy, yes. The Smirnoff Ice dancing cat, definitely. But a fucking spider!'

Patric brought the phone back towards his face. 'To be fair, Anastassia, the tarantula was a key part of the story. The contributor's brother gave it to her, along with the Gothic bedroom she needed help with. We did leave out the bat and the snake and went to considerable trouble to conceal her pierced nipple.'

'Just the viewer profile we're looking for. Not,' Anastassia spat. 'Anyway, that isn't why I really called. What's the story with the woman in the wheelchair and that awful person in the polyester tracksuit hovering beside her?'

'That was her carer.'

'Her what?'

'Carer. We had to have her carer on hand in case our wheelchair lady had a fit and was unable to speak.'

'You put a woman on TV who might be unable to speak!' Anastasia was incredulous.

'Yeah, well, political correctness and all that. As you know, we have to be seen to be reflecting all sections of society. Actually, it came down to a choice between the wheelchair lady and a chap who'd had testicular cancer, but he wanted to talk about self-examination. It was felt that this might be intrusive during an item about how to replace a U-bend.'

Anastassia was almost having a fit herself. She pulled herself together. 'Whatever. The overnights speak for themselves. Five point two for last night's show isn't good enough. I did warn you. If the figures don't get above five and a half, then I'm going to have to offer the slot to some other indies.' She slammed down the phone.

Olivia placed her hand gently on one perfect Sicilian male buttock. It was firm and round and covered with a dusting of dark hair like the fuzz on a gooseberry.

'Oleevia.' Gianni's voice was sleepy. '*Bellissima.*'

'Sssh.' Olivia leaned forward and planted a kiss on Gianni's shoulder. 'Sleepio, or whatever you say in Italian.'

Olivia was multi-lingual on a strictly need-to-know basis. She had never needed to know the word for sleep. Instead, she had mastered certain key phrases. 'How much is that?' was one. 'Do you have it in a size twelve?' was another. Her favourite was 'What discount do you do for cash?' All of these she could say in eight languages.

But being with Gianni was a new experience in many ways. Sex with Colin, if she could remember back to the Jurassic period, had been sort of friendly. Friendly and tepid. With James it had been more exciting, but on her side at least there had been a subtext of resentment. Now she was in bed with a man she barely knew and she'd just had the best sex of her life. Olivia blushed. She felt good, but also scared. She felt out of control, giddy and lightheaded, as if she'd knocked back a glass of champagne too quickly. Only she hadn't had a drop. She was drunk on possibility. If she could do this, then what else might she be capable of?

Olivia was living in extremes. Since Colin had told her about Nigel, she had bounced from dark desperation to feeling almost high. Like a skateboarder in a tube, she went right to the edge in one direction, teetered on the brink, then slid back and rode up the opposite bank, before teetering on the brink again. But the brink of what?

What had really shocked her was how Colin's affair had brought James's infidelity flooding back. It was as fresh and raw as it had been eight years ago. She'd thought she had come to terms with it. But at the moment when Colin confessed, she had felt the force not just of his betrayal but of James's too. The combined effect had knocked her off her feet and on to her knees emotionally.

Olivia needed time to recover her strength. The warm Sicilian air was part of her cure. Gianni was now another.

The Chip Inn, Stoke on Trent, had never seen anything quite like it. Liam was standing at the counter in a purple mock-snake jacket and silver studded jeans. His mohican was a vivid shade of fuchsia, as were his twenty-two-hole Doctor Marten boots.

With Liam was Saffron, who was wearing a glittery clip in her hair and a 'Boy Crazee' T-shirt. The Curse of Karen. Jeanine, the production manager, was ordering her third helping of chips, while Tim regaled her with the tale of his tightrope walk over the Grand Canyon. Ian, the sound man, was crouched in a corner, polishing his headphones.

The woman behind the counter had a beehive and sky-blue eye shadow. She looked as if aliens had kidnapped her in 1966 and only recently returned her to earth. She also had a deeply disinterested air.

Liam was pointing excitedly at something through the window of the heated cabinet set into the counter. 'Ah, you've got tempura. Marvellous. Is that crayfish tempura by any chance?'

'Saveloy,' said the beehive woman, flicking the ash off her cigarette on to the floor.

'Actually, the Savoy don't do tempura, unfortunately.'

'It's a saveloy in batter,' Miss Beehive droned.

'Oh, I see. Not familiar with that, I'm afraid, but . . .'

'It's a sausage, quite nice actually. Can I have another three?' mumbled Jeanine, but her mouth was full of batter bits and curry sauce, so neither Liam nor anyone else could understand her.

'I'm sure it's delicious,' he declared. 'Do you have any chilli oil?'

'Ketchup.' The chip shop assistant pointed towards a plastic bottle in the shape of a tomato. It was crusty round the top. She retrieved the evil-looking battered saveloy from the cabinet and put it on a paper plate.

'How charming,' said Liam, studying the tomato ketchup dispenser. 'Quite Dali-esque.'

Brrng, brrng. It was his mobile.

Liam began to have a noisy argument. '. . . Yes, well, maybe thirty-five thousand is a lot for the Croydon Playhouse, but, darling, you know I simply can't get out of bed for less than forty K a week.'

He took the paper plate off the top of the counter. 'What do you mean, Prince Charming? I'm not playing Prince Charming! That lovely director, what's his name? . . . Sam, yes Sam Mendes. Well *he* promised me Fairy Godmother . . . I'm sure Anita Harris would understand. You can manage it, darling, bye.'

Liam snapped his phone shut.

'One pound ten,' said Fag Ash Lil.

Liam looked blank. Like the Queen, he didn't carry cash.

Jeanine put down her chips momentarily and rifled through her pockets. As she did so, Liam's phone rang again. He walked towards the door.

'Olivia! Darling! How are you? . . . Me? Fine. Ooh, but there's so much to tell you. Now where do I start . . .'

Siobhan crouched over her laptop, typing. Since Jack's message asking for help, they had been bouncing e-mails back and forth like shuttlecocks over a badminton net. Jack was indeed in trouble. One of the many bored housewives whose guttering he had cleared, so to speak, had recently given birth. She was now alleging that Jack was the father of the child. If he didn't agree to pay her a hefty monthly maintenance, she was threatening to shop him to the papers and the CSA.

The reason Jack had come to Siobhan was, basically, because he had no one else to turn to. She was honest and dependable and he didn't think she would judge him. And he was right. Siobhan might have been rubbish at sorting her own life out, but she was a fantastic friend to have in a crisis. There was a reason for that. By focusing on other people's problems, it meant she didn't have to confront her own.

Siobhan had been rather pleased that Jack had contacted her. Not pleased at his predicament, obviously. But pleased he'd chosen to confide in her. She decided they had to act quickly. As a first step to pulling himself out of the quicksand he was now sinking into, she told him he had to demand a paternity test. So panicked had he been by his situation, he hadn't even thought of that. That had been five days ago. Thanks to the wonders of medical science it was possible to get a resolution that fast. Now he was e-mailing Siobhan with the results.

Siobhan squinted in the sunlight. She was sitting at a little table on a balcony that overlooked the back of the villa. Below, she could see Beth and Stanley splashing in the pool. Their happy laughter bounced off the hillside like a tennis ball against a brick wall and flew back at them, magnified, before funnelling upwards to Siobhan. It was such a simple and joyous scene, it seemed a good omen.

Siobhan double-clicked on Jack's message.

'good news. i'm not a dad. have a thirst quencher on me. jack X.'

Siobhan's smile stretched from ear to ear. 'Yes!' she exclaimed.

'What?' Beth shouted up. 'You sound like you've won the lottery.'

And that was how Siobhan felt. She was delighted for Jack, and just as delighted to have played a part in his narrow escape from disaster. Still, she wasn't about to tell Beth or Olivia that. She knew their opinion of him. After Simon and Kyle and Darren, Siobhan didn't think she was ready for any more lectures.

'It's nothing,' she shouted down to Beth.

Beth shook her head in bemusement and went back to bouncing Stanley in the water.

It had only been a few days, but Siobhan could sense a growing relationship between herself and Jack. At the moment it was just a cyber-friendship, but it was building. That was why she felt so relieved. Had Jack been the father of the baby, Siobhan would have had to confront his reputation head on. This way, she could push that to the back of her mind and just deal with the kind, sensitive, funny person she was getting to know via e-mail.

'Mama, mama!' shouted Stanley as he splashed happily in his water wings.

'Yes, yes. Well done,' said Beth, holding him under his arms.

Siobhan shut the laptop and made a mental note to pull herself together. A few e-mails does not a relationship make. Besides, now the crisis was over, she'd probably never hear from Jack again.

Olivia was standing in the kitchen of the villa. It was early, sixish. The sun, just rising, was casting a mute, greyish light over the garden. The children were still asleep and the house was quiet. Olivia was pouring hot water from the kettle into a mug with a tea bag in it.

'Can you make me one?' asked Colin.

Olivia flinched. She hadn't expected to see anyone. 'What are you doing up?' she asked.

'Oh, you know. What about you?'

'Just thinking.'

'Now, that can be dangerous,' he said, smiling.

Olivia looked at Colin. He was leaning against the kitchen worktop. His back was bent and he had one foot crossed over the other. She'd seen him stand like this a million times before. But now everything was different.

'I think we should talk,' Colin said.

Olivia smiled. Colin definitely was gay. No straight man ever offered to *talk*.

'What?' asked Colin, intrigued.

'Nothing. Yes, I think we should talk too.'

'Shall we go outside?'

Colin opened the French windows on to the balcony. They each pulled out an iron chair as quietly as possible and sat down. At first they just absorbed the view. Then Colin started to speak.

'I didn't expect it to be like this,' he said, his tone quiet, measured and reflective. 'I thought that when I came out – God, I hate that phrase – I'd feel ecstatic, you know, like those people who walk across hot coals.'

'And you don't?'

'It's complicated. I'm glad I've finally been honest. But I feel sort of lost. Confused. I suppose you can't just switch off how you feel about someone.'

'What do you mean?'

'I miss you.'

Olivia shook her head in disbelief. 'You miss me! You are the one who's turned our lives upside down. It wasn't my idea. Anyway, how can you miss me when you've got your boyfriend living with us?'

'Oh, do you want him to move out? I thought you were fine, but if you're not . . .'

'No, no, it's OK. It's just it's going to take a bit of getting used to. The fact that you're gay, I mean.'

'Am I? I wonder.'

'Well, it's a bit late to have doubts now.'

'I know, I know, but I don't think it's a case of being straight or gay. I don't think love works like that. I think you fall in love with a person and their gender is sort of accidental. You could have been a man and I'd still have fallen for you.'

'Gee, thanks,' said Olivia.

'What I'm trying to say is, whatever I am, I did love you. I still do.'

Olivia was quiet. There had been one question she had wanted to ask Colin from the moment he told her about Nigel. She hadn't because she was afraid of the answer. She decided to risk it.

'On those rare occasions when we were, you know, making love, was it me you were making love to? Really me? What I mean is – oh God, this is difficult.' She said the next bit in a rush. 'Did you fantasise about men while we were in bed together?'

Colin didn't answer immediately. When he did, he looked anguished. 'Sometimes I thought about, you know, men, but not always. I wanted to feel that way about you, I really did, but it was hard.'

'Or rather, it wasn't,' said Olivia drily.

'I'm sorry.'

There was silence between them. Olivia was working herself up to ask another difficult question.

'Did you know you were gay when we got married?'

Again, Colin paused for what seemed to Olivia like an agonisingly long time.

'Yes,' he said finally. 'But I thought it would go away.'

'Like a cold.'

Colin took Olivia's hand. 'I loved you so much. You were so brilliant and clever. When I met you, I was just bowled over. I didn't want to miss the chance to be with you because of something I thought was less important than you. And the gay thing was less important than you, it was. The thing is, over the years, it got to be not more important exactly, but as important.'

'OK, what about the children then? Did you marry me so you could have them?'

There was another awkward silence. Colin sat back in his chair and avoided Olivia's eye. 'I think one of the reasons I didn't want to be gay, or to admit it, was I knew that would mean I wouldn't be able to have children. I suppose I could have found a friendly lesbian, but I wanted to be a proper dad. So, yes, to be honest, the idea of having children was part of my reason for getting married, but isn't that why everyone gets married, rather than just living together?'

'Yeah, but they do normally want to sleep with their wives for reasons other than procreation.'

'That wasn't the only reason we made love. I did want to make you happy. Anyway, why did you marry me? You must have known, suspected at least.'

'Yeah, I suppose I did. Deep down, anyway. But we seemed so compatible. Should have known that you were really just another girlfriend.'

They smiled at each other and sipped their tea.

'So what's it like being with someone else, then?' asked Olivia.

'Weird. He's certainly a lot more tidy than you are.'

'I am not untidy!' bristled Olivia. 'I'm just not obsessed with putting things away.'

'All right, all right. Anyway, I could ask you the same question. Casanova stayed over again last night, did he?'

'Yes.' Olivia was embarrassed. 'And it feels weird too.'

'Is it good weird or bad weird?'

'Both.'

Olivia and Colin stared out into the morning light and it felt like old times. Almost.

'Changing the subject a bit,' said Colin, 'has Beth decided what she's going to do?'

'No, but I've been having a bit of a think about that. Spoke to Liam today and, well, you know how he is. Mouth like the Mersey Tunnel. Anyway, he says things aren't going well on the show. Anastassia's on the warpath, apparently. Threatening to offer the show's slot to independents, which has given me an idea . . .'

Chapter Nineteen

'D'you think we could really do it?' asked Siobhan, her voice equal parts anxiety and excitement. 'It's a bit of a risk.'

'I know, but can you imagine Karen's face if we did manage to launch a rival show to *On The House*? She'd internally combust,' declared Olivia. 'And let's not forget the Bimboid.'

'Ooh yes,' drooled Beth. 'If they cancelled *On The House*, Chastity would be out of a job. Her five minutes of fame would be cut to two and a half! It's almost worth it for that alone.'

The three of them were silent for a moment. They were sitting round a table set up outside in a part of the garden shaded by lemon trees. The branches were heavy with ripe fruit, impossibly brilliant against dark green, glossy leaves. A gentle breeze made the boughs sway above them, wafting the scent of citrus into the air.

The twins were asleep in a pushchair next to the table and Anouska and Stanley were both upstairs having a nap. Before she'd had Stanley, Beth hadn't realised how precious peace and quiet was. Now that it was so rare, when she got the chance she wallowed in it, sank her tired body into it as if it were a vat of chocolate mousse.

The debris of lunch littered the table. A loaf of coarse rustic bread that dried out too quickly in the sun sat next to a dish of unsalted butter. Plum tomatoes, the colour of a London bus, were sliced up in a bowl and speckled with shards of basil leaf. Chunks of mozzarella as soft and white as cotton wool nestled in among the tomatoes, soaking up a vivid green puddle of olive oil.

From the other end of the garden, they could just hear the distant strains of splashing and laughter from the pool as Seth, Colin and Nigel played a noisy game of piggy in the middle.

'Daddee, daddee!' squealed Seth as he threw a ball to Colin.

Olivia glanced over at Gianni, who was walking towards them from the kitchen. He was carrying a tray with a pot of coffee and three cups on it. He'd fitted seamlessly into their motley crew, coming over to the villa every day on his Vespa between shifts at the café. The children adored him. He had that natural way with them that only comes from being a member of a large extended family. Gianni was the fifth of nine children.

Gianni put the tray down on the table and smiled at Olivia from under his long eyelashes. Olivia thought how incredibly handsome he was. But he was more than that. Gianni was what used to be called A Good Man. He was honest, straightforward and uncomplicated. The age difference bothered Olivia, but not him. When he said Olivia was beautiful, he meant it. It was strange to be with a man who was so easy-going. Olivia was used to chaps who were in crisis. Had young men actually evolved, or was it to do with him being Italian? Olivia didn't know. Gianni was the most sorted male she'd ever met and the best thing was, it rubbed off on her. The more time she spent with Gianni, the more relaxed she became.

Gianni poured the coffee and they passed the cups round the

table. He bent towards Olivia and kissed her. He had to go back to work.

'Will I see you later?' she asked.

He nodded, then turned to Beth and Siobhan. '*Arrivederci*,' he said.

'Yeah, see you later,' replied Beth and Siobhan.

With a wave, he turned and walked towards the path that ran round to the front of the house. He disappeared, and a moment later they heard the whirr of his Vespa as he cranked it into life, before he roared off down the mountain.

Olivia picked up a copy of *Vogue*. 'Black is back, I see,' she mused. 'I wore loads of black when I was pregnant.'

'So did I. Pointless really,' agreed Beth.

'Yeah, I thought it would make me look thinner. But I just looked like a fat Greek woman. No wonder I was so popular in kebab shops.'

'You went into kebab shops?' gasped Beth.

'A craving, you know. For some women it's pickled onions. I was a walking shish kebab.'

Beth tried to picture Olivia ordering a shish kebab. It was like visualising Victoria Beckham at a jumble sale.

Meanwhile, Siobhan was peering over Olivia's shoulder at her magazine. 'Is that bikini supposed to be that small or do you think she shrank it in the wash?'

'You'd definitely have to have a Brazilian wax, that's for sure,' declared Olivia.

'Why do they call it that, a Brazilian, I mean?'

'Because it's so painful, when you leap off the beautician's table that's where you end up. Brazil,' answered Olivia.

They all laughed.

Then Beth looked serious. 'To get back to the matter in hand, do you really think we can get the *On The House* commission? Even if we do set up our own production company, we'll have no track record, nothing to be judged on. Who's going to take us seriously?'

'Anastassia, for one,' said Olivia. 'We'll come up with such a shit-hot idea for a show, she'll have to.'

Beth and Siobhan looked doubtful.

'Oh, come on, you two,' cajoled Olivia. 'I'm not saying it'll be easy. It'll be bloody difficult, but let's look at our assets. Beth, you know enough about formatting to prepare a treatment for Anastassia to look at.'

Beth nodded.

'And Siobhan, you're our person on the inside,' continued Olivia. 'Do you think once you get back to the office you can put your ear to the ground, find out the state of play with *On The House* and Channel 6?'

Siobhan nodded.

'If Liam's right and Anastassia is going to put the slot out to tender, we need to be first in line.'

'I tell you what, it's mighty handy that you and Liam get on so well. He's going to come in jolly useful,' said Beth.

Olivia smiled. 'Yeah. Perhaps I should get him to divorce his wife and marry me.'

'Is Liam married?' asked Siobhan.

'Oh, yes,' explained Beth. 'He's got a wife and at least five kids he wheels out every so often to impress Middle England.'

'Doesn't sound like much of a life for her,' said Siobhan.

'Oh, I don't know. Big house, loads of money and she gets to change the wallpaper as often as she likes. Sounds all right to me,' Olivia answered.

The sun felt delicious against their bare skin. They tingled with a mix of the temperature and the exhilaration they all felt about their plan.

Olivia broke the atmosphere. 'Shit! We've forgotten one thing.'

'What?' said Siobhan and Beth together.

'Money! We need to know the costings for *On The House*. If we're going to pitch against it, we don't stand a chance if we go in way over Karen.'

'Damn! If only you were still seeing Kevin the Teenager, Siobhan, you could have got him to hack into the office computer,' said Beth.

'Very funny,' said Siobhan. 'But I don't think even a seventeen-year-old techno-whizz—'

'Jesus, is that how old he was!' Olivia exclaimed.

'Yeah, well,' continued Siobhan. 'I doubt even Darren could access Futura Productions' files now. They've just upped the security. Another of Karen's bright ideas.'

There was a glum silence.

'It's so infuriating,' sighed Olivia. 'If only we knew someone with top-level access who might be willing to help us.'

'You mean like a mole?' said Siobhan.

Beth was rummaging in her bag. She pulled out a scrap of paper. 'Thank God I never clean this out.' She waved the piece of paper in triumph. 'Meet our mole.'

'Hello, Marcia? It's Beth Davies. Sorry to call you at home.'

'No, not at all. How are you? It's good to hear from you. Are you OK?'

'Yes, fine. Well, no job, no husband. You probably heard about that.'

'Yes, the party. Sorry.'

There was a pause while Beth plucked up the courage to ask what she needed to. 'Marcia?'

'Yes.'

'You know you said if ever I needed anything?'

'Yes?'

'Well I do. Can I come and see you next week, when I get back from Italy? That's where I'm calling you from, by the way.'

'Ooh, lovely. Whereabouts?'

'Sicily.'

'Never been, but I love those holiday programmes. Always fancied Venice myself—'

Beth interrupted her: 'Yeah, well, can I come and see you?'

'Sorry. Yes. Of course. No problem. But why?'

'I'd rather not say over the phone.'

'Sounds very mysterious. What do you think, Hercule?'

Beth was confused.

'Hercule is one of my teddies. I told you I collect them, didn't I? Well, this one's named after Poirot. You know, Agatha Christie. He's got a little moustache and everything.'

'Oh,' said Beth, momentarily stunned by the notion of a teddy bear dressed to look like Hercule Poirot, and even more stunned by the idea that someone would pay good money to purchase it.

'Hercule says yes.'

Their fate had been decided by a small stuffed toy.

* * *

Siobhan smiled. She had another e-mail from Jack. So he hadn't abandoned her just yet anyway.

'hiya blondie, well, it's all over. she's backed right off since the blood test. dropped the claim completely. what a relief!'

It was funny, but although Siobhan had secretly fancied Jack when they'd worked together, it was only now he'd been in trouble that she'd felt a real connection with him. Olivia would call it Siobhan's hedgehog hospital complex. And she had to admit that, looking at her romantic track record, she did tend to go for the male equivalent of Mrs Tiggywinkle with the broken leg.

Simon might have been successful, professionally speaking, but emotionally he was all over the place. Siobhan hadn't so much been his mistress as his nurse, tending to his damaged ego. Of course, had she thought sensibly about this, she would have told him the first time she'd met him to get off his sick bed and walk – right out the door. Perhaps it was she who was the sick one after all.

Siobhan was determined to break the cycle. No more wounded males. Still, she found herself increasingly drawn to Jack. If she was absolutely honest, she'd enjoyed coming to his rescue. It made her feel important, needed. Wasn't that the definition of co-dependency? Jesus! She had to stop this or she'd end up with Noel Gallagher for a husband, trawling seedy bars trying to prise her drunken spouse off his stool.

Siobhan looked back down at the screen. As she read the rest of Jack's message, a broad smile spread across her face. As it turned out, it wasn't only Jack the woman was blackmailing. *Turning Over A New Leaf* had done a garden makeover round the corner the week after *On The House* were there. Jack's accuser had Bill Patterson round for coffee! And a bit more, it seemed.

Siobhan was staggered. Bill Patterson! To look at him, you wouldn't think he could get up the energy to take his socks off. Siobhan laughed out loud, then put a hand over her mouth to muffle the sound. She was in her bedroom, but Olivia was next door and Beth was just across the hall. She didn't want them to hear. Why tell them when, now that Jack was definitely out of trouble, their little flirtation was sure to come to an end. It had been fun, but it was time to face reality.

Siobhan scrolled up to read the rest of Jack's message.

'when u coming back? thought we cld meet up. what u think?'

There was a sharp intake of breath from Siobhan. Maybe Jack wasn't about to disappear from her life after all – unless she wanted him to.

On the departures board, the dreaded word 'delayed' was flashing up next to their flight. Olivia groaned. Siobhan sighed. Beth steeled herself to cope with a fractious one year old for an extra one hundred and twenty minutes.

They checked in. The woman at the Alitalia desk was wearing a little cap set at a jaunty angle on top of hair ruthlessly pulled back into a ponytail. She took one look at the assorted children and immediately stuck them all right at the back of the plane, next to the loo.

According to Olivia, there was a rule about airlines. When choosing which one to fly, you needed to consider the nation from which it drew its staff. Air stewardesses exhibited the worst national traits in exaggerated form. So, French trolley dollies were vain and only interested in male passengers, and Italian flight attendants were snotty and status-conscious. German hostesses were grim and unsmiling. They'd got the snotty option.

Olivia wanted to say goodbye to Gianni, so Siobhan, Beth, Colin and Nigel went through to departures with the children and installed themselves in a café.

Beth turned to Colin. 'Can I just pop to duty-free? Will you keep an eye on Stanley?'

'Yeah, fine,' he answered.

Beth loved duty-frees, especially at airports on the return leg of a trip. In the same way that it was perfectly acceptable to hoover up every scrap of an in-flight meal, however disgusting, because calories didn't count at high altitude, so using up the last of the foreign currency wasn't really shopping. Euros weren't real money.

Beth wandered round looking at outsize Toblerones, mugs with pictures of gondolas on them and packets of luridly coloured pasta. Then she spotted an aeroplane mobile. Stanley would love that. As she put her hand out to pick up the box, it landed on someone else's who'd got there a microsecond ahead of her.

'I'm so sorry,' Beth said, snatching her hand back.

When she looked up, she felt the blood drain from her face. The hand belonged to Richard.

Neither Richard nor Beth said anything for about twenty seconds. The scene at the party was replaying through both their minds.

Finally, Richard spoke. 'I left a message on the answerphone at home saying I was here. But I don't suppose you got that.'

'No,' said Beth, still stunned.

Richard had the aeroplane box in his hand. 'Thought Stanley might like this. His sort of thing.'

'Yes,' said Beth.

There was another long silence. It was as if their brains were bicycles that had slipped their chains. They were both pedalling wildly, but to absolutely no effect.

With a bit of a jolt, Beth clicked back into gear. 'Sorry, but what the hell are you doing here?' she exclaimed.

'Same thing as you are, I suppose,' Richard answered defensively.

'I needed a break,' Beth said icily.

'Yeah, well, so did I.'

Beth scanned Richard's face. 'This break you needed, was it on your own, or are you here with *her*?'

Richard looked embarrassed. 'Chastity's here, yeah,'

'Don't you mean Linda? Or has she thought up yet another name for herself now? What about Marriage Wrecking Tart, that's a good name, isn't it, Richard?'

Richard flinched, but decided not to react to that. 'You know I don't—'

Beth interrupted him. 'I know, she doesn't mean anything to you. I've heard it, remember? And I didn't believe it then either.'

'But Beth . . .'

'No, Richard. While you're with *her*, I don't want to talk to you. In fact, I don't want to talk to you ever again. From now on, whatever you have to say, say it to my lawyer.'

They were standing facing each other about five feet apart. If this had been *High Noon*, one of them would now have shot the other. 'You've got a lawyer?' said Richard, sounding shocked.

'Well, no, not yet, but you obviously want a divorce, so I think we should just get on with it. No use hanging about, is there?'

'I don't want a divorce. I never wanted a divorce,' Richard replied, taking a step towards Beth.

She stiffened. 'Well, you have a funny way of showing you want to stay married. You're living with your mistress!'

Beth had spotted the essential flaw in Richard's argument. If he loved her, why was he still with Chastity? The answer was that he was in limbo. He desperately wanted Beth to take him back, but couldn't be sure if and when that might happen. So he was hedging his bets.

He knew it was pathetic, but on a purely practical level, he had nowhere else to go. Certainly, he could have rented himself a flat, but that would have been to legitimise the situation. Plus, it would mean removing all his things from the house, which would make it easier for Beth to cut him out of her life. He felt he was still in with a chance of a reconciliation if his shoes remained in the wardrobe.

Richard also had to admit it was convenient to stay with Chastity. After the holiday, they both knew it wasn't going to last, but her flat, if not big, was relatively comfortable. Much more comfortable, anyway, than living on his own in a miserable little bedsit with a twenty-four-inch TV and the smell of other people's cooking coming up the hall.

Richard took another step closer to Beth. He looked anguished. 'I know, but I . . . It's all been such a mistake. I only wanted . . .'

'What? A bit on the side? Well, you had that, didn't you? And now you can have as much of it as you like. You can have a great big dollop of it if you like. A dollop of trollop. That's what you've got. A dollop of trollop. Or isn't it as much fun when it isn't behind my back?'

A shopper with a complexion the colour of gravy browning was pushing a trolley laden with cigarettes and bottles of whisky towards them. '*Prego*,' he said. Beth and Richard flattened themselves against opposite shelves and the Bisto Kid squeezed past.

Richard looked at his watch. He appeared agitated. 'Look, I need to go, but can we talk some more when we get back to London? Sorry, but I only said I'd be gone five minutes.'

Beth exploded. 'Oh, SHE'S waiting for you, is she? Well we wouldn't want to inconvenience HER, would we?'

Richard attempted to head off the now inevitable scene. 'No, it's just, well, she's not like you. She can be a bit, er, you know, highly strung.'

Richard's attempt to damp things down had the opposite effect. It was as if he'd poured a jug of water on a chip-pan fire. Beth was incandescent.

'Oh, highly strung, is she? Sure you're not talking about what she looks like when she's hitched up her G-string, the one men shove tenners down?'

Richard's mouth opened, but nothing came out.

'And what do you mean, she's not like me? What am I like then?'

Richard said nothing.

'Well, what *am* I like?'

'Oh, you know,' said Richard, fully aware that he was now wading through shark-infested waters with the equivalent of a sirloin steak strapped to his chest. 'You're, well, *not highly strung*.'

'And?' said Beth. 'Come on. I'm waiting for your deep insight into my character.'

'What do you want me to say?'

'The truth would be a start. Do you think you could manage that?'

Richard winced. 'You're strong, sensible, you're—'

'Dull, you mean I'm dull, don't you?'

Before Richard could contradict her, Beth had spotted a display of novelty liqueur chocolates, packaged to look as if they were stored in miniature oak casks. She marched up to them, swung her shopping basket and knocked them flying. 'Is that too dull for you?' she shrieked.

'No, no,' shouted Richard. 'I never said you were dull. You said that, not me.'

Beth wasn't listening. She had moved on to a shelf of dolls dressed in Italian football kit. With one arm out, as if directing traffic, she swept along scattering soccer players in all directions.

'Still dull, Richard?' she bellowed.

By now, staff had noticed the commotion and were massing on the periphery.

'Beth, stop, please. Really. I don't think you're dull,' begged Richard.

But it was too late. Beth's eyes were wild as they settled upon a huge tower of salami. Richard watched aghast as she began to jog towards this homage to saturated fat. With both hands, she shoved. The tower crumbled and the floor became a sea of rolling sausages, like felled trees bobbing down a river.

'I'm sorry. I'm sorry. What else can I say?' pleaded Richard. 'I'm crap and useless and a bastard and everything. But I love you. I really do.'

Beth's eyes met Richard's.

'I've made the biggest mistake of my life,' he continued. 'I want to try and make it up to you, if you'll let me.'

'Before you do that, signor, perhaps you'd like to accompany the signora to the manager's office,' said an officious Italian voice.

Beth and Richard turned to see a large security guard wearing epaulettes and a peaked cap. There was another behind him. The first approached Beth, slipped one arm through hers and placed a hand on her back. The other put a hand on Richard's shoulder. Then they set off in convoy through the store.

'Well, um, this is it, I suppose,' said Olivia. 'It's been fun, but, well, all good things come to an end, you know.'

'Why you do thees?' said Gianni.

'What?'

'Pretend ees not serious between us.'

Gianni and Olivia were hovering next to the sign pointing the way to departures. Olivia was aware that in two hours she'd be back in England. It would probably be cold and rainy and Gianni and Sicily would seem a long way off.

Yes, she felt something for Gianni, but she wasn't about to make a fool of herself. She'd read those articles about sad middle-aged women falling for lithe African tribesmen, selling their suburban semis and moving into mud huts, only for their tribal lover to reveal he had eight other wives. She didn't think Gianni had a brace of spouses tucked away somewhere, but she was determined not to get caught up in a romantic fantasy.

'Oh, come on, Gianni. You're a good-looking guy of twenty-four. You can have anyone. You don't want a thirty-nine-year-old married, technically anyway, mother of four. We've had a great time, but let's not kid ourselves.'

'*Mi amore*. I love you, Oleevia.'

'I bet you say that to all the girls.'

Gianni shook his head. He was angry. '*Basta!* You have no respect for me! You think I do thees with every lady who come in the bar?'

'I don't know, do I?'

'You do know. You know me.'

Olivia wanted to say: 'Yes, and I love you, too.' Instead she said nothing. This was Olivia's chance to take a chance, but when it came to it, she couldn't. She was afraid of looking ridiculous.

Gianni shook his head sadly. He didn't say goodbye.

Karen put her dumb-bell down on a cushion trimmed with pink marabou. It was sitting, in perfect alignment, on top of a mound of co-ordinating grey and pink pillows and cushions. These were piled up on top of Karen's grey-wool-covered bed, the corners as crisp as a sheaf of photocopy paper. Another identical cushion tower sat next to it. They looked like twin stacks of brightly coloured French toast. Only a woman without children or a sex life could ever have managed this uncompromising degree of soft furnishing perfection.

But then, only a woman without a sex life would keep dumb-bells in the bedroom, or at least use them for something other than a doorstop. Karen kept a full set right next to her bed, just in case of a spare few minutes. She stared down at the note in front of her: 4.3 million. That was all it said. But it was enough. For *On The House* to achieve ratings of only 4.3 million was as good as announcing that the show's slot was now officially up for grabs.

If Futura lost the commission, then Karen could kiss goodbye to her career. She could see it now. The calls of commiseration and concern from colleagues in the industry, when secretly they'd be engaged in a feeding frenzy for *On The House*'s prime-time slot. Well, it wasn't going to happen. Karen retrieved her dumb-bell and began doing frenzied bicep curls. She was going to make sure she got another series of *On The House*. Whatever it took.

After twenty minutes and about half a box of hankies, Beth managed to persuade the manager of the duty-free store that she wasn't a criminal. Still, it took a lot of talking and a very large swipe of the credit card before he would let her and Richard go. Richard offered to pay, but Beth refused.

'I don't need your money. I don't need anything from you,' she said.

Once outside, she calmed down and they both hovered awkwardly.

'Hadn't you better run along? She'll be waiting,' Beth hissed sarcastically.

Richard nodded. 'Yeah,' but he didn't move.

Neither did Beth. Richard studied his shoes. Beth picked at a bit of fluff on her jumper. They both waited for the other to speak. Finally, Beth turned and walked away. Richard stood and watched her go.

'Sorry for the delay, ladies and gentlemen, but we'll be underway very shortly. So, if you'd just like to sit back and relax, our excellent cabin staff will do everything they can to make sure you have an enjoyable flight.'

Beth shifted Stanley on her lap so his weight didn't cut off the circulation in one leg. He murmured in protest, then fell back to sleep again. She glanced at Siobhan across the aisle. Had the pilot's announcement reminded her of Simon? Beth sighed. Please God, let Stanley stay asleep for the next two and a half hours. The odds on that happening were about the same as those on Julio Iglesias joining Black Sabbath. Still, she could hope.

Next to her, Olivia was quiet. She had Mia on her lap and she was rocking her gently. Daisy was being looked after by Colin, who was sat next to the window. Across the aisle, with Siobhan and Nigel, were Seth and Anouska, partially buried under a fast-accumulating pile of discarded toys.

As they'd boarded, Olivia had nudged Beth and pointed out a couple in First Class. They were travelling with children too, only they'd booked them into Economy along with the nanny. Beth could feel one of the little horrors hammering the seat in front of her with his little fists. She shut her eyes and tried not to imagine herself armed with a sub-machine-gun. Come the revolution, all people who earned over fifty grand would be forced to endure the behaviour of their own offspring on planes.

Beth began to doze. Half an hour into the flight, she was vaguely aware of Stanley wriggling. She put a protective hand on his tummy in an effort to calm him. He wriggled even more. Then an unmistakable aroma wafted up to her. He needed changing.

When Harry Houdini managed his famous trick of escaping from chains and padlocks while in a tank full of water, no one had yet come up with the challenge of trying to change a baby's nappy in an aeroplane loo. Beth struggled to keep a squealing Stanley still while she negotiated her tiny space. She had to remove one nappy, put that in a nappy sack, wipe him clean, put the wipes in the sack, tie it up, apply cream to Stanley's clean bottom, unfold a fresh nappy, put it on and refasten his clothes. All in a space only big enough to accommodate Elle McPherson's right buttock.

Midway through Beth's tricky procedure, there was a knock on the door.

'Just a minute,' she yelled, as Stanley placed one foot in the tub of nappy cream and then smeared the contents all over her trousers.

There was another, firmer knock.

'I said I'll be out in a minute!' Beth shouted, silently cursing, trying to hold Stanley down and wipe her trousers at the same time.

At the third knock, she lost her temper. She struggled to her feet and pulled back the door. 'Can't you see I'm—'

She stopped. Richard was standing in front of her.

'Dada,' said Stanley excitedly.

'I saw you go down the aisle and I followed you,' said Richard, pushing his way into the tiny loo before she could protest. 'At least this is one place you can't get away. We need to sort this out.'

Beth was staggered into silence by his gall. Also, with three people in such a small space, there didn't seem enough oxygen for them all to breathe and speak at the same time.

Stanley was shouting: 'Dada, dada.'

'Hello, Stanley, Yes, it's Dada. Have you missed me?' said Richard.

That snapped Beth out of her torpor. 'Don't. Just don't,' she hissed. 'Don't even think about using Stanley to guilt me out that you haven't seen him. You are the one who had the affair, remember.'

'I know.' Richard looked directly at Beth. 'I meant everything I said, you know. I do love you.'

'Yeah, well, maybe.' Beth wasn't really listening. She could hear noise outside the cubicle.

'Well, I saw a man AND a woman go in there!' said an appalled female voice not unlike Margaret Rutherford at her most strident. 'Goodness knows what they're getting up to!'

There was a sharp rap on the door. 'Excuse me. You, in there. This is the senior cabin stewardess. Would you come out immediately!'

Beth and Richard exchanged horrified looks.

There was another rap on the door. 'Hello! Hello!' said the stewardess. 'You in there. We know what you're up to!'

'They're definitely in there. I heard NOISES,' the appalled woman exclaimed. 'It's disgusting!'

There was nothing for it. Richard slid open the door and squeezed himself out.

The stewardess gave him a cold stare. 'If you'd like to return to your seat, sir.'

Beth followed with Stanley. She got an even colder look.

'Madam.'

As Beth made her humiliating progress past the queue, she heard the appalled woman say: 'And in front of a baby, too. You expect that sort of thing on a charter flight. But this is scheduled!'

When she got to her seat, Richard was waiting for her. 'Please, will you call me when we get back to London?'

Beth was exhausted. 'I don't know,' she said.

The stewardess was now right behind Richard. 'Haven't you inconvenienced enough of your fellow passengers already? You're blocking the aisle and we are about to start dinner service. Please return to your seat, sir.'

Richard walked sheepishly up the gangway and pushed open the little curtain that separates First from Economy. Beth couldn't believe it. He and the Bimboid were in First! She sat down and put Stanley back on her lap, then clipped her seat belt shut with so much force, she virtually severed a finger.

The food trolley began its slow progress to the back of the plane. When it reached Olivia and Beth's assorted party, the only thing left was the vegetarian selection. This was pretty similar to the normal meal, only the chocolate was missing.

'I mean,' said Olivia in a huff, 'since when did a veal calf die to produce a bloody After Eight!'

When the drinks came round, a good twenty minutes after the meal, by which time Beth's mouth was so dry she could have sanded a table with her tongue, the stewardess handed her a napkin.

'The, er, gentleman in First asked me to give you this,' she whispered.

Beth unfolded the napkin. 'I love you,' it said in shaky biro. Underneath, in brackets, presumably to avoid confusion lest she was deluged with tissue declarations of devotion, he'd added the word 'Richard'. The biro had run out before the end, so the last letter of his name was simply scratched into the paper. What it actually said was 'Richar', which, considering where he was sitting, was apt, Beth felt.

The napkin lay open in the palm of Beth's hand. Her first instinct was to screw it up into a very small ball, but she didn't.

She folded it up and put it in her handbag. She didn't know if there was a future for her and Richard, but she wasn't willing to rule it out. Yet.

Chapter Twenty

The drizzle was unrelenting. It seeped through Beth's showerproof mac – what sort of shower was it proof against? Asteroid? – and made her skin feel clammy. She trudged on, every so often consulting her A to Z, then trudging on some more.

When she arrived at Marcia's, she was not at her best. Marcia was ebullient, however.

'Come in, come in,' she chirruped happily. 'Is it very wet? Let me get you a camomile tea.'

Beth declined and Marcia went off to try to rustle up a shot of caffeine. Beth was left to marvel at Marcia's idea of interior decoration. Her front room was like something your granny might live in. The sofa was sage-green Dralon, with white antimacassars trimmed with crochet draped over the back and arms.

The carpet was also green, as was the patterned wallpaper, not that you could see much of that. Every inch of wall space was covered in shelves. On them sat teddy bear after teddy bear. There was the occasional break in the animal theme. Marcia also appeared to collect miniature pottery country cottages – there must have been forty of these – and plates decorated with small rosy-cheeked children in Victorian dress. It was clear that she didn't spend money on clothes and now Beth knew why. She was obviously blowing all her salary in the back pages of the Sunday supplements.

Marcia returned and gestured for Beth to sit down.

'It's a very, um, comprehensive collection,' said Beth, waving her hand in the direction of the teddies.

'Oh, do you think so?' said Marcia, sounding pleased.

They both sipped their drinks, with Beth trying to work out how to broach the subject she had come to talk about. In the end, she decided to just plunge in.

'You know you said if there was ever anything you could do, I was to call you?'

'Yes,' said Marcia.

'And you also know that I haven't got a job.'

Marcia placed her cup and saucer on a patch of cream crochet, nodding as she did so.

'Well, in the spirit of DIY, you might say, we, that is me, Siobhan and Olivia, have decided to do it ourselves. We're going to pitch for a DIY show. We want to launch a rival bid for the *On The House* slot.'

There was silence. Beth wondered whether Marcia had heard, or perhaps she'd heard and not understood; with all those teddies, she'd got kapok on the brain.

'And you need someone on the inside to help you with the money aspect, so you can match or even undercut the Futura offer?' Marcia was looking right at Beth. 'You need someone to access confidential computer files to bring you detailed costings and keep you apprised of any secret memos and minutes of meetings between Futura and Channel 6?'

Marcia had heard and understood, and if she had anything on the brain, it wasn't kapok. Underneath the frumpy clothes and the teddy bear addiction, there was a streak of pure steel.

'No problem,' she continued.

It was as simple as that. Marcia James, loyal secretary to Patric Mortimer for twelve years, had taken about ten seconds to agree to betray him. Beth had thought she would need some persuading.

'I don't understand,' said Beth.

'It's not difficult to understand. I said I'd help you,' declared Marcia.

'But why?'

'Because you asked me.'

'Yeah, but . . .'

'I have a price. If you get the commission, I want to be production manager.'

Beth looked surprised. 'I still don't understand.'

'Look,' said Marcia, 'I know that everyone thinks I'm the sad little secretary in the beige cardi.' She looked directly at Beth. 'Even you.'

'No, no. I don't,' Beth said, feeling guilty for all the things she'd said and thought about Marcia in the past.

'It doesn't matter,' said Marcia, waving Beth's guilt away. 'For twelve years I have done my job. I have typed Patric's letters for him, kept his diary, done his expenses, booked tickets for the theatre and bought presents for his wife. I have reminded him when it's his wedding anniversary, arranged family holidays, picked up his dry-cleaning, organised his *lunches* . . .'

Beth raised an eyebrow at the mention of Patric's lunches. They all knew about those. He was notorious for lunchtime shag sessions at the Milton.

'Every morning for twelve years I have placed a cappuccino and a lightly toasted smoked salmon bagel, no butter, lemon juice and black pepper, on his desk. Well, I've had enough.'

'I don't know what to say,' gasped Beth.

It had never occurred to Beth before, but the relationship between boss and secretary, the office marriage, had to be the only sort of matrimony totally untouched by the feminism of the last thirty years. No wonder male executives fought tooth and nail to hang on to their PAs. They'd never get that degree of geisha devotion at home.

'I have given up birthdays to attend vital meetings. I have spent Christmases feeding his children's guinea pigs while he's been sunning himself abroad. I have worked weekends and evenings. I have missed parties and weddings. I have cancelled dates so many times they stopped asking.'

Marcia paused, allowing Beth the time to take in the idea that she might have been asked on dates at all.

'I wasn't always like this, you know. I used to have a life outside work. But I gave that up for Patric,' continued Marcia. 'You know, sometimes I think he doesn't even see me. To him I am not a woman. I am not even a human being. I am just his efficient little ghost.'

This whole speech was delivered in the same quiet, even tone Marcia always used. She didn't get hysterical, or angry, or tearful. She could have been reciting the stationery order.

'And what do I get in return?' she continued. 'A pair of oven gloves.'

'Sorry?' said Beth.

'Oven gloves. That's what he gave me last Christmas. His wife

338

had chosen them, of course. And wrapped them. When he wraps something, it looks like he's wrestled it. It's all crumpled. And he uses half a roll of Sellotape. That's why I do most of that as well.'

Beth was totally nonplussed.

'I don't cook. He knows I don't cook and he gave me oven gloves. After twelve years, he can't be bothered to choose me something that I might actually like. Anyway, when I got the oven gloves, that was it. I've been looking for a way out ever since. You've just provided it.'

Beth was suddenly aware of the enormity of the betrayal she was asking of Marcia. 'Are you sure? If Patric or Karen find out you're helping us, you'll get the push too. Twelve years is a long time.'

'Yes, it is. Too long,' said Marcia.

By the time Beth left, she had entrusted all their futures to Marcia. She didn't know if she was right to do so. Marcia had revealed a ruthless streak. She could just as easily use this to play double agent. They were taking a heck of a risk on a woman who still remained largely a mystery to all of them.

Siobhan didn't know what she'd been expecting, but it definitely wasn't this. She did a slow 360-degree turn to take in her surroundings. The walls were covered with paintings. Huge canvases of gentle country landscapes jostled for space with small delicate watercolours of flowers and animals. More canvases were propped against the walls. Tubes of paint and pots stuffed with brushes of all sizes littered every flat surface.

'Here's your cranberry juice,' Jack said, handing her a glass.

'I had no idea that you painted.'

Jack had on a T-shirt covered in multicoloured smudges where he had wiped his brushes. His hands were encrusted with more paint. It had sunk into the crevices round his nails, so they looked as if they'd been outlined with felt tip. More paint had run up his arm to his elbow. Even his face was daubed; one eyebrow was red, the other green. Siobhan looked at Jack and thought he'd never looked so attractive.

'Nobody does,' replied Jack. 'I kind of like to keep it private.'

Siobhan did another turn round the room with her eyes. The pictures had a sweetness, a delicacy that was totally at odds with the Jack Taylor the public had come to know. If he was glib and a bit mouthy, his paintings were minutely observed and thoughtful.

'They're beautiful, just beautiful,' she gushed. 'How long have you been painting?'

'Years. I went to art school and I was going to do it professionally, but it's kind of hard to make a living at it.'

Siobhan had thought she'd got used to Jack surprising her. But once again he'd managed to totally confound her preconceptions. She would never have guessed in a million years that beneath the happy-go-lucky, one-of-the-guys-down-the-pub exterior, there was a sensitive artist. It made her wonder what else she'd got wrong about him.

Then, as she wandered round the room sipping her cranberry juice and looking closely at the pictures, something suddenly struck her. In all the images of the great outdoors, of nature and wildlife, not one was Australian. She wasn't expecting kangaroos-a-go-go, but it was odd that there was no reference to Australia at all.

'Can I ask you something?' Siobhan ventured. 'They're very English. Why haven't you painted any of your home?'

'England is my home.'

'Well it is now, but—'

'Lunch is ready,' announced Jack, changing the subject abruptly. 'Shall we go into the other room?'

Siobhan felt guilty. Jack's painting was obviously very personal to him. She had trespassed too heavily upon it. Still, as she followed Jack into the kitchen, she felt just a niggle of doubt.

Karen surveyed her staff. 'So good of you all to join me,' she said, a notable lack of fluffiness in her voice. The marabou-trimmed gloves had come off.

'As you will be aware, last week's figures were not good. Not good at all. Unfortunately, this means that, as of yesterday, Channel 6 is accepting rival bids for our slot.'

She paused for the full impact of this statement to sink in.

'*On The House* is no longer the only game in town. We have competition.'

Karen's gaze swept around the room like one of those search-lights they used to have to prevent Communist refuseniks scaling the Berlin Wall. There was no way anyone was getting out of this meeting either, although several people looked like they dearly wanted to make a run for it. Chief among them was Olivia.

Siobhan had taken the day off, claiming she had heartburn. In fact, Olivia suspected that she was avoiding telling Karen about her pregnancy. Anyway, with Beth gone and Siobhan out of the office, Olivia felt lonely. She glanced over at Saffron, and did a double take. Was there less of her these days? She certainly seemed to have shed a few pounds lately. Her clothes had also undergone a bit of a transformation. Saffron had on another of her new

T-shirts. This one said: 'Come here Big Boy!' Olivia winced.

Next to Saffron, Chastity was only dimly aware that her vertical career trajectory was in severe danger of plunging in the opposite direction. She was too busy playing with her hair, twiddling a strand round her finger, and retrieving a text message from her phone. It wasn't from Richard, things between them now being at best strained. As far as Chastity was concerned, Richard had out-stayed his welcome. She'd put up with him if she had to, but only as a stopgap before her next mission came to fruition. And she already had her next target in sight. This time she was really aiming high. Chastity's new male project was a very big fish indeed.

Elsewhere, the atmosphere was tense. This was a room full of people whose entire future depended on what happened to *On The House*. Even Liam's usual ebullience was muffled by the overwhelming sense of failure hanging over the crowd. He was the only one among them to be totally unfazed whatever happened. He had so many other irons in so many other fires, he could have run up an entire set of garden furniture and still have enough left over for a new garden gate.

Karen was speaking again. 'I am not a woman who likes to lose,' she announced. 'Correction. I am not a woman who loses. Full stop. So, I have a plan for a new show to replace *On The House* next season.'

Olivia was thinking about another plan. Their plan. They still didn't have a format, or a presenter, or anything concrete at all. Could they really take on Karen and win?

'At the moment, I'm keeping things under wraps,' continued Karen. 'Careless talk costs lives and all that. But, believe you me, it'll blow everyone else out of the water.'

* * *

Beth examined her complexion in the mirror.

'Are you sure this is how it's supposed to look?' she asked nervously.

'Of course!' declared Mira.

Beth knew this woman's name was Mira because the moment she'd stepped across the threshold of swishy cosmetics emporium Skin, she'd been greeted by a tall, fearsomely well-groomed woman announcing: 'My name is Mira.' Greeted was not quite the right word, however. With one look, Beth had been assessed, from the price of her haircut to whether her shoes needed reheeling. Not since she had had her hair picked through with a metal nit comb by the school nurse had she had such a thorough once-over.

Skin was a chain of shops selling upmarket make-up and hair unguents, with the odd scented candle thrown in for that added bit of holistic pretentiousness. Still, the real point of Skin was the staff. They took the concept of the terrifying cosmetics counter assistant to new heights.

These were no frumpy department store harridans. They were living, breathing paeans to cool. Their clothes were black, their hair discreet. They wore the sort of barely there make-up that is really, really hard to do. Some of them also wore deliberately ugly glasses as a way to demonstrate their commitment to fashion. They were scary.

Beth had only gone in for a new mascara, but, under Mira's stern gaze, had ended up having a complete makeover, Now, she was reviewing the results. The most striking feature of her new face was the foundation. It looked greasy.

Beth screwed up her courage. 'Don't you think the foundation—'

Mira interrupted her. 'Base. We call it the base.'

Twenty minutes ago, Beth had thought a base was something the army lived in. Mira had put her right on that, like so much else.

'OK, I mean the base,' continued Beth. 'Don't you think it's a bit, um, shiny?'

Mira sighed and rolled her eyes to the ceiling as if trying to explain to a five year old that if she kept throwing Barbie's pony on the floor then of course one of the legs would break off.

'Matt base is so eighties,' she said in a tone that could have frozen water at ten paces. 'This is so much more *current.*'

'Yes, but I look sweaty,' said Beth, standing her ground.

'The finish we're going for is a soft sheen.'

Beth was sure she had a can of furniture polish at home called that. But she knew there was little point in mentioning this. Instead she simply said: 'Oh, right.'

Beth didn't know why she was bothering buying make-up anyway. It wasn't as if her meeting with Richard was a date. It was more the opening of peace talks between two opposing parties. Even had Tony Blair found the time to helicopter himself in and make a scripted off-the-cuff appeal for resolution, there was absolutely no guarantee they'd reach an agreement.

The last thing Beth wanted was for Richard to think that she'd made an effort. That would be like placing a plate of egg and chips in front of his ego. She was tempted to put on an old jumper and not wash her hair. Then again, she didn't want him to think she'd let herself go either. That would be like replacing his ego's egg and chips with a lobster and a half-bottle of champagne. It was a tricky call to make.

She scrambled off her impossibly high stool. This had no back and nowhere to hook your feet, so you felt especially vulnerable and therefore more receptive to the Skin sales pitch. Then she followed Mira up to the counter and paid for her new look, the price of which would have brought her out in a sweat even if the make-up hadn't achieved that effect all on its own.

'Hello, Marcia?' It was Patric, sounding businesslike. 'Could you book the Milton for lunch?'

'Yes, Patric,' said Marcia.

'Twelve thirty-ish?'

'Of course.' Marcia paused. 'Your usual room?'

In the time Marcia had worked for Patric, she had booked him hundreds of 'lunches'. The routine was always the same. He rang her at about 10.30. She then booked Room 112 at the Milton. Always the Milton. Always Room 112. She didn't know if there was anything special about Room 112, never having stepped across the threshold herself. Maybe he liked the pattern on the bedspread, or the view was especially good from the window, not that she thought he had much time to enjoy either.

Patric always left for his lunches at 12.25. The Milton was only round the corner. He was back at his desk by half one. One hour five minutes exactly. If anyone could write the definitive book on time management it was the persistent adulterer. Marcia had sometimes wondered if Patric managed to squeeze a bite to eat into his sixty-five-minute assignations. It seemed doubtful. He had never asked her to organise so much as a round of sandwiches. He evidently regarded his company as sustenance enough.

So who was the latest female to receive the Room 112 treatment? Marcia cast her eye, metaphorically, over the female staff of

Futura. When she'd first worked for Patric he'd been quite adventurous. Waitresses, barmaids, senior television executives, he'd shagged them all. These days, however, he'd become lazy. He preferred to keep things in-house. It meant he didn't have to try too hard. He could use his boss's status to dazzle them into removing their underwear.

That Patric's conquests remained relatively discreet about his behaviour was down to two things. First, he only chose the newest, youngest and most naive members of staff. He was then adept at making them feel special so that, even after he'd moved on to the next, they still felt a bit like teacher's pet. Second, there was the embarrassment factor. Once a new recruit realised that she was not alone in having attracted Patric's attention and that, indeed, sleeping with him was tantamount to a Futura initiation rite, she was mortified. She didn't hate Patric enough to want to expose him and she despised herself too much to want to go public.

Word inevitably got round, however, and a strange sort of sisterhood had grown up between Patric's ex-squeezes. They even had a nickname for him. Marcia had heard them giggling about it. 'Mr Twenty Minutes' they called him. Marcia presumed that was how long he took, which didn't sound like much to boast about. But perhaps it was a very good twenty minutes.

'Marcia?' Patric wasn't finished.

'Yes?'

'Can you remind the Milton not to—'

'I know,' interrupted Marcia. 'Not to put a mint on the pillow.'

'Yeah. They forgot last time. Melted everywhere.'

It was definite then. Whoever she was was getting *lunch*, but not lunch.

* * *

Oona Kirkpatrick scanned the menu.

'So, how are you – haven't seen you since the transmission party? asked Liam, knowing it was a leading question. Oona was always on one diet or another.

'Well, I am detoxing,' she said. 'That means no wheat, no dairy, no salt, no spices, nothing fried, chargrilled, or boiled for more than ninety seconds. No tomatoes, peppers, oranges or lemons, no fat, obviously, but I can have asparagus. Oh, yes, and I have to take these.'

Oona put her handbag on the table and began pulling packets and jars out of it. 'That's kelp, that's green tea extract and that's African tree bark. Those people with the very long necks and lots of jewellery have ben using it for centuries, apparently, and, I mean, in all those documentaries, have you ever seen one of them with water retention?'

Liam shook his head.

'Exactly!'

The table was now crowded with pills and potions. 'Then there are the colonic irrigation sussions. I have them daily, after I've drunk my eight pints of water. And, naturally, I have my weekly vitamin injections. According to my nutritionist, I'm not fat. This . . .' Oona grabbed an handful of tummy, '. . . is an allergic reation.'

Yeah, to chocolate, thought Liam. But he didn't say it. He couldn't get a word in edgeways.

Oona had barely drawn breath since she and Liam walked into the restaurant. She was one of his closest friends, and also a superb source of gossip, which was why Liam entertained her little

347

foibles. When the waiter arrived, they ordered herring sashima, a bowl of vegetable broth each and something creative with potato.

'So how's it going otherwise, Oona?' asked Liam. 'Workwise, I mean.'

'Oh, you know. The usual. *Celebrity Squares*, *Celebrity Ready Steady Cook*, *Celebrity Sleepover*, *Celebrity Who Wants To Be A Millionaire*, *Celebrity Weakest Link* and *Songs of Praise* have all been on to my agent. Oh yes, and I had a call from your lot.'

The food arrived. Two doll-size bowls of coloured water and three huge square plates with about a tablespoon of something evil-looking in the middle of a page from *Das Kapital*.

'You know what. I'm not that hungry,' said Liam.

'No, this detox thing really kills your appetite. I feel so cleansed I don't want to disturb my chi by putting food inside me. Then again . . .' Oona took her fork and dug it into one of the grey piles.

'Anyway,' said Liam, 'what were you saying about being approached by my lot? Do you mean *On The House*?'

'Yes,' said Oona, between chews. 'Someone called Karen. Wanted to know if I was interested in being a celebrity guest on the new series.'

'Celebrity guest?'

'Yeah, she's asking everyone. The idea, apparently, is to shoot it at a celebrity home and then all that celebrity's celebrity friends pop in to help with the DIY. And it's all filmed. There is also the suggestion we bring our pets.'

'Do you do DIY?' asked a shocked Liam.

'Oh, God, no. They get a team in to do the actual DIY off camera at night. We just walk up and down holding drills and things and chatting.'

'Have you said yes?'

'Not yet. Arguing about the fee. You know, this isn't bad,' she said, picking up what remained of the food on one plate with her fingers and biting into it.

Liam leaned forward and whispered: 'I don't think you're supposed to eat the Communist tract, darling.'

Chastity leaned towards the mirror and applied another layer of mascara. Then she stepped back and admired herself, turning her head from side to side, giving herself her best coquettish glance. Finally, she puckered her lips and blew a kiss at her reflection. 'Gorgeous!' she exclaimed.

Picking her jacket up off the bed, she headed for the door. She pushed it open, giving the room a last look. Her eyes glittered in triumph; on her lips was a smug smile. Then she stepped out, letting the door shut behind her with an expensive clunk.

Once on the ground floor, Chastity strode through the lobby, her heels making a sharp *tip-tap* on the marble floor. She tossed her hair dramatically, just in case there might be a lone person who had managed not to notice her. When she reached the front, she stopped by a porter in a red jacket with enough gold rope on it to tow the *QEII*.

'Taxi, madam?' the porter asked.

'Yeah,' she replied.

Chastity climbed into the cab while the porter held the door open.

'I do hope you enjoyed your stay at the Milton,' he said. 'Do come back again soon.'

'Oh, I think I'll be here regularly from now on,' she replied.

Chapter Twenty-One

Beth took a sip of her frappuccino. It was like drinking liquidised Milky Bar. Still, she needed something artery-clogging to steady her nerves. She looked around. Café Café was full of twenty-something office workers trying desperately to look like they weren't skiving off.

Beth had secreted herself in a corner. To her right, a woman with an expensive handbag was scribbling maniacally on a Palm Pilot.

'Revolutionised my life, this thing,' she was saying to a man sat with her.

He, too, was writing on an electronic notepad.

'Barely have to talk to anyone any more,' he said, without looking up.

'Yeah, great, isn't it?' she replied.

Beth felt depressed. So, talking was obsolete, was it, like the black-and-white TV or the Sinclair C5? If she and Richard had done a bit more talking, maybe they wouldn't be in the situation they were now. She took another sip of her coffee. It tasted sweet and comforting.

The glass door swung open, delivering a cold blast of air just where Beth was sitting. It was Richard. She shivered, not merely from the draught, but from a flutter of anxiety. She was nervous! She was having coffee with her own husband and she was nervous!

Richard picked his way between the tables over to hers.

'Hi, how are you?' he asked.

'How do you think?' Beth replied.

Richard looked embarrassed. He didn't know what to say.

Beth filled the gap. 'Still, at least one woman you've slept with is working. How is *she* getting on?'

Richard sensed that, already, this was not going the way he had hoped. Beth's hostility gave him a sensation not dissimilar to having the soles of his feet jabbed repeatedly with a cocktail stick.

'I think I'll just go and get myself a coffee.' He pointed at her cup. She shook her head.

Richard walked up to the counter. Only two minutes in and it wasn't progressing as Beth wanted either, but she didn't seem able to stop herself being nasty. She wanted to appear to be together and in control, but the fury bubbled up in her like a pan of sugar syrup on too high a gas.

She had plenty of time to try to compose herself, however. At Café Café, there was an inverse relationship between price and speed of delivery. It took fifteen minutes for a dopey girl in a jaunty baseball cap to take Richard's order, pass it to another assistant, who had to actually make the coffee, which she then passed back to the first, who rang it up on the till.

When Richard finally returned to the table, Beth could have sworn her hair had grown another inch. There was a seat next to her on the sofa, but he took the chair opposite. Perhaps he wanted the table between them to act as a barricade behind which he could shelter.

At first, neither of them spoke, then Richard broke the silence.

'Are you all right? You look a bit . . .'

'What?'

'No, it doesn't matter.'

'No, what?'

'Sort of sweaty. Are you coming down with something?'

'It's fashionable.'

'What is?'

'My base.'

'Isn't that what the army lives in?'

'No, it's make-up. It's called soft sheen.'

'I thought that was a furniture polish.'

'Well, you're wrong. It's a sort of make-up.'

'Oh, right. My mistake.'

They lapsed back into silence. Beth had a look on her face that said: Be afraid, be very afraid. Richard played nervously with a sugar sachet.

'Is that a new jacket?' Beth asked after a couple of minutes.

Richard had slipped it over the back of his chair. 'Yeah, do you like it?'

'Very nice. And the jumper and the trousers, they new too?'

'Yeah.'

'So she's buying clothes for you already, is she?'

'No, I chose them.'

Beth looked disbelieving

'Well, I paid for them. Anyway, what was I supposed to do? All my stuff is at home and you won't answer the phone. I couldn't keep wearing the same pair of trousers, you know.'

Beth pounced. 'Oh, so the reason you keep ringing me isn't to grovel for a second chance. You just want some clean socks.'

Richard realised his mistake. 'No, no . . .' Then he stared into his coffee to avoid putting his foot in it again.

Finally Beth spoke. 'So, you said we needed to talk,' she said. 'Although why you want to talk when you're still living with *her*, I don't know.'

'I love you.'

'How can you say that? You're living with her! If you loved me, you'd have moved out of her place.'

'I'm going to. It's just . . .'

'What? You like her brand of washing powder, or is it something else she does for you that you'd rather not do without?'

'Look, I'm going to move out. I want to come home.'

'No.'

'Beth, please.'

'No. Next subject.'

'Oh, Beth.'

Beth got to her feet. 'If that's all you wanted to say, then we might as well wind this up now.'

'No, no,' Richard replied desperately. 'There's Stanley to talk about. It's been a few weeks now and—'

Beth was still standing. 'Hold on right there,' she ordered. 'You don't even have the right to say his name, let alone see him. I mean, do you honestly think that you are a fit role model for *my* son? And, as for *her*, you can't possibly imagine that I would let her anywhere near him.'

'Sit down, please. Surely we could work something out?' Richard pleaded.

Beth was having none of it. 'Work something out! If you'd worked out that having an affair was incompatible with living with your wife and child, then you wouldn't now be missing your son, would you?'

She could feel her anger boiling over, but she wanted to be rational. Her first instinct was always to try to be reasonable and reach a compromise, even in this situation. She tried to calm herself down. She sank back into her seat and took a slow, deliberate sip from her coffee. Richard was hunched up in his chair like a soldier in a trench waiting for the shelling to stop.

'OK, OK, I know we've got to talk about Stanley, but I think we need to clear the air on some other stuff first,' suggested Beth.

Richard prepared to step into no-man's-land, not entirely sure there wasn't a stray sniper still about.

'Um, yeah?'

Beth stared directly at him. Her look was confrontational but also nervous. 'Why don't we start with why you had an affair?'

There was silence. Richard appeared to find the design on a paper napkin infinitely interesting. Finally, he spoke. 'I don't know. I wish I hadn't. Maybe I'm having an early mid-life crisis.'

'Not that early,' Beth replied, archly.

Richard didn't react. He didn't want to be deflected from the point he was trying to make. He looked up at her. 'You do know it's not you, don't you? It's me.'

'Well, thanks. I think I'd worked that one out. I'm not the one shacked up with a topless tart,' she said.

Richard's jaw twitched. 'What I mean is, you didn't do anything wrong,' he continued. 'I was an idiot. She was there. She ...'

'What? Put it on a plate for you?'

'Yeah. In a way.'

Beth was incandescent. 'That's the oldest excuse! "Sorry, miss. She made me do it." You are an adult, Richard.'

'Yeah, but I'm a man, and maybe things would be better if we were different, but when you're offered something, it's hard to say no.'

'OK, let's say you're right and all men are potentially up for it all the time, why should we trust any of you?'

'Maybe you shouldn't,' answered Richard, staring morosely into his coffee again.

'For a man who's got what he wanted, you don't seem very cheerful,' Beth commented acidly.

'Well, maybe it wasn't what I wanted,' Richard said carefully. 'Maybe things went a bit too fast and I didn't know how much I had to lose, and now I do and if I could turn the clock back ...'

'But you can't, can you?' said Beth fiercely.

'I'd never do it again, you know. Be unfaithful.' Richard was gripping his coffee mug tightly.

'What? Been there, done that, bought the T-shirt? Bought the entire bloody shop, by the looks of things,' Beth said, indicating his outfit. 'You just said that all men are up for it all the time. You just miss Stanley. That's it, isn't it? You couldn't give a damn about me.'

Beth's voice had risen far enough to be heard across the café. The couple with the Palm Pilots looked up from their scribbling. Richard caught the man's eye. It was a brief moment of male bonding. In that one glance, Mr Palm Pilot was saying: 'Rather you than me, mate.'

'It's not just Stanley. I miss you too,' said Richard.

'How can I believe you? You've lied to me before, remember? And, presumably you're lying to *her* now. You didn't tell her you were coming to see me, I suppose?'

'Well, no.'

They were silent again. Beth punctured the atmosphere this time. 'You know what really hurts? It's not the fact you had an affair It's the fact you lied to me.'

'But I had to lie to you. I wouldn't have been able to have the affair otherwise, would I?'

Richard's logic was unarguable and yet shocking. Beth was sitting forward, cradling her cup on her knees. Richard was also hunched forward, earnestly.

'Look, said Beth, 'this isn't getting us anywhere. You can say till you're blue, red and green in the face that it'll never happen again, but until I really understand why it happened, I can't trust you.'

'Well . . .'

'Come on. I want to know.'

Richard wasn't sure total honesty was the way forward, but Beth was determined. Unless he wanted things to end right here, he had no choice but to comply with her wishes. He shuffled, lemming-like, to the edge of the conversational cliff.

'All right. I suppose it was Stanley. When we had him, I know it was really hard for you and everything, what with working and looking after him and stuff. But I sort of felt a bit, well, pushed out. I felt that you loved him more than me.'

Richard waited for Beth to reply. When she did, her voice was quiet.

'I do love Stanley more than you,' she said. 'But so do you – love him more than me, that is – don't you?'

'No.'

'Oh, come on. Tell the truth, Richard.'

'I don't. I really don't.'

Beth sighed. 'Well, maybe there is no answer to this then. Maybe it's genetic, something in the female make-up, because I have to admit that if Stanley was in danger, I would literally walk through fire to save him.'

'And me? You'd let me burn to death, would you?' asked Richard.

'I would hope you'd be trying to save me, actually.'

Now it was Richard's turn to sigh. He was exasperated. 'I don't know what you want me to be. One minute I'm supposed to be all caring and sharing and the next you want to be married to Rambo.'

'I never said I wanted to be married to Rambo. I'm more of a Gladiator girl myself.' Beth saw Richard's face. 'Sorry, go on.'

'Maybe you're better off without me. I've never really worked out why you married me anyway.'

'What do you mean?'

'Even before Stanley, you seemed to be able to do pretty much anything without my help. After Stanley, well, you picked it all up really easily. I felt like a spare part.'

'Jesus, Richard, there are always things to do – nappies to change, shopping to get. If you think I'm so bloody brilliant, it's because I've had to be. I feel like I've been married to the invisible man for the last year. I have done everything, because you've done sod-all. You've carried on as if nothing's changed and I've almost collapsed under the weight of keeping my job going and looking after Stanley, not to mention trying to prop up our relationship, although I obviously didn't do too good a job of that, did I?'

'I didn't know you were that unhappy,' commented Richard quietly.

'Neither did I,' replied Beth. 'I was too busy being Superwoman. I didn't have time to think about it, I suppose.'

They surveyed each other. Richard didn't look like the carefree adulterer now. He looked destroyed. Beth just looked tired. She took a deep breath. 'If we were to, um, get back together, things would have to change, you know.'

'Just tell me what you want me to do,' answered Richard.

Beth really lost her temper now. 'It's not about me telling you. Don't you see? That's the whole problem. This is a marriage, not a Duke of Edinburgh's Award Scheme outing. I'm not reading the map and giving you directions. I don't want to have to remind, or cajole, or nag. It's too bloody knackering. Our marriage should be a genuine partnership where you see what needs doing and JUST DO IT!'

'OK, OK,' Richard shot back defensively. 'You want it to be a genuine partnership? Let's talk about sex, or the lack of it, then.' He was shouting now. The staff behind the counter were whispering and looking over. Richard lowered the volume slightly. 'How do you think it feels to be constantly rejected by your own wife?'

'I don't constantly reject you.'

'No, but I get Heavy Leg Syndrome often enough.'

'Heavy Leg what?'

'Heavy Leg Syndrome. You know. I say: "How about it?" And you say: "Oh, all right, but I'm really tired," and you just lie there with legs like lead weights.'

'Well, why do you think that is?' hissed Beth. 'If I felt a bit more supported elsewhere in our marriage, maybe I might be more keen to have sex.'

'And if I felt you were a bit more up for it in bed, maybe I might load the dishwasher more often.'

They stopped, both exhausted.

'Jesus, and I thought we were happily married,' said Beth, glumly.

'Maybe we just got good at papering over the cracks.'

'I never wanted one of those marriages,' said Beth.

'So what do we do?'

'I don't know. I'm too tired to talk any more now.'

'What about Stanley?'

'Well, I suppose he shouldn't suffer because of all this, should he?' Beth said hesitantly.

Richard jumped to his feet with a big smile and went to kiss her.

She pulled her head away. 'My God, is that all you think it will take? A chat over a coffee, and it's all forgiven and forgotten.' She stood up.

Richard tried to recover lost ground. 'No, no. I'm sorry. I don't expect you to take me back. I was just happy that I'm going to see Stanley.'

'Rubbish. You think I'm so desperate that I will take you back whatever you've done. Well, I'm not that desperate. If I take you back – and at the moment it is a very big if – it will be on my terms–'

Richard, panicking, interrupted her. 'I'm a pillock. Let's just agree on that. I am a total pillock,' he shouted.

'Yes, you are,' Beth shouted back. 'But you're my pillock!'

They looked at each other and smiled.

'Can we sit down, please,' Richard whispered.

'All right, but only after you've got me another frappuccino with extra marshmallow. And you're paying!'

'I had no idea they even made knickers this size,' said Siobhan, aghast. 'I could parachute into a foreign country with these!'

'Yes, well, you're pregnant now,' said Olivia. 'And one of the sad facts about pregnancy is that, while you may have had sex to get you into this condition, maternity knickers are designed to make the odds of that ever happening again a million to one.'

Siobhan looked depressed.

'I'm exaggerating, darling. You only wear them for a few months.' Siobhan brightened. 'After that, your disappearing bosoms, stretch marks and the four a.m. feed will take over the contraceptive role.'

Siobhan and Olivia were in lingerie emporium par excellence Underworld. Siobhan hadn't yet reached the heffalump stage of pregnancy. However, her size 8 G-strings were under a certain strain. The ropes securing the canvas of a circus big top on an especially windy day weren't stretched as taut.

Olivia had collected an armful of horrible pants.

'Talking of sex, when are you going to reveal who your mystery man of the e-mail is?'

Siobhan shook her head. 'Sex has nothing to do with it. We're just friends.'

'Yeah, right. No man is ever just friends with a woman. He's just lulling you into a false sense of security before he sticks his hand up your skirt.'

Siobhan held up her huge pants again.

'Oh, well, maybe in this case ...' said Olivia, laughing and walking over to the bra section. 'Now, remember, no underwiring,' she announced.

Siobhan groaned. 'Can't I have just a bit of push-up?'

'Anyone would think you didn't want to be chained to the sofa for six months, wearing zip-front tops and no make-up, breast-feeding your little darling on demand and wondering what happened to your life,' said Olivia.

'I won't really wonder what happened to my life, will I?'

'No, you'll be too shagged-out to be able to manage any coherent thoughts at all.'

'Oh God, don't scare me, Olivia. I need my confidence building. I'm seeing Karen this afternoon. I'm going to tell her about the baby.'

'Well, I did wonder when you were going to broach the subject. You were pushing it a bit with the too many Hobnobs line.'

Brrng, brrng. Olivia put down the flesh-coloured maternity bra she was holding and fished her phone out of her pocket.

'Hi, Liam, darling. It's very noisy. Where are you? ... Oh, Sionara Gdansk ... You're with Oona Kirkpatrick! ... Really? ... Oh, *really*? Has she said yes? ... So who else is on the list? ... You're kidding ... Oh, OK. Get your other phone. I'll see you later. Bye.'

Olivia looked at Siobhan. 'Now we know what Karen's really up to.'

'You're what!' screeched Karen.

'Pregnant. I'm pregnant,' Siobhan answered.

'You can't be.'

'There isn't any doubt. I've had a scan.'

'No, I won't allow it.'

For Karen, the idea that a member of her staff should do anything without her approval was anathema. Add to this her child phobia and Siobhan had committed the ultimate crime. Still, Karen was canny enough to know that she couldn't be seen to be completely unsupportive. That was the fast track to the industrial tribunal. She took a deep breath, pasted a look of concern on her face and came out from behind her desk.

Putting an arm round Siobhan, Karen said: 'What I mean is, have you definitely decided to have it?'

Siobhan was shocked by the question. 'Yes.'

'Absolutely definitely?'

'Yes. I'm six months gone.'

'Well, I'm sure we could find a sympathetic doctor, a special clinic.'

Siobhan was acutely aware of Karen's arm round her shoulder. It felt as though she was wearing a straitjacket. 'No,' she said. 'It's all arranged. I'm having it. I just felt you needed to know because of maternity leave.'

Karen removed her arm. 'Maternity what?'

'The time I'll need to take off when the baby comes.'

'Do you think that's really necessary?'

'Well, I wasn't thinking of giving birth on a Black and Decker Workmate. I will have to go to hospital, and then there's the breast-feeding afterwards to think about. I wouldn't want to come straight back . . .'

The look on Karen's face was pure distaste. The mere mention of the words 'breast' and 'feeding' in the same sentence made her stomach turn over. She was a woman who prided herself on her ability to overcome her gender. Her whole life was devoted to ignoring any messages her brain sent her which didn't accord with her image of herself as the hard-as-nails natural winner. Vulnerability? The desire to nurture? Neither registered on her personal emotional Richter scale.

'I don't think we need to go into details, do we? I have to say, I am disappointed. You seemed like such a bright girl.'

'I'm not retiring, I'm just having a baby.'

'Well, we'll see, won't we?'

Karen had already decided. Siobhan would be retiring whether she liked it or not. The only question was: how?

Chapter Twenty-Two

'Marcia has come up trumps then,' said Olivia, handing the piece of paper back to Beth.

'Yup. Hell hath no fury like a woman given oven gloves for Christmas.'

They were in Olivia's sitting room. Beth was standing by the fireplace, her elbow propped on the mantelpiece. Olivia was perched on the edge of an armchair and Siobhan was lying full length on the sofa.

'Sure I can't get you anything?' Olivia asked.

Siobhan shook her head. 'I'll be all right in a minute. I just needed to rest my legs. Karen made me stand up for ages.' She raised one foot off a cushion. 'Look, I've got my granny's ankles!'

'It's just water retention,' said Beth. 'How did it go?'

'Well, she didn't sack me there and then, but I don't think she was too pleased.'

'All the more reason for making our secret plan work,' Olivia announced.

They all nodded.

There was a commotion outside the door. Whoever came up

with the phrase 'the patter of tiny feet' had clearly never met a real child. It sounded like a herd of cattle was stampeding down the hall. The door flew open and Seth and Anouska burst in. They were followed by Colin and Nigel, holding Mia and Daisy.

'Mummy, Mummy,' shouted Seth, launching himself missile-like on to Olivia's lap.

Anouska scrambled on afterwards. 'Kiss dolly!' she demanded. Olivia duly planted an ostentatious kiss on the forehead of a Tiny Tears. The doll's face had been heavily defaced and she'd had a haircut that would have been regarded as a bit butch even at a lesbian disco. Seth had attacked her with a biro and a pair of nail scissors.

The twins squeaked and gurgled. Siobhan pulled first one then the other up and they nestled in beside her belly.

'Baby,' said Anouska, pointing at Siobhan's stomach.

'Yes, darling. That's right,' said Olivia. 'Now, have you brushed your teeth?'

Anouska made a face.

'What about you, Seth? Have you done your teeth?'

'I am rather busy,' Seth declared. 'I have got a lot on my plate, you know!'

All the adults smiled, but tried not to let Seth see. Olivia kissed him and Anouska and set them down on the floor. Then she picked up the twins and put one on each hip. 'Time for bed,' she said, and like the Pied Piper of Hamlin, she led her cluster of children upstairs.

'I wonder how Richard's getting on with Stanley?' Beth mused.

'Oh, so you agreed to give him access after all, did you?'

'Yeah. He's on trial. I don't know if it was the right thing to do, but I did it more for Stanley than Richard.'

'Is *she* going to be there?'

'Dunno. I decided to try and be mature, so I pretended she didn't exist.'

Olivia reappeared with Colin and Nigel, who were both putting on jackets.

'Sure you'll be OK? We can stay, you know,' said a concerned Colin.

Olivia shook her head. 'No, we'll be fine.'

'Well, we'll be back by eleven,' said Colin anxiously. 'But we'll keep one of the mobiles on, just in case.'

'Jesus, it's like saying goodbye to Saint Francis of Assisi and Mother Teresa of Calcutta. Go and misbehave, for goodness' sake.'

Olivia shut the door behind them and came back into the sitting room.

'Where are they off to?' asked Siobhan.

'Some gay pride thing. Colin's worried all the men will have shaved heads and tight T-shirts.'

'They probably will,' Siobhan laughed.

'Thank God you didn't tell him that. It's taken me and Nigel days to persuade him to go,' Olivia replied. 'There's not much point in coming out if you're going to stay in for the rest of your life, is there?'

'How's it going between them, then?' asked Beth.

'OK, I think. I haven't been aware of any dinner plates whizzing back and forth anyway. Then again, Nigel would be too worried about making a mess. He is the cleanest person I've ever met. That nursing training, I suppose. I timed him the other day. He took three minutes and forty-five seconds just to clean his fingernails!'

'Colin's head must be spinning. He's gone from the queen of

chaos to the king of clean,' said Beth. 'But that's probably part of the appeal.'

'What do you mean?' asked Siobhan.

'It's like always having holidayed in Ibiza. After a while, you fancy a quiet weekend in Torquay.'

'I don't!' announced Olivia.

'My point exactly!' said Beth. 'Anyway, what about you? How are you managing, living with them both?'

'Oh, you know what they say. Two's company, three's a porn movie.'

'You wouldn't, would you?' gasped Siobhan.

'God, no. I can't think of anything I'd less like to do than go to bed with Colin and Nigel.'

'Why is it that for women the idea of two men together is about as appealing as day-old rice pudding, but for blokes, two girls together is such a turn-on?' asked Siobhan.

'They think lesbianism is like snooker,' said Olivia. 'A spectator sport.'

'And they just love playing with their balls, don't they?' added Beth, giggling.

'Don't make me laugh,' said Siobhan. 'It hurts.'

'Are you sure you're all right?' asked Beth.

'I'll be fine. Let's just get down to some work. How much does Marcia say Karen's pitched the new show at, per half-hour?'

Beth picked up the piece of paper she'd stashed behind the mirror on the mantelpiece. 'Seventy-five grand. That's not much.'

'And we've got to come in below that?' said Olivia incredulously.

'If we want the commission, basically, yes,' said Beth. 'We can have the best idea in the world, but there's nothing more persuasive to a TV executive than cash in their channel's pocket.'

'OK. Seventy K, then, is that what we're aiming for?'

They all nodded.

'Right, so how do we reinvent the DIY show for seventy K,' mused Beth, as she walked over to the one empty armchair and sat down.

'By not doing any DIY?' suggested Olivia.

'As attractive as that may sound, I think the audience might rumble us,' said Beth.

'Remember, according to Liam, Karen's big on the celeb angle, though how she's going to do that for seventy-five grand I don't know,' said Olivia.

'They're going to get a free bathroom, kitchen or whatever. If she goes far enough down the C-list, they'll bite her hand off at the wrist for that,' said Beth. 'Panto in Woking doesn't pay so well when you haven't been in a soap for a while.'

'As Valerie is no doubt finding out,' added Olivia, arching an eyebrow.

Siobhan sat upright and thumped a cushion. 'A presenter! We haven't even thought about that!' she gasped.

Olivia jumped up from her seat and started pacing up and down in front of the fireplace.

'We can't submit a pitch without a name on it,' sighed Beth.

'OK, let's stay calm,' said Olivia, stopping her pacing. 'Who can we afford?'

'You know who'd be fantastic?' said Beth, getting excited. 'Jack.' Her face fell. 'But he's probably too pricey, and anyway, we don't know where he is, do we?'

There was a depressed silence, broken by Siobhan. 'I think I can get hold of him,' she whispered.

'Do you?' gasped Beth. 'How?'

Siobhan smiled shyly. 'You know you wanted to know who I'd been e-mailing . . .'

'Siobhan O'Hanlan!' shrieked Olivia, running over to her and hugging her. 'You are a dark horse, a very dark horse indeed!'

'What's that smell?' Chastity waved a hand back and forth in front of a nose that was wrinkled in horror.

She and Richard were in the living room of her small flat, whose interior boasted a mix of white leather and highly polished wicker. A collection of poster-sized framed photographs decorated one wall. They featured Chastity in various states of undress, fortunately in heavy soft focus.

The room was dominated by a sofa and a smoked glass and brass effect dining table. It felt cramped. This impression wasn't helped by the presence of a large three-wheeler push chair parked in the centre of the floor. This was being shoved back and forth with glee by Stanley. He took particular pleasure in the loud banging noise it made as it hit the skirting board perilously close to the TV and the relatively softer thud as it ricocheted off the sofa.

'Does he have to do that?' hissed Chastity, getting up and going to a side table to pour herself another large vodka.

'Stanley! Come here!' ordered Richard with a distinct lack of authority. 'I think he may have pooed.' He reached forward, picked up Stanley and put his nose to the baby's bottom. 'Yup. He's definitely pooed.'

'Ugh! That's disgusting,' exclaimed Chastity, taking a swig of her drink.

'What?'

'What you just did.'

'I don't know what you mean.' Richard was genuinely mystified.

'Sniffing his . . . you know.'

'Oh, Chastity, when you become a parent, some of the normal barriers have to come down, you know.'

Chastity cast an accusing look at Stanley. 'I never want children,' she spat.

Richard's eyes glazed slightly. Beth had said she didn't want children. She'd changed her mind, though. Maybe if she hadn't they'd still be together. He transferred Stanley on to one hip and grappled for the changing bag. The strap was draped over the handles of the push chair. He gave Stanley an affectionate squeeze. Now he'd got him, Richard wouldn't be without him for anything.

'Babies do have their compensations, you know,' he said, rubbing Stanley's back.

'Really?' asked Chastity, her lip curling. 'What are those, exactly?'

Richard walked past her and headed to the bathroom to change Stanley. He knew he was living with a woman who was no longer interested in him and whom he didn't even like. However, he couldn't afford to bring things to a head until he'd talked Beth round. He was walking on eggshells in two separate locations at once.

He laid Stanley down on the bathroom floor.

Stanley wriggled. 'Diddah. I diddah.'

'You can have your digger in a minute. Let's give you a nice clean bottom first,' Richard said tenderly.

'I thought we were going out,' Chastity shouted from next door. 'The booking at Sionara Gdansk is for eight thirty. It's a quarter to now.'

Chastity had a lot to learn when it came to children. She seemed to think they were like handbags. You carted them off to your destination, put them down at your feet and they'd stay there, tucked out of the way as long as you fancied. Even on his very best behaviour, Stanley was unlikely to remain mute or static for more than two minutes.

Richard screwed up his face. 'Do you mind if we don't go?' he asked. 'I know I said I'd take you, but that was before I knew we'd have Stanley. Posh restaurants and small children don't really mix, not unless you mind me spending most of the meal sitting with Stanley in the car outside.' He laughed hopefully.

Chastity didn't reply. She was thinking that maybe an evening without Richard was quite a pleasant prospect. She had to admit he'd had his uses. If it wasn't for him, she'd never have met Karen and got her job on *On The House*. And then she'd never have met Patric ... But Richard was now pretty much surplus to requirements.

'Um. I thought we could could, er . . .' Richard was being tentative. 'Sort of pop out for a hamburger. It might be fun.'

The cold breeze of disapproval blew in from the living room.

'Diddah, diddah!' shouted Stanley, rolling over, scrambling to his feet and making a dash for the door. Richard tried to grab him. Instead, all he caught was the edge of his nappy. Father and son battled for a few seconds. Then the nappy gave way and Stanley shot like a smelly missile into the living room.

'Richard! Richard!' screamed Chastity in terror. 'It's got out!'

'He's not an it,' said Richard, walking into the room. 'Stanley is a he. You make him sound like a puppy.'

'At least you can house-train a puppy!' said Chastity, backing away from the small naked child holding a plastic truck who was advancing on her.

'He's only a baby. Give him a break.'

Richard was annoyed now. He walked up behind Stanley and scooped him up protectively. 'Come here, you,' he said, giving Chastity an accusing look.

Chastity frowned.

'What?' said Richard.

'Nothing,' she answered.

'No, what?'

'It's just, I never saw you as the nappy-changing kind of a man.'

'What do you mean?'

'I *thought* you were important, a go-getting executive, you know. Not some sort of . . .' she wrinkled her nose, 'wussy new man.'

'And now you're disappointed. Sort of like buying a Porsche and getting it home to find it's turned into a Morris Minor?' Richard said this last bit with heavy sarcasm, which Chastity missed completely.

'Exactly!' she agreed brightly.

Richard sighed. 'You always knew I had a child.'

'Yeah, but I didn't realise that you'd want to bring it round to my flat!'

'Well – what would you prefer I do? Find a cardboard box somewhere and entertain him there?'

Chastity didn't say anything. Richard retreated to the bathroom again.

'Look, I know it's not ideal. We're a bit on top of each other here, but if we all make an effort . . . I'll just change Stanley and then we can go out.'

'Great,' sighed Chastity.

Siobhan pressed the 'Send' button. Her message flew down the international superhighway and she waited for a reply.

Beep. Five minutes later Jack's e-mail popped up on the screen. 'hi, blondie. a proposition u say? tell me more. J.'

Siobhan began typing. She explained the plan she, Beth and Olivia had cooked up. Then she pressed the 'Send' button again. She was banking on three things. First, Jack was hardly Karen's biggest fan. He'd have to drop his normal fee, but that might be a small price to pay for getting even with Karen. Second, he needed the work. Since *On The House*, he had had precisely two jobs. One was posing for a government-sponsored leaflet on ladder safety. The other was a video for a DIY store on how to lay a laminate floor. Peak-time TV this was not.

Her third trump card, though she was shy of admitting it, was herself. Since her visit to Jack's flat, they had become closer. They weren't dating *exactly*. Jack hadn't even kissed her. But they were spending an awful lot of time e-mailing and texting each other. It definitely felt like something was going on. It was ironic, really, that Siobhan's most successful relationship to date was with a man who she wasn't even officially dating. So far they'd only had the one face-to-face meeting at his flat. Still, Siobhan felt she now knew Jack better than any of her 'real' boyfriends.

That was the nature of e-mail and text. Typing e-mails to someone you couldn't see was both more anonymous and more intimate than actually talking to them. It allowed you to be totally honest. Or totally dishonest. E-mails could also conceal the fact that you were lying through your teeth.

Still, if Jack was deceiving her, there wasn't much in it for him, as far as she could see. She was almost eight months pregnant. Not exactly quick-shag material. It would have taken her half an hour to get her trousers off. She was like one of those whales you see on the news that's been washed up on a beach and the local people spend days trying to haul it back into the sea again. This was actually a pretty accurate depiction of the effort it would have taken Jack to seduce her.

'You have one new message' appeared on Siobhan's screen.

Siobhan didn't know if she could trust Jack – with her heart or with the details of their bid to steal the *On The House* slot – but she didn't have much choice. She sensed he was holding something back. She just didn't yet know what.

'Did you see that? He's got four chips in his mouth at once, *and* he's chewing them. Clever boy. You're such a clever boy! Look, Chastity, he's just got another one in!' exclaimed Richard.

Chastity was staring out the window. 'Yeah, whatever,' she said, without turning round.

They were sat in Burger World, a homage to all things plastic, including the food. Richard had a tray in front of him cluttered with debris of a half-eaten Family Feast. Chastity's Feast was noticeably untouched.

'You know, you can tell he really missed me,' continued Richard.

'See the way he kept looking at me? It's not good for a child not to have a strong male role model around.'

'You never know, Beth might get herself a boyfriend,' Chastity offered, turning her head away from him and smirking.

'Oh, no. Beth wouldn't do that,' said Richard quickly, wiping ketchup off Stanley's nose. 'She's not the type.'

'Oh yes, I forgot, she's Little Miss Perfect now, isn't she? Funny you didn't think that when you were with her, isn't it?' she said waspishly. 'Anyway, can we go now? It's hardly good for my image as a television celebrity to be seen in a place like this.'

'You've only been on TV five minutes,' Richard responded. 'Anyway, Stanley hasn't finished yet, have you? You're enjoying your dinner with Daddy, aren't you? Perhaps Mummy will let us have dinner more often now. Maybe if we ask very nicely she'll let you stay overnight next time. Or maybe you could come on Friday and stay all the way till Sunday. You'd like that, wouldn't you, Stanley?'

The colour drained from Chastity's face. 'Hang on a sec . . .' she began.

Stanley also began to turn a rather odd colour.

'I never said it could . . .' continued Chastity.

Richard wasn't listening. He was looking in concern at Stanley.

'Richard!' declared Chastity.

'Yeah, one minute. Stanley's looking a bit . . .' he responded.

'Richard.' Chastity was more insistent now.

'Yeah, if you could just give me a moment. I think Stanley may be going to . . .'

'Jesus, baby, baby, baby, that's all you're interested in. What about me?'

Chastity was silenced by Stanley, who, with impeccable aim, projectile-vomited hamburger and chips all over her from a distance of at least two feet. Having done this, he gurgled with delight at his own cleverness.

It took a supreme effort of will for Richard to prevent himself laughing out loud. He couldn't suppress a smile, however. Stanley giggled and pointed at the uneaten portion of his hamburger, hoping to refuel for a repeat performance.

Chastity was not amused. She picked up a napkin and began dabbing at her front, casting Richard a filthy look.

'Oh, come on. You have to admit it is funny,' Richard said.

'I think we need to get a few things straight,' she announced coldly.

'Is that a new cardi, Marcia? It's very *you*, isn't it?' said Karen, smiling wickedly at Patric. 'Did you knit it yourself?'

'Um, yes, actually,' Marcia replied, her cheeks feeling hot.

'Well I don't think Mathew Williamson need lose any sleep.' With this comment, Karen and Patric burst out laughing.

Marcia had gone a beetroot colour. 'Coffee, Karen?' she asked in a terse voice.

Karen nodded, still laughing. When she had recovered herself, she managed to add: 'Black, no sugar.' Then she and Patric went into his office and he closed the door.

Marcia tugged at the buttons of her cardi. She had been rather pleased with it when she'd finished it. Now she hated it. It was bad enough that Karen had made fun of her, but for Patric to laugh at her too . . . She felt totally humiliated.

Still, there was no time to dwell on that. She had to find out what they were talking about inside Patric's office. She made a dash for the kitchen. It was empty. Most people had gone home, but Marcia, as ever, was working late.

'Come on, come on,' she whispered impatiently as she waited for the kettle to boil.

A spoon of coffee, a splash of hot water, a quick stir and she had the cup on a tray and was headed back to Patric's office.

'So, we've got competition from *inside* Futura. Are you sure?' Karen was saying as Marcia went in.

'Yes, Anastassia dropped a huge hint today. I think she's rather enjoying it, throwing the scraps to the starving people and watching them fight among themselves.'

Marcia put the tray down on the coffee table. Neither Patric nor Karen even acknowledged her. She was the efficient ghost again.

'Is it someone from *On The House*?' asked Karen.

'Yeah, Anastassia as good as said so.'

'Well,' announced Karen, 'I'll find out who it is, don't you worry.'

Marcia shut the door and leaned back against it. How did Anastassia know about their plan? The bids weren't even in yet. Never mind, the point was, Patric and Karen knew. Pitches were supposed to be confidential, but if Anastassia had as good as told Patric about the rival bid, once the pitches were in she wouldn't be able to resist revealing the identity of those involved sooner or later. Marcia's bet was on sooner.

She picked up the phone and ever so quietly dialled Beth's number.

'Well, the bad news is, Karen and Patric know about us,' said Beth, walking into Siobhan's living room and slipping out of her coat.

'What do you mean? How?' said a horrified Siobhan, looking as if she was about to give birth on the spot.

Olivia leapt off the sofa and rushed forward to put an arm round Siobhan's shoulders. 'Jesus, Beth, don't you know not to give a heavily pregnant woman a shock? I don't know how your forceps technique is, but I don't fancy my chances with a pair of bacon tongs.'

Olivia guided Siobhan over to the sofa. 'Sit down,' she ordered her gently.

'Sorry, sorry,' said Beth. 'Let me rephrase that. Marcia says that Karen and Patric know there's going to be a rival pitch from inside *On The House*. They don't know exactly who's behind it, though.'

'Thank God,' said Siobhan, sinking back into a sky-blue ostrich-feather cushion. 'Do they know about Jack?'

'It seems not,' said Beth. 'He has said a firm yes, hasn't he?'

Siobhan nodded. 'Don't worry.'

'Might be wise to tell him to be a bit cloak-and-dagger about it, though. When are you seeing him?'

Siobhan blushed. 'Thursday, but it's not a date or anything. I just thought we'd go over the details.'

'Yeah, yeah, yeah,' said Olivia. She and Beth exchanged amused glances.

Siobhan's flat was a real single girl's pad, down to the beige sea-grass flooring and the cream sofa. Neither Beth nor Olivia had liked to point out what baby wee would do to off-white linen. They thought it better to let Siobhan find out for herself.

'What I don't get is how Karen and Patric know about us,' said Olivia suspiciously. 'We haven't even submitted the final pitch yet.'

She had joined Siobhan on the sofa.

'Anastassia told them,' Beth replied, turning to Siobhan. 'Remember, you had to call her PA to get the submission date.'

'I knew I shouldn't have used my own name, but I don't lie very convincingly,' Siobhan said, wringing her hands.

'It doesn't matter,' said Beth. 'The thing is, Marcia's not sure, but she reckons Anastassia might dob us all in when she gets the proper paperwork. You know how she loves to ferment discord?'

Siobhan put her head in her hands. 'I thought if we got it, great, but if we didn't, no one need ever know. I could go on maternity leave and it would all have blown over by the time I got back.'

'You two need to think about this really carefully,' said Beth, sounding grim. 'We can stop right now and you're safe. But if we go on with it there is the very real chance that you will lose your jobs like me and Jack.'

Siobhan and Olivia looked at one another, trying to gauge each other's feelings.

'Fuck it,' announced Olivia.

'Yeah,' agreed Siobhan. 'Let's do it.'

'As long as you're sure?' said Beth hesitantly.

'Yeah,' they both said.

Karen plodded ahead. She was on her third lap of Hyde Park. It was pitch dark, but that didn't worry her. She was wearing her miner's helmet and the lamp on the front was casting a beam of light ahead of her. Karen liked running at night. It gave her something to do of an evening and it allowed her time to think.

Anastassia had said one of the rival bids was coming from inside Futura; inside *On The House* no less. Who could it be? She considered the likely candidates. Saffron? Too stupid. Jeanine? Too busy eating. Siobhan? Pregnant, so her brain was only working at half capacity. Olivia? Maybe, although she always seemed a bit airy-fairy to Karen. This left Liam and Chastity. The former had the nous and the contacts but probably not the time, the latter had the ambition, but frankly the IQ level of a dairy cow.

Karen reached a T-junction. She skirted a taxi and ran straight over the top of a Smart Car. As she leapt on to the bonnet with the driver, too stunned to speak, looking on, she noticed a laptop lying on the passenger seat.

Karen needed to find out who the traitor was and she'd just worked out how she was going to do it.

'OK, we need a format,' Beth announced.

Siobhan sat upright, clasping her hands in front of her as if praying for inspiration. 'What about doing up homes abroad?' she suggested.

'Too middle class. Our viewers drink lager not Beaujolais,' declared Olivia. 'But we could still go out of the UK. Concentrate on the sympathy angle. You know, do a children's home in Albania, a garden for blind people in Kosovo. That sort of thing.'

'Compassion fatigue,' announced Beth. 'Plus, it still costs an arm and a leg to take a crew overseas, even if they are sleeping in bunk beds in a bombed-out building when you get there. Too many kickbacks.'

'OK,' said Siobhan. 'What about this? Two sets of neighbours who hate each other. We get them to bond by doing DIY together. We could call it "Love Thy Neighbour".'

'And what if they *don't* bond?' asked Olivia. 'Would you really want to hand an irate neighbour a heat gun, or a strimmer for that matter?'

'This is hopeless,' said Siobhan.

'No it's not,' insisted Beth.

'We'll just have to lock ourselves in here until we come up with something.'

'My God!' shrieked Olivia. 'That's it. We lock them in! We lock a group of people in a house and—'

Beth interrupted her. 'They have to do the DIY! Of course. We film them on secret cameras.'

'Jack can comment on their work through two-way mirrors,' added Siobhan excitedly.

'Yes!' shouted Olivia. 'And the viewers can vote one person out of the house each week.'

'The person who's most rubbish at DIY!' they all shouted together.

They were on their feet now, dancing dementedly round Olivia's living room. Admittedly, Siobhan's dancing was a bit less energetic than the others', but she was giving it a good go.

'It's *Big Sister* meets *On The House*. It's brilliant,' said Olivia.

'Even better,' said Beth, 'it's cheap! We don't have to pay for a building team. The punters do all the work for us. Plus, we don't have to pay *them*, because they get their shot at small-screen fame. AND we can sell the house afterwards!'

Siobhan stopped doing her jig and levered herself back on to the sofa. 'But will Anastassia go for it?'

Marcia was standing in the middle of her living room. Her feet were planted wide apart, her arms hung down at her sides and her eyes stared straight ahead. She'd been like that for fifteen minutes. She was so stiff and still, she could have been carved from stone. 'Portrait of Middle-Aged Woman 2002', paid for by vast sums of lottery cash and stuck on the top of a hill.

But Marcia wasn't made of stone. She was human, something that people like Karen tended to forget. Karen's jibe about Marcia's cardigan, and Patric's collusion in it, was typical of the sort of casual cruelty she had had to put up with over the years. She never complained and her tormentors never thought to wonder if she minded. 'Good old Marcia, she can take a joke,' they said.

Well, she was tired of being good old Marcia. As she stood there, her coat still on, her door keys in her hand and her supper sitting defrosting in a carrier bag at her feet, something happened inside Marcia. A great ball of pain and disappointment and regret and pure, pure rage exploded inside of her.

The sound that came out of Marcia's mouth was a cross between a growl and a bellow. It came from deep within her. It was raw, elemental, the very opposite of Marcia's usual careful, controlled speech. And that was the point. For the first time in her life, Marcia was out of control. The normal Marcia would have pulled herself together. This Marcia didn't. She tipped her head back. 'No!' she shouted as loud as she could.

It was the no she should have said to all the late nights and weekends, the little favours done and the big secrets kept. It was the no she had swallowed when someone asked if she minded being teased, or patronised, or ignored. More than anything, it was the no she was now saying to the future as mapped out for her. Good old Marcia was gone and the new Marcia wanted more.

Marcia looked round her living room at the shelves crowded

with the teddy bears and pottery cottages she'd so lovingly collected. Now she hated them. They symbolised everything wrong with her life. They were pointless, a way to fill space, occupy time. Instead of relationships with living, breathing people, she had invested her emotions in ceramic and wool.

Marcia was only thirty-eight, but when she looked round this room, she felt ancient. It was like a tomb, a cosy little tomb. Well, no more. She was exhuming herself. Marcia James was going to be born again.

She went to the kitchen and came back with a roll of dustbin liners. Slowly, methodically, she began to clear the shelves of teddies and cottages. She did it carefully, but without nostalgia. As first one shelf, then another and another became empty, she felt a lightness. She didn't stop to admire the empty walls. When she'd finished in the living room, she went to the bedroom and opened the wardrobe doors. She began pulling things off hangers, putting them in her dustbin bags too.

Finally, when there was almost nothing left, Marcia looked down at her beige cardi. She went back into the kitchen and got a pair of scissors. She stood in the middle of the room, took off the cardi, held it aloft and then started hacking at it with the scissors. Small holes became great gashes as the cardigan disintegrated. Bits of fluff were flying in all directions. A sea of beige swirled around her.

Anyone looking in and seeing a woman tearing a piece of knitwear to shreds would have thought Marcia was mad. She wasn't. She felt free, free enough to embark on some unfinished business. But first she needed to do a little shopping.

Chapter Twenty-Three

Olivia pressed the bell.

Marcia shifted nervously from foot to foot next to her. 'I'm really grateful for this, you know. I usually buy from catalogues,' she said.

'Exactly,' replied Olivia crisply.

Olivia had been somewhat surprised to get the call from Marcia asking her if she'd take her shopping. She had never seen Marcia as a closet fashionista. Still, Marcia had been adamant. She wanted a new image and Olivia couldn't resist the opportunity to do a *Pretty Woman*. So here she was, standing outside London's hippest store, waiting to play Richard Gere to Marcia's Julia Roberts.

Cheap was a shop that sold clothes, very pricey clothes. The name and the stock were an expensive in-joke. Cheap operated a treat-'em-mean-to-keep-'em-keen approach to retailing. There was so little stock and the shop was open such irregular hours, it was difficult to buy anything.

Rumour had it that Valerie had once attempted to purchase a skirt, only to be told the one on display had already been sold. She attempted to salvage the situation by pushing used tenners into the owner's hand and offering to sleep with every male member of her family. The cash was snaffled up, but her other offer was declined and she still didn't get the skirt.

'Olivia, darling. How marvellous to see you. Come in. Come in.' A woman with a tan so deep she appeared to have fallen into a vat of chocolate ushered Olivia into the shop. When Marcia attempted to follow, however, she barred her way. 'I don't think so,' she hissed, giving Marcia the kind of disgusted look Rosemary Conley might adopt on being offered a slice of pepperoni pizza with extra cheese.

'But I'm with—' tried Marcia.

The shop assistant slammed the door in Marcia's face. She then snapped the lock shut from the inside, just in case Marcia hadn't got the message that she wasn't welcome. She was left on the doorstep like an especially desperate Jehovah's Witness.

Marcia peered through the glass of the door. Olivia and the perma-tan woman were talking. Olivia was gesticulating towards Marcia. Finally, after what looked like a huge amount of persuasion, the assistant consented to walk very slowly to the door and open it just wide enough for Marcia to squeeze through.

'This is Tonadella,' said Olivia, giving Marcia a look that said: 'Grovel, for God's sake.'

'Hello, what a wonderful shop,' said Marcia weakly.

Tonadella cut her off. 'Olivia tells me you're here for a restyle,' she announced brusquely, casting a long look up and down Marcia. Without making eye contact with her, she turned back to Olivia.

'I see what you mean. The first thing we've got to do is get rid of that blouse. And as for the skirt . . . What length is that anyway?'

'Mid-calf, I think they call it,' said Olivia.

'Where? Outer Mongolia?'

Tonadella shook her head in despair. Then she saw Marcia's cream stilettos and had an actual physical reaction. Her whole body shuddered and she closed her eyes like an exorcist attempting to get rid of an evil spirit.

'How long have we got?' Tonadella asked when she finally opened her eyes.

'A couple of hours,' replied Olivia.

'A couple of days and we might do something, but this . . .' She paused, struggling to find the right word. 'This needs so much work.'

'I know, I know, but just ignore what she's got on at the moment. We'll just bin it all, or send it to Oxfam or something,' Olivia said.

'Even the starving in Africa have their standards,' Tonadella declared acidly.

Marcia listened to herself being discussed and then, without a word, she started to unbutton her blouse. She slipped her arms out of it and tossed it on the floor. Then she unzipped the side of her skirt and watched as it fell into a heap at her feet. She stepped out of it, put one hand on a hip and stood, in her bra and knickers, looking defiantly at Marcia and Tonadella.

Tonadella was stunned, but not half as stunned as Olivia.

'Marcia? What has come over you?'

'Those are what I used to be,' Marcia announced, indicating the pile of discarded garments. 'I don't want to be that woman any more.'

'Yes, but . . .' said Olivia.

'I don't want to be the woman in the cardi she knitted herself that people make fun of, and the skirt that's the wrong length. I want to be the kind of woman who shops in places like this, the one who wears the right skirt and the right top and people come up to her and ask her where she got her jacket because it's so great. I want to be able to wear a pashmina without it looking like a bath towel. I want to wear the right jeans. I want to wear sunglasses on the top of my head and for it to look good!'

Marcia looked at Tonadella and Olivia, who were speechless.

'I'm not saying I think I can be a supermodel. I just want to be like everyone else, to be able to blend in and do what other women do. I want to go out to lunch with my girlfriends and buy shoes on the way back. I want to have one of those conversations in the Ladies' about lipstick. I want to be part of all that. I want to be a member of the club. But I need your help, because I don't know any of this. I don't know where to start.'

Olivia and Tonadella still didn't speak.

'Forget the old Marcia. I want you to turn me into the new, improved version.'

Olivia smiled and, slowly at first, started clapping.

Tonadella joined her. '*Bravissima!*' she declared.

Marcia was shivering, but not from the cold. She was excited, but also terrified – of Tonadella, of this shop, of herself. Here she was in the middle of a shop in only her knickers and bra and she didn't care. She should have been mortified, but she felt exhilarated by her own daring. Still, she was a bit wobbly in her new persona. She was like a radio with no volume control. One minute she was still the quiet little doormat, the next she was Scary Spice. It would take her a bit of time to find something in the middle.

'OK, let's get started,' said Tonadella. She led the way to the back of the shop. As Marcia followed her, clutching the bundle of discarded clothes to her tummy to protect her modesty, she surveyed the empty racks on either side of her. There was the occasional garment laid on a sheet of perspex suspended from the ceiling, looking like a Caribbean holidaymaker having a nap on a hammock. Marcia wondered if the store had been burgled recently, or maybe Elton John had been in.

'There doesn't seem to be a tremendous amount of choice,' she whispered to Olivia, who smiled.

'It's always like this. This is fashion as art, Marcia. You wouldn't crowd Picassos together, would you?'

Marcia glanced at a peculiar pleated thing tied in a knot and placed next to a large gourd. She wasn't quite sure what bit of the body it was meant for, but she feared she might end up looking like one of those pictures with three noses.

When they got to the changing room, Marcia gasped. It was bigger than her entire flat, only with a lot less furniture. What was it with this place? It was like a building on a diet. It didn't have enough of anything. Furniture, clothes, customers.

She cast her eye over a charcoal suede sofa on spindly metal legs. They looked like they'd break if Kate Moss perched on it. To one side were two huge round balls – were they chairs? – and what appeared to be a pogo stick. A coffee table sat nearby, displaying a vase containing a green anthurium wrapped in barbed wire. What she couldn't see was anywhere for her to change. Then Tonadella pressed a section of white wall. It pivoted to reveal a hidden room. Marcia poked her head inside while Olivia and Tonadella chatted.

'We need to go minimal. Sexy minimal,' declared Olivia. 'Gwyneth Paltrow.'

Tonadella looked at Marcia and raised an eyebrow.

'Well, maybe Catherine Zeta Jones then.'

Tonadella nodded. 'That's more realistic.'

'Obviously,' continued Olivia, 'the hair needs help—'

'Help?' interrupted Tonadella. 'It needs open heart surgery.'

'Yeah well, we're booked in at Aidan Smurfitt at two.'

'VIP suite?'

'Of course. He had to bump Oona Kirkpatrick, though. She wasn't happy.'

There was a sharp intake of breath from Tonadella. 'I bet.'

Olivia laughed. 'It's all right. Aidan sent round a tray of fat-free muffins and one of his best-looking young assistants, stripped to the waist.'

'Really? Stripped to the waist?'

'Well, he will be within five minutes of Oona getting her hands on him.'

They both laughed, before turning their attention back to Marcia.

'The legs aren't bad,' pronounced Tonadella.

Now Marcia was embarrassed.

'Yeah,' agreed Olivia. 'I'm thinking leather. I'm thinking knee boots.'

'*New Avengers* with a twist?'

'Exactly.'

Marcia spent the next two hours being pulled and pushed, pinched and patted. Given that the shop was so empty, Tonadella managed to come up with a surprising number of options. Marcia climbed into halter necks and boat necks, V-necks and polo necks.

She tried boot-cut trousers and cigarette-leg pants, pedal pushers and culottes. She walked up and down in a mini, a maxi, a pelmet and a bias-cut knee-skimmer.

When Marcia and Olivia left Cheap, she was loaded down with carrier bags. Olivia had negotiated a generous discount. Even so, Marcia had spent more in one morning than she'd spent on clothes in her entire life. Fortunately the cost was more than covered by the sale of all those teddies and pottery cottages. In fact, Marcia had made rather a nice profit on them. It turned out they'd become quite collectable. She felt light-headed but happy. In the shop's full-length mirror, she'd glimpsed a version of herself that she'd never seen before. The woman who had looked back at her was a member of the club.

'Right, that's stage one,' announced Olivia on the doorstep. 'Now for stage two.'

Anastassia leaned forward. In front of her she had a neat pile of documents – alternative treatments for the slot currently occupied by *On The House*. She picked up the first and scanned it for about five seconds.

'No,' Anastassia declared, tossing it dismissively into a bin by her feet.

She picked up another. 'No,' was her verdict again.

And again and again.

When she had finished chewing up and spitting out the efforts of a good proportion of London's best TV brains, she had just two pieces of paper left in front of her.

The first was *Celebrity On The House* from Futura Productions. It was impressive. *The Time of Your Life* meets *DIYSOS*. It was a definite ratings builder. The viewer got to have a good gander at some celeb's nick-nacks and there were tips on how to strip wallpaper thrown in. The addition of pets was brilliant. Should deliver some of the *Animal Hospital* audience as well.

The second piece of paper was marked *Real DIY*, from Phoenix Productions. Anastassia had never heard of Phoenix Productions. The format was pretty good though, sort of *Big Sister* meets *On The House*. It might just be a huge hit. Even better, it was bloody cheap to do. Unlike *Celebrity On The House*, where they'd insist on smoked salmon morning, noon and night, with reality DIY you could bung them a can of corned beef and they'd be happy, so long as they had enough cider.

Anastassia thought it over. Celebs were the safe option, *Real DIY* was a risk, but one that could pay dividends for her programme budget. Which was it to be?

Jack flipped the velveteen seat down and held it there. Siobhan lowered herself slowly on to it.

'Ever hear that line about trying to fit a quart into a pint pot?' she said as her bottom finally hit the seat. She relaxed.

'I think you look beautiful. You're glowing,' replied Jack, sitting down next to her.

Siobhan rolled her eyes.

'No, really, you are. Do you mind if I ...?' The flat of Jack's hand hovered about four inches from Siobhan's tummy.

'No, go ahead,' said Siobhan. She was getting used to total strangers putting their hands on her stomach as if they were fortune-tellers laying hands upon a crystal ball. Still, she was touched by Jack wanting to do it.

As Siobhan was discovering, pregnancy was a centrifugal force. It separated men into two types: those who were repulsed and those who were attracted. The first group were either body fascists or their mothers breast-fed them too long. Those blokes who liked pregnant woman were either really well-adjusted and, therefore, able to see women as multi-faceted creatures, or their mothers had breast-fed them too long.

Jack put his hand on Siobhan's bump. He did it gently, tenderly, so that he hardly touched the surface. He didn't want her to think he was being pervy. He was fascinated by what was inside. Fascinated and awed. Not that he didn't fancy Siobhan. Even at this stage of her pregnancy, he found her attractive. Perhaps all the more so for being pregnant. The fact that she was carrying another man's child didn't come into it. Jack felt hugely protective of her, she brought out the best in him. He rather enjoyed the opportunity to gallop in on his white horse to save a damsel in distress. He'd have had a heck of a job getting her into the saddle, but he'd have given it his best shot.

There was a sharp intake of breath from Jack. 'It kicked! I felt a kick!' he declared, totally astounded.

Siobhan smiled. 'Yes, they do, babies, that is.'

'That was amazing. Do it again! Do it again!'

' 'Fraid tadpole doesn't kick to order. Mind you, pop round at three in the morning. Regular as clockwork then.'

Siobhan looked down at Jack's hand on her bump and she felt a tingle of excitement. She tried to pull herself together. She was a pregnant woman, for goodness' sake. She had a complicated life already, without adding another man to it, and yet, what if Jack was the one? What if he was the man she'd been waiting for and she missed him? She looked at her tummy again and told herself not to be silly. No man could possibly fancy her in her current state.

The lights in the cinema went down and the heavy velvet curtains ahead of them whirred apart. They'd come to see Nicole Kidman's latest movie. What with Jack's nationality, it seemed fitting. The film was up for multiple Oscars in that it featured Kidman as a sexually repressed toff, no make-up and an unflattering wig – 'See, I'm brave enough to play ugly!' – and mooching about nineteenth-century Queensland. At some point she would have some sort of mental breakdown, become mute, have an affair with a rough local and take up the violin.

Neither Jack nor Siobhan could really concentrate on the screen. This was their first proper date and they were acutely conscious of each other. They navigated their arms and legs round the other's like expert synchronised swimmers. Any accidental touch triggered an electric shock. Both knew this was going on, but neither acknowledged it. Perhaps relationships were like kettles, mused Siobhan. They only worked if you didn't watch them too closely. Neither she nor Jack had explicitly commented on the change in their friendship. They had both pretended not to notice the amount of messages going back and forth, or the affectionate little P.S.s on the end of them.

Nicole Kidman was looking depressed in a headscarf and Russell Crowe was shearing a sheep nearby in an aggressive manner. Both their accents were impenetrable. Perhaps nineteenth-century Queenslanders communicated by beating drums, forming pebbles into interesting shapes, or hanging coloured petticoats on a washing line. They certainly didn't seem to speak any sort of English Siobhan had ever heard.

In desperation, Siobhan turned to Jack. 'Can you make head or tail of what they're on about?' she whispered.

'Beats me,' Jack replied.

'But you must be able to, you're Australian!' Siobhan declared.

'Ah, well, not exactly . . .'

'What do you mean?'

A man in the row in front of them turned round. 'Do you mind?' he demanded.

'Sorry,' Siobhan whispered, but she couldn't leave her conversation with Jack in mid-air. She leaned over so her lips were an inch or so from his ear and cupped her hand around her mouth to further muffle the sound. 'What do you mean, you're not Australian?'

'I was born near the Old Kent Road.'

'But . . .' she ventured.

'Shhh,' said the man in front again, giving Siobhan a filthy look.

Jack now put his lips to Siobhan's ear. 'Remember the paintings at my flat? You said they were very English?'

Siobhan nodded.

'Now you know why. I *am* English.'

Siobhan frowned. She could barely believe what she was hearing.

'Listen to my accent?' asked Jack. 'It's English. This is the real me. The English me.'

Siobhan thought about it and yes, Jack did sound English. Then she remembered all his mails and texts. She'd wondered at the time why there'd been none of his usual Australianisms in them – no cobbers, or Sheilas or tinnies. She'd thought it was odd, but had let it go.

'I only pretended to be Australian because I needed the work. There was already a cheeky cockney handyman knocking about when I started, so I reckoned I might do better as a cheeky Aussie handyman. And it worked, didn't it?'

Siobhan had to admit it had.

'Actually, it's a relief not to have to lie to you any more. Obviously, I'll have to go on being Australian in public, but do you mind if I give all that cobber stuff a miss when I'm with you?'

'I'd be honoured.'

The man in the row in front was tut-tutting now. Jack and Siobhan ignored him.

'I'll tell you a secret,' continued Jack, still whispering. 'I never liked all that Aussie malarkey.'

'I'll tell you another one,' Siobhan said. 'Neither did I.'

'If you're not going to watch the film, would you just leave,' said the man in front, now incandescent with rage. Even in the gloom, Siobhan and Jack could see his complexion had gone a deep cherry red.

Jack looked questioningly at Siobhan, as if to say: 'Do you want to go?' Siobhan looked at the screen. Nicole was now trudging across an arid landscape in a grubby corset and maxi skirt. She nodded. Jack smiled back.

'Before we go in, can I ask you something?' said Marcia.

'Yeah?'

'Aidan Smurfitt?'

'Yes?'

'He's not going to do anything too weird with my hair, is he?'

'Weird? No. Why?'

396

'Well, I've seen these TV programmes where they do dreadful things – these celebrity hairdressers.'

'Come on,' said Olivia. Smiling, she hooked her arm though Marcia's reassuringly. 'Let's go in.'

Olivia led the way. She stepped through a doorway and Marcia found herself in a glass tunnel snaking over banks of chairs and basins and people snipping and sweeping and rushing about looking busy.

'They call it the catwalk,' confided Olivia. 'Aidan had it built so his celeb clients would feel at home.' She pointed down.

The carpet was red. Either side of it, set into the glass, was gold velvet rope. When they reached the other end of the tunnel, a deafening clicking noise exploded from concealed speakers.

'Paparazzi camera shutters,' explained Olivia. 'Recorded at the premiere of *Die Hard 27*. Wait for it.' There was a surge in the noise level. 'Some girl from *Hollyoaks* arriving in a dishcloth.'

They turned a corner and approached a desk guarding access to a long flight of stairs leading down to the salon itself.

'Olivia, darling. How are you?' oozed a man wearing a Madonna-style telephone headset and with a coif so brutal you didn't know if he was going to cut your hair or your throat.

'Hello, Carlos,' said Olivia. The pair exchanged a showy air kiss. 'This is Marcia.'

Carlos nodded, but he was already tapping into a keyboard. '*Uno momento*,' he instructed. 'Aidan's with a client.' He leaned forward. 'Linda Watson. Going to be very big in DIY TV.' He adjusted his microphone and then spoke into it. 'Hi, Aidan. Olivia's here.'

Olivia bent towards Marcia. 'Trust that bitch Chastity to get an appointment with the hottest crimper in town. Is there anything she's not capable of?'

'TV presenting isn't her strong suit, I hear,' answered Marcia.

Olivia smiled. This new Marcia was turning out to be fun.

At that moment there was a commotion downstairs. 'You look fabulous, sweetie. You are a DIY diva!' exclaimed a large, unshaven man with a broad Scouse accent and a sleeveless T-shirt that showed off arms covered in tattoos.

'That's Aidan,' Olivia said.

Marcia was flabbergasted. 'But he looks like . . .'

'I know, a roofer or something. The female clients love it. He's their bit of rough. Mind you, he's making a mint. Seven figures last year, I heard. Not from the salon, of course. That's just window dressing. It's the product line that pays for the ex-wife and the villa in Barbados.'

'We must have lunch. Sionara Gdansk is fab . . .' Chastity was coming up the stairs. A few more feet and she would be face to face with Olivia and Marcia.

'I am not saying hello to that cow,' hissed Olivia, grabbing a magazine off the counter and indicating that Marcia should do the same. The pair of them opened the glossies and held them up to their faces.

'Why don't you give Carlos a call. We'll set something up,' said Aidan, kissing Chastity again as she swept past two shifty-looking women with magazines shielding their faces.

'Olivia, is that you?' asked Aidan, pulling her magazine down. 'What are you doing?'

'Just had the lips done, a bit puffy, you know.'

'Well, you look fabulous, darling. Very Liv Tyler,' he cooed. 'So is this your friend? I see what you mean. Fashion car crash or what?'

Marcia was getting used to being insulted by people she didn't know.

'This is Marcia,' said Olivia, putting a protective hand on her shoulder in much the same way she reassured Seth on his first day at nursery. 'Now, you're going to be fine, Marcia. Aidan's a genius.'

They followed Aidan into the VIP room, which reminded Marcia of a school kitchen. Every surface was stainless steel. Ricky sat her down and stared over her shoulder into the mirror.

'So what do we think?' he said to Olivia.

'It's got to go, hasn't it?' she answered. Then, seeing the horrified look on Marcia's face, she added, 'Don't worry. Aidan's a genius.'

Aidan had begun picking up bits of hair and running a comb through them. 'Dreadful!' he pronounced. 'Appalling!' He went round her head finding ever more reasons to be rude about her hairstyle. Marcia said nothing.

What Marcia was experiencing was the crimper's version of the builder's standard 'So what cowboy did this then?' speech. Except that, instead of pointing out potentially lethal wiring and the beginnings of dry rot, Aidan was remarking on dodgy highlights and a bad parting. He took it just as seriously, however.

At the end of his follicular assassination, Aidan paused, then announced: 'Choppy!'

'Oooh, yes, we like choppy,' purred Olivia.

'Do we?' asked Marcia, who thought choppy was what you called a bad crossing on the Dover–Calais ferry.

'Yes, we do,' Olivia insisted.

A small Japanese woman came into the room carrying a pile of towels. She bowed.

'This is Raiku. She's our shiatsu shampooist,' explained Aidan. 'She's new. Her head massage is out of this world. You can start now, Raiku,' he ordered. There was a lot of bowing and smiling, but no action. 'You shampoo now,' ordered Aidan again. 'Oh, for God's sake. Needs a few more English lessons.' He marched to the door, opened it and bellowed, 'Wayne, you're doing a VIP shampoo.' Then he turned back to Olivia and Marcia. 'Shiatsu's off, I'm afraid. Wayne's from Luton, but don't hold that against him.'

Once Wayne, a hormonal beanpole in a Sex Pistols T-shirt, had finished shampooing, Aidan got to work. Marcia looked terrified as he darted first towards her then away. In and out he swooped, cutting great chunks from her coiffure. To take Marcia's mind off the matter in hand, Olivia engaged Aidan in polite conversation.

'So Chastity, I mean Linda, Linda Watson, is a client of yours now, is she?'

'Yeah, fab, isn't she? Do you two know each other?'

'We've, um, met, yeah.'

'Oh, yes, you're on the same show, aren't you? Well, don't you just love her to bits?'

'To bits,' answered Olivia drily.

Aidan carried on snipping and burbling. 'I mean. Linda, well, she's so out there, isn't she? Going to be a huge star, HUGE! If she can find time between all the men in her life, that is. Oops! Wasn't supposed to say anything about that.'

Olivia was intrigued.

'*All* her men? But I thought she was sort of settled with that TV guy?'

'Which one?' laughed Aidan.

'Oh, you know, what's his name? Richard, Richard Davies from *Smart Talk*.'

Olivia and Marcia exchanged looks in the mirror.

'Oh, no,' said Aidan, waving his scissors dismissively. 'That's all finished. She dumped him. Ex-wife from hell apparently. Total psycho and with some awful brat.'

Olivia had an urge to snatch Aidan's scissors, bolt up the stairs to find Chastity and then cut her heart out with them.

'She's got herself a new one now,' continued Aidan. 'Also married, unfortunately. Why don't these girls ever learn?'

'Who is he?'

'She swore me to secrecy, I'm afraid. So my lips are sealed.'

'Oh, go on, Aidan. What's the point of having gossip if you can't pass it on?'

'Well . . .'

'I'll get you into the press preview of the Prada sale.'

'I don't know.'

'Front-row ticket to Dior?'

'Well . . .'

'OK, you know that jacket you want from YSL, that there's a waiting list of a hundred and twenty for?'

Aidan nodded.

'Well, I can get you bumped to the top.'

'All right, but you didn't hear this from me and you can't tell anyone and . . .'

'Yes, yes,' Olivia promised impatiently.

'Linda's new man is, well, I think you know him actually. He's called Patric. Patric, oh, his surname's something beginning with M.'

'Not Patric Mortimer by any chance?'

'That's it. Patric Mortimer.'

Marcia choked on her coffee.

'Are you OK?' asked Aidan.

Marcia waved a hand in front of her face. 'I'll be fine.'

'It's all very hush-hush, of course,' continued Aidan. 'Linda says he's going to turn her into the next Carol Smillie.'

'Why not Vorderman?' Marcia asked.

Aidan and Olivia looked at Marcia for a moment. They'd both more or less forgotten she was there. Then Aidan stepped back and took a look at his handiwork.

'Fabulous,' he announced. 'I'll be back in ten,' and he walked out of the room.

'Where's he gone?' asked Marcia. 'I haven't had my blow-dry yet.'

'Oh, Marcia, you have so much to learn. Celebrity hairdressers don't do blow-dries,' Olivia explained. 'That's like asking Gordon Ramsay to peel a pound of potatoes.'

'But I saw how much this haircut cost . . .'

'Yeah, and for two hundred and fifty pounds you'd expect him to practically grow your hair for you as well, wouldn't you? But that's not how it works. There are eight VIP rooms here. He's cutting eight people's hair simultaneously. He hasn't got *time* to do blow-dries. Don't worry, there'll be a minion along in a minute.'

A stressed-looking woman with multicoloured hair extensions and a pierced tongue blow-dried Marcia's hair, and then Aidan reappeared to do the final adjustments. When Marcia saw herself in the mirror, she barely recognised the woman who looked back at her. She *was* one of those women who shopped at Cheap and knew how to tie a pashmina.

Olivia was ecstatic. 'Didn't I tell you he was a genius!' she exclaimed.

Marcia simply kept saying 'thank you', over and over.

Aidan already had two other clients waiting, so he bustled out. However, before he left, he turned back to Marcia. 'Whoever he is, the way you look now, you're way too good for him,' he said.

'She never said there was a he,' Olivia declared.

'There's always a he,' replied Aidan. 'Isn't there, Marcia?'

Patric peered at the computer screen. Now all he needed to do was . . . He clicked his mouse and waited. Nothing. He pressed the return key. Still nothing. The screen had frozen. Frantically, Patric began hitting keys at random.

Damn Marcia for having the day off. She never had the day off. Perhaps if she did, only occasionally, mind, then he would know how to use the bloody computer. It was her fault his screen was now frozen. Marcia had deliberately created a situation where, by selfishly not ever taking the day off, she had made herself so indispensable that he could never sack her.

Brrng, brrng. Now the sodding phone was ringing.

Patric abandoned his useless computer for a moment and picked up the receiver. 'Yes!' he hissed into it. 'What?'

'Patric, is that you? It's Anastassia.'

Patric swallowed and then started back-pedalling fast. 'Oh, Anastassia. Sorry about that. In the middle of a computer crisis. Pressed the wrong bloody button. I mean, um, must be a mainframe fault. Whole system is kaput. Server down and all that.'

Anastassia sounded amused. 'And I just thought Marcia had stepped away from her desk for a nanosecond.'

'Well, yes, she is actually off today. You know, I'm not one of those bosses who expects their staff to work *seven days a week*, ha, ha, ha.'

'I am,' replied Anastassia, pointedly not laughing. 'Which is why I'm Director of Factual Entertainment, Commissioning Leisure and Lifestyle Programming and Production, National and Regional, at Channel 6 and you're not. Anyway, let's get down to business. This *Celebrity On The House* idea of yours, it's not bad, but, as you know, I have been looking at other formats.'

'So you haven't made a decision?'

'No, it's between you and one other, from Phoenix Productions. The budget is just that interesting bit under yours.'

'Phoenix Productions, who are they?' Patric was rattled, but tried not to show it.

'They're new. But, well, there is something about Phoenix I thought you might like to know.'

Anastassia paused, like a cat who had dragged the Sunday chicken off the kitchen table and was preparing to tuck in.

'The pitch has Jack Taylor's name attached. Didn't you get rid of him?'

'Yes,' Patric said.

'Oh, and Beth Davies's name is on it too. She used to be one of yours, didn't she?'

Patric's face tightened. 'Yes.'

Patric thought for a moment. Beth and Jack. How could they do this to him? He had conveniently forgotten that he had sacked both of them.

Anastassia couldn't resist making more trouble. 'And then, of course, there are a couple of people who are still with you, I believe.'

'Who might they be?' Patric asked, as lightly as possible, annoyed at being manipulated by Anastassia.

Anastassia rustled a piece of paper. 'You know bids are confidential, Patric. Don't be impatient. All will become clear soon enough.'

Chapter Twenty-Four

When Beth got home, Olivia was sitting on the doorstep.

'Where've you been?' she demanded. 'Your mobile's turned off as well.'

Beth parked the pushchair containing a sleeping Stanley, and put her key in the lock on the front door. 'You sound like my mother. Come to think of it, you look like her too. What is that frumpy coat you're wearing?'

Olivia stood up and did an Anthea Redfern twirl, giving Beth a 360-degree view of salmon-pink tweed. 'I've been to Cheap today, with Marcia actually.' Beth looked surprised. 'I'll explain later. Anyway it's not frumpy. It's fashion frumpy. There is a difference, you know.'

Beth was not convinced. She pushed the door open and walked back past Olivia to retrieve the pushchair. 'If you want to have sex ever again, I suggest you don't wear it when you go and see Gianni.'

'I never said I was going to see Gianni,' protested Olivia, following Beth into the house.

'Oh, Olivia, you've been mooning about over him for weeks. Why don't you just call him?'

'Yeah well, maybe. Anyway, that's not why I'm here. Have I got news for you?'

Beth wheeled Stanley down the hall, then put the brake on and began to unzip the Cosytoes, so he wouldn't boil alive.

'Well, aren't you interested?' Olivia asked impatiently, shutting the front door.

'Yes, sorry. What news?'

'Well, Marcia and I were in Aidan Smurfitt's today. She's got a fab new haircut by the way and you should see the clothes we got in Cheap. Anyway, who do you think was at Aidan's?'

Beth didn't answer.

'Chastity!' announced Olivia. 'Chastity was at Aidan Smurfitt's.'

Beth was only half listening. She was attempting to remove Stanley's coat without waking him, a feat that made that trick where you tug the cloth from a fully laden table look easy.

'Anyway, she told Aidan, who told me, that she and Richard have broken up! She's dumped him!'

Beth didn't react.

'Didn't you hear what I said? Richard and–'

'I heard,' replied Beth. 'I'm just wondering why you think that would mean anything to me. It's not as if I'd ever think of taking him back or anything.'

Now it was Olivia's turn to be disbelieving. 'Beth! Remember, I've been where you are.'

Beth removed the last bit of coat with a silent flourish. 'I refuse to be that much of a doormat.'

'You don't have to be a doormat to want to save your marriage.'

'It's him who broke it up. He humiliated me.'

Olivia walked towards Beth. 'Look, tell me to sod off if you like, but in my experience, you should never make a decision about a relationship based on pride. Don't worry what other people might think. There is only one question you need to ask yourself – do you love him? Well?'

Beth sat down at the foot of the stairs. She frowned. 'I don't know. At the moment I just don't know. I hate him for what he's done and I don't know if underneath that I still love him as well. I know I can't trust him.'

'Can you honestly say that you trusted Richard a hundred per cent before all this happened?'

'Yes!'

'Oh, come on. Be honest. If he was locked in a room with the Corrs and Britney Spears and Christina Aguilera and–'

'You're depressing me now.'

'OK, well, if Richard had been locked in a room with these gorgeous, nubile women and he knew you'd never find out, would you honestly not have had a twinge of doubt about his behaviour?'

'Well, maybe just a twinge.'

'There you are then. The only totally trusting woman is an idiot.'

Beth sighed. 'So what's the answer, never to trust a man ever again?'

'Not exactly, just don't focus on trust as the be all and end all.'

'But that would mean he had won. He could go out and shag anything he liked because I wouldn't expect any better of him. I'd be a doormat.'

'The definition of a doormat is a woman who has no choices. You do. If he behaved badly again you could sling him out, or leave yourself. And you have a choice right now. Ask yourself this question: can you contemplate a future without Richard? If so, then divorce him and be done with it. If not, well, with Chastity out of the way, you're at least in with a chance of getting him back.'

'And this one has a harelip,' said a large woman in a batik tunic and African pendant. Her name was Audrey and she was holding up a photograph of a frightening-looking infant. She handed it to Siobhan, who blanched.

'Do pass it along, dear,' Audrey ordered, before scanning the rest of the group. 'It's important you all see all the pictures.'

A man called Sebastian, in a jumper and cords, was gripping a photograph with both hands. Shock was etched across his face. Audrey spotted him. 'I said pass them along,' she chided. 'I think someone may be hogging the malformed testes.'

Siobhan was at a National Childbirth Trust antenatal class. It was being held in Audrey's sitting room in Fulham. She'd pushed the sofa and table to one end of the room and littered the floor with a collection of Kashmiri rugs, kilim-covered cushions and, yes, beanbags.

Audrey was a formidable woman. Physically, she was intimidating. She had the sort of no-nonsense monobosom that entered a room thirty seconds before she did and brooked no argument. Hers were breasts as battering rams. Her attitude was brusque. When not lecturing on the wonders of water births, Audrey was running her local branch of Help the Aged with ruthless efficiency.

The reason Siobhan was beached on one of Audrey's ethnic soft furnishings was that she had announced to Beth and Olivia that she was thinking of doing without pain relief during the birth and opting instead for a CD of dolphin sounds and a paddling pool. They had exchanged horrified looks and booked her these classes as a kind of aversion therapy.

One look at a room full of control-freak women clutching birth plans in one hand and TENS machines in the other and they reckoned she'd be begging for an epidural. And it was working, perhaps rather too well. As Siobhan studied a picture of a baby with webbed feet, she was going off the idea of motherhood completely.

She was handed a snap of a baby gorilla. She hadn't realised the National Childbirth Trust worked with animals. Still, she didn't say anything. It was a relief to have a break from human misery. Audrey leaned towards her and indicated the picture. 'Some babies are born with quite a lot of hair,' she announced. Jesus! It was human!

Siobhan had been signed up for eight classes, but this was the first she'd actually attended. She'd kept putting it off, fearing that, without a partner, she'd be the odd one out. And, indeed, when Audrey had brought her in, her heart had sunk at the sight of the room full of perfect couples. The women were all in suits, having dashed from their high-powered jobs, which they were all still doing marvellously despite the fact that they were on the point of giving birth.

The men were more of a mix, but what they did share was an almost Moonie-like devotion of their wives. When not rubbing their other halves' backs, these Stepford Husbands were writing down Audrey's pronouncements in a notebook or asking eager, pertinent questions.

Do these blokes behave like this at home? wondered Siobhan. Were they really cushion-plumping, elbow-squeezing, ice-cream-from-the-petrol-station-in-the-middle-of-the-night-getting para- gons of spousal virtue? Not likely. They were probably too busy getting pissed down the pub with their mates in front of the foot- ball. In front of Audrey and, more importantly, each other, how- ever, the men vied for the title of Most Cringingly Earnest Other Half.

Siobhan would have smothered herself with a kilim-covered bolster were it not for the lesbian couple in the corner. Everybody was really, really nice to them and pointedly didn't ask about turkey basters. This took some of the heat off Siobhan as the only person not part of a conventional couple, although at least there were two of them.

The subject for discussion at tonight's class was: 'What will my baby look like?' The idea, explained Audrey, was to get everyone used to the possibility that their offspring might not necessarily emerge Hollywood-perfect. To illustrate her point, she had produced her selection of unhappy snaps.

For an hour, they indulged in a sort of macabre pass the parcel, only in this game, people were only too keen to pass things along. The shots of the newborn with a third nipple and a full set of teeth weren't too bad. Anything featuring gonads, however, and the resolve of even the most Stepfordian husband was tested to the limit, with a couple of the guys going a funny green colour.

When Siobhan's mobile beeped, she offered a silent prayer of thanks and excused herself from the group. Out in the hall, she saw that the message was from Jack. 'Hi Blondie. Hw r u & TP?' it read. Since their night at the cinema, Jack had taken to calling the baby Tadpole or TP, just as Siobhan did. She rather liked it.

Siobhan and Jack's date had ended chastely. A peck on the cheek and a hug were as far as it went. But anything else would have felt wrong. There were other, more important ways to establish intimacy. He held her elbow when they went up and down kerbs, and when she got a twinge of sciatica and had to walk in a really peculiar way, he didn't laugh.

The crowning moment for Siobhan came when they were in the taxi on the way home from the cinema and she had got a sudden craving for chocolate. She had shyly confessed and he made the cab take a detour. He didn't say: 'Are you sure you really need that?' as one of Siobhan's exes had once said when she went to finish the last biscuit in the packet. Jack went in and got her sweets and came back without comment. It was at that moment that Siobhan knew she either had to marry him or lock him in the cupboard under the stairs. She'd never find another like him.

She composed the briefest of replies to Jack's message – 'Me and TP good, u?' – and pressed the 'Send' button. At this point, she could have gone straight back into the meeting, but she couldn't face it. She loitered by the coat rack, attempting to conceal as much of herself as possible behind one of Audrey's many cloaks. Almost immediately, her phone beeped again. She fumbled about under layers of wool. When she looked at the screen, she saw it was another message from Jack.

'Fancy dinner 2morrow?'

They hadn't done dinner before. Things were moving up a rung on the romantic ladder. Siobhan was excited, but also apprehensive. Were they right to throw away a great friendship for something that might never work? She still wasn't entirely convinced by the English Jack who liked to paint in his spare time. It was such a massive shift from the man she'd known before.

Plus, there were two pieces of the Jack jigsaw that clearly didn't fit with this new, wholesome image: Beth – and the woman in Cardiff who'd blackmailed him. Jack had slept with them both. If he really was the sensitive romantic, why had he done that? Siobhan hadn't had the courage to tackle him about it yet, but she knew she had to – or turn back now. Jack's night with Beth made Siobhan especially uncomfortable. It felt like bigamy. The three of them could appear with bouffant hair and loud clothing on Jerry Springer.

But this was the sensible part of Siobhan talking. Deep down, she was desperate to take that final step with Jack. Now he'd given her the chance to do that. The sensible voice said, 'Don't do it.' The romantic in Siobhan urged her on. She crouched in Audrey's Fulham hallway, half a ton of tweed draped over her, and vacillated about dinner. From inside the living room, she could hear Audrey's voice.

'Hermaphroditism,' Audrey announced. 'Not as uncommon as you might think . . .'

Siobhan looked down at her mobile. Tapped the keys and pressed 'Send'. Then she found her coat and slipped it over her shoulders. She tiptoed to the end of the hall, opened the front door and stepped out.

Richard's kiss landed as awkwardly as a Cuban tourist jet with engine trouble. He'd been unsure whether to aim for Beth's lips or her cheek. He'd dithered a second too long, until Beth decided to avoid the issue altogether by turning her head away. His lips collided with her cheekbone and then ended up somewhere in her hair.

Richard pulled his head back and swiftly looked down. He was embarrassed. He could also taste Beth's shampoo. It was familiar and curiously poignant.

'Shall we go?' said Beth briskly, launching herself and the pushchair along the pavement.

Richard scuttled after, catching up and walking beside Beth, but careful not to allow his body to touch hers. They moved together, separated by a tiny strip of space as crucial to them as the layer of air under a Hovercraft.

'So, how're things?' asked Richard, as casually as possible. He, like Beth, found the beginnings of their meetings now awkward, jerky almost, like the first few pulls on a rowing machine.

'Oh, fine,' said Beth, a touch too brightly. 'And you?'

Beth had decided not to bring up the Chastity situation until Richard mentioned it. Even if she was dying to gloat, she didn't want to appear too interested.

'Yeah, you know,' replied Richard noncommittally, changing the subject. 'You, um, working?'

'Irons in the fire, projects in development, meetings, you know,' said Beth.

'If you need money, I could put a bit more in the joint account,' Richard offered.

'No, no. We're fine,' Beth lied.

Beth was sure there was a technical, psychological term for what she'd just done. Ah, yes, it was called cutting off your nose to spite your face. In truth, Beth could have done with some extra cash, but she couldn't bear to appear pathetic in front of Richard. If, and it was a very big if, there was to be a rapprochement between them, she wanted it to be negotiated on her side from a position of strength.

When they got to the park, Beth unclipped Stanley from his pushchair and lifted him on to a swing. Richard pushed and she looked on from a nearby park bench. Stanley gurgled delightedly as his father played peek-a-boo and tickled his feet. Richard, too, was clearly enjoying himself. Seeing them together, Beth had to admit that they blossomed in each other's company.

Beth sometimes wondered if Richard's relationship with his child would have been different if they'd had a girl. Was there something particular about fathers and sons? There was a sense, when she saw Richard with Stanley, that having a son gave him the chance to revisit his own childhood. Stanley's toys – cars, fire engines, balls and drums – allowed a legitimate regression.

For Beth, giving birth to a boy had been like being given a chemistry set for Christmas. She had unwrapped it, unsure of what any of the bits were really for. Early experiments resulted in peculiar smells and the odd explosive episode, but she was learning as she went along.

'Mama, mama,' shouted Stanley, as he came tottering towards her. He threw his arms round her knees and laid his head in her lap. She stroked his hair.

Richard sat down beside her, announcing: 'I'm knackered.'

'You try doing it twenty-four hours a day, on your own,' said Beth crisply.

'I know, but you don't have to be on your own.' Richard paused, unsure whether to make a more explicit plea to be allowed back into the house so soon into the conversation.

It didn't matter; Beth had understood perfectly. 'No. It's too quick,' she declared, getting up and taking Stanley's hand. 'Shall we go and play in the sand pit?'

'Why?' said Richard, following her. 'You need help with Stanley, and you can see how pleased he is to see me.'

'I don't want a baby-sitter, I want a husband,' said Beth, lifting Stanley into the sand pit. He staggered off, picked up a scoop and began digging.

She turned and looked directly at Richard. 'Anyway, I thought you were with *her*.'

Richard looked embarrassed. 'No, no, that's all over.'

'What do you mean, over?'

'I ended it.'

'She didn't dump you then?'

'No.'

Maybe Chastity had lied, but Beth doubted it. Even now, Richard was still trying to save face. She almost smiled at his ridiculousness.

'It was never right,' continued Richard. 'We had no history. I couldn't say: "Do you remember the time when . . ." It was as if the last ten years of my life had never happened; as if they were written on a blackboard with chalk and someone had just wiped a wet cloth over it.'

'Very poetic, except it was you who did the rubbing-out.'

Richard clasped his hands together in anguish. 'I know, I know.'

They say you should never kick a man when he's down, but

Beth knew that when it came to having a serious emotional conversation with someone of the male gender, about the only time he was willing was when he was already in crisis. He'd be too shell shocked to run away. There was another time, and that was when he was drunk, but then he wouldn't remember any of it the next day.

Beth seized her chance. 'I want us to be together,' she ventured. 'But I don't know whether I can get over what you did. You're not the man I thought you were. The man I thought I married was bright and well-read and passionate about his work. He wouldn't have gone off and had a sordid little fling with some girl who prances about in a G-string for a living. He'd have been too bloody embarrassed.' She paused. 'I don't know who you are.'

Richard gazed imploringly at her. 'I am the same man. I just went mad for a while.'

'Olivia says that she never loved Colin and he knew it,' said Beth. 'He knew she'd settled for him. I couldn't bear it if you were settling for me.'

'I'm not, I love you,' Richard answered.

He wanted to put his arms round Beth, but he didn't dare. The two of them had shifted to opposite ends of the bench and the thin layer of air that had separated them had swollen to a couple of feet of space. It was as if the more intimate the conversation became, the more exposed they felt and the greater their need to pad themselves with protective air, like bubble wrap on a pair of precious antique vases.

'You say you love me, but I don't know whether I believe you,' Beth said.

Richard sighed with exasperation. 'Well, if you don't believe that, then there really isn't any hope for us.'

'I didn't say that. It's just, I need to find a reason to like you again. At the moment, I am struggling not to hate you.'

'What about Stanley, isn't he a reason?'

They both looked over to the sand pit. Stanley glanced up and his face creased into a big smile. He burbled something unintelligible.

Beth looked back at Richard. 'I need to find a reason that's not about Stanley. I need to find a reason for me.'

Richard had no answer to that. There was an anxious gap in the conversation.

'Look, maybe it's my turn to have a mid-life crisis, the one I never had time for before,' said Beth. 'You said you got a bit lost in our marriage after Stanley. Well, so did I. Suddenly I'm a mother and that's what I'm supposed to be and I don't even know what that is. And I'm feeling trapped and panicky and I'm having real trouble remembering who I am. Beth. Who's she? What is she? So, anyway, you had your affair, and I went off and ended up in bed with Jack, and—'

'You did *what*?'

Beth hadn't made a deliberate decision not to tell Richard about Jack, but she hadn't meant to let it slip out quite like this.

'You said you ended up in bed with Jack.' Richard was incredulous.

'Yes, but—'

'Don't tell me. It didn't mean anything? And to think you made me grovel, and all the time you've been having an affair with that . . . that Australian simpleton!'

'Oh, well, if we're talking IQ, I think you'll find your bimbo is slightly closer to the green crayon level than Jack.'

'It isn't his IQ you're interested in, though, is it? So, how is he in bed? Good, is he?'

'Oh, Richard. Don't be so ridiculous.'

'Well, if you won't answer that, at least tell me how long it's been going on.'

'It only happened once. I don't even know if—'

Richard interrupted her. 'You expect me to believe that?'

'Yes.'

Richard had a look of total disgust on his face. 'My wife, with that—'

Beth exploded in fury. 'Your wife! Your wife! If you'd remembered I was your wife, maybe you wouldn't have shagged that tart!'

Richard shook his head. 'This changes everything. I thought you were the good one. The loyal wife. Now I find—'

'Oh, excuse me for falling off the pedestal on to which you shoved me WITHOUT MY CONSENT. I am a human being, not just your wife, or Stanley's mother, come to that.'

At the sound of his name, Stanley stumbled through the sand towards them.

'Mama,' he said, looking anxious and putting his hands in the air.

Beth reached forward and picked Stanley up. She felt a wave of guilt. Arguing in front of their child. They'd always said they'd never do that.

Richard had stood up. 'Look, I've got to think about all this,' he said, backing away from Beth. 'Frankly, it's come as a shock and, well, I'm disappointed. You say you don't recognise me; well, I don't recognise you either. At the moment, I don't think I can bear to be in the same room as you, let alone live with you.'

Richard walked out of the playground and out of the park. The question was, was it out of Beth's life as well?

Chapter Twenty-Five

The roses were sitting in a vase in the centre of the kitchen table when Olivia got back. Colin or Nigel must have arranged them. A small white envelope with her name on it was propped up against the base of the vase. Olivia ripped it open.

'*Mi amore*, Gianni XX,' it read.

Olivia sighed and tossed the card on the table, next to the other four. The house was beginning to resemble a florist's. Wherever you went, you were followed by the heavy scent of roses. This wasn't the way it was supposed to go. British woman old enough to know better has holiday fling with Italian waiter. She buggers off back to her real life in England and he moves on to the next tourist. That was what was supposed to happen. So why was Gianni determined to do things differently?

Olivia sat down. She reached over and picked up her little stack of cards and reread them. '*Mi amore.*' That was what they all said. '*Mi amore.*' What if that was how he really felt? She'd been lied to by James and now even by nice old Colin, so could she trust any of them? But maybe she was letting cynicism poison what could be her future happiness.

She got up and carried the cards over to the telephone. She hesitated, then picked up the receiver. She didn't need to look up the number. She knew it by heart. She'd rehearsed this moment so many times. The line clicked and then she heard the ring tone.

'*Prego?*' It was a woman's voice. A woman was answering Gianni's phone.

Olivia froze.

'*Prego?*'

Olivia's jaw clenched. She put down the phone, walked over to the bin, put her foot on the pedal and tipped the cards inside. It shut with a definite-sounding clatter. She opened the fridge door, took out a bottle of wine and poured herself a glass.

'Just because you're paranoid it doesn't mean the bastards aren't out to get you,' she announced before taking a very large sip.

Marcia smoothed down her skirt. The black leather felt slippery to the touch. She gave her charcoal polo-neck a tug and pulled back her shoulders. Was this how Boudicca felt on her way into battle? She knocked on the door to Patric's office.

'Come!' Patric shouted from the other side. (Marcia had often wondered if he used the same imperious tone with women he was in bed with.) 'Come!'

She pushed open the door and approached Patric's desk. He was reading a paper and didn't look up as she put a pile of post down.

'Thanks,' he said, absent-mindedly.

Marcia hovered for a moment, hoping he might put the paper down and look at her.

'Has Anastassia called?' Patric asked, still engrossed in his newsprint.

'No,' Marcia replied.

'When she does, can you put her straight through. It's a very important call.'

Marcia's stomach turned over. Had Anastassia come to a decision? She made a supreme effort not to show her anxiety, turning and beginning her retreat from Patric's office.

'Oh, and there was something else. My wife's birthday. You couldn't pop out and . . .'

Patric had torn himself away from today's news. Marcia looked round to see him with his mouth open, the sight of her bottom in a leather skirt having rendered him incapable of speech. After five seconds or so, he managed to close his jaw.

'Yes, Patric, you were saying could I pop out,' said Marcia, embarrassed, but also enjoying the sweetness of the moment.

'Jesus, what happened? I mean, you look . . . Your clothes. They're so, well, different. Jesus, Marcia, you're wearing leather!'

'I know what I'm wearing, Patric,' said Marcia.

Patric got to his feet and peered over his desk for a full-length view. 'Turn around,' he ordered.

'Oh, Patric.' Marcia was blushing now. She had wanted him to notice her, but this was too much.

'No, turn around.'

Reluctantly, Marcia did a slow 360-degree turn.

'You've got legs, Marcia. You've got legs!' declared Patric.

'I have had for the last twelve years,' said Marcia drily.

Patric was flabbergasted. 'Yeah, but . . .' He shook his head. 'You look fantastic.'

Marcia's embarrassed blush turned to a flush of triumph. She could hear her phone ringing outside. 'I'll just get that,' she said, walking out with almost a sashay.

Brrng, went the doorbell.

Beth picked up Stanley, swung him on to her right hip and walked up the hall. On the doorstep was a motorcycle messenger, still in his helmet.

'Da!' shrieked Stanley delightedly, pointing at the helmet.

What was it about little boys and motorbikes, or big boys for that matter? Was there an extra male chromosome that decreed an obsession with dangerous wheeled objects? Beth suddenly had a terrible vision of her beautiful child crushed under a bus, a mangled Harley lying nearby. It was not going to happen. Stanley might be the only eighteen year old still strapped into his baby seat, but at least he'd be safe.

Beth signed for the package and walked back downstairs into the kitchen. Stanley ran about chasing his favourite bin and she tore open the padded envelope. Inside, there was a typed letter.

'Dear Beth, Since you won't pick up when I call – again – I have resorted to this.'

'Resorted, bloody cheek!' Beth was about to throw it in the bin, but it was just too tantalising.

'No, don't throw this away,' the letter continued.

Beth smiled.

'I've thought about it and I think I can put your affair with Jack behind us.'

Again, Beth had the urge to throw the letter in the bin. It wasn't an affair! It was one night! She went as far as to crumple up the paper. Then she uncrumpled it and read on.

'I'm not saying I forgive you. But for Stanley's sake, I think we should try to move forward.'

What was that warm sensation round Beth's ears? Oh yes, it was the steam coming out of them.

'I'm willing to try and I hope you are. Please call me. Richard.'

Beth sat down. She let out a hoarse laugh. Richard was unbelievable. Her affair! What about his? He made it sound as if he was willing to take her back out of the goodness of his heart!

She looked down at Stanley. Could the man who'd sent that letter really be his father? And her husband? Maybe she'd just kidded herself that he was even a moderately modern man. Maybe Olivia was right, and deep down all men were unreconstructed. All that stuff they spouted about how, of course, women were equal was just flim-flam to get you to take your bra off in the first place.

But if that was true, Beth could trade Richard in for a newer model, and in eight years' time she would be facing the same grim realisation. Richard was better at the flim-flam than most. She'd spent eight years training him, for God's sake. If he was a racehorse, he'd be a Cheltenham Gold Cup winner by now. Even if he had begun to falter, with that pedigree you wouldn't put him out to pasture – unless he'd broken a leg, in which case you'd shoot him. This was an option Beth hadn't entirely discounted.

The dilemma facing her was simple. Did she abandon her romantic notions of marriage for the sake of her son and, she had to be honest, herself as well? To be single in your thirties was not the fun-packed adventure it was in your twenties. She only had to look at Siobhan to see that. All the thirty-something men were dating twenty-something women and all the thirty-something

427

women were reading self-help books and getting their eggs frozen. To be a thirty-seven-year-old single mother in that environment was as good as wearing a skull and crossbones on your forehead.

The faint vestiges of a feminist conscience stirred themselves into life. 'So what?' they said. 'You don't need a man to be fulfilled!' And, of course, that was true. But the reality of parenthood was that it was a whole lot easier if there were two of you. Compromise was one of those words, like 'electric blanket' and 'carpet sweeper', that made Beth feel like her granny. It sounded so 1950s. But this was what Beth was faced with. Should she compromise her notion of what a good marriage ought to be, or did that make her a failure?

Beth looked at Stanley.

'Dada,' he said.

'You must be Steve the computer whizz. Hi, I'm Karen from *On The House*.'

Karen was leaning over the shoulder of a man in a polycotton shirt. Ordinarily, she would have given any man in mixed fibres a wide berth, but needs must.

'Um, yes. Hi,' said Steve nervously, wiping his palms on his acrylic slacks before accepting the hand proffered by Karen. As soon as he could, he withdrew from the handshake, though, so as to push his glasses up his nose.

'Well, Steve, I've got a teeny-weeny problem,' simpered Karen in her best little-girl voice. 'Do you mind if I sit down?'

Before he could answer, Karen had perched herself on the edge of his desk. He shifted uncomfortably. Being a computer nerd,

Steve was unused to physical contact of any kind, especially female. He preferred his women virtual.

'I find all this computer stuff terribly confusing. But I hear you're an expert,' lisped Karen.

'Well . . .' said Steve, uncertainly.

'The thing is, I wondered whether you could have a little peek at some e-mails for me.'

'Are these e-mails yours?'

'Not exactly.'

'You want me to access someone else's personal e-mail files?'

'Yes! How clever of you! Only, it's not just one. I need a sweep of all my staff, really.'

'I don't know if that's quite ethical,' said Steve, frowning, a fine sweat just visible on his upper lip.

Karen took a piece of hair and twiddled it round her finger. 'But Steve, I know you could do it, and it is only little me asking.'

'I'd like to help, I really would, but . . .'

Karen leapt off the desk and placed a hand, claw-like, round Steve's throat. She pinned his head to his keyboard so that it gave off hysterical beeps and whirrs and the screen flashed alarmingly.

'Listen, you sad excuse for a human being,' she hissed. 'If you don't do what I want AND DO IT NOW, I will tell Human Resources you've been surfing porn in company time. GAY PORN!'

Steve wavered. 'Well, I still think—'

'When I've finished with you, you won't be able to get a job sweeping up in an internet café!'

'All right, all right,' said Steve. 'Just give me the names.'

Karen smiled, let go of Steve's neck and smoothed down her own clothing. She produced a three-page list from her pocket.

'By five o'clock, sweetie, OK?'

'Have you heard anything?' asked Olivia.

Beth shook her head.

'God, it's worse than my GCSE results,' sighed Siobhan.

'Hopefully we'll do rather better than I did in my O-levels,' said Olivia, ruefully.

The three of them were sitting on a park bench in Soho Square. To their left, two men with thick Scottish accents and open cans of Special Brew were abusing passers-by. To their right, a noisy argument was going on between a man and his much younger boyfriend: 'I am not buying you a Porsche! You can have a Fiat Punto and that's it!'

'Nice spot,' said Olivia.

'Sorry, but I couldn't very well come to the office, could I?' answered Beth.

Brrng, brrng. It was Beth's mobile.

'Hello, Beth Davies speaking.'

Beth put her hand over the receiver and mouthed the words 'Anastassia Frink's office.' Olivia and Siobhan instinctively clutched each other's hands and held on to them.

'Yes ... Yes ... No ... Really?'

'What's she saying?' whispered Siobhan to Beth.

Beth waved the question away with her hand.

'Well, the reason Anastassia hasn't got a CV for Phoenix Productions is that we are rather new ... Very new ... We haven't actually made any programmes yet ...'

Olivia and Siobhan exchanged an anxious glance.

'But our team is very experienced . . .'

Olivia and Siobhan nodded wildly.

'. . . and the good thing about being a new company is that we're not jaded. We are raring to go!'

'That's good,' whispered Siobhan.

'Right . . . OK . . . Later today . . . Fine . . . Bye.'

Beth ended the call. Olivia and Siobhan were staring at her like a pair of hungry puppies.

'Well?' asked Siobhan. 'What did they say?'

'It's between us and one other company. Didn't say who, but they've got more experience,' said Beth. 'We should hear later today.'

'God, I wish I had a religion,' wailed Olivia.

'You do. It's called shopping,' said Siobhan.

'You've heard of Christian Scientists?' said Beth, laughing. 'Well, you're a Christian Lacroix.'

Olivia smiled. 'Well, I wish I had a proper religion. Then I'd start praying.'

'Start praying anyway,' said Beth.

Marcia's phone was ringing. The flashing red light said it was an internal call.

'Marcia?' said Patric.

'Yes,' she replied.

'I was just wondering if you, you know, um, fancied lunch?'

'Lunch?'

'Yes. You know. At the Milton.'

Marcia didn't answer. She was too shocked. Was Patric asking her what she thought he was?

'Are you still there?'

'Yes, yes,' said Marcia, recovering herself. 'When you say lunch, do you mean . . .'

'Room 112. Can you book it, and remember . . .'

'I know, I know. No mint on the pillow.'

Siobhan and Olivia walked back into the office and were immediately spotted by Karen.

'Oh, what a coincidence. I was hoping to speak to both of you and here you are together!' she declared. 'Could you just come into my office for a moment?'

Siobhan looked at Olivia and Olivia looked at Siobhan. They were like a couple of murder suspects being brought in for questioning who hadn't had time to synchronise their alibis. They braced themselves.

When they got into Karen's office, she motioned them to sit on the sofa.

'How are you both?' Karen asked, full of mock concern. 'Are you all right? Are you happy? You know, I do think it's so important to be *happy* in your work, don't you?'

Siobhan and Olivia muttered something vague.

'If you weren't happy, you would tell me, wouldn't you?' said Karen.

Again, Siobhan and Olivia just mumbled.

'Rather than . . .' Karen's voice had begun to rise, in both pitch and volume '. . . go behind my back and attempt to steal . . .' it was getting even louder '. . . the *On The House* slot out from under me?' Her speech ended in a bellow of a force steelworkers might use in a particularly busy foundry.

'I don't know what you mean,' said Olivia, trying gamely to save Siobhan and herself from certain death.

Karen reached into her office drawer and pulled out a sheaf of papers.

'Siobhan, perhaps you'd like to explain these?' she said, as she dumped them into her lap.

They were Siobhan's e-mails to Jack, including the one outlining the plan to make a rival pitch to Channel 6. Siobhan stared at the pile of paper. Their geese weren't so much cooked as charred beyond recognition.

'Clear your desks and get out!' Karen spat.

As they left Karen's office, Olivia's mobile went. It was Beth.

'Anastassia's office just called. She's come to a decision.'

Chapter Twenty-Six

Olivia and Siobhan sat slumped on their Fresh and Earthy bamboo stools, shrouded in an all-enveloping blanket of depression. They barely had the energy to sip their drinks. Occasionally one of them would say something along the lines of 'I can't believe this has happened', or 'Karen will burn in hell.' Otherwise, though, they just stared at hugely enlarged pictures of vegetables on the wall and sank into an intellectual torpor not unlike that enjoyed by the average savoy cabbage.

'Why are we back here? I thought we hated it?' It was Beth, pushing her way through the front door.

'We do, but everywhere else is packed at this time,' answered Olivia. 'This place is so horrible, at least you can find somewhere to park your bottom.'

'If you don't mind it going numb,' added Siobhan, lifting her bum off her bamboo seat and rubbing it.

'I got you a Bark Booster,' Olivia continued, pointing at a paper cup filled with a brown, sludgy liquid.

'I would say "That looks delicious", but it doesn't,' said Beth. 'What's in it?'

'It's supposed to pep you up,' announced Olivia.

'Well, looking at you two, it doesn't seem to be working, does it?'

Olivia and Siobhan sighed.

Beth unwound her velvet scarf and sat down. 'Look, we gave it a go and it didn't work out. We didn't get the deal. Nobody died.'

'I know, but I really wanted it to work,' said Siobhan.

'Besides, now Karen's won,' added Olivia.

'No she hasn't. She's only won if we give up. There are other programmes, other channels,' said Beth.

Brrng, brrng. Olivia's phone was ringing.

'Hi, Marcia . . . It's OK. Well, it's not OK, but you know what I mean . . . Oh, they're, um . . .' Olivia glanced at Siobhan and Beth '. . . bearing up. What about you? Where are you? I can't hear you very well . . . The Milton? What are you doing there? . . . Sorry, Marcia, the line's getting worse. What was that about Patric? . . . Look, just call me later, bye.'

Olivia turned back to the others. 'Marcia's at the Milton.'

'With Patric?' asked Siobhan incredulously.

'Apparently so,' said Beth.

'Bloody hell. I did a better makeover than I thought!' exclaimed Olivia. 'She's shagging the boss now.'

'Oh, come on. This is Marcia we're talking about,' Beth said. 'She's probably gone there to drop off some papers or something.'

They all nodded.

Siobhan looked at her watch. 'Oh God, I've got to go. Meant to be going out tonight. Don't really feel like it now.'

Olivia was amused. 'Jack *again*?'

Siobhan looked embarrassed. 'Yeah, well, you know—'

Beth interrupted her. 'Jack! He doesn't know we didn't get it!'

'It's all right. I'll break the news,' said Siobhan, getting up off her seat with some difficulty and starting to walk to the door.

'Don't do anything we wouldn't do,' shouted Olivia.

Siobhan turned round. 'I haven't seen my feet for at least twelve weeks, and when I roll over at night I unleash a tidal wave that could flatten several of the smaller Caribbean islands. I'm not capable of doing anything you *would* do, let alone anything you *wouldn't*!' She smiled. 'Talk to you later.'

Beth and Olivia stayed for another half-hour or so. They couldn't bear to go home straight away. There, they would have to get on with things, talk to other people and pretend it didn't matter. And it did.

When they did finally lever themselves upright and head for the door, Beth stopped halfway.

'There's something I've got to do,' she said.

She walked back to her table and picked up her more than half full Bark Booster. Then she went up to the counter. Behind it, a very thin girl in a vest was practising yoga poses with her eyes shut. Beth jerked her hand forward and brown sludgy liquid landed all over her.

Patric slid the credit card key into the slot, waited for the light to go green then withdrew it. This act of unlocking the door was performed with the sort of slick wrist action the maître d' of an expensive Italian restaurant might use to shake a napkin out of a swan shape and place it across a female diner's lap. Patric even wore the same half-deferential, half-arrogant smile as he pushed the handle down and opened the door to Room 112 of the Milton Hotel.

'After you,' he said.

Marcia felt a twinge of irritation. Patric's showy chivalry was supposed to make her feel special. It didn't. It reminded her that she was simply the latest recruit to his chorus line of sexual conquests.

How many times had he opened the door like that before? How many times had he said 'After you'? How many times . . .

She didn't need an answer to any of these questions. She knew how many times. She was the one who'd booked the room. Then, while Patric got up to whatever he got up to in Room 112, she was the one who'd sat at her desk, like a Pekinese outside a supermarket, patiently awaiting her master's return. She had eaten her miserable cheese sandwich and answered his phone. 'No, he's not in,' she'd told people – Anastassia, his wife, even his kids – 'he's in a meeting.' And afterwards, she'd filled in his expense form. 'Lunch meeting, £95,' she'd written, having, of course, secured a half-day discount.

But now she was here. The heels of her boots were sinking into the soft cream hotel carpet and it was her breath muffled by the peach-coloured international executive-style soft furnishings. Marcia had always been curious about the room itself. In her mind, Room 112, the Milton Hotel, had attained an almost mythical status. It was like the inside of the Queen's private apartments in Buckingham Palace, or Madonna's en suite. She just wanted to see what it was like.

Had Patric not been there, Marcia would have rushed into the bathroom and checked out the soap and shaken up the little bottles of shampoo. Then she'd have liked a good look at the contents of the mini bar – champagne or Asti Spumante? Pistachios or salted peanuts? Finally, she'd have done a circuit of the room, feeling the fabric of the curtains and the sofa, running her hand over the polished surfaces of the coffee table and the marble tiles in the bathroom. After all those years of booking this room for other women, Marcia wanted to feel a sense of ownership of a space that had for so long remained off limits.

She breathed in the scent of furniture polish and faded rose petals coming from a dish of pot-pourri on the window sill. She tried to feel the magic, experience the mystique. She closed her eyes. Room 112. She was in Room 112. But she might as well have been calling bingo numbers. She felt nothing. When she opened her eyes and looked around, all she saw was an anonymous hotel room with a dent in the carpet next to the sofa where it had been moved to do the hoovering and not put back in quite the same place afterwards.

'Shall we?' said Patric, gesturing towards the bed. He had taken off his jacket and hung it on a wire contraption designed so the busy executive didn't have to manage the arduous task of walking ten feet to the wardrobe to keep his clothes crease-free.

Marcia stepped towards the bed. In the hotel room gloom, she didn't spot the shoe-cleaning box in her path. She bashed her toe on the edge.

'Ow!' she shrieked.

Patric didn't look up. 'You OK?'

'Yeah, it's nothing,' she answered, embarrassed by her clumsiness.

Marcia felt a shiver of excitement. Twelve years she'd waited for this moment. She'd watched Patric in seduction mode, putting a hand on the shoulder of one woman, an arm round the waist of another. She'd seen the intimate whispers and the discreet, or not so discreet, shared smiles. She'd watched and said nothing.

Patric was taking off his shoes and placing them on one side of the bed. He'd peeled back the covers and they were folded in a neat V-shape.

Marcia felt awkward. Normally, she knew what to do. But here, in this situation, she was completely out of her depth. She groped desperately for something to say or do to fill the silence. Calm, she just had to stay calm. Patric was now removing his socks. She could see his naked ankles. Oh God!

Marcia had an idea. 'What about some champagne?' she asked.

Patric laughed. 'Are you all right? You know the expenses situation as well as I do, well, probably better, don't you?' He shook his head in disbelief.

It hadn't occurred to Marcia that Patric would expect to put *everything* on expenses. After twelve years, wasn't she worth a measly bottle of Moët? Apparently not.

'If you're thirsty, why don't you get some water from the bathroom?' he added.

Since they'd arrived in the hotel room, Patric had barely spoken to her. If this was how he operated, then Marcia was amazed he'd been so successful. She would have been annoyed if she hadn't been so nervous. Patric was now starting to unzip his trousers. She panicked and darted for the bathroom. 'Just getting that, um, water then,' she said, fleeing.

She shut the bathroom door and walked over to the sink. She turned the tap on in case Patric could hear her nerves jangling through the wall. They seemed deafening to her. She put one hand on either side of the sink and leaned forward and stared at herself in the mirror.

'Pull yourself together,' she whispered.

Studying her reflection restored some of Marcia's confidence. She didn't scrub up too badly. Of course, much of it was down to Olivia. She'd done a heck of a job. Marcia ran her fingers through her hair, and grimaced to check there was nothing caught in her teeth. There wasn't.

'He's not good enough for you.' That was what Aidan had said to her.

She took a tube of raspberry-flavoured lipgloss out of her handbag and smoothed on another layer, rubbed her lips together and took a deep breath.

When she re-emerged, Patric was wearing only his pants. He was bending over the trouser press. His back was hunched and his tummy formed a peanut shape over the top of his burgundy mini briefs. His legs were thin and white. He looked like a turkey foraging for grain on the farmyard floor. His trousers were folded inside the press and he was just shutting the door.

Marcia walked over to him, as nonchalantly as possible.

'So, what did you have in mind?' she asked, as suggestively as she could muster.

'Can you just hang on a minute. Just need to . . .' said Patric. He was concentrating on the dial that controlled the time on the trouser press. The maximum number of minutes available was thirty. Patric turned it to twenty. 'Now, what was that you were saying?'

Marcia was stunned. It wasn't just the fact that he only thought she was worth twenty minutes, which was insulting enough; it was the exactitude of it. Not twenty-five minutes, or fifteen, but twenty.

After twelve years of these lunches, he had obviously worked out the bare minimum amount of time needed for his mission to be accomplished, and it was twenty minutes. A bit of foreplay, the sex itself and then a quick peck on the cheek, and he could be back in the office in half an hour. Except he wasn't. When Patric had a lunch meeting, he was away for at least an hour. So what happened in the missing thirty minutes? Then Marcia remembered the carrier bag.

When Patric returned from his assignations, he invariably did so clutching a carrier bag from the upmarket deli next to the hotel. Marcia had assumed his bottle of olive oil or loaf of rosemary focaccia were guilt purchases for his wife. Now, she knew it was because he had time to kill and he'd rather browse the balsamic vinegars in Deli-cioso than have to actually talk to the woman he'd just slept with.

Of all the self-centred, egotistical, lazy, arrogant bastards, she fumed silently. Patric was oblivious to her rapidly deteriorating humour. He put his arms round her and began kissing her neck. Then another thought occurred to her. She giggled. Patric carried on nibbling. He had now begun to slide a hand up her jumper. The giggle turned into a laugh, and before long, it became a full-flown guffaw. Marcia's shoulders were shaking so much, Patric couldn't get a firm grip with his lips. It was like trying to apply a plunger to a wet spaniel.

Patric gave up. He was annoyed. 'OK,' he announced, 'is this nervous laughter or what? I mean, I know you're not very experienced . . .'

Marcia was laughing too much to be annoyed. 'Twenty minutes. You put it on for twenty minutes,' she managed, before collapsing into hysterical giggles again.

Patric frowned, at a loss to know what she was going on about. He considered his options and decided to plough on regardless. He extended a hand towards Marcia's breast. He was getting cold in just his pants and he thought a spot of nipple tweaking might silence her giggles.

She waved his hand away. 'Mr Twenty Minutes. That's why they call you Mr Twenty Minutes,' she wailed. 'The trouser press. Mr Twenty Minutes.' Tears were now rolling down her cheeks. She disentangled herself from Patric and staggered into the bathroom to get a tissue.

There was a knock at the bedroom door. Marcia put a hand over her mouth to muffle her laughter and staggered into the bathroom.

'Oh, for God's sake,' fumed Patric. 'What now?' He marched over to the door and flung it open.

'Linda! What are you doing here?' he exclaimed.

'What do you mean?' asked Chastity, pushing past him. 'I got a message to meet you here.'

Patric was confused. 'You, here, today? I don't think so.'

Chastity registered Patric's pants and the fact that they were all that he was wearing. 'What's going on? Who's here with you?' she asked.

'Nobody,' replied Patric unconvincingly, recognising the precipice over which he was now dangling.

'I don't believe you. Where is she?' demanded Chastity, stalking the room, looking behind curtains and peering under the bed.

'There's nobody, really . . .' said Patric.

Chastity turned and faced the bathroom door. 'She's in there, isn't she?'

'No, no. I mean, who?' gabbled Patric, darting towards the bathroom and standing in front of the door.

Forget the Incredible Hulk; a woman who thinks she is being cheated on has superhuman powers of sight, smell, hearing and, most useful in this case, strength. Chastity brushed Patric aside like a piece of fluff off her lapel. When the bathroom door swung open, Marcia was standing in her underwear.

'Marcia!' exclaimed Patric and Chastity together, in shock.

'You didn't think you were the only one, did you?' said Marcia. 'Patric and I go back such a long way.'

'You don't understand,' stammered Patric.

'Oh, I understand,' said Chastity. 'I understand perfectly well. You've been having an affair!'

The look on Patric's face was one of pure panic. He was cornered. Had it been his wife standing where Chastity was, then maybe he might have got out alive. Wives of persistent philanderers, having on the whole come to terms with their other half's behaviour, are pretty much unshockable. But Chastity was Patric's mistress, and however hardbitten a mistress is – in Chastity's case, very – she still harbours the fantasy that she is the one and only. It is this that keeps her warm at night. To find she is not the one true love exposes the whole relationship as a sham.

'But I haven't been having an affair. At least, not with Marcia.'

'Oh, there's somebody else *as well*, is there?' Chastity was moving into Bette Davis mode now.

'Yes, no. Well, you know, I never said we were exclusive.'

In the background, Marcia had put her clothes on and picked up her handbag from the sofa.

'How many others are there? How many?' Chastity was screaming as Patric cowered.

Marcia tiptoed out.

Chapter Twenty-Seven

Siobhan surveyed her less than rich and varied selection of maternity wear, searching for something that didn't make her look like Demis Roussos. She chose a red jumper and black trousers. She took the jumper off again when she realised she resembled a very large tomato and put on a black jumper instead. Then she rifled through her jewellery box.

In one of the mother and baby magazines Olivia had lent her, it said that to draw attention away from your bump, you should wear striking earrings. Frankly, she'd have needed a naked Chippendale dangling from each ear lobe to distract attention from her tummy. In the last couple of weeks, she seemed to have doubled in size.

Siobhan abandoned the jewellery idea and opted for bright red lipstick instead. This was another way to create an alternative focal point, according to Olivia's magazine. It did that all right. Had she been sitting in a coal hole, her lips would still have been visible.

Siobhan was having dinner at Sionara Gdansk. She hadn't been here before, but, according to Liam, the herring sashimi marinaded in vodka was fabulous. It didn't fill you up, but you were too pissed to notice. When she arrived, the miniature Japanese maître d's eyes almost popped out of their sockets. After much bowing, he rushed her to her table to sit down. He clearly felt that if he made her wait, she might give birth on the spot.

Once in her place there was more bowing and she was left to contemplate a potato – an ironic reference to the Polish influence on the menu – sitting in the middle of the tablecloth.

Her King Edward not being that riveting, Siobhan decided to visit the Ladies'. In her condition, her bladder had shrunk to the size of a Sindy handbag, so it was wise to go as often as possible. It was then that she learned the down side of eating in a minimalist nirvana. Sionara Gdansk's designer had vetoed conventional signage, indeed, any signage at all, on the grounds that it would interrupt his clean lines. Finding the loo was therefore an impossibility. Siobhan wandered up and down for a while before a member of staff darted forward, bowed and pointed.

When she got back to the table, Jack had arrived. Next to the Lilliputian staff, he looked enormous. He also looked un-comfortable. Although he'd chosen the restaurant, it wasn't his sort of thing at all. He had selected it because he knew how much Siobhan wanted to eat here. She thought this was sweet.

Siobhan was suddenly gripped by self-doubt. He must think I look like a hippo, she thought.

But Jack put her at her ease. He negotiated a route round her frontage and kissed her on the cheek. 'Hi, Blondie.'

'I can tell you hate it. Let's go somewhere else,' said Siobhan.

Jack waved away her concern. 'It's fine,' he drawled. 'Let's have a drink.'

A Sapporo for Jack and a glass of mineral water for Siobhan later, and they were looking at the menu.

'What d'you reckon to potato latka sushi?' asked Jack.

'Probably comes with a complementary side order of weeping gypsy violinist, which actually might come in handy tonight,' said Siobhan. 'We didn't get the show. Sorry.'

'Oh, bad luck. You must be gutted,' Jack sighed.

Siobhan crouched forward over the table. She groaned.

'Look, it's not that bad,' said Jack.

'I'll be fine. Just give me a minute,' said Siobhan. 'Touch of heartburn, I think.'

Five minutes later, she was bent double again. And five minutes after that. An ominous pattern was emerging.

'Jack?' said Siobhan, her voice distorted due to the fact that she was hugging herself so hard, her face was squished against the potato in front of her.

He nodded.

'I think my waters just broke.'

Up to that moment, Jack had been able to kid himself that maybe Siobhan wasn't in labour. Now, there was no doubt. He leapt to his feet and began waving to a waiter.

'Hey, mate. Could ya rustle up the bill and a cab?'

Siobhan struggled to her feet. 'No time, Jack. It'll be quicker if we hail one outside.'

When they got outside, which took some time because Siobhan had to keep stopping and the waiters had to keep bowing, there was a taxi drought.

'You know, I'm really annoyed,' said Siobhan, as they hovered on the pavement.

' 'Cause there are no cabs?'

'No, because my waters didn't break in Marks and Spencer. They give you a free gift voucher. If only I'd known, I'd have spent the evening hanging about in the food hall until it happened. Even better, if I'd actually had the baby in store and I decided I didn't like it, they've got that no-quibble refund policy. Do you think I could have swapped a newborn for a cashmere jumper?' The last few words were slightly strangulated, as Siobhan was gripped by another contraction. She groaned and sat down on the pavement.

Jack crouched beside her and stroked her forehead. 'There, there,' he said, as if she was a seven year old who had just fallen off her bike.

It was a scene that they both should have found acutely embarrassing: Jack because he was a bloke, and the last thing a bloke wants on a date is to be faced with a woman's gynaecology in crisis; and Siobhan because her feminine veneer was being stripped away to reveal her as a woman at her most basic, instinctual and, well, messy. Neither of them had any control over the situation.

But, sitting on the pavement, as people walked round them and traffic roared a few feet away, Siobhan felt calm.

'You stay there,' said Jack, getting to his feet and scanning the horizon for a cab.

Siobhan decided it was now or never. 'Can I ask you something?'

'Yeah,' said Jack, absent-mindedly.

'You and Beth, you know when you, um, slept together—'

Jack interrupted her. 'Ah, well, I haven't been *entirely* honest about that.'

'What do you mean?'

450

Another contraction was building. Siobhan pulled her knees to her stomach and hugged them.

'We *slept* together. That was true. But we didn't exactly sleep together, if you know what I mean.'

Siobhan was rocking back and forth on her bottom. 'Whoo, whoo, whoo,' she panted.

'It's not that I wanted to lie to you, although I seem to have done a lot of that, haven't I?' Jack bent down on his haunches and looked desperately into Siobhan's eyes. 'I didn't tell the whole truth at the beginning, and then I couldn't change my story . . .'

Siobhan's contraction had eased. She sat up.

'Are you telling me that you and Beth didn't have sex?'

Jack nodded. 'Sorry.'

'What about all the others – the lonely housewives?'

'No, nothing ever happened.'

'What, with none of them?'

'No.'

'What about that woman in Cardiff? She said you were the father of her baby, so you must have slept with her.'

Jack shook his head. 'She was pissed off because I *wouldn't* sleep with her.'

Siobhan's next contraction had started. The pavement felt cold and clammy, but she barely noticed it, the pain was so intense. 'Whoo, whoo, whoo,' she panted.

The panting was all NCT Audrey's idea. She said it would ease the pain. Siobhan was puffing like a steam engine, without the slightest effect.

'I know what people think of me,' said Jack, sitting back down. 'They think I'm this Jack-the-lad, any-port-in-a-storm, wherever-

I-lay-my-hat cliché. And I'll admit, I have played on that. It was part of the persona, the TV persona that I made up. But then it became a prison. I was trapped inside this stereotype and I couldn't escape. Everywhere I went, women expected me to rip their clothes off.'

'And you said no?' Siobhan managed to whisper.

'Yes. It may seem difficult to believe, but some of us men like to get to know a woman before we take it to that level. We want more than a quick fumble on someone else's sofa.'

Siobhan would have laughed, had she not been racked with pain. Instead, she leaned forward and planted a kiss on Jack's lips. He put his arms round her and she squeezed him tight. Too tight. When she eased her grip, it took several minutes for the feeling to return to his shoulder.

The contraction over, Siobhan looked quizzically into Jack's eyes.

'So with all those women on our shoots, when you told us you went round supposedly to put up shelves, you were . . .'

'Putting up shelves.'

Now Siobhan smiled.

'So how many women have you actually slept with, then?'

Jack looked embarrassed. 'Seven,' he announced, running a hand through his long fringe.

'Seven!'

Jack nodded and Siobhan began to laugh. She'd been scared of taking things further with him because he was such a Romeo, and he'd had fewer lovers than his shoe size.

Jack looked anxious. He was with a woman who might be having a baby at any moment and they were sitting in the middle of the pavement.

'Can you walk?' he asked, scrambling to his feet.

Siobhan nodded and they began to shuffle forward, albeit slowly. Jack had spotted one of those little green huts up ahead where taxi drivers get cups of tea. There was a tantalising line of cabs outside. When they reached them, however, all the drivers were missing.

'I hate to worry you, but this is getting serious,' moaned Siobhan. She reached out and grabbed the nearest taxi door handle as another contraction kicked in. 'Whoo, whoo, whoo,' she panted, bent double.

'Wait here!' Jack ordered.

'Well, I'm not, whoo, whoo, exactly going to, whoo, whoo, do a runner, whoo, whoo, am I?'

Jack sprinted up to the green hut and threw the door open.

Siobhan could vaguely hear him saying something, then he emerged with a cabbie in tow.

'Thank, whoo, whoo, God,' Siobhan whispered under her breath.

Jack and the cabbie approached. Then the cabbie stopped dead.

'You're that bloke off the telly, aren't you?' he announced excitedly. 'Now, don't tell me, don't tell me. What show is it again?'

'Does it really matter, mate?' asked Jack, automatically going back into professional Aussie mode.

'I'll get it in a minute, I will,' said the cabbie.

'Ugh!' Siobhan groaned, as another contraction hit her. They were now two minutes apart.

'Look, mate—'

Jack was interrupted. 'I know! You're that Jason Donovan, aren't ya? Off *Home and Away*. You are, aren't ya? Mind you, yer hair's looking better these days. 'Ad a transplant? What's Kylie like, then?'

'I'm not Jason Donovan,' said Jack firmly, the seriousness of the situation making him abandon his Crocodile Dundee impression. 'Now, if it's OK with you . . .'

'Ugh!' groaned Siobhan. 'Whoo, whoo, whoo.'

The cabbie didn't notice Jack's change of accent. 'I've got a pen and paper in the cab. Can I 'ave yer autograph? D'you think you could get me Kylie's? Always fancied 'er.' As he said this, he unlocked the driver's door of the taxi and reached inside.

Jack opened one of the back doors and helped Siobhan in.

'You OK?'

Siobhan smiled weakly.

'Could ya put: "To Barry"?' said the cabbie, holding out a biro. 'An' then could ya do one for me mum, Shirley. She's sixty-eight, just 'ad a hip operation. Then there's me sister Jean and her daughter Suzanne. Suzanne won't know who you are. She's only nine and you 'aven't been on *Home and Away* for a while, 'ave ya? Must get right up yer nose when people say: "Didn't you used to be Jason Donovan?" Do you get that? Bet you do. I dunno how . . .'

Jack snapped. He snatched the car keys and jumped into the front seat.

'Oi, Jason, what ya doin'? You 'aven't got me address to send me Kylie's–' The cabbie was cut off by the sound of the ignition starting.

'Hold on, Blondie!' Jack shouted, before screeching away from the kerb.

In between panting, Siobhan breathed a sigh of relief. Technically, what Jack and she were doing was car theft, but there couldn't be a court in the land who'd convict them, especially when they heard the Jason Donovan bit. At least they were on their way.

'Dreadful man! I thought he'd never stop talking,' said Jack, catching Siobhan's eye in the rear-view mirror. 'Still, shouldn't be too long now.'

Jack guided the cab through the central London traffic. Progress was slow, but Siobhan still felt every bump. She slumped down on the seat and closed her eyes, trying to imagine she was somewhere else. She was on a beach in St Tropez. The sea was gently lapping her feet.

There was a click, then a squeak, followed by a male voice with a thick American accent.

'Gee, Marge, these taxi cabs are too damned small!'

'Stop whining, Randy,' answered a female voice with the same thick Midwest accent. 'Hey, bud. Lice-ester Square.'

To Siobhan's horror, a large man of about sixty in a Nike baseball cap and shorts, and his wife, wearing an 'I've Been To Blenheim Palace' T-shirt, climbed into the cab. They hadn't seen her slumped in the seat. When they did see her, they froze, then thought better of it and carried on.

'Gee, honey, ya don' mind if we share ya taxi, d'ya? We're in kindava hurry,' Marge asked. Then they plonked themselves down next to her.

Siobhan felt another contraction kick in. 'Whoo, whoo, whoo,' she panted.

'Must be another foreigner,' declared Marge. Then she bellowed, 'Hey, honey, you been to Buck-hing-ham Palace yet? We're only here three days and we wanna know if it's worth the bucks.'

'Whoo, whoo, whoo,' went Siobhan.

Jack watched the scene unfold, but was powerless to act

because there was a police car behind him and he didn't want to arouse suspicion. So when the lights changed, he simply put his foot on the accelerator and moved off. For what seemed an age, he drove, aware of the bizarre happenings behind him.

Finally, the panda car veered off to the left. Jack slid back the glass window behind his head. 'Um, sorry,' he said to the Americans, 'but you're going to have to find yourselves another cab.'

He went on to explain why Siobhan was making such funny noises, why they'd stolen the taxi, and that they couldn't go to Lice-est-er Square because they had to get to a hospital. Pronto.

'Gee, it's just like *Thelma and Louise!*' declared Marge.

'Except they were both gals,' pointed out Randy.

'You always have to split hairs, don't you, Randy?'

'Whoo, whoo, whoo,' went Siobhan.

Neither Randy nor Marge were keen to miss this exciting experience, one with which they planned to regale their friends just as soon as they got back home. They were staying put.

'Get the camera, Randy,' instructed Marge.

Randy looped his arm out from under a strap and put a camcorder up to his eye, pointing it at Siobhan.

'Smile, honey, you're on candid camera,' he announced delightedly.

As it turned out, Randy had a cattle ranch in Oklahoma.

'I done my share o' foalin' and calfin', ain't I, Marge? Bit of a dab hand, y'might say! Now, let's have a lookee here at this little filly.' With that, he handed the camera to Marge, placed a hand on Siobhan's stomach and asked: 'How ya doin'?'

Siobhan shrugged her shoulders, as if to say: 'Not too bad.' Then she let out a groan not unlike that of a cow in severe pain.

'Y'know, Marge, it's a cryin' shame I ain't got my calfin' gloves with me.' Randy leaned forward and tapped on the glass partition. 'Hey, you. You ain't got five or six feet o' good strong rope an' a bucket on ya, have ya?'

Siobhan's panting went up an octave.

Marge took her hand. 'Never you mind, honey,' she said. 'You jus' hol' on as tight as you damn well please. An' you go ahead an' holler.' She adjusted the zoom on the camera. 'We got sound on this thing, ya know!'

'What the hell did you think you were doing?' Patric was so angry he was practically levitating. 'I never told you to call Linda and ask her to come to the Milton. It's Tuesday. That's not her day, is it? How could you be so stupid?'

Marcia looked at Patric and said nothing. They were in his office. It was late. She'd taken the rest of the afternoon off, reasoning that it might be wise to let Patric calm down. When she'd come back, however, he'd been sat outside his office, waiting for her, not so much like a Pekinese as a Rottweiler.

Patric dropped his voice to a whisper. 'Today was supposed to be just you and me, Marcia. I know you were nervous, but really, I don't understand how you could have got things mixed up like that.'

Marcia still didn't answer. She was looking at Patric and pitying him.

'I mean, it really was rather awkward, wasn't it? Her bursting in like that and you in your, um, well, without your clothes on, you know. Shame she arrived just when you'd got over the giggles. Still, maybe another lunch. Only next time, no mistakes, eh?'

'It wasn't a mistake.'

'What?'

'I said it wasn't a mistake. I meant for Linda to catch us. I organised it.'

Patric gasped. 'Why?'

'I thought she should learn to take what she dishes out.'

'What's she to you?'

'Let's just say I did it for a friend.'

'But you must have known how embarrassing it would be for me. Why would you do that to me?'

'Oven gloves.'

Patric was mystified.

'I have worked for you for twelve years. I've watched all your little affairs. I've organised them for you. Bought the presents, booked the hotel rooms . . .'

Patric adopted a self-satisfied smile. 'Ah, so you're jealous. I had no idea you'd been in love with me for twelve years. My, my.'

Marcia ignored his smugness and continued: 'I was jealous and, yes, I was in love with you. There, I've said it. For twelve years I was in love with you and you didn't even notice. But you know what? I'm not any more.'

Patric wrinkled his brow. 'But why did you agree to meet me at the Milton?'

It was Marcia's turn to feel smug. 'You didn't actually think I was going to go through with it, did you?' She laughed. 'And be just one more of your conquests? I don't think so. I'm worth more than that. You're not good enough for me. It was a ruse. A trap. And you fell right into it.'

Patric was now totally confused. 'I still don't understand . . .'

'I don't care who you sleep with but I wonder if your wife feels the same.' She waved a piece of paper in front of him. 'Remember, Patric, I do your expenses. In triplicate. You've always taken my efficiency for granted. Well, my records are impeccable and they go back a long, long way. Seven years, for example.' Marcia placed the sheet of paper in front of him. There was writing on it, and a column of figures on the right-hand side. Some were highlighted.

'I'm sure your wife would be interested to know that seven years ago you spent a certain weekend in a hotel room in Blackpool with Anastassia Frink.' Marcia flipped the paper over to reveal a photocopied page stapled to it. She pointed to a signature. 'Interesting to note that even then you didn't like paying for champagne, although you were quite happy to claim for it. That is Anastassia's signature, isn't it?'

Patric looked at the paper, then at Marcia, then at the paper again.

'As for Anastassia's husband, I understand he used to wrestle professionally,' Marcia added. 'And then, of course, there are the other directors of Channel 6. How would they feel if they knew that one of their colleagues was giving preferential treatment to an ex-boyfriend? Not very ethical, is it? Not to mention the newspapers.'

'OK, OK. What do you want?' sighed Patric, putting his head in his hands.

'I want you to call Anastassia Frink and withdraw Futura's pitch for *Celebrity On The House*. And then I want you to recommend Phoenix Productions' bid. Phoenix Productions, got that?'

'Never heard of them.'

'It doesn't matter. Phoenix Productions, remember.'

'But why?'

'You don't need to know that. All you need to know is that I have other copies of that expense form, and if Phoenix Productions don't get the commission, I will be posting them to your wife, Anastassia's husband, the board of Channel 6, and a wide selection of tabloid and broadsheet newspapers.'

Patric nodded. He knew he was beaten.

Marcia turned on her heel and walked to the door. 'By the way, I quit. From now on, you can do your own sodding typing.'

Siobhan was being pushed through Casualty at speed in a wheelchair. 'Now, if you're ever in the big ol' US of A,' bellowed Randy from the other end of the room, 'you come on down t'Oklahoma, purdiest state you ever did see.' Marge was admonishing him: 'OK, Randy. You can stop filming now. Cain't you see the poor girl's got other things on her min'. Now let's go an' get one of those little ol' shep-herd's pies we heard so much about.'

Siobhan raced down corridors, into lifts, and down more corridors. Jack was running alongside, as was a midwife, pulling a wheeled trolley with canisters on it.

'How advanced is her pregnancy?' the nurse asked Jack. Siobhan had a mask delivering gas and air clamped to her face and was thus indisposed to answer questions.

Jack looked blank.

'How many weeks?'

'Oh, um, eight months, I think,' said Jack.

'You don't know?'

'Well, I . . .'

The midwife shrugged, as if to say: 'Fathers, complete waste of space.' What she actually said was: 'A bit early.' She sounded worried. 'If we have to section, Dad will have to step outside, OK?'

'I'm not . . .' Jack paused, looking at Siobhan.

The last thing Siobhan wanted was to be left alone to have the baby. She wanted Jack with her. She ripped the mask off her face. 'Squeamish. He's not squeamish,' she screamed.

Jack smiled and squeezed Siobhan's hand again.

'That may be so, but it's hospital regulations.'

When they got to the delivery suite, the midwife patted Jack on the arm. 'Is there anybody else she wants at the birth? Somebody we should call?'

Siobhan managed to pull the gas and air mask from her face again. 'Olivia and Beth!' she gasped, desperately. 'I want them!' Then her face creased in pain again and she clamped the mask back on.

'What are you doing here?' said a shocked Olivia.

'Ees a nice welcome!' said Gianni, giving her a broad smile before planting a kiss on her lips. 'Ees OK if I come in?'

'Oh, yes,' stuttered Olivia. 'Sorry, I'm just so surprised to see you.'

Olivia and Gianni walked down the hall into the living room.

'Gianni!' shouted Seth in amazement when he saw him. Gianni put his bag down and dropped on to his haunches. He and Seth hugged warmly.

Then Anouska ran over. 'Dolly not well!' she announced. Gianni picked Anouska up and gave dolly a compensatory stroke. Seth clung to his leg. 'Gianni, Gianni!'

'Hi, good to see you,' shouted Nigel from his position on the floor, where he was building a soft brick wall to be knocked over by Daisy and Mia.

Then Colin appeared at the door. 'What's going on?' he asked. 'Oh, Gianni! Why didn't you say you were coming?' He put a hand through Gianni's hair and ruffled it playfully. 'The risotto should stretch, though. You don't mind Italian food, do you? You are staying for dinner, aren't you?'

'I don't know. Ees up to Oleevia.'

Olivia felt all eyes lock on her.

'Gianni can stay, can't he, Mummy?' implored Seth.

'G-anni, G-anni, G-anni,' chanted Anouska, pulling his hair.

Gianni laughed and looked shyly at Olivia.

'We'll see,' Olivia finally declared.

'Oh, Mummee!' wailed Seth.

'I said, we'll see,' repeated Olivia. 'But first, Mummy and Gianni need to have a serious talk. Upstairs.'

Gianni put Anouska down and disentangled his leg from Seth's grasp. He and Olivia climbed the stairs and went into her bedroom. Olivia shut the door firmly.

'OK, what's going on, Gianni? Why are you here?'

'I come to see you, Oleevia.' He walked towards her. '*Mi amore.*' Gianni cupped Olivia's chin with the palm of his hand.

'Yeah, yeah,' said Olivia, brushing his hand away. 'I got the flowers.' She crossed her arms over her chest protectively.

'An' you called, but you no speak, Oleevia, why?'

'How do you know I called?'

'My mother, she say someone call and no speak. I press last number redial. I see ees you.'

Olivia dropped her hands to her sides, tipped her head back to the ceiling and sighed. 'Your mother! It was your mother who answered the phone!'

'Yes,' Gianni said. 'Who you think?' Then he laughed. 'You think, what, ees another woman? Oh, Oleevia. *Mi amore.* I told you.'

Gianni walked over to Olivia and put his arms round her. He moved his face close to hers. She brushed her nose against his affectionately.

'Why didn't you tell me you lived with your mum?' she asked.

'I think you no respect me,' he replied.

Olivia shook her head in disbelief. After all the grief she'd given Siobhan about going out with a boy who lived with his parents, she'd ended up doing exactly the same thing.

'Say that *mi amore* bit again,' she said.

'Would you like to hold her?' asked Siobhan. She was sitting up in bed, high on adrenaline, cradling her new daughter in her arms. The baby was perfect. A bit small, the midwife had said, but nothing to worry about.

She handed the tiny wrinkled bundle to Jack. He laid her in the crook of his arm. She looked very small. Head to toe, she barely spanned his forearm.

'She's a beauty, just like her mum,' he said.

It was corny, but it didn't matter. Siobhan didn't think she could get any happier.

There was a knock at the door, then it was pushed open. Beth and Olivia came in, carrying flowers and chocolates.

Jack handed the baby to Beth. 'Anyone fancy a coffee?' he asked.

They all shook their heads.

'Well, I'm a bit thirsty. I think I'll just pop to the cafeteria,' he announced, before disappearing.

'That was nice of him,' said Beth.

'Yeah,' replied Siobhan. 'He is nice.'

'Jack reborn as a sensitive new man!' declared an astonished Olivia. 'And what the hell happened to his accent?'

'Oh, it's a long story. Actually, there is something you should know, Beth. You and Jack, you didn't actually do it.'

'You mean . . .'

'Yeah. You didn't sleep with him. Thought you'd want to know.'

'Yeah, thanks,' said a relieved Beth.

The baby stirred and snuffled in Beth's arms. Olivia and Siobhan formed a tight huddle around her.

'She's fantastic,' said Beth.

'Amazing,' said Olivia. 'What are you going to call her?'

Siobhan thought for a minute. Then she smiled. 'Marge. I think I'll call her Marge.' She laughed.

'You still on the gas and air?' asked Olivia.

Drrng, drrng. Beth cocked an ear in the direction of her handbag.

'Can't be mine. It's switched off,' said Olivia, looking at Beth. 'They're not allowed in here, you know.'

'Sorry, I'm waiting for a call from Richard. He's looking after Stanley.'

Beth carefully handed the baby to Olivia.

'Sounds like things are moving in the right direction between you,' Olivia said.

'Yeah, well,' mumbled Beth, trying to find her phone in her bag.

'Can we use the R word?' continued Olivia. 'R for reconciliation?'

Beth smiled and winked, then found her phone and walked to the far corner of the room. 'Hello?'

Olivia and Siobhan went back to gazing at Marge. They were so engrossed, they didn't even notice when Beth rejoined them.

'You're not going to believe this,' Beth said. Her face was ashen and her hands were trembling. 'That was Anastassia Frink.'

'What did she want?' hissed Olivia, still not looking up from the baby. 'To rub our noses in it?'

'No. You don't understand,' said Beth. 'We've got the commission!'

Chastity was pacing up and down, wearing a nasty groove with her stilettos into the shagpile of her living-room carpet. 'What do you mean I'm out of a job? I can't be . . . I thought Karen had got the new show. But Patric, you're the head of the bloody company, surely you can . . . OK, what about other programmes? Can't you get me on that pets one? I like that Ralph Morris. Can't stand his drawings, and the singing's a bit naff, but . . . Look, why don't we talk about this tonight? . . . What do you mean, you're cancelling . . . Cool it, why? . . . I know I went a bit mad, but it was a shock. I thought . . . So when will I see you? . . . What does that mean? . . . No, I won't calm down. Patric, Patric, are you there? You said you were going to turn me into the new Carol Smillie . . .'

Olivia's knees buckled.

'I think I'll take Marge,' said Siobhan. Olivia handed her back.

'But I thought we hadn't got the commission!' she exclaimed.

'That's the really weird thing,' explained Beth. 'We hadn't. And now we have. She's changed her mind.'

'What do you mean, she's changed her mind?' asked Siobhan,

the baby now safely settled in her arms. 'Channel bosses don't change their minds, or at least, they don't admit it.'

'Yes, well, it seems that Anastassia has decided to take a risk on us after all,' said Beth, shaking her head in disbelief. 'That's why we didn't get it the first time, by the way. We were too big a risk.'

'And now . . .' said Olivia.

'They want to be daring. That was the word she used. Daring.'

'It still doesn't add up,' said Olivia, suspiciously. 'I'm not complaining, but there's got to be more to it than that.'

There was a knock at the door.

'After the stuff you've seen today, Jack, you don't need to knock!' laughed Siobhan.

The door was pushed ajar. Marcia's head popped into the gap. A hand appeared, holding a bottle of champagne.

'Congratulations,' Marcia said.

Then she stepped into the room. She was holding another bottle of Moët in her other hand. 'I understand this is a double celebration.'

'How did you know?' asked Siobhan.

'It was you, wasn't it?' gasped Olivia. 'Outfit looks great, by the way.'

The others nodded in approval.

'You got to Anastassia,' continued Olivia. 'But how?'

Marcia looked down. 'It was Patric who persuaded Anastassia, actually. After what Karen did to you, let's say his conscience got the better of him.'

Siobhan, Olivia and Beth exchanged befuddled looks.

'This doesn't sound like Patric. Are you sure you had nothing to do with it?' said a puzzled Beth.

'Well, I may have pricked that conscience ever so slightly.' Marcia smiled enigmatically. 'Now, let's get this open.' She waved her bottles of champagne. 'Actually, I just ran into Liam on the way in, visiting Oona. She's had another face lift.'

'How are they?'

'Oona? I don't know,' answered Marcia.

'No, Liam,' said Beth.

'Oh, didn't you hear?' exclaimed Olivia. 'Liam's gone New Age. He's building an eco house on Sark out of egg boxes and old newspapers. Says recycling is the new rock and roll.'

'How long d'you reckon that'll last?' asked Beth.

'About long enough for him to work out his mobile doesn't pick up there, they don't do fresh pasta at the local shop – if there is one – and the best-dressed things on the island are the seagulls, I should say.'

The door swung open again.

'I found this lot in reception,' announced Jack. Gianni, Colin and Nigel appeared, with Seth, Daisy, Mia and Anouska. They crowded excitedly round Siobhan, the twins poking delightedly at the baby.

'Baba, baba,' they burbled.

No sooner had the door clunked closed than it was pushed open again, this time by Richard, holding Stanley. Beth looked at them in the doorway. They were so alike, they were like the first and last of a set of Russian dolls, the middle ones having unaccountably gone missing. Stanley saw Beth and waved.

'Mama!' he exclaimed.

Richard smiled shyly and walked over to Beth. He didn't attempt to kiss her, but she reached up and pushed a curl of his hair off his cheek. Then she kissed it.

'What's that for?'

'Oh, I don't know,' Beth said. 'But if you're going to move back in, you'd better get used to it.'

Richard wrapped his free arm around her. 'I love you,' he whispered in her ear.

'I love you too,' Beth said.

She could have used this intimate moment to tell him what she now knew, that she hadn't, in fact, slept with Jack, but she decided not to. She might be letting him move in, but she wasn't ready yet to forgive him completely for the way he'd behaved over Jack. She'd let him stew for a little while longer. Maybe she'd never tell him, keep that as her little secret.

There was the pop of a champagne cork, and then the fizzing sound as it was poured into glasses. Beth and Richard joined the others round the bed.

'To two new arrivals,' declared Beth. 'One very small and another which is going to be huge!'

'Cheers!' they all chorused.

It took five cardboard boxes to contain all of Karen's stuff. When the woman herself appeared in the doorway, Saffron was just throwing in a marabou-trimmed picture frame. It missed the box and landed on the floor, cracking the glass.

'Sorry about that.'

'What the hell are you doing?' gasped Karen in horror.

'I would have thought that was obvious,' declared Saffron.

'Wait till Patric hears about this!'

'It was Patric who asked me to do it. Actually, he also asked me to give you this.'

Saffron handed Karen an envelope. She ripped it open and took out a sheet of paper.

'No, they can't!' She looked up from the letter. The shock was written on her face. 'We got the commission. Anastassia called Patric. He told me.'

'Seems she changed her mind. Commissioning editor's prerogative, I'm afraid.'

'But why? I don't understand.'

'Oh well, never mind. The thing is, Patric did say he wanted your stuff out of here by five o'clock.'

'But . . .'

'It's in the letter.'

Karen looked down at her piece of paper again. 'No, no, he can't. After all the work I've done.'

'No one likes a failure, do they, Karen? It's like a bad smell. It follows you around.'

Karen tried to push past Saffron to get to her desk. 'I'm calling Patric. He must have made a mistake.'

Saffron was immovable. She picked up the phone on the desk. 'Hello, Security? Could you send someone up to Karen Newsome's office, please. ASAP.'

'No, no,' shouted Karen, trying to wrestle the receiver from her.

Saffron struggled to continue. 'We have an, um . . .'

Karen got custody of the phone, but Saffron then kicked her in the shin and she dropped it.

'We have a situation up here. OK, bye.' Saffron replaced the receiver.

Karen was hopping around on the carpet, cradling her knee and moaning. 'I just want to talk to Patric. I just want to talk to him, that's all.'

'Well, you can't,' snapped Saffron. 'He's gone away.'

'Gone away? That was a bit sudden.'

'Yes, well, second honeymoon, I'm told. Still, they say Nice is lovely this time of year.'

Karen had now managed to put two feet on the ground, but it didn't make her look any less dejected. 'I don't care about Nice,' she wailed. 'Patric doesn't want to sack me. He needs me.'

Saffron was merciless. 'Apparently not,' she declared imperiously.

Karen was downcast. She reached over and began picking up the boxes containing the debris of her life. A security guard was already approaching her office. She looked at Saffron. She seemed different. Karen hadn't noticed before, but Saffron was slimmer. Over the last few weeks, she'd shrunk three dress sizes. She was wearing tight jeans and a tiny T-shirt. It said 'Fluffy Bunny' on it.

Karen pleaded with Saffron. 'Well, at least I'm not on my own. You'll come and have a few drinks with me, won't you? We can plot a comeback.'

'Sorry, Karen, I've got work to do,' replied Saffron.

'Work?'

'Oh, I forgot to say. I'm the new series producer of *Pet Alert*. Apparently they were looking for some new blood.'

The security guard had reached the office now. Saffron nodded towards Karen and he put a hand on her shoulder.

'There's an easy way to do this and there's a hard way,' he said, having obviously seen too many episodes of *The Bill*.

Karen ignored him. She was focused on Saffron. 'You, a series producer?' she bellowed. 'It's only five minutes since you were a bloody runner!'

The guard took hold of one of Karen's hands and pulled her middle finger back so far, she yelped in pain. Then he twisted that arm behind her back and began frog-marching her out of the office. She was forced to carry the box she was holding with one arm. All those press-ups finally had a use.

'After everything I've done for you!' shrieked Karen, as she disappeared from sight. 'I made you!' And of course she *had* made Saffron. In her own image.

'Welcome to Alicante,' said a very familiar female voice from somewhere in the far corner of the hospital room.

The adults turned to find the source of the noise. The TV was on and Seth was holding the remote, flicking channels.

'Seth! Turn that TV off,' ordered Olivia.

'No, no. Go back, Seth,' said Beth.

Seth looked to his mother for permission. She nodded. The screen flickered as he worked his way back through the channels.

'Stop!' said Beth.

A woman in an expensive-looking swimsuit was standing on a packed beach. Every inch of it was covered with people on towels and sun loungers. Behind her, a throng of holidaymakers, who appeared to have had one too many sangrias, jostled to be on camera. One man was mouthing, 'Hello, Mum.'

'. . . and affordable fun for all the family is exactly what you'll find here in sunny Spain,' the woman was saying.

The camera was down low, shooting upwards, affording the viewer the unappetising sight of her jowls wobbling as she spoke.

Just visible on the periphery of the screen, a teenager with a lobster complexion was making a V-sign at the camera.

'...I'm Valerie Chancellor, and you're watching the Travel Channel.'

Beth, Olivia, Siobhan and Marcia looked at each other and grinned.

'Does this champagne taste a bit sweet to you?' asked Siobhan.

'Yes,' said Beth. 'Very sweet indeed.'